THE SAVANNAH LADY

First published in Great Britain in 2003 by
The Book Guild Ltd
25 High Street
Lewes, Sussex
BN7 2LU

All characters in this publication are fictitious and any resemblance to real people, alive or dead, is purely coincidental.

Typesetting in Baskerville by
Keyboard Services, Luton, Bedfordshire

Printed in Great Britain by
Bookcraft (Bath) Ltd, Avon

A catalogue record for this book is
available from the British Library

ISBN 1 85776 795 0

Dedicated to my son Lee for all his help with the computer; without him, I could never have finished this book.

Also to Tyrone Walkes for his help and patience.

1

The lightning zigzagged across the sky and the thunder rumbled, then an enormous clap shattered the peace of the small Caribbean island of Barbados. The lightning flashed again and again, lighting up the cloudy early morning sky and the rain began to fall – it beat down heavily and the wind howled tossing the palms, and in minutes, the Caribbean Sea was whipped up into a raging torrent.

The sloop was tossed like a cork, and twisted like a paper sail boat on the rolling waves, the wind whistled through her rigging. Her timbers creaked and groaned under the strain of the sea and the lashing rain as mountainous waves thundered against her hull. The spray rose high into the air and rained down on the deck, and the men that were on it disappeared under the deluge, as the power of the gale-force wind blew the ship nearer to the hazardous coral reef.

The treacherous lightning, and the tremendous noise of the thunder, the booming of the sea on the shore kept George Kingsley awake for hours. His wife and 16-year-old son lay helpless, and terrified in their beds, with their heads buried under the pillows and their hands clapped tightly over their ears.

George was a native of Barbados, a big man over six feet tall, with broad shoulders and a massive chest. He stood at the open cottage door, and his black skin shone as the lightning flashed across the covered verandah which sheltered him from the driving rain. The cottage had weathered many such storms over the years: it was made of coral stone, and George's father had built it with his own bare hands when he was a free man.

George had been born into slavery; his father had been captured by white men and brought from Africa on a slave ship to Barbados, and with hundreds of other men and women he had been sold in the market place, where plantation owners had bid high prices for strong and virile men to work in the sugar cane fields, and for years he had planted and cut sugar cane, every day from morning until evening, under the fierce heat of the Caribbean sun. It was here on the plantation, that he met Annie, a young and beautiful African girl, who had been enslaved like himself; they had fallen in love and married. George was the youngest of their four children. He had also worked in the cane fields from the age of five. The master, Mr Cunningham, was an Englishman; he had settled in Barbados, with his wife, who had died many years before of a fever, and he had lived on in the plantation house quite alone. He had been a good master, and when he had died, he had left a will stating that on the day of his death, all his slaves would be free men.

George had been 18 then and, being a free man, he had decided to go to sea. From the port at Bridgetown, he joined the crew of a merchant ship called the *Coral Queen*, which was due to sail to the Americas with a cargo of molasses and cotton. For ten years he enjoyed the seafaring life, the cool, fresh, salty air, and the docking in different islands and countries he never knew existed, places beyond his wildest dreams. He would come back to his homeland, bringing presents of silk and perfume for his mother and his sisters, and enthral his family and friends with tales of faraway places. It was on one of these occasions that he had met Marianna, a friend of his sister; they had fallen in love, and they had been married one year later on his next return home. He left the sea and his merchantman life when his son Joshua was born, and for a while they lived in a small chattel house, and then, when his father died, they moved into the cottage with his mother, and he took over the running of the small farm, growing a little sugar cane for their needs, and raising a few chickens and pigs.

Standing on the verandah while the storm raged, he could hear his horse neighing in the stable, and the chickens clucking; he knew they were afraid of the thunder.

The cottage stood about 20 feet above the beach, on coral stone rock. Lightning crackled and streaked across the cloudy sky, lighting up the whole cove and rocky shoreline. This was a tropical storm like no other, as the mountainous waves crashed like the thunder itself onto the sand, smashing into the rocks, and shooting spray 30 feet into the air. As the lightning flashed, he could see small fishing boats, anchored some way off shore, lifted high on the swells, and then they disappeared out of sight, only to appear again on the crest of the next mountainous wave. He caught a quick glimpse of one filling with water, which would certainly sink before the light of dawn. George's own fishing boat which, earlier in the day, he had brought up onto the beach, was tossed over and over, and was blown along the beach with the force of the wind, and he saw that it was surrounded by swirling water as the sea rushed in violently.

The heavy rain hammered on the wooden roof above his head and bounced off onto the verandah, running down the coral stone steps before him, leading down on to the beach like a fast-running river, and wound its way down towards the sea, making deep grooves in the sand. The gale-force wind ravaged the trees, breaking twigs, which flew in the air, and heavy branches came crashing down all around; coconut palms swayed, and their willowy trunks were bent almost in half as their feathery arms waved in a frenzied dance.

George blinked his deep brown eyes and flinched in the grey light of the early morning, as the lightning continually flashed across the sky, blinding him for a second, as the storm raged on violently. He saw the ship out there, halfway to the horizon, near the reef, being tossed this way and that, and the faint sounds of all hands on deck, and shouts and cries of the seamen floated across the torrential sea, and wafted away on the wind. He watched in flashes of lightning as shadowed figures of men battled against the wind and the driving rain, he saw silhouettes of men rolling and stumbling on the slippery deck as the ship pitched and rolled, men cursed and screamed to each other, he heard odd words which were distorted, as the elements raged on, he saw the slanting and driving rain and knew that it beat down cruelly onto their bare backs, and must have stung like a thousand pointed arrows.

Onboard, the men cursed the weather, they cursed the ship and shouted obscenities at each other, and the Captain cursed them all, shouting orders for them to put their backs into it, but the orders were lost on the wind and rain, and unheard. The rain stung into their bare backs, got into their eyes and their mouths, and the wind whistled deafeningly in their ears, and as the heavy waves crashed down onto the listing deck, booted feet lost their grip and strong, muscled arms and legs were stretched and strained to the limit as they fought with all their might to keep the ship from listing and being dragged onto the coral reef. The figurehead at the bow plunged her streaming red-gold hair deep into the depths of the raging torrent, and then rose high again on the crest of the next mountainous wave, and her sightless blue eyes looked to the heavens for mercy, while the cries of the seamen were carried high and lost again on the howling, screaming wind, which ripped violently through the sails, tearing them to shreds, as the men struggled with ropes and rigging.

There was a tremendous clap of thunder and George ducked his head, as the lightning lit up the whole sky, and in that moment he saw the main mast fall, and he saw that she was flying the black flag, and the wind snatched it, whirling it higher and higher into the air, until it was lost to his view.

As the heavy mast crashed across the wet and slippery deck, George heard the screams and cries of agony, as the pirates were pinned down amongst the tangle of the rigging, and their bones were crushed under the weight of the heavy oak. Some were now possibly dead, some would be badly wounded, some trying desperately to free themselves, fighting for their lives as the cruel sea thundered down upon them, and the ship heaved and rolled right into the clutching arms and the evil embrace of the rocky coral reef. She fought back bravely, but her timbers creaked and groaned in pain, before they were finally dashed to splinters, and the last pitiful screams of the seamen were lost to the elements... And George heard no more. In the raging tumult there seemed to be a peaceful tranquillity as the sea pounded on the shore and the wind howled around him, and the rain hammered on the roof above his head. George closed his eyes in sorrow. In this year of 1721, this was the third ship to be wrecked on the hazardous coral reef.

George himself had been shipwrecked, many years ago, when the *Queen of the Seas* had run aground on a reef off the coast of Jamaica in a bad storm, but not nearly as bad as this one. Luckily he and most of the crew, including their Captain, had managed to swim ashore. He felt for the poor devils in peril, some probably out there now, struggling and swimming for their lives in the raging and furious waters of the blue Caribbean, which looked so beautiful and enticing in the brightness of the sunshine – but the sea showed men no mercy, be they merchantmen as he had once been, or pirate. When the sea was angry, it claimed all souls. George turned away from the fast coming of the dawn light, a sadness in his heart, and went inside his cottage, closing the verandah door.

Later that morning, the sun was bright in the blue sky. George looked up; there was not a trace of the early-morning storm clouds, although the sea was still very rough, but it was going to be another scorching hot day.

Marianna had baked fresh bread and picked mango and bananas from the garden, and set the table for their breakfast. Afterwards, George and his son, Joshua, looked down from the verandah on to the beach; the debris from the sloop, which now slept peacefully on the sea bed, was strewn along the sand in a long line amongst wet and soggy seaweed. They walked along the wooden verandah, and their hardened feet felt nothing of the rugged and sharp coral stone as they walked slowly down the steps onto the warm soft sand. Joshua ran wildly down to the water's edge, where pieces of wood floated in and out on the white foaming heavy surf, which dashed it to splinters on the rocks.

Joshua waded into the white fluffy surf and swam a few yards out, to where two barrels of rum bobbed up and down, almost submerged in the heavy swells. He swam, pushing them before him into the white surf, which washed them out again; he tried again, and then with his father's help they managed to roll them one at a time up on the dry sand. One had *Savannah Lady* painted in black letters on the side. 'It was a pirate ship, Papa.' George nodded, seeing the painted name. They collected more wood and laid it out to dry, so that Marianna could burn it on the fire for cooking.

Joshua swam out several times, collecting and bringing in

pieces of wood, rope, articles of clothing, pieces of sail cloth, yards of torn canvas and a bolt of purple silk, which he rolled over and over in the surf until he reached the sand, dragging it up onto the beach; his mother would be pleased, she would make new dresses with it. One odd shoe turned over and over in the surf. And straw bedding, of the brightest yellow, now that it was wet and soggy, floated limply out of its filthy cotton covering, and strands of straw were entangled with wet seaweed, as it was left on the sand by the rolling tide. Joshua looked around him and then saw something red bobbing and rolling out in the deeper water; he swam out to it and found that it was seven or eight feet long. He reached out and it rolled away and rolled over, and he could see that it was the figurehead of the ship – the face of a woman was brightly painted, and the body was of the brightest red. He swam pushing it slowly before him, first with one hand and then with the other, guiding it with difficulty towards the beach, until his feet touched the sand and he was able to stand. He held onto it as the rough surf tossed it high, and his father came into the water to help him with it.

'Wha' have e there, Josh?' George was splashing in the water up to his thighs, calling loudly above the sound of the waves which swirled around him, and then he could see what his son had, and he went deeper into the water, and between them they hauled the great piece of carved wood up onto the beach and then dragged it further up onto the sand, where they had laid the rest of the wood to dry.

They stood either side breathing heavily from their efforts, and looking down on the beautifully carved face and curvaceous body of the goddess as she lay, looking with sightless blue eyes towards the sky; her full red lips had a secret smile, and her long, red-gold curling hair was carved as if blown back by a strong gale. The face and the large bosom were painted a shiny pink, and the nipples showed through beneath the low-cut neckline of the red dress, which was carved in swathes and clung tightly around the body. The arms and hands were straight down and close to her side, and the fingers were perfectly carved, as were the shapely feet, which were crossed at the ankles, showing beneath the dress.

Water dripped from Joshua's ragged knee-length cotton

pants onto the legs of the goddess. 'She beautiful, Papa! Look how she carved.' His African accent was short and clipped. 'We don't chop her up for de fire, Papa?'

George ran his hand down his thick black beard thoughtfully, 'Yes, Josh. She carved beautiful,' he pursed his lips, 'but maybe we need de wood at some time. We keep her for now, go now see what else ye can find.'

Joshua left his father standing over the figurehead, and walked back down to the water's edge, picking up pieces of wood as they rolled in onto the shore; some pieces were intermingled with thick rubbery seaweed. He collected armfuls of wood and threw it down in a heap and went looking for more, and then he spied part of the flag, the Jolly Roger, clinging to a rock, which disappeared every second as the waves rushed over it. He waded out up to his thighs to reach it, and pulled it from the rock and put it into his pocket.

George was down near the water's edge now, and amongst the seaweed which was strewn along the waterline he found an empty keg which had held rum, and tangled into it was a pair of torn trousers. He left it there and walked on a little further, and then sticking out from under a wet and broken palm frond he found a leather-bound book. He tried to turn the soggy pages, but they just dissolved in his hand, and the writing which was on them was faint and completely unreadable. He thought it could be the ship's log, but there was no name written on it to identify it; he decided to keep it anyway. Kicking his feet about in the seaweed, he uncovered another piece of wood; he was about to fling it up onto the dry sand, when he noticed the name painted on it in bold black letters, SAVANNAH LADY. He held it up to show Joshua, who was some way along the beach, waving back to his father.

Joshua was standing up to his waist amongst the rocks in the rushing white foam. He called to his father, waving frantically, and beckoned him to come quickly. George, thinking his son was in some kind of trouble, began to run towards him.

'Papa! Papa! Look! Look!'

'Wha' is it maaan, wha' is it, Josh? Wha'ave ye found?' George shouted, and was relieved to see that his son was not in any difficulty, but could see the anxious look on his face, as he came closer.

The whites of Joshua's dark brown eyes were showing as he shouted hysterically and pointed excitedly below the water, shouting, 'Look! Look! Papa, look!'

His father splashed boisterously into the surf, and his hardened feet felt nothing as he trod on hidden sharp rocks, 'Wat' is it, Josh? Maaaan!' Looking to where his son was pointing, he could see, caught between the rocks and clutching a piece of wood, a hand, and as the sea washed over it, it moved back and forth. George dipped his long strong arm deep into the water, and grabbed at the wood, dragging it up through the swirling surf, holding it away from him, as they both stared. Joshua had a horror-stricken look on his young face.

The hand had been severed at the wrist, and the fair hairs lay flat against the blue-grey colour of the skin; the nails were black, drained of their life's blood, and the bones and sinews stuck out from the wrist.

Joshua turned his head away and grimaced in horror, and then looked back at the hideous sight. It was a white man's hand, a left hand. A hand that had not been hard-working, but now the lifeless fingers, bound with rope, clung tightly to the splintered wood, which if it had not been severed from the arm, might even have saved his life. There was a ring on the third finger – a heavy gold ring, with a jade stone carved in the shape of a falcon – and in the eye was a sizable ruby.

Joshua winced in horror, feeling the pain as he watched his father prize open the lifeless fingers. He squeezed his shoulders up to his ears as the bones cracked, and he felt a nauseating pain in his stomach and his own hands as he clenched them into tight fists.

George pulled the ring from the finger and held it up between his fingers; the piece of wood, with the hand still attached, he held at his side, the surf rushing over it. They both examined the ring closely.

'Id datt a reeeell RUBY, Papa?' Joshua looked amazed; his big brown eyes were wide, knowing what it was and knowing it was a valuable stone, but never having seen one in his life before.

'Yeah, dat be a real ruby, son,' and as George moved the ring, it sparkled in the sunlight. Joshua held his breath as they waded out of the sea and up onto the wet hard sand.

'Whatcha gonna do wid dis horrible ting, Papa? Throw it far out into de sea?' his voice was raised to a pitch, and his eyebrows raised high in horror. His lips were pulled back tight, showing strong clenched white teeth, and he felt a sickness in his stomach as he looked at the lifeless blood-drained hand.

'I t'ink, son,' said George, carrying the wood with the hand attached further up the beach onto the soft warm sand, and to the rocks, 'dat we should buried it.' He began to unravel the rope which held the hand fast to the wood, 'Start to dig a deep hole, Josh, if we bury dis horrific ting, hopefully the man will rest in peace, and may be forgiven for all his sins and bad deeds.'

Joshua finished digging a deep hole with his hands. 'Go and find somet'ing to wrap dis in,' he looked down onto the sand where he had laid the gruesome specimen, and Joshua ran quickly down to the water's edge, where he had seen a torn shirt, and brought it back, and his father wrapped it carefully round the hand and laid the hand deep down into the hole beneath a big rounded rock, and covered it with some large pebbles which were close by, and between them, they filled in the hole with sand. He pulled out a knife from his belt, and scratched a deep cross high up on the large rounded rock, and then he knelt down, indicating that Joshua should kneel as well, and he said a quiet prayer.

'Do a pirate deserve all dis, Papa?'

George looked solemnly at his son. 'He was a maaan, Joshua, my son, just like you and me.' He shook his head gently. 'God turns no maaan away ... and we have peace of mind, and I believe that I have done de right ting...' He turned and walked away, and Joshua followed him back down to the water's edge.

William Cotton was the nearest neighbour and friend, who lived a few yards away in a similar cottage to George. He was walking along the beach carrying a long stick, which he was poking into the wet seaweed and then into the surf, dragging out pieces of driftwood, much the same as George and Joshua.

'Mornin', George, mornin', Joshua, rough night,' he had also watched the storm from his verandah. 'De ship was lost, den?' he called.

'Yeah,' George nodded his head as he came nearer, and then came right up to them.

'She was a pirate vessel,' Joshua said eagerly. 'We got de flag, well part of it anyways, look!' He pulled it from his pocket, 'Yeah! And a maaan's hand, we jest buried it didn't we, Pa?' His young face lit up, and his eyes were wide with eagerness, as he told William Cotton about the gold ring which had been on the finger. 'Show it to him, Papa. It got a reeeel RUBY in it, Mr Cotton, ain't it, Papa?' He looked at his father and then into the face of Will Cotton, who saw his eyes light up.

George smiled at his son's exuberance as he reached into the pocket of his light cotton trousers, which clung tightly to his thick thighs, now covered in wet sand, and showed the ring to his friend.

Will's brown eyes widened and his eyebrows raised in surprise, and his black shiny face creased into a huge smile, showing a set of strong yellow teeth.

'Dat'll make ee a fortune, George ... if it real ... you tink it real, George, eh? Eh! George? You tink, you tink?' He looked into George's face, his eyes bright, and then back at the ring and then back at George again, enquiringly.

'Yeah, it real, maaan, a real ruby, feel de weight of de gold, maaan.' He dropped the ring into Will's open hand. Will weighed it in his palm, and rubbed his thumb over the jade and the ruby, relishing the feel, and then handed it back with a nod.

'Yeah, maaan! It real right enough. Watcha gonna do wid it? Sell it?'

'No, I don't tink I sell it, Will, I have no needs for great fortune, we lives comfortable, on de fish I's catch, and I makes a fair boat if anyone wants to pay me. I tink I keep de ring, maybe young Josh may need to sell it some day.'

Will nodded. 'Well, maybe you's right, George...' he rubbed his black beard thoughtfully; he knew what he would do. 'Have ye found anything else worth keepin', George? I wonder what ship it was out their early dis mornin'? Has ye found anyting wid a name oni?'

'Yeah! Will, the *Savannah Lady*,' his heavy drawl was bitter as he spat out the name.

'Ooooh. Dat rogue! Captain Jack Barneby!' He said the

name with disgust. 'He would kill his own kin, dat one ... I wonder what she was carryin'?' His face twisted. 'Stolen silver, most like, I have no pity, it's just one less pirate ship, and it's all they deserve, preying on innocent folk like dae duzz, stealin' and killin' and the like, it's all they deserve. I say the only way for pirates is down, down deep.' He pointed his thumb to the sand, in a forceful gesture.

'I don't know what she was a-carryin', Will, but you are probably right, most likely silver, but it is now in de deep, but as you can see there is plenty of wood for our fires, not much else, though,' he grimaced. 'Although, Will, there is a barrel of rum up there, you can take maaan ... Josh, see it a-bobbin' out dare in de ocean, and he bring it in.'

'Tanks, maaan,' Will Cotton's black and shiny face beamed with delight as he looked up the beach to where two barrels stood side by side, and then he bent to pick up a piece of driftwood which was about to float back on the tide, and George went on to collect wood and lay it out to dry as he had been doing before Will had come along.

Joshua, who was way down the beach, looked up and saw Will Cotton's two sons, Thomas and Matthew, running down the beach towards him. He stepped out of the surf with his arms full of pieces of wood and some clothing and a rusty lamp, which had been rolling in on the surf. He came towards them, smiling and anxious to tell them about the hand and the ring. He asked his father to give it to him so that he could show them.

The boys, huddled together, marvelled at the ring. 'Papa say, it a reeeel RUBY,' Joshua's deep brown eyes goggled at his friends, as they each took the ring in turn and examined it, and their eyes goggled at him as they listened to him telling them about the gruesome hand, and showed them where they had buried it, and Matthew wanted to dig it up again to look at it, but Joshua said that his father had given it a proper burial and said prayers, and it would not be right or proper to disturb it now. So they all went off along the beach, searching for wood and anxious to find something of value.

'Did ye git much damage to ye house, George?' Will asked, as he bent to pick up a tattered waistcoat, which was covered in wet sand, and half-buried. He had lifted it from amongst the seaweed with his stick, and he put it into the surf to wash off the sand, but it floated away and he grabbed again with the stick, trying to keep his cotton trousers dry, but it proved impossible.

'Only mar boat shipped a bit o water, and I lost mar oars, but I can soon make some more,' George nodded.

'Yeah, maaan, we lucky too, de house was all right, but mar boat git a bit tossed but not much damaged, more an I kin say for dem...' He pointed to the debris that was washing up on the shore, that had only a few hours ago been the possessions of men, even though they were pirates.

They had turned now and were walking back along the water's edge towards their homes. George's big feet splashed in the shallow surf as it ran back and forth, and Will, much shorter of the two, walked beside his friend, carrying an armful of wood and the waistcoat in an old wet canvas bag, which he had found; in it he had stuffed a shoe and a red wet silk ladies' shawl, and a small boat which someone had carefully carved was sticking out of the top.

'Wat's dat?' asked Will, looking up the beach to the large piece of painted wood.

'The figurehead from de ship,' said George; they walked further up the beach, their powerful feet sinking deep into the soft dry sand. 'Josh got it out of de water.' They stood either side of the brightly painted goddess.

'Maaan,' Will drawled, 'dis is e prize.' He kicked at the legs with his bare foot. 'Lota firewood dare, maaan.'

'I gonna keep her, maaan,' George drawled back, with a slight smile. 'I ain't gonna chop her up.'

'Waaye gonna do wid her, den?' Will asked, looking first at his friend and then back at the large red bosom.

George was about to say that he didn't know yet, when the three boys came running up the beach, shouting excitedly to their fathers to come quickly – they had found a body.

2

Richard was in the kitchen. The phone rang on the table beside him, and he picked up the receiver. It was his mother, wishing them a safe flight.

Alison had the bag on the hall table; she was doing the last minute check on the hand luggage, tickets, passports. She was muttering to herself, and she had stuffed a good book in for the eight-hour flight ahead of them

The front door bell rang. She went to open it, calling over her shoulder, 'Richard, the taxi is here.'

'Good morning, Ma'am,' the smiling taxi man greeted her, lifting his eyebrows admiringly. He didn't see too many beautiful women on these early-morning trips, but her face was glowing with excitement, and her long dark hair was tied up into a ponytail with a red ribbon, and the light grey trouser suit, easy for travelling, suited her slim figure. She smiled back at him, wincing as the cold March wind came rushing through the open door.

Richard came out of the kitchen and down the hall, and picked up one of the Louis Vuitton suitcases, which were standing by the front door.

Alison threw the strap of her bag over her right shoulder, and carrying the hand luggage bag in her left hand, closed the front door and followed them out to the waiting taxi.

'Gosh! It's cold out here,' she shivered, as the strong March wind whipped at her jacket and rustled what few leaves were left on the cherry tree, which stood in the very small front garden of their London flat.

'It won't be where we are going,' Richard assured her, as he climbed into the back seat beside her, tucking his long legs in behind the driver's seat.

* * *

Robert Bentley, Alison's 17-year-old nephew, was waiting for them at the check-in desk when they arrived at Gatwick Airport. He greeted them happily, gave Alison a peck on the cheek, and shook hands enthusiastically with Richard.

'Thanks for letting me come with you, Ali. I'm really looking forward to it.'

'Oh, you know it's no problem,' said Richard with a smile, handing the tickets to the girl at the desk. 'You know you are quite welcome, but you will have to take pot luck; even we don't know what it is going to be like.'

Robert smiled down at his aunt, 'I bet it's going to be great,' he said excitedly.

Alison smiled up into his fresh, handsome face; she would be proud to have a son like Robert, he was tall and slim, like his father Peter, almost as tall as Richard, and still growing, 'Well, lets hope so.' She smiled, 'How's your Mum?'

'Fed up.' Robert wrinkled his nose.

Alison had been most surprised when her sister Sue had called only yesterday, to say that they would not be coming to the Caribbean with them, as her husband Peter had been called away to Germany on some urgent business that could not be put off, and he wanted her to go with him. Sue had sounded bitterly disappointed, and she said Robert had been stomping about the house in a black mood all morning, uttering words she didn't even know that he knew, and he would have to go and stay with a friend for couple of weeks, as they couldn't leave him at home on his own, or would they mind very much if he came out to the Caribbean with them?

They were going to stay in a cottage which had been left to Richard's father by an old aunt who had died a few years ago; the affairs had only just been settled, and no one had been out to look at the cottage yet. It appeared that Richard's Great-aunt Emily had been married to James Kingsley, a Barbadian doctor, who had died in his forties, and since then Aunt Emily had lived alone except for a housekeeper who came in daily, and she was still there, looking after the cottage, and that was all they knew.

The flight had been smooth, and Alison looked out onto blue

sea and golden beaches as the aircraft flew along the coastline, and the 'Fasten seat belt' sign was switched on. They touched down gently, and the mighty engines roared as they raced along the runway, then moving slowly and finally to a standstill.

They collected their hand luggage, standing near the door, and when the doors were opened, the sun streamed in hot and oven-like. They stepped from the aircraft and proceeded down the steps, and a strong, warm tropical breeze blew across the runway as they made the short walk into the terminal building. After waiting in line for ages to have their passports checked, a smiling porter stood with them, patiently waiting for their luggage to come round on the carousel, which also took ages. They were finally in a taxi, tired after the eight hours' flying time, and now on their way to the cottage.

They were met at the cottage door by a rounded smiling Bajan lady in her fifties, dressed in a pale pink overall dress which showed off her shiny black skin. She welcomed them shyly, with 'Hello, Master, hello, Mistress. I am Selena, and I am de maid and de cook,' she spread her arms proudly, showing them into the spotlessly clean and well-furnished sitting room. Alison smiled, with delight; it was lovely, and much better than she had expected. They then followed Selena up the stairs, to where there was a choice of four sizable bedrooms, each with a bathroom and separate shower, which had obviously been modernized over the years, each room with a sea view. Richard and Alison took the master suite, which was just to the left at the top of the stairs, and Robert took the room at the end of the hall.

Selena smiled to herself as she stood just in the doorway, as Richard dumped the heavy suitcase on the floor, and Alison went straight to the window and looked out at the sea, saying what a lovely view; she had seen so many of Mrs Kingsley's guests do the same thing when they first arrived. She thought to herself that it was nice to have guests again, there had been quite a few over the years, but she had looked after the cottage now for three years quite alone, and she still missed Mrs Kingsley, she had been a good mistress. She asked them if they would like a cold drink, most people were gasping when they first arrived in the heat.

'Thank you, Selena. Could you bring us a Coca-Cola with

ice, please, and I am sure that Mr Robert would like one too?' Selena went off to the kitchen. Richard lifted the heavy suitcase up onto the bed and unlocked it. Alison came away from the window and began to unpack the case. Richard lifted the other one upon to an armchair. He was putting his shirts into the dressing table drawer when Selena came back with three drinks on a tray.

In the evening, Selena proved to be a very good cook, and Alison, Richard and Robert relaxed in the comfortable white painted rattan chairs on the wooden verandah. The night was still and humid. Richard got up and poured the last of the white wine into his and Alison's glass; Robert had had a small glass of wine, but was not really very keen. Richard sat down and lit a cigarette.

Selena poked her head round the door and said that she was going, and would see them in the morning. They wished her goodnight, and she went back to the kitchen to leave by the back entrance.

Alison got up and walked through the door into the hall. The stairs went up straight in front of her, and to the left of the banisters was a small highly polished dark mahogany table, on which stood a telephone, and the directory, a notepad and pencil. Selena had put fresh flowers into a cut-glass vase. To the right of the stairs, a door opened into the dining room. 'Nice dining room, darling,' she called out to Richard to come and have a look.

'Nice isn't it?' He nodded, looking round the room at the highly polished mahogany table and ten chairs with blue flowered seat covers. To the right were blue curtained windows with sheer white gauzy drapes, and to the left, facing the window, stood a mahogany polished sideboard, with thin spindly carved legs, and on the top of it was a white lace doily on which stood a silver tray with a silver coffee pot and matching milk jug and sugar basin. Above the sideboard a glass cabinet was mounted on the wall. Richard peered into it; it contained some relics from a ship. The name was painted on a piece of board: *Savannah Lady*.

'I wonder what this is?' said Alison, looking at the cabinet. 'Something that Aunt Emily treasured, I expect.' Richard nodded; he didn't reply, and he wasn't very interested.

They came back onto the verandah; Robert was dosing in the chair. He looked up sleepily, easing himself out of the chair with great effort, and said, 'I'm going to bed, goodnight.'

'Sleep well,' Alison called after him.

Richard yawned as they both sat down again, either side of the coffee table, on which a candle burned steadily in a glass hurricane shade. The night was becoming quite dark as they sat together under the star-studded velvet sky, with the sound of the tree frogs whistling loudly and the crickets buzzing in the trees, and not a leaf moved. There was a new moon, which did not give much light; they looked out into the blackness of the night, at small lights twinkling on fishing boats as the sea shushed gently on the shore.

'Oh this is bliss,' said Alison, laying her head back on the back of the chair and closing her eyes. 'Just to think we have got three whole weeks of this,' with her eyes closed she was smiling. 'Tomorrow, I am going to sit down on the beach and paint the sea and those fishing boats.'

At six o'clock the next morning, they were both awake, and the early-morning light streamed in through a gap in the curtains; outside they could hear the sea shushing on the beach. Richard got out of bed and went to the window; the sky was a clear blue, and it was already a nice day. He could see Robert down at the water's edge paddling his feet, so they both joined him, and their first day began with an early-morning swim.

When they came back, Selena had arrived and had already set the breakfast on the verandah table.

After breakfast, Richard and Robert carried sun beds down onto the beach and Richard set up Alison's easel, and they sat beside her in swimming shorts, reading the papers, while she painted, until Richard looked at his watch and suggested that they take a stroll along the beach to the Sunset Hotel, and have lunch. He and Robert took the sun beds up onto the verandah and also Alison's painting equipment, and Alison went up to get her T-shirt. The beach seemed deserted apart from two fishermen who were unloading the day's catch from their boat, and they stopped to watch for a few minutes, then they walked on, reaching the hotel.

They sat at the beach bar on high stools, where a pleasant barman asked what they would like to drink, Richard smiled and asked what he would recommend, and he beamed and said, 'Try a rum punch, Sir.' Robert ordered a Coke.

They were the only ones sitting at the bar, and they agreed that a rum punch was a good drink. The beach was a hive of activity, people swimming, water-skiing, and jet bikes roared, in and out. Then two people came to sit opposite them at the bar.

The man smiled and called loudly, 'Hello,' and came round the bar, hand outstretched for Richard to shake, 'Mr Price, isn't it? I am right, aren't I? It is Richard Price, isn't it?'

Richard took the hand, which he offered, then said, 'Hello.' Alison and Robert exchanged puzzled glances.

'It was your agency that sold us our house,' the man was saying. 'We met you about four years ago, do you remember?'

'Oh yes, of course.' Richard was struggling for a name, he vaguely remembered meeting him before, and then, it suddenly came to him, 'Oh yes it's...'

'John Turner,' the man volunteered.

'Of course,' said Richard, relieved that he had not said a name and made a mistake. He quickly introduced Alison and Robert.

John introduced his wife Carol, and there were smiles and handshakes all round, and Richard bought them a rum punch and ordered another one for Alison and himself.

Alison and Carol sat chatting, while the men were discussing business. Alison was saying that Richard had taken over the business since his father had retired, and she suddenly stopped as two youths arrived at the bar.

'Dad,' said the younger of the two, 'we are going on a jet bike, it is OK?'

John Turner said that it was all right for them to go, and then he said, looking at Richard, 'These are our sons, Gareth and Timothy; this is Mr and Mrs Price and Robert.' They all exchanged hellos and smiles, and John asked them if they wanted a Coke.

'No thanks, Dad,' Gareth shook his head. 'Can't stop, we

have the guys waiting with the jet bikes.' They were half turned to go off, and Gareth said to Robert, 'Do you want to come?'

Robert looked eager to go, but first glanced at Richard, to see if it was OK.

'Go on, Rob,' Richard nodded his head sideways. Robert smiled, and went off with the lads, and Richard called after him, 'Have you got some money, Rob?' He was about to say no, but John Turner said, 'Oh, don't worry about it, it's on our hotel bill.' Then he ordered another drink, and suggested that they all have lunch together when the lads got back, saying that the food in the hotel was quite good, and that they had stayed in the same hotel several times. It turned out to be a very enjoyable lunch and a very good first day, and Richard invited the Turners to the cottage for drinks the next evening.

The morning was quiet, apart from the rolling of the sea, and a ski boat had just raced by with a skier, who had now splashed into the water, and the boat was coming back to pick him up. Richard looked up; he had been absorbed in a good book, and was sitting on the sun bed on the verandah. He put down the book, stretched and yawned as if he had had a hard day. He looked at his watch, it was eleven o'clock; he stood up and stretched again, and walked stiffly across the verandah to the corner of the house, to where Alison was sitting in the garden under the shade of the trees, painting the figurehead of an old sailing ship, which had stood against the north wall of the cottage for years. It had weathered rain and high winds, and the everyday heat of the blazing sun. It was painted completely white.

Alison was just putting the finishing touches to the painting when Richard came up behind her; she jumped, turning to look at him.

'Sorry darling, didn't mean to creep up on you.'

'Oh, it's all right,' she smiled up at him. 'It's been so quiet here all the morning. What have you been doing, reading?' He nodded, looking at her painting. 'Is Robert with the Turner boys?' she asked.

'Yes, he went down to the hotel about an hour ago.'

Alison nodded. 'She has something eerie about her, don't you think?'

'Who?'

'The White Lady,' said Alison. 'She almost seems to move, don't you think? I am sure she is longing for something.'

Richard pulled a face. 'Oh, I am sure she is,' he said with a mocking tone.

'Don't be like that, Richard, she really does seem to have a presence about her, and can't you feel it? There's a kind of buzz around her, listen.'

Richard listened. He thought that he could hear something. A bee, possibly buzzing nearby, 'Yes, yes, I can hear something, but I don't know what it is.' He put his head on one side, looking at her painting, 'You know, darling, that is very good,' he nodded with approval, then stood back to get a better view. 'Mmmm, yes, I like it, but why did you paint its dress red?'

'Well that's how I visualize her, with blue eyes, and red-gold hair. Why, what colour would you have painted her, then?'

'Oh, well,' he considered for a moment, 'ummm,' he bit his lip with a comical gesture, and raised his eyebrows. 'BLUE, yup!!' He nodded his head, 'Blue, she would wear blue. Mind you, I didn't know her, of course,' he pulled a face. 'She's a bit too old for me, you're more my type,' he mused, and bent down to give her a peck on the cheek. 'I wonder why they whitewashed it all over?' He thought for a moment. 'I suppose the original colour was wearing off, and someone had a surplus of whitewash.' He looked up at the statue with its white painted face, its mouth with the secret smile, the white painted eyes, that seemed to be straining through the whitewash. He didn't say anything to Alison, but he understood what she felt, there was something weird about it.

'Well!' he said suddenly, sort of shaking himself out of a trance, if you could call it a trance. 'Look ... are you nearly finished here? I am going down for a swim, are you coming?'

'Yes, I am just finishing,' she said, leaning down to the paint box for a rag to wipe the brush, swizzling it round in the jar of water, and then putting the cap back on the paint tube. 'You go, and I'll be down in just a minute.' Richard went off.

Alison studied her painting and then looked up into the

face of the white goddess, was she smiling at her, mocking her perhaps? She looked away, and finished putting the paints back into the box, then she stood up and took the pad off the easel; she looked at it and then held it to her side, then looked up again deep into the white painted wooden face. She felt she could look into her mind. 'There is something about you, you're eerie,' she almost breathed the words. 'You're eerie. I wonder if Great Aunt Emily ever felt like this about you. I wonder?'

'Sorry Mistress, you say sometin'?'

'Oh! Selena!' Alison turned quickly with a quick intake of her breath, and put her hand to her throat. 'You made me jump! I didn't know you were there,' her breath came in short bursts and she felt embarrassed. 'I, er, I was talking to myself,' she smiled.

Selena had a mysterious smile.

Alison recovered from her embarrassment. 'Selena, what do you make of this goddess, has she stood here in the garden for a long time?'

'Many, many years, Mistress,' she grimaced, and her tone was low. 'She could tell many tales of de sea.'

'Mmm ... she seems to be longing to go back,' said Alison thoughtfully, with her head on one side.

Selena stood beside her looking up at the statue; she pursed her lips, nodding silently. There was an atmosphere between them. Alison felt her skin creep. 'Well!' she said and turned so quickly that Selena was startled and stepped back a step.

'I must go and have a swim, my husband is waiting for me. Would you take the easel and the little stool in for me please, Selena?' She walked off carrying the painting and took it into the dining room, and stood it just inside the door against the wall to dry. She stood for a moment, looking round the room; it was dim, the curtains were closed, and it was very cool. She glanced at the glass cabinet above the sideboard; the things in the cabinet must have come from the same ship as the figure-head. Perhaps Aunt Emily's husband had owned the ship. She raised her eyebrows thoughtfully, and then left the room. She went out onto the verandah; she could see Richard out there swimming. She slipped easily out of the pink shorts, tied the strings of her bikini a bit tighter round her neck, and set off down the coral stone steps, leaving her flip-flops on the bottom step as she walked down to the water's edge. Richard was floating on his back and she swam out to him, the cool water caressing her tanned skin. 'Gosh, this is lovely,' she called.

'God, you were a long time, I thought you weren't coming.'

'Sorry, I was talking to Selena.'

After the swim, they came back up on to the verandah again. Alison sighed, the heat was intense she felt languid, and she laid back down on the sun bed, taking off her sunglasses and closing her eyes to the brightness.

A shadow fell across her face, and she opened one eye to a slit, it was Richard, he was smiling down at her.

'I've just had a walk round the garden. It's a fair size, not enormous though, there are mango trees and bananas and breadfruit.'

'How would you know?' she jeered. 'You wouldn't know a mango tree from a rose bush.'

'Oh, they're all labelled, that's how I know, and there must be gardener that looks after it, it's all neat and tidy. Come and have a look.'

They walked to the end of the verandah, and looked up at the coral stone walls, once white but now creamed and yellowed, black and patchy and weathered with age. 'I suppose it has been extended,' said Richard.

They walked the spacious garden. Selena had told them it once was part of a sugar cane plantation, but there was now an orchard of tropical fruit trees, all varieties. They looked at the names on them, Avocado, Pomelo. 'What's that?' said Alison.

'Don't know,' said Richard, looking at another tree with a label, Mandarins, Soursop. 'They make drinks of this, don't they?'

The mangos hung heavily from the branches of a large tree. 'Mmmmm, must be the mango season,' said Alison, looking up at the fruit and then at the tall coconut palms where, under the outstretched green palm leaves, clusters of very green coconut clung tightly together. 'I wonder how they get those down?'

The guys climb up the trunk with a big knife, haven't you seen it on the telly?' Close to the wall of the house, bougainvillea climbed higher than the roof, its rich, vivid pink flowers ablaze in the brilliant sunlight. Hibiscus nodded their scarlet heads in the breeze; tomorrow they would be gone and new blooms would flower. A large frangipani tree, covered in beautiful pale pink blossoms, wafted a delicate perfume as they came near, and beneath it stood the White Lady.

'Must be about seven or eight feet tall, I should think, wouldn't you?' said Alison.

Richard was looking at the bougainvillea. 'Much higher, it's above the roof.'

'No, it's not.'

'Yes it is ... aah, what is?' he couldn't see what she was looking at. 'Oh that thing, yes I suppose it must be about seven feet tall ... mmm, yes.'

Alison looked open-mouthed at him. 'Don't call her THAT THING, like that! You will hurt her feelings! She is really quite beautiful, but there is something strange about her, don't you think? I wonder just what she is thinking?'

'THINKING?' Richard blurted out. 'It's a bloody block of wood! For God's sake, Alison, how the hell can it be thinking, it's wooden. What's the matter with you?' he shook his head and started to walk away.

'NO! Look! There is something in that sort of smile, something in the face, a sort of longing. I am sure she wants to go back to the sea, it is as if she moves, look at it. Richard, please, you must be able to feel it.'

'Feel what?' He pulled a face. 'I can't see what there is to feel, what am I supposed to feel? I agree she might be longing to go back to the sea, but then that is because she has been standing here facing it all these years, she's got nothing else to look at. Oh God, just listen to me, discussing the feelings of a block of wood. You're making me as daft as you.'

'Oh, really, Richard,' Alison frowned with frustration, 'you have no imagination at all.'

'Well, I think you have enough imagination for both us.' He was about to say 'a weird one', but Robert came up the steps from the beach and interrupted him.

'Hello, I'm back,' he smiled.

'Had a good morning, Rob?' Richard nodded to him.

'Yes, I haven't skied for a couple of years, it was good fun.

Gareth and Tim are good skiers, Mr Turner has been in the boat with us as well. They are looking forward to coming up here this evening for a drink. I might go back down to the hotel again after lunch; they are going to get jet bikes again.'

Selena had heard Robert come back, and appeared round the corner of the house with three Cokes on a tray. They each took one, thanking her, and Robert drank his straight down, saying skiing made him thirsty.

Selena had seen Alison staring wonderingly at the goddess. Emily Kingsley had had many guests to stay at the cottage over the years, and she had seen many of them looking at the goddess. But very few had felt the power of the White Lady, but she knew that Mrs Price could feel it, by the look on her face. She had felt it many times herself, but she knew that Mrs Price had not yet heard the moaning and the wailing.

The Turners would be arriving in a few minutes.

Richard got the glasses and set them on the glass top table. Robert was slumped into a chair, a cassette player on the coffee table beside him, the headset clamped tightly to his ears; he was nodding and tapping his foot to sounds unheard.

John and Carol Turner and their sons came up the coral stone steps.

Robert snatched at the headset and jumped to his feet, tucking the back of his shirt into his trousers.

'Hello,' said Alison in surprise, 'I didn't expect you to come along the beach.'

'Well, we were going to get a taxi,' smiled Carol. 'But the boys insisted on walking along the beach. We are certainly going back in a taxi. Look at this,' she said, tipping the sand out of her shoes over the balustrade. 'Be warned, if you ever have children, don't have boys,' she laughed, 'especially two. What with them and John, I am totally outnumbered.'

Richard handed the women a glass of cold white wine and then poured one for John and himself. Alison and Carol sat down while Richard and John rested themselves on the balustrade, a drink in hand. The boys were standing together by the balustrade. 'Had a good day, lads?' Richard asked.

'We've been water skiing,' Tim said, his eyes sparkling. 'Dad

hired a boat, didn't Robert tell you? It was good fun, wasn't it Dad?'

John smiled, 'Yes, we had an hour or so out there, the lads enjoyed it. Cheers,' he raised his glass all round.

'Cheers,' they all raised their glasses.

'Now what do you lads want to drink?' asked Richard. 'There is Coke, beer or orange juice, or you can have a glass of wine, if your Dad says it's OK.'

'I'm going to have a beer,' said Robert, 'would you like one, Gareth?'

'Yes please, and the name is Gary. I don't know where Mum ever got that name from. I think it was Auntie Lynn who suggested it.' He looked at his mother with raised eyebrows and pulled a comical face.

'Oh,' Carol sighed, raising her eyes then looking at Alison, 'you can't win can you?' Alison smiled.

'Can I have a glass of wine please?' said Tim.

'Oh no you can't,' said his father. 'You can have a Coke.' Tim turned away, shrugging his shoulders, and pulling a face.'

Richard grinned. 'Sorry,' he said to John, 'they are both so tall, and you forget they are only young. How old are they?'

'Gary is just seventeen, and Tim's almost fifteen. But I agree, they look so grown up, don't they?'

Robert came back from the kitchen with two cans of beer and a can of Coke for Tim. 'Oh, I forgot the glasses. Get the glasses, Gary, they are on the sideboard in the dining room, Richard got them out earlier.' Gary started to move away, and Robert pointed, 'Just there on the right.'

Gary was gone a few minutes, and came back with three long glasses. 'I say, that's interesting,' he nodded his head sideways, towards the dining room. 'I mean all that stuff in that glass cabinet. Off an old ship, isn't it?'

'I don't know,' said Robert, 'I haven't really looked.'

'Neither have we really,' said Richard, looking at Robert and Gary. 'Alison and I were in there yesterday. We glanced at it, it looks like a lot of old junk, but I expect it is something that my aunt treasured.'

'Well, it might be valuable,' said Gary, 'there's a piece of paper rolled up, it looks very old, it's brown with age. It's got

Captain Barn or something on it, that's all I could see, and the piece of wood looks ancient; it's very dry, looks almost grey, it must have come off a ship. It's got the name *Savannah Lady* painted on it, and there is something that looks like the Jolly Roger.'

'*Savannah Lady*!' Tim's eyes were wide. 'We did a paper on that at school a couple of terms ago,' and he began to talk very quickly and excitably, and they listened stunned and speechless, drinks held steady in their hands.

'The Captain was Jack Barneby. He was a pirate.' He was putting lots of expression into his voice, spitting out the word with venom. 'A notorious pirate who stole jewels and silver and gold, and he captured Sir Hugo Fotheringay, who was a very rich man who owned several ships, and traded in tea and spices, in the Orient and...' Tim took a breath and then went on. 'Barneby stole two of his ships and kidnapped Sir Hugo ... well ... I think he did,' he put his hand to his lips and thought for a split second. 'Yes, I think I am right. Then ... this Barneby, being tall and handsome, dressed himself up in the finest clothing, silk and satin and velvet.' His tone changed. 'You know, like they used to wear, like they do in films, curly wigs and things. Then, looking like a gentleman of honour, and being a charmer with the ladies, he got Sir Hugo to introduce him to all the best people and went to all the best parties, knowing that the houses were loaded with valuable items, and that all the guests, the ladies would be wearing their finest jewels. There would be drinking and music and dancing, and then that's when his cut-throat crew would come creeping up. And then they would break in through the doors and windows, causing havoc, stealing and breaking everything and killing all the servants, and grabbing the ladies' jewels. They even burnt down the house of Lord and Lady, emm, err ... oh, I can't remember.'

'But Sir Hugo Fotheringay arranged all this, and everyone thought that he was their friend, a gentleman of honour and all that. Some friend; I bet he did well out of it. Most of his so-called rich friends were left broke and homeless. He even, would you believe, arranged a party in his own home, asking all his so-called wealthy friends, who innocently came thinking it was his wife's birthday; actually his wife and children were away at the time visiting relations. Of course Jack Barneby was there, being charming, and then, his pirate crew burst in, terrifying everyone; some of the ladies fainted, as the men tried to fight off the pirates, and then Sir Hugo was kidnapped, or they thought he was, but he probably arranged it all, and as far as anyone knows he joined forces with Barneby and became a pirate. The *Savannah Lady* rammed ships on the high seas, taking gold and silver and supplies like salt and sugar; they stole barrels of rum from ships leaving Jamaica, they stole anything they could get their hands on, and they killed for the sake of killing. Apparently Sir Hugo was a good swordsman, but he wasn't in the same league as Barneby and his cut-throats, so he arranged all the on-shore stuff, like ravaging and pillaging villages and houses ... and ... you know, stuff...' It suddenly went quiet for a minute as they were all waiting for him to go on. 'Can I go and have a look at the glass cabinet, please?' he addressed the question to Richard.

Richard nodded. 'Yes of course, you seem to know much more about it than we do.'

They all looked amazed as Tim went off to the dining room.

'I didn't know he learnt things like that at school, did you Carol?' John looked at her with surprised eyes.

Carol shook her head. 'It's amazing what they teach them.'

'Sounds a bit more exciting than when we were at school,' laughed Richard, 'all I can remember is doing maths.' John chuckled in agreement.

'Well, we haven't paid much attention to what is in the cabinet,' said Alison, 'we had a quick look, but we have been too busy sunbathing.'

Robert and Gary followed Tim into the dining room; he was peering closely through the glass into the cabinet.

Robert opened the cabinet and took out the brown and yellowed rolled-up, aged paper, and slipped off the pale blue frayed and faded ribbon. He handled it very carefully, unrolling it and looking at the scratchy writing, which was written in English, but was not easy to understand. He began to read very slowly as they sat down at the dining room table. Tim and Gary listened.

To my son Joshua.

It was on dis tent daey of July, in de year of our Lord seventeen hundred and twenty-one. De big hurricane did strike de Island, I watch from de Cottage door as de pirate shipe Savannah Lady did founder on de coral reef, her Captain Jack Barneby did die on dis daey and all he crew.

On de rise of de sun de storm did blow away.

Wid Joshua my son we de go on e beach. We find much wood for de fires, and barrels of rum afloatin in de sea. To e plank was tyde e white man hand on e finger a golden ring, de stone be jade, carved of e birds head, Wis a ruby eye.

We did keep e ring, and bery de hand, below de big rock in de sand near de cottage we did mark e cross. Me think, dis be de hand of Sir Hugo Fotheringay a English gentleman much hated so tales tell. He did turn to piracy on de sea, and land, he did rob and kill wid de Pirate Jack Barneby. De goddess Savannah Lady we did find arollin' in de sea. We stand her on de north wall o dis cottage. William Cotton and son Thomas did help.

De red dress and red golden hair and de eyes so blue look out to sea from whence she did come.

She do cry a mournfully above de crashing of de waves.

When de storm come, lands men heers de crys.

She did take my deer wife Marianna and Joshua deer mother yet e yeer after de big storm did come again. Take heed, and be ye warned, lock away all e women folk when she wail. I rite dees words Joshua my son, dat ye will remember and tell de tale of e goddess and e wailing to ye children and ye children's children when e time doth come.

Dis daey de shipe Savannah Lady lays deep and sleeps a peaceful sleep below de waters, never again to prey on innocent folk.

And also poor poor Mathew nair will be forgotten.

Heer I rite my name.

George Kingsley merchantman.

Gary and Tim exchanged glances.

'Well, what do you make of that?' said Robert, letting the paper curl back up as it had been for years, and slipping the faded blue ribbon back over it.

'Don't know.' Gary shook his head.

'Who's Matthew?' Tim had a deep frown on his young face.

'Don't know,' said Gary.

Robert put the faded paper back in the cabinet. 'Well, here is the ring.'

'Let's have a look,' Gary was looking into the cabinet, just as Robert picked up the ring and put it onto the end of his finger. 'It really happened, then?'

'Can I hold the ring?' Tim was looking on in wonderment. Robert gave it to him, 'Oooh, it's quite heavy,' he weighed it in his hand, looking at the ruby, 'and it sparkles, doesn't it?'

'Let's feel,' said Gary, taking it from his brother. 'Yes, it's weighty.'

'Its marvellous,' said Robert. 'Just think, all those years ago, can you just imagine, this old boy standing right here on this verandah watching a ship go down in a storm, and then sitting down, probably in this very room, to write it all down so that people like us could read it all these years on. And what was that bit about locking up women when you hear the crying?'

'What was that about Matthew?' said Tim. 'I wonder who he was.'

'Yeah, sounds weird.' Gary grimaced.

'What is it that wails then?' Tim looked puzzled.

'Well, that thing in the garden, I suppose,' said Robert.

'What thing?'

Robert nodded his head towards the door. 'That thing, that figurehead off an old ship. This, I expect, all came from the ship.' He pointed his thumb over his shoulder at the glass cabinet. 'It's standing in the garden, just out there under that pink flowering tree, a frangipani I think Alison called it. Come on, I'll show you.'

'Gosh yes.' Tim was looking up goggle-eyed at the figurehead. 'She's great. Coo, Old Smythe would love to see this. I will have to take a picture.'

'Who's Old Smythe?' said Robert.

'He's the history teacher, the one who gave us the papers to do on this pirate thing. I can't wait to get back and tell him that it is all true.'

'Well, of course it's all true, stupid, if you had it in a history lesson.' Gareth shook his head.

'Yeah, but we didn't believe half of what he was telling us. I don't think Old Smythe really believed it, he just gave it to us for something to do. You see, he is into old ships and things, it's his hobby, and he was talking to us about Nelson and the *Victory*, and then somehow it got round to pirate ships when someone asked if Nelson ever ran into Blackbeard. It was all a big laugh, and the whole class was getting out of hand, you know. Throwing bits of paper at each other. Someone threw a paper dart, and Old Smythe banged on the desk, and then said if we were into pirate ships, he had some paintings that he would bring in and show us, and in the meantime, we could research into ships. He picked a subject, and it happened to be the *Savannah Lady*. We did it for weeks, but we would all have sooner been into space age stuff, you know like who was the first man in space, and who walked on the moon. But really the pirate thing did get a bit interesting, and now I can't wait to get back and tell them all about this. I wonder if the cross is still marked on the rock. Come on, let's go and have a look.'

Alison was handing round the canapes, and Richard was opening another bottle of wine, when the three came back to the verandah and started down the coral stone steps to the beach.

'Where are you going?' Alison looked up in surprise. 'Do you want some canapes?'

'No thanks, we have been reading that old scroll in there,' he indicated the dining room with his thumb, 'and there is supposed to be a cross marked on a rock.'

'Come on you two,' Tim called up from the bottom of the steps. Gary, taking a sip from the Coke can, was halfway down the steps.

They walked along, carefully checking every rock.

'I expect it has worn off by now anyway,' said Gary.

'Bet it hasn't,' said Tim, walking off a little way in front of them. 'What about inscriptions on old gravestones? They last for ever.'

Robert stopped to look at a large rock which had been smoothed over the years by the elements, as were most of the rocks, but this one was more rounded and there seemed to be a cross marked on it; he wasn't sure, it was very faint.

'This might be it,' he called. Gary walked back to look.

'Yeah,' he said in surprise. 'Yeah, it could be; looks something like a cross, doesn't it? Hey! Tim, I think we've found it.'

Tim came running up to them. 'Where, where?' he said excitedly.

Robert pointed to a faint mark about six or eight inches long. 'That's a cross, isn't it?'

Tim had to stand on his toes to see it; even though he was tall, he was not quite as tall as the other two, 'Yes, yes,' he smiled. 'Looks like it, doesn't it?' Then he dropped down on his knees and began digging into the sand with his hands excitedly.

'What are you doing?' Gary looked down on him.

'Well, help me!'

'What on earth are you looking for? What do you expect to find after a couple of hundred years, old bones or something? Oh! Come on, Tim. Wake up!'

Tim stopped digging and looked up at them. 'Well, you never know,' and then he went back to digging again.

'Don't be stupid, there must be a hundred tons of sand covering what is buried there, if anything is there anyway.' Gary dropped down onto his knees with a chuckle, and began to help his brother scrape away some of the sand, while Robert stood looking down on the pair of them, his hands on his hips and a sceptical look on his face.

The hole was now quite deep, they were reaching down as far as their shoulders and bringing up wet sand and shingle. They reached some large rocks, then suddenly there was a terrible smell and they both jumped back quickly. Robert pinched his nose and Gary stood up, holding his hand over his mouth, and Tim lost his balance and fell back flat on his back, as a swift gust of wind took them by surprise and swirled around them with a howl and whipping up the sand, and was gone in a minute. It seemed to have come from out of the hole.

'Pooh!' Gary turned away, holding his nose and pulling a terrible face. 'Smells like something has died.'

They began to laugh. 'Cor', you're right,' Tim laughed, picking himself up, holding his nose and shielding his face from the wind and the sand that stung him.

'It's the hand...' Robert said slowly, leering at them with a sinister 'HAAA, HAAAA HAAAAAAA', his arms spread and raised high and his fingers stretched out, imitating Count Dracula.

'Ooooooh, don't,' said Tim, gripping his neck and choking, shaking and pretending to be frightened. 'Sounds scary, come on, quick, let's fill it in again.'

The three of them kicked the sand back into the hole again with their feet, laughing and giggling, then pushed each other up the steps, not noticing the strong chill wind which was swirling around them.

Alison was chasing paper napkins across the verandah as the sudden wind whirled them off the table; Carol caught one and put it on the table under her glass.

'Well, I think we should be going now, John, we have to be back for dinner,' she smiled.

'Yes, come on, we don't want to outstay our welcome.' He put his glass down on the table.

Thank you, Alison, it has been lovely,' said Carol, standing up and picking up her bag. 'We have a table booked at eight in the restaurant.'

'Can I ring for a taxi, Richard? I know that Carol won't walk back along the beach, especially now as it is dark.'

'Oh, I'll drive you back, John,' said Richard. 'No need for taxis; we have a hire car, it won't take me five minutes, let me just get the keys.'

'We will have dinner one night,' said John as they got into the car, Richard and John in the front, and Carol squeezed into the back with the three boys. Robert went with them and Alison waved, saying goodnight.

Selena had left an hour ago, and Alison put the glasses onto the tray and took them into the kitchen, leaving the empty wine bottles in the ice bucket on the table.

As she came back down the hall she saw that the dining room door was open and that the boys had pulled the curtains back. In the morning, the light from the window would be shining onto her painting; she turned it to face the wall. Tomorrow, if the sun streamed in, it would fade the colours. She looked into the glass cabinet: the Jolly Roger flag was hanging over the piece of wood half-covering the name of the ship, and the rolled-up scroll was in front of it, lying on a piece of coiled rope, and in front of that was the jade ring on a piece of grubby sail cloth. As she moved, the ruby eye caught the light and twinkled.

She picked up the scroll, slid off the faded blue ribbon and unrolled it carefully, looking at the thin and scratchy writing, and then letting go of one end, it snapped back into a roll again. She turned back to the cabinet, picked up the gold ring and slipped it onto her finger; it was too big, but she held her hand out in front of her and the ruby shimmered in the electric light. Then she looked at it closely, it was of heavy, thick dark gold, certainly a man's ring; the large pale green jade stone was carved with the head of a bird or she thought it was a falcon, and the one ruby eye seemed to sparkle, much more than any other ruby she had ever seen even in a jewellers' window. She thought it must be quite valuable, and very old – they didn't make jewellery like that these days, although she didn't think it was beautiful, not ugly, but no she couldn't say there was any beauty in it, even if the ruby was a super stone, and it did sparkle a lot.

She took it from her finger, and as she turned to put it back in the cabinet a creepy feeling came over her. She looked at the scroll, and was just about to put that back into the cabinet when there was a terrific draught, and the dining room door slammed with a shuddering bang, and the paper in her hand crackled. As the gust of wind whirled around her and the curtains blew in and up, she realized that the window was not even open. She felt strangely cold. She flung the ring back into the cabinet and rushed to the dining room door, but it was stuck fast; she twisted the handle, pulling it hard, but it would not budge, then it suddenly came open and she rushed out through the door and onto to the verandah.

She turned, looking back to see if she was being followed, her heart beating so fast and drumming in her ears. Her head felt hot, her hands were clammy, and yet she shivered, and sat down on a chair at the table shakily. She took a few deep breaths, still looking in the direction of the verandah door, expecting any minute for something or someone to come through it. She changed her seat, and sat in a chair with her back to the cottage wall, knowing that no one could come up behind her.

She sat still for a few minutes, taking deep breaths and thinking how stupid she was, panicking just because the wind blew the door shut, and it wasn't as if it was really dark yet, although the light was beginning to fade fast as it does in the tropics, but these sudden blasts came and went so quickly. Everything around her was now so still, there was only one fishing boat out on the water, and the sea seemed to shush gently on the beach, birds twittered hidden in the trees, which were very still, and she saw a few small bats flying swiftly from tree to tree, as they had done on the first night about this time in the evening. It was a sign that the night was coming on, and the small tree frogs would start their nightly whistling as soon as the real darkness came.

She was still holding the scroll in her hand, she unrolled it carefully and began to read, her hand still shaking gently, and then looked up nervously, almost jumping out of her skin, as the car pulled up outside the gate and Richard and Robert came on to the verandah. They had been gone about five minutes.

'What's the matter, darling?' Richard saw her large frightened eyes.

'Nothing! You just made me jump that's all.'

He looked at her quizzically. 'Are you sure?'

'Yes,' she said. 'I just had a bit of a fright, that's all. The wind blew the dining room shut, and I couldn't get it open.'

'Oh,' he nodded. He screwed up the side of his mouth and his right eye, putting his head on one side. 'What's that humming noise? Can you hear it?'

'Sounds like an electric appliance,' said Robert. 'Maybe the fridge or something.'

'Well, there was this terrific draught just now, just seemed to come from nowhere. It shuddered all the doors and windows, probably triggered something off.'

'Perhaps ... sounds more like a buzzing now,' said Richard. 'Bees or,' he pursed his lips, 'crickets.'

'Crickets! No, crickets don't sound like that,' Robert frowned. 'Do they?'

'Bees, then,' said Richard, leaning over the verandah rail listening. 'Funny, it seems quite quiet out there, apart from the sound of the sea of course.'

A soft breeze blew, ruffling Alison's hair, and the scroll fluttered and crackled as she held it on her knee.

'Sea sounds a bit rough out there,' said Robert, listening over the rail the same as Richard

'You should read this,' said Alison, looking up as Richard walked past her on his way to the kitchen.

He came back with a glass of water. 'What is it?'

'It's the paper that was in the cabinet in the dining room. You remember, Gareth mentioned it.'

'It's the scroll we were reading,' said Robert. 'It tells you about the ship that went down in 1721. It's quite interesting. Tells you about the pirate, and there is a grave down on the beach, well, a sort of grave. They buried a hand or something, and there is a cross on the rock, and we found it. Tim said he had done it all at school. Well, not the hand bit, of course. It's interesting, you should read it, Richard.'

'Oh, yes, Tim knew a lot about the things in the cabinet, didn't he? The pirate ship and the pirate, what's his name?' He took the paper from Alison, and putting the glass of water down on the table, he sat down and began to read. 'Switch the other light on please, Rob.'

He scanned the paper. 'Sounds a bit weird, doesn't it? Hands and rings and things. What else is in that cabinet?'

'Well, the ring is there,' said Alison, 'looks quite valuable. There is some string and rope, and a tatty leather-bound book, looks like a Bible, but I'm not sure.'

'It's a ship's log, actually, Ali,' said Robert, 'but there is nothing on it. The sea has washed the pages clean, they're all stuck together anyway, and yellow with age. And there is part of the Jolly Roger flag, which Tim felt very excited about. Well, we all were really, not many people can say that they have actually handled a Jolly Roger flag from a pirate ship, can they?'

Richard was half-listening and half-reading. 'Where is that painting you did of that statue in the garden, Ali?'

'In the dining room. I left it there to dry. Why do you want to see it?' She jumped up quickly and went off to the dining room. She stood for a second in front of the door, and then opened it cautiously, putting her hand round the door to switch on the light, and then pushing the door wide open. She peered in; there was nothing; she had a quick glance at the cabinet, then picked up the painting and came out of the room quickly, closing the door.

Richard took the painting from her and stood it up, resting it against the back of a chair. He looked at it and then back at the scroll in his hand, and shook his head. 'It's really uncanny, Ali. How did you know to paint her dress red? The statue is completely whitewashed, and you have painted it exactly, red-gold hair and blue eyes. How on earth did you know?'

'I don't know. You asked me that before, and I just don't know. It's eerie, isn't it? You know I had a funny experience while you were taking the Turners back. I was in the dining room and suddenly there was this draught, and the door slammed, and I couldn't get it open, and it suddenly felt icy cold in there, and I felt as if there was something in there leering over me. It really did give me a fright, Richard ... do you believe in ghosts?'

'Ghosts!' Richard frowned.

Robert lifted his eyebrows, a slight smile touching his lips.

'Why, do you?' said Richard looking up from the scroll.

'Well,' she said a little shyly, 'I thought that it may be Aunt Emily, you know, perhaps she doesn't like us touching her things ... or being in her house...'

'Rubbish! I expect it was just a gust of wind that slammed the door.'

'Well, after reading that,' said Robert, pointing to the scroll, 'we went down on to the beach, Tim and Gary and I, and we found the rock with the cross on it, and Tim wanted to dig down and see what was there. Both Gary and I thought he was mad, but Gary helped him dig. They dug down quite deep, and when Gary moved a big rock at the bottom, there was the most atrocious smell and a terrific gust of wind. We all laughed about it, but it seemed to come straight up from out of the hole. And I must say I found it quite eerie. I don't think I believe in ghosts, but it does make you think, and I wonder now if we might have disturbed the grave. What do you think?'

Richard looked at him open-mouthed. 'No! It couldn't be ... could it?' He looked at them. 'I think we need another drink.' He got up with a disbelieving smile on his face. 'What have we got for dinner, Ali?'

She swallowed hard, then went to the fridge and took out the cold roast chicken which Selena had left for them, and there was salad. She called to Robert to come and help her. He laid the table, and the three of them sat round talking about everything, but they all avoided the subject of ghosts.

After they had eaten, Alison cleared the table and they sat in comfortable white-painted rattan chairs, finishing off the rest of the bottle of white wine. The moon's silvery light shone across the water and the waves rushed on to the sand, and the evening was alive with whistling tiny tree frogs, and the buzzing of the crickets. The night was humid; there was not a breath of air, and not even a leaf moved.

It was in the middle of the night when Alison woke and heard the wailing. She sat up in bed.

'Richard?' she said quietly, looking at him; he had his back to her, but he was fast asleep. The wailing seemed to be all around the house. She froze. 'Richard! Richard!' She shook his shoulder, 'Richard what is it?'

'Mmm what?' he mumbled into the pillow.

'Richard?'

He turned towards her sleepily, half-opening his eyes, then suddenly alarmed, he opened them wide, and sat bolt upright. 'What's that noise?'

'I don't know,' said Alison. She got up and went to the window, pushing aside the curtains. 'It sounds like the wind, but the trees are not blowing.'

Richard came up behind her, looking out of the window over her head, 'It looks a bit misty out there, doesn't it?' He rubbed his hand over the glass.

'They don't have fog in the tropics, do they?' She turned to look up at him.

'Well, they must do, it's a swirling mist.'

'Oh, Richard.' Alison's tone was low; she was worried, as the noise got louder and louder and to a screaming pitch and howling, like something in great pain. It kept on and on, and then it gradually died away to a humming, buzzing sound, the same sound as Richard pointed out earlier in the evening. Then there was a sudden banging on the verandah door, and someone was shouting. They looked at each other in alarm. 'What the hell's that?' Richard exclaimed, rushing out of the bedroom door, just as Robert came rushing out of his.

'Oh don't go down, Richard,' Alison cried in alarm, but he was already to the bottom of the stairs, Robert close on his heels, as he pulled open the verandah door.

Alison grabbed her pink towelling housecoat, struggled into it and came down the stairs, still tying the belt.

'Oh! Thank God you are all right,' exclaimed the younger of the two men standing at the door, a look of relief on his face. He was looking at Alison as she joined them at the verandah door.

Richard was taken aback to see them, and was breathing heavily. 'Yes, yeah, we're OK, thanks,' he stammered. 'What is that terrible noise?'

Alison stood nervously between Richard and Robert, fiddling with the ties on her housecoat.

The tall, slim dark-eyed Latin-looking man, dressed in a blue T-shirt and denim shorts, looked at Alison with relief, 'God, I'm glad you are OK.' He looked then at Richard, 'I'm Nick Cotton and this is my grandfather Bill Cotton, we live almost next door just along the beach. We heard the wailing and come as quick as we could, we knew you would be alarmed ... but as long as your wife...' he stopped. 'I mean as long as you are all OK.'

Richard put his arm around Alison's shoulders. He could see she was shivering, although the night was humid; he knew it was the shock. 'Do you know what that noise was?'

'Yes,' said Nick a little hesitantly. He took a breath, 'Yes, it was the ... er ... White Lady in your garden.' He saw Richard's look of puzzled alarm. 'Yes, I think something must have upset her, she usually wails when there is a storm coming, but it doesn't look stormy tonight,' he looked up at the sky. 'Something has upset her. We saw the mist swirling around your door, but when we got here it had gone out to sea. I expect the ship is out there.'

Richard looked at him with a puzzled expression, not knowing what on earth he was talking about. 'White Lady?' He shook his head. 'What ship? I'm sorry, I don't really know what you mean.'

'We saw the mist from the window,' said Alison softly. 'We thought it was a sea mist. What was it, then?'

'Well, it is, sort of,' said Bill Cotton; it was the first time he had spoken. 'You see, it doesn't happen too often, and usually when it is stormy, there is really no harm in it, it has been wailing for years, ever since I was a young lad. But the wailing is very eerie, we know, and it frightens folk who do not understand it. Most folk stay in their houses when she wails, well, women I mean, the men usually come to see if they can help with a ship that is in danger. We have been out in our fishing boats on many a rough night to help survivors, when a ship gets caught on the reef.'

They were all startled as Selena and a very tall young black man came rushing through the gate and up on to the verandah.

'Oh! Selena,' Alison gasped, putting her hand to her throat.

'We come to see you all right, Mistress,' she said hastily, looking at Alison, then at Richard and Robert. 'Dis my son Joseph. Hello, Mr Cotton,' she nodded her head. 'Hello, Mr Nick,' she nodded again, nervously, giving them a half smile and looking a little flustered, and then turning back to Alison. 'Are you all right, Mistress?' Her concern seemed only for the mistress, then she looked at Richard for confirmation. He nodded, saying, 'Yes,' and then she looked at Robert, who just nodded.

'Yes, we are fine thanks, Selena,' said Richard. 'What an eerie sound, really had us worried, but thanks to Mr Cotton and his grandson, we are beginning to understand a bit, and, of course, thanks to you and your son for coming out at this late hour, we are very grateful to you all.'

Alison looked at her watch; it was just gone three o'clock.

Knowing that they must be worried, Selena said Joseph would stay the rest of the night out on their verandah. He was a handsome young man of 21; at least six foot six tall and built like a house, he towered over Richard, Robert and Nick Cotton, who was the same height. He had broad shoulders and muscles that bulged from the sleeves on his white T-shirt. He obviously worked out, probably a body builder, thought Richard, as the light from the open doorway made his black skin shine, and his body seemed to fill the whole of the door frame.

Joseph smiled, showing a set of white teeth, and his large eyes sparkled at the thought of helping them. 'Yes, Mr Price, I will stay on de verandah till de mornin'.' His voice was deep but soft, and the West Indian accent was strong. His large brown eyes were kind, and he seemed a gentle giant.

'Well, thank you, Joseph, that is very kind of you,' said Richard with a smile. 'But I think we will be OK now we know more or less what to expect.'

'Well, I don't think I could sleep now anyway,' said Alison.

Nick smiled. 'Well, we will be getting back then. I'm glad to see everything is OK.'

'I don't think she will give you any more trouble tonight,' said his grandfather, as his thick grey whiskers broke into a smile and his deep brown eyes crinkled at the sides and almost disappeared under the shaggy grey eyebrows.

Richard, Alison and Robert thanked them for coming, and said goodnight as they all moved away, back to their own homes.

Richard closed the door and they went into the lounge.

'Oh, Richard, it's a bit eerie, isn't it?' Alison sat down in an armchair.

'Yes, a bit,' he said, raising his eyebrows and nodding thoughtfully. 'Anyway, darling, come on, let's go back to bed, it will be all right now, come on,' he coaxed.

'Oh, no. I don't think I want to go back to bed now. No, not now, I couldn't possibly sleep,' she shook her head.

'Oh, come on darling, don't worry, it will be all right now I'm sure.' He tried to make his voice sound casual; he was feeling a bit worried himself, but didn't want her to know that. He looked over Alison's head, and nodded to Robert who was standing near the door. 'Make some tea, Rob, will you, please?'

'It's so eerie, Richard, how can a statue just suddenly start wailing in the middle of the night?'

'Well, I expect it is the breeze or something, that just suddenly whips up and whistles around the statue. It most probably has holes in the old wood, and the wind whistled through them.'

'Well, they were all worried about us, weren't they? And how can you explain that mist? It was swirling outside the window, wasn't it, and when you opened the door it was gone. Mist doesn't disappear just like that, does it?'

'No.' Richard looked concerned, but she didn't see it. 'But at least,' he said brightly, 'we know that we have friendly neighbours that are looking out for us. Come on, let's go back to bed.' He was trying to put on a cheerful air, knowing that she was scared.

'No, I couldn't go back to bed now. There's no way I could sleep, could you?'

'No, but you would be resting.'

'Resting!' She leaned back in the armchair just as Robert came through the door with a tray of tea and put it on the coffee table, and handed her a cup and saucer.

'Cheer up, Ali,' said Robert, 'we've only been here a couple of days, and these people have lived here for years, and they have all heard this wailing before, and they are still OK.' She smiled, taking the tea from Robert.

'Richard?' she said slowly, 'You know that scroll we were reading this evening, it said something about...' she thought for a moment, 'something about locking up womenfolk when the wailing starts. It's strange, isn't it? I mean, that mist, and the wailing... Do you think it was coming after me?' She looked up at both of them.

'Why, just cos it's a bit misty?' said Robert in surprise.

'Oh! Alison! Darling! Please,' Richard was shaking his head in despair. 'Please stop worrying. I know it was eerie, we didn't like it much either, did we Robert? It's not funny being woken up in the middle of the night, it's unnerving, I know. But I bet you it is the wind that whistles through the holes in the wood, probably just a freak gust. It happens on islands, it happens all the time. And the neighbours came running, they knew there was nothing out there to be afraid of, they just knew we would be alarmed at the noise, that's all.'

'Well, what about the womenfolk thing, then?' said Alison.

Richard thought for a moment, 'Well, Selena was out there, she's a woman, besides you are not alone,' he smiled, punching his chest. 'You have us two he-men here to protect you.'

'Yes,' laughed Robert, lifting his arms, flexing his muscles and throwing out his chest. 'Just look at the two of us.'

'Yes,' Richard chuckled, 'just look at the two of us, all of our muscles couldn't come anywhere near that Joseph. Did you see his arms?'

'Yeah, he works out, you can see that,' said Robert.

Alison wasn't smiling. She felt far too serious; these two seemed to be making a big joke of it. 'Richard? You know when you took the Turners back, well, I was in the dining room, looking at the things in that cabinet in there. I told you there was a terrific draught and the windows and the door shuddered ... and...'

'Well, there you are then. A freak gust of wind, I told you.' He held out his hand to her. 'Come on, if you won't go back to bed, let's go and sit out on the verandah, it's too hot in here.'

Robert said he was going back to bed, and Alison and Richard sat out on the verandah holding hands. She looked around her nervously, but there was nothing but the black starry sky, and they sat watching as the faint light of the dawn came up and the birds began to twitter and the sounds of the night gradually faded away; one small bat flew into a tree to sleep until the night came on again. As the sunrise came up from behind them over the roof, the grey dawn sky blossomed into a misty blue tinged with pink and apricot, sending shafts of pale golden sunbeams down into the sparkling turquoise blue water. It was going to be another scorching hot day.

Gareth and Tim arrived mid-morning at the cottage; they were with Robert in the dining room, and he was telling them the events of last night, the wailing and the moaning, and the neighbours banging on the door.

'I bet it was scary,' said Tim, 'but I wish that I had been here.'

'So do I,' said Gareth. 'It sounds incredible. I wanted to

have another look at that figurehead, can we go in a minute?' Tim was photographing the scroll, and Robert and Gareth were holding it out flat for him; he took a close-up picture, hoping that the scratchy writing would be visible. He also took close-up photos of the ring and the Jolly Roger and the name painted on the piece of wood, and then a picture of the whole display in the glass cabinet.

'Old Smythe will go crazy when he sees this lot. I know he won't believe his eyes, and I can't wait to show him. How old is this house, Robert?'

'I really don't know, but the date on this scroll is 1721, and George Kingsley watched this ship go down from this verandah, so it must be pretty old.'

Alison was on the verandah, lying on a sun bed reading. When the boys came out, she looked up at them through sunglasses, shading her eyes. 'Finished the filming, Tim?'

'Yes thank you, Alison.' He had a huge grin on his face. 'This will be great when I get to school, they'll be talking about it months.'

'We are going for a swim now, Ali,' said Robert. 'Leave the camera on the table, Tim, Alison will look after it. You can collect it later.' Tim put the camera onto the coffee table, and the three of them darted down the coral stone steps, and went charging down the beach, shouting who was going to be the first one in.

Alison smiled to herself as she watched them. Richard had gone for a walk along the beach; he had much more energy than she had this morning after being up most of the night. She thought about the night, why had Nick Cotton and his grandfather, and Selena and Joseph, come; why had they been so concerned about them? Maybe to save them? But to save them from what?

She got up slowly, and walked to the side of the cottage and turned the corner, walking towards the White Lady. It was quiet in the garden, just the shushing of the sea as it rushed up onto the sand; she walked cautiously as she neared the frangipani tree under which the White Lady stood, with the pink blossoms hanging over her shoulders. She stopped, feeling a little apprehensive. It was bright sunshine. She looked around the garden, but nothing seemed threatening, so she stepped a little closer, looking up into the white wooden face and the unseeing eyes, which seemed to pierce right through her, making a shiver run down her spine. She hunched her shoulders to shake off the cold chill.

'What is it?' she whispered. 'What are you thinking? What are you trying to tell me? You don't really want to hurt me, do you?' She was whispering so quietly, it was almost a thought. She stared into the white-painted face, she was sure that the eyes were straining to see out, and the mouth seemed to curl at the corners. Alison blinked her eyes and shook her head. No, it couldn't be, but there was a faint humming around the Lady. Alison put out her hand gingerly to touch her, but as she did, she saw a movement out of the corner of her eye. 'Oh! Selena!' she gasped; she felt a bit silly – could Selena have heard her talking to a statue?

'Sorry Mistress, but it good I come, or she have you in her power.'

'What! Who?' Had she heard what she was saying?

'SHE! Sheee! She have you in a trance,' Selena said angrily, pointing a sharp finger at the statue. 'I see you. And I watch you, and I see it all before. She takes you too?' She was angry. 'Be careful, Mistress.' Her voice came down to a whisper, and her brown eyes flashed.

'Take me?' Alison frowned. 'Take me where?'

'To sea!' Selena said sharply, then her voice went down to a whisper again, and she stopped short as the master approached them.

'Oh! Hello, Selena.'

'Hello Mr Price, Sir,' she drawled slowly, lowering her brown eyes shyly, as a slight smile caught the corners of her thick lips.

Alison smiled. 'Hello darling, had a nice walk?' Alison was glad to see Richard, and he had relieved the tension between her and Selena. Selena was right, she was feeling transfixed. And she wondered what Selena was about to say.

'Yeah, it was nice down on the beach. I met John down by the hotel and had a chat. I told him about last night. I'm going for a swim now, just come back to see if you wanted to come, the boys are already down there in the water, they're having a great time. I'm glad Robert has found some friends. Are you coming?'

'Yes, I'll come.' He was beginning to walk away. Alison took a deep breath, looked at the Lady, pulled herself together and started to follow him, and then she hesitated. 'What were you saying about the sea, Selena?'

Just then Richard turned, calling her, 'Come on, Ali, the sea looks lovely,' interrupting them again.

Alison and Selena were both looking towards Richard, then they turned back to face each other again. Alison was waiting for Selena to speak.

'I have work to do, Mistress.' She lowered her eyes, then looked up, 'Would you like fish for your lunch? Joseph got a fresh big fish, dis mornin'.'

Alison swallowed hard, 'Err ... yes! Yes, oh ... yes, Selena, that would be lovely, thank you.' She hesitated for a moment, sort of hovering on the spot; their eyes met, she was about to ask Selena again and then thought better of it. Walking past Selena, her mind racing, as she reached the corner of the cottage, she turned. Selena was watching her, their eyes met again just for an instant. She went down the coral stone steps and walked to the water's edge, where she could see Richard and the three boys splashing about. The water was cool, as she waded in and then swam out to them.

After the swim, Alison went up to the bedroom, changed into a dry bikini, then decided that she would do some more painting. She asked Richard to take her easel and the small fold-up stool which she had found standing against the wall in the kitchen, down on to the beach; he could carry it down more easily than she could, even though the easel folded up small enough to fit into the suitcase. Carrying a large pad, a box of paints and brushes, and a large jar of clean water, she followed Richard down onto the beach, where he set her up under the shade of the mahogany tree, which overhung the verandah. She sat for about three hours; the beach was quiet, not many people walked past, and mostly they stayed further along the beach near the hotel.

She was just putting the finishing touch to the white billowy sails of the ship, and she called to Richard to come and look at what she had done, but he was asleep on the verandah, just above her; the walk on the beach and the swimming, plus being up since three in the morning, had taken its toll. She dipped the brush in the water and touched in a small grey cloud, and was concentrating on getting the shading just right, when a large black dog came sniffing by and began to drink thirstily at the water jar.

'Hey,' she turned quickly with a surprised chuckle, 'where did you come from?' He was wagging his tail and slopping noisily at the water.

'That is very good,' said a voice from behind her. 'Sorry about Jojo. Come away, Jojo,' he grabbed the dog's collar.

She turned to see Nick Cotton, the man who had banged on the door last night. He was standing now with his arms folded, his head on one side, frowning though dark glasses and scrutinizing her work.

'I didn't know you were an artist,' he smiled. 'Fancy you being able to paint a galleon like that. You have painted it perfectly.' He sounded very surprised and impressed.

'Well,' she smiled, 'I only paint what I can see. She really is beautiful, isn't she?' nodding and pointing with the brush out to sea, then a look of surprise, 'Oh! She's gone. That was quick, and I must have been putting in the finishing touches longer than I thought.'

Nick looked out to sea; there was a large yellow catamaran sailing by with about 20 people on board. He looked back at Alison, a strange frown across his dark, handsome face. 'Gone?' he queried, looking down at her and then back out to sea.

'Hello Jojo,' Alison was patting the dog, who was nosing at her with warm enthusiasm and his tail wagging excitedly. 'He is lovely, isn't he?' she said looking up at Nick with a dazzling smile, and squinting her eyes in the sun. She reached for her sunglasses, which were on top of her paint box, and now quite sandy where Jojo's feet were dancing about in the sand.

Nick looked down at her thoughtfully. 'Look, umm, err ... I'm sorry if Gramps and I scared you all last night,' he said cautiously, a bit uncertain whether he should have brought up the subject again.

'Oh! No!' She looked up from the dog, 'Well ... yes, Mr Cotton, yes, it was a bit of a shock, you knocking on the door at three in the morning.'

'Sorry, but we were worried. The name is Nick by the way.'

She smiled, nodding. 'Alison Price.' They shook hands. 'It

was a terrible noise though, wasn't it? And the mist, we saw it from the window, and then when we opened the door to you it was gone. Funny that, wasn't it? I mean the statue wailing, you did say it was the statue, didn't you? Weird. Richard says it's probably the wind that blows through the holes in the old wood, and it makes a whistling sound or a wailing. It's probably just a freak gust. What do you think?'

'Yes,' he nodded with a frown. 'Maybe he's right, it could be the wind.' He looked away out to sea; he knew differently, and hoped that it did not show on his face. He looked back at her painting. 'You mentioned something about the ship not being there now?' He frowned and a quizzical smile touched his lips.

'Mmmm, yes,' she smiled, raising her eyebrows. 'It was out there nearly to the horizon. It looked so lovely I just had to sketch quickly, and then I got engrossed in trying to match the colours. But I think I have captured it all right.' She stood up and stepped back to admire her work. 'It looked wonderful out there in full sail,' she had her back to him, 'but it looks as if it was blowing out there a bit, don't you think?' She half turned to look at him. 'A bit stormy, I think.' She turned back to look at her painting, 'Or perhaps it is just the way I have painted it, but that is what I saw, and I think I have got the right red on the dress of the figurehead, don't...' she stopped abruptly, turning quickly to face him. 'Nick!' she breathed, putting her hands to her face in alarm. 'Nick!' her voice rose, 'What have I done? What is happening? What have I seen?'

She looked back at what she had painted – the ship was tossing under grey storm clouds, the figurehead, with her red-gold hair flying in the wind, and the bright red dress billowing. She had painted white full sails, the Jolly Roger flying in the wind, a row of cannons, small figures of men pulling at ropes, hardly visible, but they were there.

'Oh! Nick!' her eyes were wide. 'Oh Nick, I could not possibly have seen a galleon out there, could I? Could I?' She looked at him intently, hoping he had an explanation. 'Nick, a ghost ship?' she said quietly. 'Could it be?' A peculiar tingle came into her stomach, as her wide brown eyes looked searchingly into his for an answer.

Nick took a breath; he was shaking his head slowly and was about to say something, but Jojo broke the tension by nuzzling his hand, and Alison looked down at the dog in a stunned silence. Then looking up at him again, she said, 'Tell me, why did you and your grandfather come knocking on our door last night? You were worried – but why were you worried? And Selena and her son were worried too, weren't they?'

His dark eyes looked at her, and he said thoughtfully, 'Well, you see it's the Lady. She wails sometimes ... it's happened for a couple of hundred years. I thought it was terrible the first time that I heard it, but Gramps reassured me. I don't live here, I am only visiting. I live in New York, and I'm here for a month, maybe two. The legend says that she wails when a ship is in distress on the reef, and she wants to go back to the sea. I believe it's an old wives' tale, myself. Luckily it doesn't happen very often, I've only heard it about three times, and Gramps said that we have had ships in distress on the reef, and she has wailed, but I really don't know if there is any connection. I personally have never seen a ship go down on the reef, but now I think they have marker buoys out there, which they didn't used to have years ago. But Gramps said that other people have been alarmed when they have stayed in the cottage. I think he meant when Emily was here, and I expect that she has lived with this wailing for years, but I have never really thought much about it. I remember her, though. I was here a year or so before she died, she was a very nice little lady, she always came over for a cup of tea with Gramps, and Gramps was very upset and quite lonely, when she went...' He stopped for a minute, and kicked his feet thoughtfully in the sand.

'As I said, when we heard the wailing start up, we knew you had just arrived, and we knew you would be alarmed, so we came over. Silly really, banging on your door at three in the morning. As you said, it is probably just the wind whistling though the holes in the old wood. Oh! Come here, Jojo!' The dog was chasing off down the beach after another dog. 'I'd better go, see you later,' he smiled and walked away quickly, and then broke into a run.

She looked back at her painting, wondering just what she had seen; it was a mystery. She shook her head very slightly and sighed, biting her bottom lip. She bent to pick up the empty water jar. Jojo had been very thirsty. She walked down to the water's edge, and washed out the jar in the sea, brought it back half-full, swizzled her brushes around in it, and then emptied the water on to the sand. She looked at the large sketchpad again; how could she have painted a galleon? She must have seen it out there, or she would not have known how to paint it so perfectly. The rigging. Just look at the rigging. Now what did she know about rigging? Nothing, it had always looked like bits of string hanging from one stick to another, but now on the pad it looked perfect. She had painted cannons; did galleons have cannons? Yes, of course they did, she had seen pirate films, she had even got shadows of men, pirates she supposed. She had got the figurehead, with the red dress billowing and the red-gold hair streaming out behind her as if the wind was blowing full in her face. The sea was rough and the waves were high around the hull, and bursting into white foam, the sails were full blown, and the Jolly Roger seemed to be wavering in the strong gale-force wind, and she was listing to port.

Alison bit her lip, and looked out to sea, it was calm, turquoise blue and clear, the sun caught each ripple, it shone like diamonds, She clenched her hands into tight fists. Was it a ghost ship? Impossible. But it must have been there. She shook her head thoughtfully; she could not even imagine a galleon in such detail, and in fact she had never painted a boat before she came here. It was mostly trees and flowers and still life, vases and things, never a boat.

She came back to reality as a jet bike zoomed by. She bent to pick up her paints and brushes and the water jar, balanced it all on the stool and carried it back to the bottom of the steps, and then she went back for the easel. Leaving the stool and the easel at the bottom of the steps, for Richard to bring up, she carried the pad and the paints. She came up onto the verandah, her footsteps arousing him from his deep sleep.

He yawned, stretching his arms in the air, 'Hello, Ali, I must have dozed right off.'

'Could you bring my easel and the stool up for me, darling, please? I left them at the bottom of the steps, I couldn't manage them. Don't mind, do you?' she smiled; she could see he was hardly awake.

'No, course not,' he yawned, swinging his long legs over the sunbed, standing up lazily and stretching again, reaching right up to touch the roof of the verandah. He let his arms flop back down heavily to his sides, and then went off down the steps.

Alison took her painting into the dining room. She got a cover from the bedroom to match the bikini, and came downstairs; Selena said it was lunchtime.

Richard came to the table. 'Thanks, Selena, I'm starving, had a busy morning.'

'Busy?' Alison looked open-mouthed. He looked at her, pulling a face and chuckling.

'Well, I did have to bring your easel and the stool up, didn't I?'

'Oh, Richard,' she gave him an exasperated sideways glance. They sat at the glass-topped table and Selena brought them quiche and salad, and a glass of light wine with lots of ice in it.

'Where's Robert?' said Richard, looking around.

'I don't know, I haven't seen him all the morning, he must have gone off with the Turner boys ... I met Nick Cotton down there on the beach.'

'Who's he?'

'He is the guy who was banging on the door last night.'

Richard smiled, 'Oh, yes, I remember his name now.'

'I saw a galleon out there on the horizon, and I painted it. I'll show it to you after lunch. Nick Cotton said it was good and I seemed to have got every detail, but I can't understand it because I wouldn't know what a galleon looked like in detail, would I? Nick Cotton seemed to think I saw a ghost ship, can you believe that?'

'This quiche is delicious.' He took a sip of the wine, 'Selena certainly is a good cook.'

'Would I, though?' she frowned. 'I wouldn't know what it looked like, would I?'

'Know what?' he looked up from his plate, and took another sip of the ice-cold wine.

'About the galleon!' Her voice rose. 'How could I know, if I hadn't seen it?'

'What galleon?'

'Are you listening to me?' She put down her knife and fork,

looking annoyed. 'Did you hear what I said? It does seem strange, don't you think?'

'Yes darling, of course, you painted a galleon, and Nick from next door came along and said it was strange, but I think you paint very well, darling, you put a lot of time and effort into it.'

'Oh! You're not listening,' she shook her head with annoyance. 'I told you, there was a galleon out there.'

'Is there? Where?' He looked out to sea.

She put down her knife and fork with a clatter on the plate, the meal only half-finished. She got up from the table and marched off into the cool dining room, picked up the painting and brought it back, holding it up in front of him.

'Oh darling!' he exclaimed, finishing the last piece of tomato, and putting down his knife and fork. 'That is brilliant.' He looked at the painting admiringly. 'It's perfect. How can you paint like that? It beats me, it's wonderful, and how can you remember every single detail? It's wonderful. You have a marvellous imagination, darling; I wouldn't know what a galleon looked like.'

She sighed with annoyance. 'I told you, Richard, I saw it out there, and I told you I actually saw it out there on the horizon. I know it sounds crazy, but it was there; how on earth would I know how to paint it if I had not seen it? Besides, I think it is the first time I have ever painted a boat in my life. It's a ghost ship. You know, like the *Flying Dutchman*.'

'You couldn't have seen it?'

She sighed, again clicking her tongue irritably. 'That's what I keep trying to tell you, and you just don't listen. I thought I saw it out there, in fact I am sure I saw it. I sat there and sketched it out, and then I was just finishing off painting it, when that Nick guy from next door came along and said it was good. By the way, he apologized for banging on the door last night, he explained about the statue in the garden, and said that it has wailed for years, but that they hadn't heard it for some time. I said that we thought that it was a freak gust of wind whistling through the old wood, and he said that was probably just what it was.'

He looked at the painting again. 'You know, you have a wonderful imagination. Perhaps you did see the *Flying Dutchman*.

I read somewhere that it had been sighted; I thought it was rubbish, though … I wonder where Robert has got to.'

'I saw it, Richard.' She stormed off to the dining room and slapped the painting down on the table, feeling very frustrated. Did men ever listen? She was sure that Richard had not heard a word she had said, even now. She went back out: he was stretched out on a sun bed with his eyes closed, and she sat down on the other bed beside him, gazing out to sea, hoping to see something, but the only thing she saw was a large container ship making its way slowly toward the harbour in Bridgetown. It seemed as if it was perched on a dark blue line, with a background of light blue sky. The sea had many shades, dark blue to black, streaked in silver and turquoise blue, and shades of green; each ripple sparkled like a diamond, until it got near to the shore a bright ultramarine, and then turned over, splashing into fluffy white foam, and rolling up onto the golden sand. Her artist's eye saw every colour.

Richard sat up and picked up the book he had been reading; he turned the pages, found where he had left off and settled himself comfortably.

Alison continued to gaze dreamily out to sea; she was deep in thought, hoping that she would get a glimpse of the galleon, which she knew must have been a figment of her imagination.

The sound of the phone ringing jolted her back to reality. Selena poked her head around the door, and said, 'De phone is for Mr Robert, Sir, but I not see him.'

Richard looked up. 'I'll take it, Selena.' He put down his book, swung his legs over the side of the sun bed, and walked into the hall, picking up the receiver which Selena had left on the table. 'Hello.'

'Oh! Hello, Richard, Gary here, sorry to bother you, but would you tell Rob to hurry, the ski boat will be here in five minutes. He was supposed to be down here by three-thirty, I thought he might have forgotten. Oh, and Tim says would he bring his camera, he left it on the table on your verandah. Thanks, bye,' and he rang off.

Richard quickly dialled the hotel number which was in front of him on the pad. Gareth was still near the phone when it rang; he picked it up saying, 'Hello.'

'Hello, Gareth, it's Richard again. Look, we haven't seen

Robert since you were here this morning, and when he didn't come in for lunch, we thought he was with you.'

'Well, we haven't seen him. Tim and I came back to the hotel hours ago after the swim, we swam back half the way and walked the rest along the beach, and Robert swam in, we haven't seen him since then.'

'Oh!' Richard was surprised. He touched his forehead, frowning, and pushed the dark curl back, which was always falling over his eye. 'Oh, perhaps he is in his room then, perhaps he's asleep, I'll check. You go ahead and ski, don't wait for him, and I'll give him the message.' They rang off, and Richard dashed up the stairs two at a time and opened Robert's door sharply.

'Who was that?' asked Alison, looking up as he came back onto the verandah.

'It was Gareth,' he frowned. 'Robert should have been down there at half past three to go water-skiing, they thought he was here, but he's not. I have just checked his room, and he's not there.'

Alison frowned. 'Funny, where is he, then? I've not seen him and I have been down on the beach all the morning. The last time I saw him, he was dashing down to the water with the boys. I wonder where he is, then?'

'See you later, Rob,' said Gary, as they began to swim away from each other. It was almost lunchtime, and he had arranged to meet Tim and Gary for water-skiing at three-thirty.

Rob came out of the water and started to walk up the beach. He smiled to himself as he saw a big black dog drinking the water out of Alison's water jar, and her face was a picture. He guessed the dog belonged to the guy she was talking to; he recognized him as the same guy who had knocked on the door in the middle of the night. He was probably asking her if they were all right after he and his grandfather left them. He didn't like to butt in, and they didn't see him as he walked past them and ran up the coral stone steps. He stood under the shower, which was at the corner of the house, for a minute, to take the salt water off his body and the sand off his feet, then grabbing a yellow towel off the back of a chair, he walked quietly past Richard, who was flat out on a sun bed. He went into the house and up the stairs to his room; he could hear Selena in the kitchen, rattling plates.

Going into the bedroom, he took a clean pair of swimming shorts out of the drawer, and went into the bathroom to dry off and change. He was going to hang the wet ones in the shower, but the sun was streaming in through the window and he thought they would dry quicker if he hung them out over the bathroom window sill; the red ones were his favourites, and if they dried he would change back into them for water-skiing. He leaned over the wash basin and flipped the shorts over the window sill. They slipped off and fell down into the garden. He leaned over, stretching his neck, but he could not see them; he would have to go down and get them.

He went back into the bedroom and put on his trainers; walking round the garden would be too hard on his bare feet. He came out of the bedroom and ran quickly down the stairs, tiptoed past Richard, who was still dead to the world, walked round the house, past the shower and down the garden path, and stopped in front of the White Lady. Alison was right, there was something about her, something odd, but he didn't know what it was - but Richard had said it was a block of wood, and he had to agree. But there was this strange sort of buzz about her. He looked at her with his head on one side, and then decided that the buzz was an electrical sound, she was standing against the kitchen wall, and the buzz must be coming from the fridge. Anyway, he had to find his shorts; it was almost lunchtime. He started to walk on just as Joseph came through the trees with a few mangos in a box; his face creased and broke into a broad smile when he saw Robert.

'Hi Joseph, what you doing? What have you got there?' Robert peered into the box.

'Hellooo maaan,' Joseph drawled, showing Robert the box.

'Are they mangos?'

Joseph nodded. 'Mama asked me to pick um, dey for you lunch.'

Robert nodded with pleasure at the thought. 'Do you work in the garden? We wondered who kept it tidy.'

'Yeah maaan, I duzz de heavy work, and help Mama, like de

liftin and tings, and I does de garden.' He looked round with a smile at the trees and plants, feeling happy with his work.

Robert smiled up at him. Joseph was a giant, towering over him. 'I bet you didn't need a ladder to pick those mangos.'

Joseph chuckled, lowering his eyes shyly, 'No, maaan.'

Robert said he was looking forward to them, as it was nearly lunchtime, and Joseph, realizing, dashed off into the kitchen with the mangos. Robert watched him go, a smile on his face, looked back up at the White Lady, and then went on his way round to the back of the house to look for his shorts.

This part of the garden had been unattended for years, here the bushes were dense; he pushed his way through tangled tall grasses, and thick plantation with heavy leaves. It was like a jungle, and he smiled, imagining himself with a big machete hacking his way through dense undergrowth, like he had seen in films, not knowing if there were lions and tigers, ready to spring upon him; he imagined himself like Tarzan, and then he spied his red shorts, hanging precariously on a high twig which overhung part of the wooden tiled roof. He put his foot on to some thick and tufty grass, it felt soft and springy under his size 12 trainers. He tried it again, making sure it was solid, and then being tall, he managed by putting his right hand onto the low roof, and leaning over he grabbed his red shorts, and as he did this the soft grass beneath his feet gave way and he slipped down a hole with a shout.

Sitting there a bit shaken, and rubbing his elbow with his shorts, he looked up and discovered that he had fallen down about ten steps which led down to a door in the wall of the house. It was covered with thick greenery; the grass had grown up over many years, and thickly matted vines had twisted and climbed, and the ancient roots had adhered to the brown wooden door. Standing now in the well of the steps, he began to pull the greenery away from the door, sending ants scattering from their nest in a frenzied mass. He jumped back as black beetles and cockroaches left the quietness of their homes and ran for cover into the undergrowth. Trying again, he pulled hard at the clinging vines that refused to leave their life's support, and he sniffed at the pungent smell of damp earth and greenery and dry rot, which puffed up into his nostrils, smelling musty like grey decaying talcum powder.

He eventually moved the undergrowth and found a heavy rusty iron handle, which the matted vines had hidden for many years, and to his surprise, it moved reasonably easily. He pulled hard at the handle and the door opened towards him, the bottom scraping on the uneven ground, and the dry and red rusty hinges squeaked.

He peered into the darkness and clouds of dust flew up. He closed his eyes tight, then opened them again and sneezed twice; it smelled old and damp and musty, and it was thick with grime, and cobwebs hung like thick grey curtains. He jumped with an 'Eeeek!' and a shiver ran down his spine as a huge black spider ran to one side of a very large web for safety, frightened by the sudden light of the bright sunbeam which shot down the wooden stairway like a searchlight into the gloom, where millions of dust particles danced in the yellow beam, glad to be free of the many years of darkness.

Robert strained his eyes but could not see the bottom of what quite obviously was a cellar. Holding onto the door frame, he put his right foot out and tested the stairs. They seemed pretty safe, he didn't want to fall down again. He began to walk carefully, as they were a bit rickety. As he neared the bottom of the stairs, with the sunbeam behind him, he could see in the right-hand corner an oar and a bundle of fishing nets. Reaching the bottom of the stairs, he found the earth floor damp and springy beneath his trainers. He touched the fishing net, and clouds of musty smelling dust rose, clogging his throat, and he coughed. There was a small mast, and the grey sail was still attached and rolled around it; it was threadbare. Beside it was a coil of rope which looked new, as if it had just been put there.

He looked around him and to the left, but beyond the brilliance of the sunbeam it was hard to see. He made his way treading carefully across the earth floor, blinded by the sun, and then in the gloom he could see a barrel, and then three barrels. He inspected them; the first one had no lid and spiders had made webs across the top; it smelled mouldy, and he suspected that at one time someone had used it for storing vegetables which had shrivelled. The wet and soggy pulp had dried years ago, and the barrel was a quarter full of grey decayed dust.

The next barrel had a name painted on it, and with closer inspection he could see only half the name, as it was turned to the wall. He tried to move it, but it was too heavy, probably full of rum, he thought, fancy all those years, it would be pretty potent now. He smiled at the thought, and although he could see only half the name, he was sure that it said *Savannah Lady*. His heart leaped and he couldn't wait to tell Tim, who he knew would be so excited and would come down and bring his camera to take pictures for Old Smythe. He smiled to himself and moved on to the next barrel, which was simply marked 'RUM'. There was a wooden tap on the side; he gave it a small turn, and the strong-smelling rum flowed out. He put his hand under it and then put it to his mouth, pulling a face as the strong amber liquid burned his tongue and his lips.

Looking round, his eyes now accustomed to the gloom, there appeared to be nothing else down here in the cellar, so he made his way carefully back across to the stairway, where the sunbeam shone down like a light shining onto a theatre stage. He was almost halfway upstairs when the wood beneath his feet began to creak and crack. There was a loud snap, and he fell backwards, thudding heavily onto the earth floor, with the wooden stairs, rotten and decaying splinters, dry mud and cobwebs showering down on top of him, wood beetles scurrying, and termites in their millions covering his chest, neck, face and hair. He brushed at them frantically, as they were running all over his body.

He lay shocked, flat on his back, for a minute or two, his eyes closed to the dust which was settling down on him, covering him and clogging his nostrils, mouth, ears and eyes. He tried to open his eyes, but the red mahogany dust lay thick on his eyelids. He wiped it away with thick dust-covered hands, easing his eyes open slowly to slits against the strong sunlight which shone down, blinding him. He managed to sit up, and looking down at himself he knew he would have frightened anyone, looking like a zombie rising from the grave.

He brushed the red dust off his chest, arms and shoulders; his hands went to his face, and he ran them though his hair. He pursed his lips and blew upward, and the dust flew out of his hair, and down again in a cloud. He coughed and choked, unable to take a really deep breath; he covered his mouth with his hand and waited again for the dust to settle, but as soon as he moved to lift the heavy rotten wood of the stairs, which was across his legs, the dust flew up again, and then he felt the pain on his shin bone. He moved his right leg, and winced loudly; he bent the leg, slowly putting his hand tightly over the wound to try to stop the pain. He found on inspection that it was a bad graze and luckily not broken, but a large bump was turning quickly into a very blue bruise, and the thin skin on his shin was torn and beginning to bleed. He didn't think it was broken, but the pain was so great that he held it even tighter, and tears streamed down his face, making rivulet lines in the red dust from his eyes to his chin.

Looking up, he could see the open doorway above him, and knew that he could not possibly reach it. His leg hurt, and he rocked back and forth, holding it tight, but it didn't deaden the pain. But he had to get out of the cellar, and he needed something to stand on. The rum barrel – that would do. He managed to get to his feet and hobble to the barrels; the one with the tap was only half-full, and if he was fit he could have rolled it but, as it was, it was too heavy. He turned on the tap to empty it, but the fumes in the confined space were so strong that he almost felt drunk on the smell, so he turned the tap off quickly. There was so much debris strewn across the floor that it would be impossible to manoeuvre a barrel anyway, and nowhere to stand it. He tried to lift the empty one; it was still heavy, but he would be able to roll it, but first he would have to set about clearing a space, so he hobbled about, first lifting the heaviest pieces of wooden stairs, which proved to be a major task, because as he moved each piece, the dust rose and choked him.

He gradually cleared a space for the barrel to stand, but he worked slowly and moved clumsily about, bending and lifting. It was hot and dusty and he needed a scarf or something to tie round his mouth, but he had nothing; he could see his red shorts, hanging up near the door and way out of his reach. The bruise on his leg was getting bluer, and the lump was now as big as a tennis ball; blood was running from the grazed skin in a stream down to his ankle, and his leg was throbbing, and the intense heat made him exhausted. He sat down amongst dirt and the rubble, away from the sunbeam, for a rest, and cooled off for maybe five or ten minutes, then he started again. He had not moved very much after an hour, but he had made a small space, enough for the barrel to stand steady. Clambering clumsily over the rotten wood, he managed to lift the empty barrel to the space near the door, and as he turned it upside down, the red dust from the rotten wood mingled with the grey dust from inside the barrel, flying up straight into his face. He coughed and spluttered, eventually getting his breath back, then making sure that the barrel was secure, he climbed up onto it very slowly, dragging his injured leg with a groan, and then finding that as he reached up he was still quite a few feet short of the door, he got gingerly down off the barrel and found a piece of the wooden stairs, which he balanced on the top of the barrel, but then he found that it was not very safe, and trying to climb up on it might result in a broken leg, so he didn't chance it.

It was now, after all this time and effort, that he decided to shout for help – he had been so confident that he would get out on his own, but it was no use, so he began to shout. But then he found that his throat was so parched with the dust that hardly any sound came out, but he shouted again and again until he was exhausted. He sat down sullenly on the barrel and folded his arms, prepared to wait. His leg was throbbing, and he put his hand gently over the wound, wincing. Soon Richard and Alison would miss him, or probably they were already looking, then why hadn't they found him? He knew why; because they had never been round to this part of the garden, and they didn't know about the cellar. Oh God, he might be down here all night, and his leg was throbbing; he held it again, knowing that if he didn't get it cleaned up, it might turn poisoned, he had heard of people in hot climates having their legs off when gangrene had set in. The thought frightened him, and he began to shout again; he listened, but all he could hear was the shushing of the sea. Surely Gary would phone when he didn't turn up for water-skiing. God, he was hot, he wiped the sweat from his brow; surely someone would come round this side of the garden. Joseph would, but when? He would just have to wait.

He sat down on the coil of rope. He was hot and exhausted from the heat, and he needed a drink. His throat was parched, but it was the first time he had really thought about water, and the more he thought about it the more thirsty he felt. He could drink the rum from the barrel, but he knew he would get drunk; he could do without a headache just now. His leg was painful enough; he looked down at it, and it looked red and angry, then a thought struck him; the rum would clean it – he had seen that many times in films, cowboys always poured whisky over their gunshot wounds, then drank from the bottle to deaden the pain. He went to the barrel and turned on the tap. The liquid flowed out and the strong aroma filled his nostrils; he found it nauseating, and quickly turned off the tap again, then hobbled back to the coil of rope, and sat down, holding his leg gently – it was too painful to touch. He sat waiting and listening, his ears straining for the slightest sound, but the cellar was very quiet. He must have dozed off.

He woke with a start, looking up. A large black dog was barking at him furiously from the open doorway. It was the guy next door's dog, the one that had been drinking the water from Alison's paintbrush jar. He licked his lips, he thought he wouldn't mind a jar of paintbrush water, just at the minute, his mouth was so dry and he would drink anything. He stood up, coming nearer to the door space, and shouted 'Help, help,' and the dog barked even louder, then someone must have called it away, for it suddenly looked to its right and then dashed off. It must have been Nick Cotton who had called it; he stood listening and then shouted, and listened again, hoping to hear Nick Cotton's voice. But there was nothing. He shouted and shouted, and then sat down again, exhausted and thirsty. His head ached with the heat, and every time he moved the dust flew up, choking him; he sat with his head in his hand, the sweat dripping from his body, the only sound the shush and an occasional thud as a heavy wave crashed on the shore.

Alison phoned the hotel and asked the operator for the room number. When Carol answered, she asked her if she had seen Robert yet.

'No, we haven't seen him,' she could hear by the tone of Alison's voice that she was really worried. It had been hours now since the boys had been skiing.

'Well we can't find him,' said Alison. 'We have looked everywhere, and Richard has been walking up and down the beach for ages. He came back, and he is down there again now. I am so worried, Carol, where on earth can he be?'

'Look, em, Gary and Tim are here, they are just going down to get jet bikes. I'll tell them to come up and help you look, he can't be far away.' Carol hesitated. 'He is a good swimmer, isn't he, Alison?' she held her breath, waiting for a reply and tapping her fingers on the table beside the phone, and wishing that she had not suggested such a thing.

'Oh, I am sure he has not got into any trouble in the water,' said Alison, shaking her head. 'He is a strong swimmer, and the sea looks quite calm, and in any case, when Gary phoned about water-skiing, he said that Robert was swimming towards the beach, he was coming in for lunch, but no one has seen him, and I am getting really worried, Carol. Oh, there's Richard just coming back, I'll have to go. I'll ring you back if there is any news.' She put down the receiver and rushed out of the hallway, calling down to Richard over the balustrade, 'Any luck?'

Richard looked up at her, raising his hands hopelessly and shaking his head. He came up the coral stone steps, talking to her all the way. 'I met Nick Cotton, he was walking his dog. He says he hasn't seen him, and he has been miles up the beach, but he said he will keep his eyes open as he goes along, but I don't think he is there, I've been everywhere.'

'Well, I phoned Carol and she said the boys are coming up to help us look.' She put her hand to her forehead and pushed her hair back. 'I am beginning to get really worried now, Richard. Carol asked if he was a good swimmer, I said he was. He is, isn't he? Do you think we should call the police?'

Richard sat limply in the chair. 'Yes, I'm sure he is a good swimmer, but I don't really know what to do. I think we should wait a bit longer before calling in the police, he can't be far away. Perhaps he has met someone on the beach and is sitting chatting, and he has forgotten the time.'

'What, all this time?' Alison's voice rose. 'No. It's not like Robert, though, is it? He wouldn't be gone this long. What, and miss his lunch? Never!'

Richard raised his eyebrows, and gave a little chuckle. 'You never know, he might have met some pretty girl on the beach, and taken her out for lunch.' His eyebrows came down and then up again comically, and he grinned at the thought.

'Oh! Richard!' she gasped, not believing her ears.

'Well, why not?' he looked up at her. 'He's growing up, isn't he? He is nearly eighteen, isn't he? It's possible.'

'Yes, but he wouldn't go off like that, without telling us. Gosh, Sue would have a fit. Besides, he was supposed to go water-skiing with the boys. He's out there somewhere.' Alison looked along the beach, as if expecting to see Robert coming or clambering over the rocks. 'Perhaps he has fallen on the rocks and broken his legs or ankle or something. He might even have hit his head and is lying out there unconscious, between the rocks.'

'No,' said Richard, looking at her as if she was stupid, 'he is not on the beach or the rocks. I've looked everywhere.'

Alison waved, as Nick Cotton was coming up the beach towards the cottage with the dog. When he got close enough he shouted up, 'Did you find Robert yet?'

'No,' Alison shook her head sadly.

A very concerned looked came on his handsome features, and he frowned deeply. 'How long has he been gone?'

'Ages,' said Richard looking at his watch.

The dog by Nick's side saw Alison and bounded up the steps, and Nick shouted at him to come back, but the dog took no notice. Nick came up the steps two at a time after him, but Alison was already making a fuss of him, and his tail was wagging excitedly.

'I'm sorry about the dog,' Nick said, 'he is a nuisance. I walk him for Gramps, and he has a mind of his own, he won't take a bit of notice of me. I should keep him on a lead really.'

'Oh, it's all right, it's no problem,' said Richard. 'Alison loves dogs. Look at the two of them.' They watched as Alison patted the dog, and the dog turned round and round in circles, wagging his tail excitedly with his mouth open in a wide doggy smile, showing a long pink tongue and a set of white sharp teeth.

'You haven't found him yet, then?' said Nick with concern.

'No.' Richard shook his head, biting his bottom lip, and sighing, he took a deep breath, and rubbed the back of his neck nervously. 'I really don't know what to think. Sit down, Nick, do you want a drink?'

'Yes, please, a glass of water or a Coke, I don't mind, thanks.'

Alison went into the kitchen and asked Selena to bring three Cokes. Selena turned to her quickly, 'You found him?'

'No. Mr Cotton from next door has just come up.'

Selena nodded. 'I bring de Cokes, Mam.'

Selena brought a tray, and Alison, Richard and Nick sat round the table in the shade. Jojo was panting with his tongue hanging out, and Alison followed Selena back into the kitchen, and came back with a large salad bowl of water for him. He lapped it up greedily, splashing and slopping noisily.

'We really don't know what to do about Robert, Nick. Do you think we should call the police?' She sat down.

'Well,' said Richard, 'we really don't want to make too much fuss, darling. I know we are worried, but I'm sure he will come back. I think we should leave it a bit longer.'

'Yes, he's got tied up somewhere,' said Nick with a smile. 'Probably found a girl.'

'Oh, no! Not you too. Richard said that.'

They sat chatting, and the conversation got round to Alison's painting of the galleon, and Alison insisted that she had seen it. Richard asked Nick about the White Lady, and Alison asked him if he had ever felt a presence about her.

'No, I don't really know,' he shook his head. 'I have never really stood that close to the statue, the only time I ever think about it is when it wails, and that is not very often. What you ought to do is to come and have a chat with Gramps. He loves to ramble on about the past, he'll tell you all the old wives' tales about the White Lady. Whether they are true or not, I don't know, but he makes it sound intriguing.'

'I suppose Robert is not over at your house, chatting to your grandfather, is he?' said Alison hopefully. 'He might have just forgotten the time. The time goes so quickly here, I just don't know where the days go.'

'No, when I came out with Jojo, Gramps was asleep in the chair.'

Jojo, after quenching his terrible thirst, had settled himself down by Nick's feet and gone to sleep with his head between his paws. He suddenly stood up and gave a low growl, then he gave a soft 'Woof, woof,' just enough to puff out his soft black jaws. He listened, and then shook his head, flapping his right ear back.

Nick laughed. 'He always flaps his ear back like that when he's listening. I've noticed him do it several times since I have been back this trip. What's the matter boy, eh? What can you hear?' He stroked the dog's head, and took hold of his collar, he didn't want to go chasing after him, down on the beach again. 'Sit, sit,' and Jojo sat down beside him; his eyes and his ears were alert, his mouth was open, showing his white teeth, and he looked as if he was smiling, his tail was wagging. He suddenly stood up, and Nick reached for the lead and was just about to clip it onto his collar when he gave a loud bark and took off, pulling away from Nick's grip on his collar. He went tearing round the side of the house, his tail held high in an air of excitement. Nick jumped up quickly from the table and chased after him, calling, 'Jojo, Jojo.' As Nick turned the corner of the house, the dog was bounding past the White Lady and almost collided with Joseph, who was running towards him.

Joseph, catching his breath, was pointing. 'Quick, Maaan, quick, it Mr Robert.' He was pointing in the direction of the dog, and then turned to follow Nick, who had now passed him, following Jojo as he disappeared round another corner of the house.

Richard and Alison heard the commotion, and Richard jumped up and rushed off the verandah, followed by Alison. Selena, who was in the kitchen, saw them all running past the window, and came quickly out of the kitchen door.

'What is it? What's happened?' cried Alison in alarm.

'I think they have found him,' Richard shouted over his shoulder.

Joseph stopped, standing aside to let Richard and Alison past. 'I tink it Mr Robert, Sir, it Mr Robert.' He could hardly get the words out, his eyes were goggling and he was pointing to the back of the house, where Nick was just disappearing round the corner, following Jojo, who had now disappeared in the long grass and the dense bushes. He couldn't see him, but the dog was barking frantically. He pushed his way with difficulty through the undergrowth, Richard now close on his heels, and when they reached the dog, he was barking down into the open doorway of the cellar.

Everyone was relieved, especially Robert, as he looked up into the four anxious faces which crowded the doorway, blocking out the light of the sun, which had now moved round, and was no longer sending an intense beam down though the doorway. Jojo continued to bark excitedly.

'Thank God you came,' said Robert, sighing with relief and taking deep breaths of the fresh air, after Joseph had got a ladder and he and Richard had helped him out. 'And thank God for dogs,' he said, bending to pat the excited Jojo and showering red dust all over the dog's back, but he didn't seem to mind a bit; he danced round in a circle wagging his tail, while Robert ruffled his ears and told him he was a good boy, and he wagged his tail even harder, knowing he had done something special.

'Good boy, good boy,' said Robert. 'At least you have good ears. That's more than I can say for this lot,' he laughed at everyone. 'I have been shouting for hours, and you were the only one who heard me, good boy,' he said, still patting the dog.

'I hear you, Mr Robert,' said Joseph; 'but I not know where to look.'

They were all concerned and asking questions about how he got down there, and what had happened, and Alison was fussing round him, saying that she was glad he was safe, and asking if he was all right, and looking at the gash on his leg.

Robert explained about his shorts falling out of the bathroom window, and finding the cellar and the stairs collapsing, and how he had tried to get out, and then they were all looking at the huge bruised lump on his leg and could see that he was limping badly. He ruffled the dog's ears again, telling him he was a clever boy, and then he said to Nick, 'Your dog came round hours ago, he was barking, and I thought you would have found me, but you must have called him away. But you are a very good boy, aren't you?' he said, patting Jojo again.

'Oh I am sorry,' said Nick. 'I was down on the beach, and I saw him come bounding up your steps, and I didn't want to come up and disturb you,' he said to Alison and Richard, 'I saw you at the table having your lunch. I heard him barking so I whistled him, and he came back probably to tell me, he doesn't usually come when I call him, he has a mind of his own. But I wish now that I had come up to see why he was barking.'

'Well, we never saw him come up,' said Richard, 'or go back down again.'

'Anyway, thanks everyone,' said Robert, shaking his head with a grateful smile. 'I'm OK now, thanks to my hero here, Jojo,' he patted the dog again. 'Gosh, you don't know how glad I am to be out. It was stifling down there, and you can't believe the dust, and I am so thirsty,' he chuckled and coughed, catching his breath. 'There is a barrel of rum down there, but if I'd had a drink I would have been legless, and you might never have found me.'

'At least you would have died happy,' laughed Richard.

Alison was looking at Robert. He was filthy, covered in red mahogany dust and grime, and the wound on his leg looked angry. 'You ought to go in and have a shower, Rob, and clean that leg up, you don't want to get that dirt in it, it will go poisoned. I'll bring you up some ice to put on it, and then I'll put some antiseptic on it and bandage it up for you.'

'Oh, thanks, Ali,' he said gratefully, 'but I need a drink first, I am absolutely gasping.'

Richard and Nick came either side of him and helped him to walk. 'Oh, it's OK, I can manage, it's not that bad.' But they could see that he was limping badly. 'By the way, did anyone find my shorts?'

'I go an look, Maaan,' said Joseph.

He was in the shower when Gary and Tim arrived. They pushed the jet bike well up onto the beach so that it would be safe and not float away, then ran up the beach and then up the coral stone steps to the verandah, with their trainers hanging round their necks.

'It's all right, it's all right,' said Alison, holding up her hand. She knew they were anxious to help. 'We have found him, he fell down into the cellar, he's OK, he will tell you about it. He is in the shower now, but you can go up.'

They went upstairs into Robert's room, and Gary banged on the bathroom door, calling 'Rob.' He called back that he would only be a minute. He came out of the bathroom wrapped only in a large white towel, and they sat on the bed while he told them what had happened, and Tim's eyes lit up when he told them about the rum barrels.

Richard, Nick and Joseph were on the verandah, all feeling relieved to be free of the anxiety, now that they had found Rob, and he was safe, and OK apart from the gash on his leg.

'Time for a drink, I think,' said Richard. 'Rum and ginger, Nick?'

'Please,' said Nick, nodding his head with a smile.

'Joseph, go into the kitchen and ask your mother to bring us three rum and gingers, please, and you can have one yourself if you like, or take a Coke or beer or whatever you want from the fridge. And thank you for your help.'

'You're welcome, thank you, Mr Price, Sir,' and Joseph went off to the kitchen, feeling happy inside and pleased with himself. His mother asked if everything was all right now, and he nodded with a happy smile, his big eyes shining with delight.

The phone was ringing on the hall table and Richard picked up the receiver.

'Hello, White Lady Cottage.'

'HELLO RICHARD,' the raised voice at the other end was loud in his ear. 'Sue here. Are you all OK?' He smiled to himself; Sue always shouted into the phone, thinking that no one could hear her.

'Oh, err, yes, Sue ... we are all fine, thanks. Oh, just a minute.' Alison came down the stairs. She had taken a Coke and some ice up to Robert to put on his leg; it would take the swelling down. She had also taken him a tube of antiseptic cream, but he had refused to let her put a bandage on it. She could see that he was still a bit shaken but otherwise all right, and was pleased to have Gary and Tim there with him.

Richard put his hand over the mouthpiece, and whispered to her, 'It's your sister.' She winced through her teeth, clenching her fists and hunching her shoulders as if in pain. This was the worst time for Sue to call. She took the receiver from him.

'Hello, Sue,' she said in a flowery voice, trying to smile into the phone, then she looked at Richard and mouthed, 'You didn't tell her about Robert.' She pointed anxiously up the stairs, in case he had not understood what she was trying to say, but he shook his head and walked away.

'Hello, Ali. Having a nice time, are you dear? What's the weather like?'

'Oh it's wonderful, Sue, hot and sunny, and we are all getting a nice tan.'

'What's the matter with Richard? He sounded a bit, sort of funny and sharp. Is he all right?'

'Yes! Yes, he's OK. He has just got someone here with him at the moment,' Alison said quickly, trying to make excuses for Richard. She did not want to tell her that her son had been missing for five hours and had hurt his leg badly, even though, at this moment, he was safely upstairs. And she hoped that Sue could not hear anything amiss in her tone either.

'Was the flight good?'

'Yes, very good thanks, Sue, eight hours.'

'How is that son of mine, is he behaving himself? Can I have a word with him?'

Alison had a quick intake of breath. 'Umm, umm, no. Sue ... he's, err ... not here just at the moment. Err, he is with some friends. They are swimming in the sea,' she said very quickly. 'How was your trip to Germany, Sue?' she said quickly, changing the subject.

'Boring, as usual, you know what business trips are like. It was freezing cold, and I kept on thinking about you all out there in the warm sunshine. And I said to Peter, we should come out there for a few days, but then he said he had too much work on, and then he said it was too far for just a few days, you know men,' she sneered. 'Any excuse, except if it's business or golf. What's the house like?'

'Oh, it's lovely, Sue, right on the beach. Nicely furnished, a lot of antiques, lot of Aunt Emily's treasures, you know, jade pieces and silverware, and a few photos of her. She looked a nice lady. And we have Selena, she has been the housekeeper here for years, she is very nice too, and a good cook.'

'Sounds nice. Well I must go, Ali, it's getting late here, and Peter has already gone up to bed. Give my love to Robert, and tell him I will ring him tomorrow. Bye, Ali. Bye.'

'Bye, Sue.' She put the receiver down, and winced; she hated having to tell lies, but she didn't want to explain about Robert. It would sound much worse over the phone, much better to let Robert tell her. She joined Richard and Nick at the table, and sipped gratefully at the rum and ginger that Richard pushed towards her.

'Did you tell Sue about Robert?'

'No,' she shook her head, and raised her eyebrows. 'You know how she worries about him. I thought it better to let him tell her tomorrow; she said she would phone him. I just said he was with some friends.' She looked at Nick and nodded. 'Robert's an only child. I think Sue thinks he is still a baby.' She smiled.

Richard added more ice to her rum and ginger. She sipped at it and Jojo put his head on her knee, and she stroked his ears. 'You're a good boy, Jojo,' she smiled down at him. 'Do you need a drink too?' She looked at the water bowl. It was almost empty. She got up and took it to the water tap by the shower at the corner of the house, and the dog followed her and watched while she filled it up, and then followed her back, anxiously waiting for her to put it down, then lapped at it noisily, splashing water over Nick's bare feet.

Robert, now showered and refreshed, came limping down the stairs and out on to the verandah, followed by Tim and Gary.

'Come on, I'll show you,' he was saying.

'Are you all right, Rob?' Alison asked, looking first at his face and then down at his leg.

'Yes, fine thanks, Ali,' he said cheerily. 'Thanks for the ice, it feels a lot better.'

The wound looked angry, the graze down his shin was bright red, and the bruise and the huge blue bump looked very painful. 'You ought to let me put a bandage on that, Robert, you don't want to get the sand in it.'

'No, it's OK. I don't need a bandage.' He started to limp away. 'Come on, Tim, and bring the camera.'

'Where are you going?' Richard looked up at the three lads. He could see that they were anxious to get away.

'I'm going to show them the cellar, Tim wants to take some pictures of the barrel.'

'What barrel? You're not going down in the cellar again?' Alison's voice rose sharply.

'Oh, didn't I tell you, there is a barrel of rum down there off the *Savannah Lady*, and Tim wants to take a photo.'

Alison looked at him open-mouthed. 'Well, you're not going down there again, are you, Robert? What about your leg if you get the dirt in it, it will go poisoned, then what are we going to do?' There was despair in her tone. 'By the way, your mother has been on the phone; she says she will ring you tomorrow. And I didn't tell her about the accident, I thought it would worry her.'

'Oh thanks, Ali. I won't tell her. Come on guys.' They began to move away.

'Robert!' Alison shouted after them, as Tim picked up his camera from the coffee table where he had left it. 'Robert!' her voice rose; he looked towards her from the end of the verandah. 'Don't you go and get stuck down there again.' She looked distraught, and knew he wouldn't take a bit of notice of what she was saying.

He just smiled, 'We'll be OK. I'll get Joseph to hold the ladder,' and they disappeared round the corner.

'Nick smiled at Richard. 'At least if they don't come back you'll know where to look.'

'Did you know that cellar was there, Nick?' Richard asked.

'No. I have only been over here about once, maybe twice, but I expect Gramps would know about it, he was very friendly with the Kingsleys. I think he spent a lot of time with James. I think they used to enjoy rum together and a cigar, and I think James used to go fishing with Gramps when he had the time. I don't remember James Kingsley, but I remember Emily. I saw her a few years ago when I came out to see Gramps.' He smiled at Richard, 'Your aunt was a quaint little lady, kindly, she looked a little fragile. Gramps has talked a lot about them, especially now you are here, and I expect it has brought back memories for him. And he was talking the other day about the tales his grandfather used to tell him about the White Lady. She hasn't always been white, you know. And I just can't figure out how you painted that ship, Alison?'

'Well I saw it, I told you.'

'I should like to have a chat with your grandfather, Nick,'

said Richard. 'I should like to find out a bit about my aunt; I expect my father would like to know too. She left him this house, but he hasn't seen her since he was at school. He said he came here once, when he was about nine years old, and can just remember Aunt Emily taking him down to the beach. Why don't you and your grandfather come over one night and have a drink with us?'

'Well,' said Alison, 'why not come over to dinner one night? You can come tonight if you would like to. Selena is a very good cook. And I am sure Robert would be interested, your grandfather will probably know about the things in our glass cabinet. We could ask John and Carol and the boys, and make it a dinner party.' She looked at Richard, nodding.

'Well, that sounds nice,' Nick smiled. 'I am sure Gramps would like that, he doesn't get out much, you know. He's eighty, but he doesn't look it. He still goes out in his fishing boat, and he loves to sit on the beach and mend nets, just as he has done all his life; if not he will just sit by his boat and smoke a pipe, or occasionally a cigar. I bring him a box when I come over.' They finished their drinks, and Nick stood up, saying that he would see them later.

'About seven-thirty, for dinner,' Alison called after him, as he went down the coral stone steps, followed closely by Jojo, his tail held high and wagging. Nick turned and looked up from the beach, and gave them a wave.

Richard went to phone John. It was a bit short notice, and John said that he was sorry they could not come, as they had already booked the table for tonight in a restaurant in the town, and he had ordered a taxi as well. He asked if the boys were on their way back yet. Richard grimaced. 'I'll tell them.'

The camera flashed, lighting up the cellar, just for a split second. Tim was excited about the barrel with the name painted on it.

'Do you think that Jack Barneby put these barrels down here in this cellar?'

Robert knew where the barrels were, but after the flash of the camera all he could see was purple and red spots. He was just beginning to focus again when Tim flashed the camera again, and both he and Gary held their eyes.

'Well, I don't know how these barrels got down here, but I would hardly think that a pirate would come ashore and dump barrels of rum in somebody's cellar. I would think that they were washed ashore when that ship went down, and that George guy picked them up. What do you think, Gary?'

'Yeah, I should think you are probably right,' said Gary, shining the torch around the cellar into dark corners, and walking towards one, leaving Tim and Robert near the barrels in semi-darkness, as the long sunbeam was broken by Joseph's huge bulk in the doorway at the top of the ladder.

'There's something down here,' said Gary, kicking his feet about and making the dust fly.

'Where?' said Tim. 'Shine the light then, so we can see.'

He shone the torch in their direction and they stood beside him, almost under the ladder, with Joseph above them. 'Look, what's that? Looks like an old lamp.' It was rusty, and Tim bent to pick it up from the dirt and grime and beetles that ran away from the torchlight. He picked up the old iron oil lamp; it was heavy. 'It's not an oil lamp, look, it's got a burned-out candle still in it.' Gary gave the torch to Robert, and bent down to move a piece of the wooden stairs, and under it was a piece of a wooden box, with a rusty iron catch and the word 'SALT' printed on it in faded black letters.

'What's that?' asked Robert, waving the torch at something pink. Gary picked it up, shaking off the red dust. It looked like a small jewel box, hand-painted in red and pink roses. He rubbed off some of the dirt and the grime. The catch was broken, and he lifted the lid; one of the two hinges was twisted. Inside it was covered in blue velvet, and there was a small pocket in the back, and hanging from it was a thin chain. He pulled at it, and held up a small oval locket, possibly silver, but black with age. He tried to open it but his fingers fumbled in his haste. He managed to open it, then in the torchlight all three looked at the miniature oil painting of a woman wearing a low-cut, off-the-shoulder green dress, and a white curly wig. Round her neck she wore a pendant, a large ruby surrounded by diamonds and pearls.

'I wonder who she was,' said Gary. Tim and Robert were twisting their necks trying to see.

'Can I hold it?' said Tim. 'I can't see it properly.'

'What have you found, Maaan?' Joseph's deep voice came from the doorway above them; he could not see down into the darkness, but he could hear Tim getting excited.

'A box and a necklace,' Robert called up to him. 'I'll show you in a minute.'

Gary kicked his feet about and the dust flew up choking them all, including Joseph. They found the remains of the wooden salt box – it had all fallen to pieces – and then the toe of Gary's trainer struck something sharp.

'Shine the torch down here, Rob.' He bent to pick up the object.

'What's that?' said Robert, trying to bend a little but his leg was throbbing.

'It's a dagger!' He was flabbergasted. 'Look!' He ran his palm over the hilt, which was covered in damp earth and grime. Robert shone the torch. 'Look,' Gary breathed, 'it's got stones on it...' He rubbed it again, and they shone in the light.

'Gosh that's super, super!' Tim shouted, his voice echoing off the walls in the darkness. Gary stood up and the three huddled together as Rob held the torch close over the magnificent dagger; the stones sparkled.

'What you found, Maaan?' Joseph was leaning down from above, but no one answered him. They were speechless.

'Do you think they are real rubies and sapphires?' Gary whispered, looking up into Robert's face, although he could not see him behind the torchlight.

'Yeah, I would think so.' Robert's voice was amazed as it came out of the darkness. 'They used to have those sort of things with precious stones in them years ago.'

'I bet that was washed up off that ship.' Tim's eyes were wide; he moved round nearer to Rob for a better look. 'It must be worth a fortune.'

'Yeah,' said Gary, 'I bet it is. But if it is off the ship, what's it doing down here?'

'Yeah, why isn't it up there in the cabinet with all the other stuff?' Robert looked puzzled.

'They didn't make a very good job of burying it, did they?' said Tim.

'Well, I expect it was packed in that box marked "Salt", and over the years the box has disintegrated.'

‘Maybe they didn’t know the value of it.’ Tim still sounded amazed.

‘Maybe it’s not real,’ said Gary. ‘But it certainly looks fabulous.’

Joseph was getting agitated. It had gone quiet, he could barely hear them mumbling. ‘Wha goin’ on, Maaan?’ he drawled, looking down into the darkness; he could see the torchlight but nothing else.

They didn’t answer him. Tim was down on his knees fumbling, and Robert shone the torch down on him.

‘I’ve found an old leather belt, here look, got a buckle on it.’

‘Hey! Maaan.’ Then, thinking he was not very respectful, Joseph called again, ‘Mr Robert, Sir.’

‘We’ve found a knife and a belt,’ Gary called up. He held them up for Joseph to see, and Joseph nodded his head with a smile, but he really didn’t see anything, and he was wishing that he didn’t have to stay up there holding the ladder.

Tim was rummaging around amongst tangled rope, and the dust was flying up, choking them. Even Joseph was coughing, and moved away from the entrance to get a breath of fresh air. Tim picked up some rusty nails and bolts and another black-painted, half-rusty lamp with a candle in it. It was half-buried in the earth, and beside it he spied a piece of thin chain. He dug his finger into the damp earth to loosen it, and then pulled. The damp and black earth parted, leaving a long, thin shallow channel, until it stopped. ‘Shine the light down here, Rob,’ he said anxiously, scraping away the earth. Rob came closer with the light, as Tim dug up a watch. ‘Look!’ he said, standing up quickly, and both Gary and Rob came closer to look at what he was holding up.

Tim put it to his ear.

‘You don’t think it’s still going, do you?’ Gary sneered.

‘You never know; it might be one of those watches that never go wrong, you see them advertised on the TV.’

‘Yeah, but I don’t think they had TV on a galleon.’ Gary raised his eyebrows and they all burst into laughter. Tim held the watch in his earth-encrusted hands and rubbed a dirty thumbnail across the back of the watch, which was black with age.

'Looks like silver,' said Robert, holding the torch steady over Tim's hand, as Tim pressed a spring and the front flew open. It had a white face, now yellow with age and watermarked, and the hands, that had stopped at 3.45, were black, as were the Roman numerals. He closed it with a click and turned it over, rubbing it again with his thumb. The dirt was embedded into the engraved vines, which surrounded a circle in the middle, with a scrolled letter 'H'.

'Fotheringay!' Tim burst out loudly. 'H for Hugo. I bet it was his.'

Gary looked down onto the ground again, and bent down quickly. 'There is something else shining down here, look, shine the torch. Looks like a button.' Tim put the watch down beside the dagger and went down on his knees beside his brother, feeling the excitement of it all in the pit of his stomach. Robert shone the light down, but swished it around until he found the right place, where Gary was already scraping away at the earth.

'It's not a button,' Gary gasped, 'it's much bigger.' Tim was on his knees, helping to scrape the earth away.

'Cool! Look! Look!' shouted Tim, his voice rising to hysterics, and he began to dig frantically, making the dust fly up choking them.

Joseph could stand the suspense no longer and came quickly down the ladder. 'Wha have you found? ... oh! Maaan...' he drawled out a long drawn-out whisper of astonishment; in the light of the torch the white of his eyes shone. He was standing beside Robert.

They all looked up, surprised. 'What are you doing down here?' Robert's surprised voice came out of the darkness. 'What about the ladder?'

'It OK, Maaan, I tie it to de tree, it safe, Maaan.' Robert saw his strong white teeth flash in the torchlight and the whites of his eyes as he looked at the magnificent sword that Gary and Tim were holding between them. The blade was bright and shiny as if new; the earth had preserved it. The hilt was encrusted with red and blue stones, which were caked with thick mud and grime. Gary ran his fingers across them, and some shimmered in the light from the torch.

Their eyes were wide with amazement. 'Do you think the

stones are real?' Tim whispered as if he was afraid even to breathe. He stood with his mouth open.

'I would think they are real...' Robert answered Tim in the same low and amazed tone, as if he were in a dream. There were no words to describe what their eyes were taking in, no words to describe each of their thoughts and their feelings, as they stood close together in the darkness, with just the light of the torch playing onto the sword. The sunlight from the open doorway shot a beam over their heads to the far corner.

'Ooooh ... Maaaaan...' Joseph drawled out the words in a long low breath, his large brown eyes had never been wider. 'I never knowed bout dis cellar. Ooooh ... Maaan. If I'd only knowed,' he was shaking his head in despair.

Gary stood like a statue, straight-backed and motionless. He let his breath out slowly. In a dream-like state he let go of the blade end, and Tim held the jewelled hilt in both hands.

Tim suddenly came back to reality. 'I bet this was stolen from some rich lord, even a king, and I bet you Jack Barneby has killed a lot of people with it. On guard,' he demanded in a deep voice, 'stand on your liver.' He lunged forward in the semi-darkness, and they all laughed loudly.

'Be careful, Tim,' Gary was still chuckling and recovering from the shock of what he had found, thinking that the one ruby, which was embedded into the earth, was a button. 'Tim, be careful, put in down,' he said with a chuckle. 'You will cut someone's legs off if you are not careful, stop swishing it about.'

Tim lowered the blade to the ground, still holding the earth-encrusted hilt. 'It's really weighty. I bet Barneby was a strong guy, and if he fought with this it would take some wielding about.' He lay it down beside the box and the dagger. 'Look. I think it matches the dagger.' Robert turned the torch onto the things that they had found, and they all agreed that in this light they did seem to match.

It was getting hot in the cellar, and Tim flung off his T-shirt as the excitement was really mounting now. All four were on their knees searching the ground, digging their hands into the red dusty grime, not caring as the dust flew up into their faces, or if they disturbed beetles and spiders or mice or rats; their only thought was to find something, anything. Robert had wedged the torch against one of the barrels so that they could see, and he too was scrabbling about in the grime, but he found it difficult kneeling only on one knee, as the throbbing pain gripped his leg.

They worked very hard with their hands, digging into the dust and the earth for what seemed ages, but they found nothing much, just a bolt and lock, a few pieces of rusty metal, and pieces of string. They decided to give up.

They wrapped the treasured pieces in Tim's T-shirt and mounted the ladder. Joseph went up first to hold it steady, followed by Gary, carrying the T-shirt under his arm. Robert, with the torch stuffed into the pocket of his shorts, gripped the sides of the ladder with both hands tightly, stepping up and slowly dragging his right foot onto the next step; on reaching the top, Gary and Joseph helped him out. And climbing slowly behind him, Tim, gripping the ladder with only one hand; his left hand held the fabulous sword over his shoulder, and as Joseph gave him a hand out of the doorway, the sun dazzled their eyes after being down in the dark for so long, and the stones on the hilt sparkled like fire in the brilliant light of the still very hot evening sunshine.

Alison and Richard were stretched out on sun beds; they had been reading since Nick had gone home. Alison yawned, 'I suppose I must go in and have a shower.' She swung her legs lazily over the side of the sun bed. 'Nick and his grandfather will be here in a couple of hours, and I want to wash my hair.'

Just then Nick came up onto the verandah, apologizing for disturbing them again; he had left his cigarettes and lighter on the table.

They were surprised as the four dirty youths came quickly and excitably round the corner and onto the verandah, and Jojo came running up the steps after Nick, jumping excitably up at Gary, who was the first on the scene.

'Look what we've found!' Robert shouted as he half-hobbled, half-skipped behind Gary, who was putting the T-shirt with the treasure in it carefully onto the table.

Richard and Alison jumped in alarm at the excitement in Robert's voice and the excitable barking and jumping of Jojo. They looked aghast at the state of the four boys, with filthy

T-shirts and shorts, and hands and knees encrusted with dirt.

'Good God!' exclaimed Richard. 'Have you been down in that cellar all this time? I thought you two had gone back to the hotel. Your father was expecting you over an hour ago.'

'Come and look at this,' they were all screaming with excitement. Richard and Nick exchanged glances with open mouths, in awe of the sword which Tim was carrying proudly over his shoulder, his young and fresh face beaming.

'Good God!' exclaimed Richard again, as they gathered round the table. 'Where did you find all this, in the cellar?'

Tim nodded his head enthusiastically, grinning from ear to ear.

'Robert,' Alison's voice was somewhere between a gasp and a whisper, astounded and bewildered.

'Yes, just look at this,' Gary said, flinging open the T-shirt to reveal the things that they had found. The dagger shone as Tim laid the sword gently down beside it on the table. They gathered round, gasping at the beauty of it all; even the lads gasped. It was the first time that they had actually looked in the daylight at what they had found. As the sun caught the stones, even through the red dusty grime and black, heavy earth, they shimmered. The blade was still sharp, and the steel bright and shiny as new, where the earth had preserved it, and as Richard picked it up, it gleamed and glinted. Richard held it up in front of him, it was breathtakingly magnificent. He weighed it in his hands. 'Just feel the weight of it,' he said, handing it to Nick.

Nick took it in two hands, holding it up in front of him as Richard had done, and as he moved, it glinted and sparks of fire shot from it.

'I should think it has been some sort of ceremonial piece at one time, wouldn't you?' said Nick, not taking his eyes off the magnificence before him.

'Ooooh, Maaaan,' Joseph standing just behind Nick, breathed the words in a low drawl.

Nick turned to him. 'Fabulous, isn't it? Would you like to hold it?'

Joseph nodded as if in a trance. His face was a picture, and Tim grabbed his camera and snapped him as he stood motionless, goggling at its beauty. Selena came to the verandah door and exclaimed a loud 'Ooo!' and clapped her hand to her mouth, holding her breath at the sight of her son, standing like a mighty giant with the sword clasped in both hands, the hilt up in front of his face, as if making a sacrifice. They smiled at each other, as they watched him marvelling at such a prize, and Tim snapped him again.

Joseph stood in awe of its beauty. He felt an empty pain in his stomach, and his heart leaped, and there was a tingling all over his body, and tears welled in his large brown eyes, 'Oh, Maaan,' he drawled in a low tone, 'oh, Maaan.' He lowered it gently down onto the table and stood back to admire it in stunned silence, knowing he would never again hold such a beautiful thing in the whole of his life.

'Do you think that the stones are real?' said Robert. 'We thought they were, down there in the dimness of the cellar, but they look fantastic out here in the daylight, don't they?'

'Oh, I am sure they must be,' said Richard, running his finger lovingly over the stones. 'Look how they shine. Just wait until they are cleaned up.'

Alison stood just looking at the table; she was speechless.

'Look,' said Tim excitedly, 'the dagger matches the sword. I found this,' he said picking up the dagger, 'and Gary found the sword. He thought he had found a button, but when he dug it up it was the sword. Isn't it just fab, can you imagine fencing with this, you couldn't lose, could you? The stones would blind your opponent. Perhaps that's why they covered it in stones? Do you think?'

'No, Tim,' said Nick. 'I should think this was made for special occasions. Just to be carried, not for use as a weapon.'

'Mmmm,' said Richard, 'could even possibly have been made for a king. Obviously stolen by a pirate. I expect they overtook a ship, and it was being transported to a king or a nobleman. They used to take things such as this from one country to another as a gift to a king or a prince, who was about to be betrothed to a daughter or some such thing. Yes, I think you're right, Nick. It wasn't made to be a weapon.'

Alison picked up the pink and red rose-painted box. 'This is pretty,' she said. The men were not paying attention, they were more interested in the sword. She lifted the broken catch and the lid nearly fell off; one of the hinges was detached.

Inside, the pale blue cushioned velvet was frayed and worn and badly discoloured, with a brownish and yellow tinged watermark. And at one corner the velvet had rotted away.

'Oh! Look at this,' said Alison, holding up the locket by the chain. They all looked up, and watched as it twizzled round.

'You can open it, Ali,' said Robert with enthusiasm. 'There's a miniature painting inside, and although it looks black, I think it will be silver when it's cleaned up.' Alison pushed the spring and the locket sprung open. 'I wonder who she was?' she said, showing the locket to Richard. He looked at a woman in a white curly wig and a green low-cut dress. Round her neck was a large ruby locket surrounded by diamonds and pearls, and from her ears hung ruby and pearl earrings.

'She must have been a very rich lady, I should think,' said Alison, 'and the painting is well preserved, even though the box is battered.'

'Yes,' Richard agreed, handing the locket back to her, and then turning his attention back to the sword.

Alison put the locket back into the pocket of the box, closing the broken lid carefully. She examined the box. It was quite thick, probably made of oak; there were five roses painted on the lid, two pinks, and three red, and the two pink ones were partly scratched off. She opened the lid again and, not knowing what she did, suddenly a secret drawer popped out. She exclaimed in such surprise, almost dropping the box, and the men looked up. She set the box down on the table, and lifted a piece of the blue velvet. 'Look!' She held up a pair of ruby and pearl earrings.

'Good God!' Richard breathed; he could think of nothing else to say.

'They are beautiful, Alison.' Nick shook his head, 'Almost takes your breath away.'

Richard was looking down at the table again and shaking his head. 'This surely must be a pirate's treasure. How on earth did all these fabulous things get down into the cellar?'

'Do you think this Jack Barneby put it there?' said Tim, with his eyebrows raised high. The thought of a real live pirate having been down there in the cellar of this house, gave him quite a thrill. What would they say when he told them all at school? He could feel the excitement mounting in his stomach.

'No! Don't be daft,' said Gary. 'Pirates don't bury treasure in people's cellars. Besides, this George guy says he was dead.'

'Yes,' said Tim, 'but he could have buried the treasure first.'

'No.' Robert shook his head. 'George would have said that he killed him.'

'Yeah, it said that he died when the ship went down,' said Gary, rubbing his chin thoughtfully.

'Well, how did it get there, then?' said Tim.

No one answered him, they just stood round the table looking, while a gentle breeze wafted across the verandah and the sea pounded in on the shore.

Robert looked at the earrings twisting round and round as Alison held them between her fingers. 'Try them on, Ali,' Robert broke into the silence.

'Oh, no! No! I couldn't,' she said softly, putting one hand to her throat as if in shock. 'Oh, no, I couldn't.' She put them gently back into the drawer and snapped it shut, not knowing how she was to open it again.

'Why not?' said Robert.

'Well, because I feel I have intruded on someone else's secret, someone's personal things, they are not mine.'

'Oh, go on, Alison, she won't mind, she's dead,' said Tim.

'Yes, long gone,' said Richard with a smile.

Nick was handling the watch. 'I think that belonged to Sir Hugo Fotheringay,' said Tim pointing a dirty fingernail. 'Look, it's got the initial "H" on the back. Turn it over, Nick.'

'Why?' said Robert. 'The "H" could stand for Henry or Horace, or something.'

'No, he was on the ship,' said Tim. 'It has to be Hugo's.' He was convinced that he was right.

'But we don't know if this stuff came off that ship,' said Gary. 'And pirates used to steal from anyone, not only on the high seas; we are only guessing.'

'Well, I think it did come off that ship.' Tim was indignant.

The next morning after breakfast, the Turners were at White Lady Cottage.

'What are you going to do with all this stuff?' asked John. 'It's simply amazing.' They were gathered around the dining room table, where the treasure was laid out on a white tablecloth. Richard and Robert had washed away most of the dirt and grime, and the stones on the hilt of the sword and dagger shone brighter than the stones in a jeweller's window, as the sun streamed across the table.

'Well,' said Richard, thoughtfully, 'I think I shall have to get on to the museum. This is not the sort of thing that you could keep, or would want the responsibility of having in the house. I couldn't even think of selling it, it must be priceless, what do you think?' he turned his hands palms up.

'Absolutely priceless.' John was shaking his head. 'I think you are right about the museum, though, seems the only thing to do.'

Alison was showing the painted box and the locket to Carol.

'Oh, it's lovely,' said Carol, holding the locket which Richard had cleaned; it was now a bright silver. Carol opened it. 'I wonder who she is?'

'Was,' said Alison with a smile. 'And what do you think of this?' She pushed the pale blue velvet in the box and the secret drawer flew open, and she held up the ruby earrings for Carol to see.

'Oh! Alison, aren't they beautiful? Oh, they are fabulous,' Carol sighed as Alison handed them to her. She held them up to her ears. 'How do I look?' she smiled. 'They must be worth a fortune. Have you tried them on?'

'No,' Alison smiled. 'I would like to, but I have a funny feeling about them. I feel they are so expensive, and they are not mine, I feel like a thief,' she smiled again.

Carol nodded. 'I think I understand what you mean, but I would.'

'Shall I?' Carol nodded, raising her eyebrows, and they went into the hall and stood in front of the mirror behind the telephone table. Alison tried on the earrings, and moving her head from side to side, they both admired them.

'Would you like to try them on, Carol?'

'Oh! Yes please.'

Nick and his grandfather had arrived at seven-thirty for dinner, with Jojo, who was now sleeping peacefully on the floor beside Nick's feet. They all sat round the glass-topped table on the verandah, feeling relaxed and full.

Nick and Gramps were puffing away on cigars which Richard had brought especially for them earlier in the day. Richard had shown Gramps the treasure when they had first arrived; Nick had told him all about it. He had just raised his eyes and nodded with a smile.

The aroma from his cigar filled the air as he sat puffing away and pondering on how he should start to tell them all the things he had learned over the years from his great-grandfather and his grandfather who had sat him on his knee and talked to him for hours. He had also learned a lot from his father, and now he would relate all these things that they wanted to know about White Lady Cottage and Emily Kingsley.

He was about to start and paused, puffing smoke into the air, and leaned forward. They all leaned forward too, resting their elbows on the table, waiting in anticipation for him to speak.

'Well,' he said, leaning back in the chair again, watching the smoke rise. 'Well, I was not surprised when you showed me what you had found in the cellar. I was more surprised to think that you had actually found the cellar.'

Gramps' brown eyes twinkled under his bushy grey eyebrows; he nodded his head gently and smiled into his grey whiskers, as he remembered things from the past. Then he began again.

'Well, as I said, I was not surprised at the things which you have found, it just brought back sweet memories for me. You see, it was me that put all those things down in the cellar, for dear Emily.'

'Oh, it's not all that old then?' said Robert.

'Oooh, yes, my boy, oh, yes, it is very old. You see, Emily asked me to take the stuff away.' He looked at Richard. 'She was a lovely lady, your Aunt Emily, a small and gentle soul. She came here as a young bride from London, England, after marrying James Kingsley, a black Barbadian man who was a medical doctor. She was a nurse, and they had met while working in a hospital in the Orient. She came back to London, and then after a year he came back and they met again and were married. My wife Ella May and me had only been married for six months when James and Emily came to live here, in this cottage. Emily and Ella May became very good friends; they would sit here on this very verandah, or on our verandah over there.' He pointed a finger towards his own house. 'And they would sit together and sew, and swap recipes for cakes and pies and the like. I would go fishing. Sometimes James came with me, but he had a surgery up there over yonder,' he pointed a finger away up into the hills, which really meant nothing to any of them, and then he continued. 'Then the gals would git together, and we would have dinners together, either here or there,' he pointed a finger again towards his own house. He nodded again, remembering, and puffed on the cigar before he started again. 'Folks around here talked a lot about the doctor marrying an English woman, a white woman, I mean, you know, it weren't done then. But they soon got used to it. They used to talk a lot about me and Ella May too. My Ella May came from Cuba.'

'I guess that's where I get my Latino looks,' Nick said with a smile, and Gramps nodded genially.

'But Emily,' he went on, 'being the doctor's wife, was different, and sometimes she was able to help him in the surgery, and folks got to like her. I mean the fisher folk around here. Most of us are still fishermen, like our fathers and forefathers. Things don't change much here on the island, it's a simple life but a good one, satisfying.' He paused for a moment, nodding to himself and smiling into this grey whiskers, puffing on the cigar and thinking of his younger days. 'Then poor James passed away,' he nodded sadly. 'He was only in his early forties; he was a few years older than Emily and me and Ella May. He died of a fever – he was bitten by a mosquito, or that is what they thought. He was ill for weeks. Emily did all she could to save him, but the fever got worse. There was a young doctor down on the south coast, he came from Guyana, settled here with his wife and family, his name was, er...' He looked at the ceiling, 'er, Thomas, I think. No, no! Not Thomas, err ... Thompson. That's it, Thompson. Well, he came to help Emily, but then it was too late. Emily was never the same after poor James passed away. The sadness showed in her eyes, she was lonely. But folks around here used to come to her for advice and medicine when they felt the need, and she was a great comfort to many of them, but then that all fizzled out when a new Doctor Granger came from England to take over the practice. Emily wanted to go back to England, but she could not afford the passage on a boat, so she kept herself busy in the house and in the garden. I helped her plant all these fruit trees. Tom Wiley came down to help us too. And then Selena came here as a very young girl to help Emily in the house, and then Emily began to relax and enjoy life a bit more. She and Ella May used to sit here on this verandah and do embroidery. Emily embroidered all the linen here, you know?' He looked at Alison. 'She made all the cushions and curtains, these are all fairly new, she finished them just before she died.'

'Really?' said Alison, 'I didn't know that Aunt Emily had done them; they are beautiful.' She looked towards the windows, but she couldn't see the curtains. She shifted her position and sat forward, leaning her elbows on the table. She was feeling a little tired after drinking the wine, and the cigar smoke was getting to her and prickling her eyes. She wondered why men enjoyed it so much.

'What about the stuff in the cabinet?' said Robert. 'And the treasure, tell us about that. Was it all washed up on the beach? I read the scroll, and it said something about a hand and a ring, and what about the White Lady?'

'Yes, go on, Gramps,' said Nick, taking the cigar out of his mouth and puffing smoke. 'Tell them the stories that your Grandfather used to tell you. Rob wants to know about the pirates and things, don't you, Rob?'

Gramps smiled, tapping grey ash off his cigar into the ashtray and then looking slowly at the red glow. He sat back and smiled through his whiskers.

'Well, I am surprised that you found the cellar. It has been shut up for years, and no one has been in that part of the garden for years.'

'Well, I fell down the steps,' said Robert. 'You see, I dropped my shorts out of the bathroom window and went round to find them. That's when I slipped down the steps.'

Gramps smiled. He was not in a hurry, but they waited anxiously while he sipped rum and blew smoke into the air, and composed himself before going on with the next part of the story. Then he began again slowly.

'It was all in the cabinet, you see. James liked to keep it there, because his great-great-grandfather had collected it and kept it. James had the cabinet made and put all the things in it. He said it was sentimental value. But Emily always thought it was evil; she told Ella May many times she hated to go into the dining room – it was always cold in there. She had asked James to move it but he wouldn't, he said he could see no reason why, and he thought the sword and the dagger beautiful to look at. Emily had to agree to the beauty, but still felt that it was evil.

'So when James had been gone some months, she decided to get rid of the evil things, as she called them, and asked me to throw them away into the sea. But I couldn't. I took them away for her, out of sight, and took them to my house. I didn't know what to do, these precious gem stones must have been worth a fortune, and they belonged to James and Emily, not me. So I came over here on a moonlight night, and I found an old wooden box and I dumped all the stuff in it and put it down into their cellar. I knew Emily would never go down into the cellar alone, so I left it there. There were a couple of rum barrels down there, painted with *Savannah Lady*. Did you find those, son?' He looked at Robert.

'Yes,' said Robert eagerly.

'Well, they must have been put down there by George Kingsley after the storm. I tried to move them but they were too heavy.'

'I know,' said Robert. 'I tried to move them too.'

'Do you know whose picture it is in the locket?' asked Alison.

'Well,' said Gramps, scratching his forehead, 'James and Emily thought that it could possibly be the wife of Sir Hugo Fotheringay, but no one really knows. But Emily said that she thought it was painted by a young man friend of the Fotheringays, an Italian artist who stayed with them, once, by the name of Giovanni Colletto. She said that she had heard it or read it somewhere. He was killed when pirates raided the house, possibly by that rogue Barneby.'

'What about the rest of the things in the cabinet?' asked Robert. 'Why did she keep all that, why didn't she let you get rid of the lot?'

'Oh, well, that didn't worry her, that was only the stuff that was washed up on the beach.'

'It was all washed up on the beach, wasn't it?' said Richard.

A smile split Gramps' whiskers, and he stroked them gently. 'Yes,' he nodded, 'you might say that they were washed up on the shore, but in a different way... You see, they were taken off Jack Barneby ... he ... was washed up on the beach, and one other member of his crew, who was not identified. My grandfather told me that my great-great-grandfather, William Cotton, who I am named after, by the way, he and George Kingsley came down on to the beach with their sons the morning after the storm, to collect wood for their fires and anything that they could find, knowing that things would float in from the ship that had gone down in the night. They found the barrels of rum and they found the figurehead off the ship, they also found the two men floating in and out on the rough surf. It was George Kingsley and my great-great-grandfather who pulled them out of the sea, and laid them down on their backs alongside the figurehead of the ship. They were going to give them a decent burial. They were amazed when they saw the hilt of the sword in the scabbard at his side sparkling in the sunlight, and they did not know who either of the men was. But then they guessed that this one was Jack Barneby.'

'We never found the scabbard,' said Robert.

'Shush, Rob!' said Alison, leaning forward to put her elbows on the table again, and resting her chin in her hands.

Gramps went on. 'He also had the dagger stuck in his belt. And they say that the dagger and sword sparkled like a million stars, and that William's eldest son, Matthew, bent down to touch the sword, when SUDDENLY,' Alison jumped when Gramps shouted out the word, 'Barneby regained consciousness, and in a flash grabbed at the boy and stabbed him in the chest with the jewelled-handled dagger. Of course there was a struggle with William and George, as you can imagine, and then William's younger son, Thomas, sprang on Barneby as he was still lying on the sand. But Barneby was a young and very fit man, even though he was exhausted from almost drowning. Pushing Thomas off him, he got to his feet and in a flash drew the sword, while the unfortunate Matthew lay in pain at his feet. Kicking him away, he swung the sword round on George Kingsley, dropping the dagger onto the sand beside Matthew, who was writhing in pain, with blood pouring from his chest wound. George's son Joshua was quick to grab the dagger from the sand, and was going to defend his father, as Barneby was beating back both George and William, who was waving a stick as Barneby waved the sword, which he had done so expertly many times before.

'He must have been an excellent swordsman, and he would have killed them both if George's wife Marianna had not come screaming down the beach when she saw her husband being threatened. Jack Barneby was caught off guard and, losing his balance, he tripped head first over the figurehead of his ship, just as Joshua lunged forward with the dagger in his hand to defend his father. As Jack Barneby fell the dagger plunged into his heart, and he lay face down slumped over the ship's figurehead, and his dying words were: "A curse on you. A curse on all your womenfolk, death to all your womenfolk..."'

It went quiet, and then Gramps went on, 'And my Grandfather said that his blood flowed over the bosom of the carved goddess, as he lay face down arms outstretched before him, with the jewelled sword still in his hand. It took them some minutes to recover from the thought of near death, as neither George Kingsley nor William Cotton had ever been threatened with a sword before, and were gentle folk and not fighting men, and Marianna tried to do what she could for poor Matthew, and Thomas ran off to tell his mother.' Tears welled in Gramps' old eyes. 'They carried Matthew back to his home, and Marianna and Lucy, Matthew's mother, tried to do what they could for the boy, but alas he died next day, he was only sixteen...' His voice trailed off in sadness.

Alison inclined her head, looking at Robert. He was 17, almost 18, and she could imagine the grief that William Cotton and his wife Lucy must have felt at losing their son so tragically, as Gramps had said, these were people who lived quiet and simple lives; they knew nothing of fighting and killing.

'George and Joshua stripped Barneby of his possessions.'

'Did they bury him?' Robert asked Gramps anxiously.

Gramps shook his head. 'William and Thomas came back to where George and Joshua were, still shaking from the shock of it all, and young Joshua was very shaken by the whole affair, and collapsed in tears, knowing that he had killed a man, even though it was the notorious pirate Jack Barneby ... and I would think that it took him a long time to get over such a terrible experience, wouldn't you?'

They all nodded silently.

'Well, George and William got Barneby and the other crewman into William's fishing boat, while Joshua and Thomas collected some heavy rocks and filled the large pockets of Barneby's frock coat, and they tied the other man's feet with ropes which were strewn along the beach, and stuffed rocks under the ropes. And then Joshua and Thomas rowed the boat out to the reef to where the ship had gone down, and between them they lifted the heavy bodies and threw them over the side. They say they watched Jack Barneby sink slowly below the clear water, and his eyes seemed to stare back at them with hatred, until he finally disappeared into the deep, to join his ship and his ruthless crew, where they could never harm anyone again.'

There was silence for a few minutes. Then they began to move. Nick stretched, and Alison sipped a little wine, which was warm now, and she pulled a face.

'It's a tragic story,' said Richard. 'But why did you put such valuable things down there in the cellar? Why did you not sell them, they would have made Emily a fortune, and then she could have bought a passage back to England.'

'No, no, Richard, you don't understand.' Gramps shook his grizzled head. 'Emily didn't want any part of it, she thought it was all very evil. The sword must have killed many men, innocent men, and it would have killed both George and William had he not slipped and been killed himself by the dagger. The things he had on him, the sword for instance and the dagger, the silver watch, even the silver buckle belt, must have been taken from dead men or Barneby would not have had them in his possession. Besides, Emily had really no desire to be rich, and neither did I. We live a simple life here on the island – we live mostly on the fish we catch and the vegetables we grow, and the riches from blood money would be no good. And in any case, years ago, there was no one on the island who could possibly afford such treasures. Emily asked me to get rid of the evil things, and they were not mine to sell anyway, they had belonged to James and his ancestors. I really did not know what to do, so I wrapped them in some material, actually it was some old curtains which Ella May had packed away,' he smiled. 'I remember that I brought them out here, and put them on the table, there was an old wooden table here then. Then I wrapped up the things, and I wrapped the sword separately because it was sharp, and then I took them away down onto the beach, I was going to bury them in the sand, and then I thought of the cellar. I knew that Emily would never go down there. I put them there just for the time being, really, and I thought for weeks what I could really do with such valuable stuff. Then I thought that if she ever did have second thoughts about them, being as they had belonged to James, then I would be able to get them back. So I left them there . . . I packed them into an old wooden box, which was already down there.'

'That was the one with "Salt" painted on it?' said Robert.

'Yes, that's right.' Gramps smiled. 'And I put them right under the back of the stairs, just in case Emily should ever go down there. But I am sure she never ever went near, always said the stairs were unsafe.'

Robert grinned knowingly.

'So there, you see the treasure has remained untouched since then. I don't even think Selena knew about it, and Joseph only does the main part of the garden.'

'Well,' said Alison thoughtfully, 'why did you not send them to the museum?'

'Because, my dear, when I was younger there wasn't a museum on the island.'

'Well, do you think they should get in touch with the museum now, Gramps?' asked Nick. 'What do you think?'

Gramps looked at Richard. 'Well, it is yours now.' He inclined his head. 'And you must decide what is best. But I personally think you would be wise not to keep it or try to sell it. Remember that the sword must have killed many a good and honest man, and that the dagger cost Barneby his life. It is evil. Well, in my opinion it is, anyway. I think the museum would be the best place, but, as I say, is up to you.'

'What about the watch?' asked Robert. 'Do you think that was Barneby's?'

'No,' said Richard and Gramps together.

'Obviously stolen,' said Gramps. 'Could have been Sir Hugo's, with the "H". He most likely killed him for it.'

'And the box,' said Alison, 'it's so pretty. Why would Emily want to throw that away, and the locket? Did she know about the earrings?'

'I don't know,' said Gramps. 'But the box was in Barneby's pocket. They found it when they put the rocks in to weigh him down. I expect it was full of jewels, but they were probably lost in the sea – he would hardly have grabbed a box with just a locket in it, before he jumped overboard, or before the ship went down, would he? I think the earrings and the locket are lovely, my dear.' Gramps smiled at Alison, 'I should keep them if I were you. I would not think of them as evil. But the sword and the dagger...' He looked at Richard. 'I would phone the museum if I were you. To me, they have bad vibes. But I am sure that they would jump at the chance to have them.'

Alison got up and went into the dining room. She took the locket from the box on the table and noticed that the cabinet door had been left open. She went to close it and then took out the ring; she would show it to Gramps, although she knew he had seen it before. As she walked out of the dining room, the door slammed shut behind her with great force, and she hunched her shoulders as the loud bang rang right through the house. She came back out onto the verandah.

'Gramps? Do you know who this woman is?' She held the open locket for him to see.

Gramps nodded. 'Well, I am not sure, but I think it is quite possibly Lady Fotheringay.' He was looking closely at the woman in a white curly wig and green silk dress; the eyes looked sad and the mouth was firm, not smiling. Round her neck hung a ruby and pearl pendant, and from her ears hung ruby and pearl earrings.

'Mmmm,' Gramps nodded, 'yes, James and I did discuss this once, and he thought it was Jane Fotheringay, but there is no knowing. She was the daughter of the Fotheringays; she was killed in a riding accident a few days after her twenty-first birthday. Maybe that is why the Italian artist was staying in the house, perhaps he was there to paint her birthday portrait, but we will never know, will we?'

Robert was standing behind Gramps, looking over his shoulder. 'It must have been someone very special, just look at the jewellery; it was only the very rich who had their portraits painted, wasn't it?'

'Yes,' Richard was looking closely, and Gramps handed him the locket. 'It wants a good clean. I would think it's silver; it's worth keeping, Ali, even if we send the other stuff to the museum. Hey, wait a minute, aren't these the same earrings that you found in the box?'

'I don't know, are they? I'll go and get them; they are still in the drawer.' She went once again into the dining room, taking the box quickly off the table, and rushing out. She waited for the door to slam behind her, but it didn't. She brought the box to the table and when she took the earrings out Richard took them from her, comparing them with the painting. 'They are, look.'

Nick took the locket from him. 'Yeah, they are the same. But I wonder why the earrings were in a secret drawer and the locket wasn't.' He handed them back to Alison.

'Well, she probably wore the locket more.' Alison compared the painting and the earrings, and put both pieces of jewellery into the drawer and snapped it shut.

'What about this jade ring?' said Robert, picking it up off the table. 'Why was this left in the cabinet? Was this the ring that was found on the hand? We read about it in the scroll.' As he held it between his thumb and forefinger, a strong breeze blew across the verandah, rustling the leaves on the low branches of the mahogany tree. Something made them all look up, but no one spoke, and Robert put the ring down on the table.

'Well, Emily wanted to keep that,' said Gramps, putting just one finger on the ring. 'James wore it all the time, he loved jade. I expect you have noticed several pieces that are around the house; he collected it, brought most of it back from the Orient with him. She didn't like the ring because of its history; you know, the hand and such. But she said she would keep it in the cabinet, it was part of James, and they were very much in love.'

'They were very happy, then?' Richard raised his eyebrows.

'Very,' Gramps nodded, and smiled in his whiskers, and his brown eyes twinkled at some hidden thought. Alison thought she could see a tear in his old eyes. 'Very happy,' he was nodding, then quickly out of his reverie, he looked at the end of his cigar; it had gone out, and Richard struck a match and relit it for him. He puffed hard until a bright red glow appeared on the end. Taking it from his mouth, he sighed, 'Yes, it was all such a long time ago,' he was shaking his head gently.

'Did they have any children?' Richard asked, moving the ashtray nearer to Gramps.

'No, they had no family,' Gramps said sadly. 'And Emily was very lonely when James passed away, but she spent many hours with my dear Ella May and our two boys, who were very young then, and Emily loved them.' He went into a thoughtful daze again, then he sighed. 'They used to call her Aunt Em. Ella May and Emily used to sit on our verandah with their patchwork. It filled in the time for her, and the boys would play on the beach, where Ella May could watch them.' And then he said quietly, taking in a deep breath, 'Then I was left alone, when my dear Ella May was taken, and Emily used to come over every day and help me with the boys, luckily they were growing up a bit then. And then Selena came here as a very young girl, to help us both. She would come to my house one day and Emily's the next. She brightened up both our lives, with her young and lively ways; she would sing about the house quite happily, while she was cleaning, and then she would cook us a meal and we would eat together, either here, or over at mine.' He nodded towards his house. Gramps was rambling on and on. He drained his rum glass, and Richard refilled it. He filled Nick's glass too, and poured more wine for Alison and himself, while Robert went off to the kitchen to get another Coke.

'What about the White Lady?' said Nick, changing the subject, and stubbing out his cigar in the ashtray. 'Tell them how she came to be out there in the garden.'

Gramps nodded his head, and raised his eyebrows. 'She's not always been white, as you know.'

'Did Joseph paint her?' asked Richard.

'Gramps smiled into his grey whiskers, and his brown eyes

twinkled. 'I suppose he has given her a few coats of paint over the years,' he chuckled.

'Alison is a good artist,' said Nick. 'You should see her painting of the goddess, Gramps, it's good. Show Gramps your painting, Alison.'

Alison went back into the dining room once again. Her paintings were dry now, and she brought them out and stood them up against the balustrade for all to see. Richard, Robert and Nick stood up, and Gramps leaned back in his chair to get a better look.

'Yes,' Gramps nodded, 'yes, very good, mmmm.'

Richard looked at Alison with admiration. 'Alison painted the lady in those colours before she ever knew about the colours, didn't you, darling?'

'Yes,' said Robert, 'and she saw the galleon out there on the horizon and…'

'What?' Gramps frowned – he could not keep the alarm and the dismay out of his voice. He looked at Alison earnestly. 'You actually … saw the ship?' he said slowly.

'Well … um, yes,' she said nervously. 'Well, I think I saw it. Well, I must have done, or I would not have been able to paint it like that … I mean,' she shrugged her right shoulder, 'all that rigging and cannons and things. I don't know anything about boats, I just sketched out what I saw, and then I painted it … but come to think of it, I don't know how I got the colours, I don't remember seeing the colours out there. I know that the lady is right because now we have read the scroll.'

'Yes, but she hadn't seen the scroll when she first painted it, had you?' said Richard.

'Tis a very good painting, my dear,' said Gramps, nodding his head. 'Very good.' And he mumbled under his breath, 'But a bad sign.'

'A bad sign,' Richard questioned, 'why?'

Gramps stood up slowly and wearily, holding onto the table for support and stretched his old legs, and his back to his full height of five feet eight inches, and squared his shoulders. There was a tight smile on his whiskered lips, 'You are a very good artist, my dear. But I must go now … feeling tired,' he nodded. 'Old age, you know,' he chuckled to himself, and then thanking them for a nice evening, he walked unsteadily towards the end of the verandah.

'Thanks for a super meal,' said Nick, taking Gramps' arm. 'It's been a nice evening.' He guided Gramps towards the gate. 'Better get Gramps home, he is a bit tottery, too much rum,' he smiled.

Gramps turned to see if Alison was listening, then he whispered to Richard, 'Look after her,' he nodded winking his eye.

Richard frowned, looking puzzled, then over Gramps' head to Nick, he whispered and mouthed, 'What does he mean?'

Nick was about to answer him, but Alison came round and he changed his mind. Then she walked away again as Robert called her back up on to the verandah.

Nick spoke quietly and quickly to Richard. 'My grandmother said she saw the galleon, and she was drowned soon afterwards. Gramps connects the two, but I don't know if there is any truth in it.'

Richard looked open-mouthed with amazement at Nick, and watched as he guided his grandfather carefully along the pathway, a short walk to his house. As Alison came back, he let the wrought-iron gate shut with a clang. There was an unusual squeal, and they both turned quickly to look at the frangipani tree; the fine mist was swirling around the figurehead. Then a seagull flew low over their heads, so close that the thud from its wings caused a draught.

'That was a funny cry,' said Robert, leaning over the verandah rail, 'seagulls don't fly at night, do they?'

'No!' Richard said abruptly. 'Come on, let's go inside.' He took Alison by the arm, and quickly and gently propelled her towards the door. 'Bring those paintings in, will you, Rob?'

Rob picked up the paintings and the box and the ring from the table, followed them in, and took them into the dining room.

'You know, I wish I had seen that galleon, Alison,' he was saying. 'It all sounds a bit mysterious, but I am going to look out for it tomorrow, I would love to see it.'

Richard looked at Rob and shook his head very slightly, warning him not to talk about it. Robert got the unspoken message. Richard was also wondering what she had seen out there on the horizon, and then there was this eerie-sounding seagull; it crossed his mind that the house could be haunted, and then he put that silly notion quickly out of his mind, although Gramps had made a quick retreat when she said she had seen a galleon.

'It was a nice evening, wasn't it?' said Rob. 'Gramps is very interesting. I wish Tim and Gary had been here. But I will tell them about it tomorrow.'

'Yes,' said Richard, 'very nice.' He looked along the hallway to where Robert was opening his bedroom door.

'Goodnight, Rob.'

'Night.' He closed the door with a click.

Gramps' words were worrying Alison. Richard knew by her attitude – she had said nothing. And he wouldn't dare to mention haunting; he didn't even dare to think about it.

The days were going fast now towards the end of their holiday. John and Carol and the boys had been gone almost a week, and Robert was missing their company. They had said that they would keep in touch, and Rob and Gary had arranged to go to a football match together when they were all back home in London, as they didn't live too far from each other, and they had become good pals over the last two weeks.

The sun had been in and out all the morning, the sky was cloudy and it had rained quite hard earlier on, and there was a strong breeze blowing. Richard and Rob had gone swimming; there was a swell on the water, and the wind was whipping the waves into white peaks. Alison had said that it was too rough for her, so she sat on the verandah thumbing through a magazine, but she felt unsettled, her mind kept going back a few days. Nick had been up with Jojo, but they hadn't seen Gramps since the night of the dinner party. His words kept ringing in her ears, and she felt she could not touch her paints.

She got up and looked over the rail down across the beach and out to sea. She felt a bit lethargic; she picked up her cover from the back of the chair and slipped it on over her bikini, and then she strolled slowly down the steps to the beach. The coral was hard and sharp under her bare feet, until she reached the sand, which was warm and soft. She shook her head as Gramps' voice engulfed her again, it kept on repeating, 'It's a bad sign, it's a bad sign. You're a good artist, my dear, but it's a bad sign.' She had to find out what he meant – why was it a bad sign to see a ship out there with white sails? It was her own imagination, surely, thinking it was a galleon; it did seem uncanny though, that she had painted it so well, her imagination had just run away with her.

She found herself at the low rocks near the water and climbed over them, wishing that she had put her sandals on. She could see the top of Gramps' head; he was sitting beside his fishing boat looking out to sea, wearing a navy blue fisherman's cap which covered his grey curls, protecting his head from the fierce rays of the sun. She walked over to him. 'Good morning, Gramps,' she smiled.

'Good morning, my dear,' he smiled up at her, wiping the sand from his hand down the front of his navy T-shirt and beige shorts and offering it to her. He smiled though his whiskers as she sat down beside him in the shadow of the boat, which did nothing for the heat of the morning.

'Gosh,' she smiled, 'it's so hot, isn't it? But we have had a lot of rain, though, in the night.'

'Yes,' Gramps looked up at the sky, 'I think we will have some more. It's a bit cloudy, but it will get better as the day goes on. We do get these funny days on the island, but it doesn't usually last very long.'

'I hope not, we haven't got much longer.'

'Oh! When do you leave then?'

'We leave on Saturday,' she smiled. 'Back to the cold weather, I expect. It's never very warm, especially after this. Have you been to England, Gramps?'

He chuckled, 'Oh no, my dear, and I don't suppose that I will go there now at my age.'

'Oh, you don't know, perhaps you will be able to come and visit us one day, perhaps Nick can arrange it.' A strong gust of wind suddenly whipped up and around them, wavering the coconut palms, and a few spots of rain blew into their faces.

'Come on,' said Gramps, getting to his feet and walking

swiftly towards his house. She followed him, and just got inside when the rain poured down like a monsoon, clattering on the red-painted corrugated iron roof.

'We were lucky there,' said Alison. 'Richard and Robert are in the sea, but then they are already wet.'

Gramps smiled. 'Yes, the rain comes down so quickly here, the clouds come over, and then the breeze starts. When you feel a few spots of rain, it is better to move quickly,' he chuckled into his whiskers. 'But it will stop in a few minutes, you will see, and the sky will be blue again. But you have been very lucky with the weather, it's the first heavy rain that we have had for weeks. Would you like a drink, Alison?'

'Err, yes please, it's very hot down there on the beach.'

Gramps pottered his way to the small kitchen at the end of the hallway, leaving her alone in the living room. The cottage was very much the same as White Lady cottage, but this room was not furnished as well: there were two brown leather armchairs, either side of the window which looked out over the verandah onto the beach. They were both frayed and worn on the arms, and the seats were very low and had been used a lot over many years. Between them stood a low mahogany coffee table, and on it was a chipped flower pot, the plant in it gasping for a drink. Around the coral stonewalls hung brightly coloured paintings of African dancers; she knew this was Haitian art. On the corner of a bookshelf there were photos, one of a baseball team, in the centre a young-looking Nick holding a crash helmet. Alongside this was a picture of a smiling bride and groom; she could see that it was Gramps' wedding. He had been a handsome man, and the bride a beautiful girl, with coffee-coloured skin and long dark hair. The bride was wearing white, with a veil, and holding a bouquet of red flowers. Below, on the next shelf, was a picture of a smiling lady in a red dress; her dark hair was piled on top of her head and secured with a red flower, and Alison could see that it was the bride in later years. Next to this was a picture of a smiling lady with grey hair wearing a blue and white spotted dress, holding a bunch of flowers. Alison turned round as Gramps came through the door, with a tray and two glasses of Coke filled to the brim with ice.

He smiled as he offered her the drink, and nodded to the

photographs, 'That's Emily in the blue and white spotted dress, that was taken just a few years ago.'

'Is it?' said Alison in surprise, although she had guessed that it was Emily. 'We have a few photos over there in the cottage, but they are much younger.'

'Well, this is how she was in her later years,' Gramps smiled. 'She was a lovely lady.' He put down his Coke and, picking up the picture of the lady in the red dress, 'And this is my Ella May,' he said lovingly and proudly. 'Oh! She was a beauty. We fell in love when we were in our twenties, and I still love her, and miss her so much to this very day.' A small tear welled in the old eyes, but then he sniffed and took a breath, shaking his head. 'Yes, it's been a long life without her,' he nodded thoughtfully, and shook his head again in a sort of despair, 'but I suppose I am lucky to have Nick for company. He comes and he goes,' he nodded with a smile, 'he has been here a couple of months now, but will go back to New York again soon, I expect.'

'Oh, so you really live here on your own,' said Alison. 'What about your two sons, you mentioned them the other night. Do they come to stay here?'

'No,' Gramps shook his head. 'I hear from them from time to time. Nick's father is Philip, somewhere in South America or Brazil, or Mexico, I think, when I last had a card. And Martin has a wife and family of four, they moved to Australia over twenty years ago. I hear from them occasionally.'

Alison put her head on one side. She smiled, feeling a little sorry for Gramps, he seemed to be alone, his family miles away; apart for Nick, he had no one. It must be awful to be old and alone.

'But,' he nodded and smiled happily, 'I fish every day, and Selena cooks me a meal every day, and comes to clean once a week, and I potter around the garden. I grow a few vegetables, enough for my needs and Selena's, and Tom Wiley comes down and we play cards or dominoes and have a few rums together. We have been friends for years, since we were at school. Ha, ha,' he nodded with a grin, 'that was a long time ago. Sometimes his wife Sarah used to come, but she can't take the walk down the hill now. She used to come and sit with Ella May and Emily, with her sewing. Tom and I couldn't stand the chatter, we used to go fishing, but what I would give to hear Ella May's chatter now.' He shook his head again, in a sort of remembered sorrow, then looked up at her with a smile.

'Gramps?' She was looking at the photo of Emily. 'Gramps, was Aunt Emily worried about, this ... umm ... err ... this mist that occurs in the garden sometimes? And about this wailing noise, she must have heard it many times, and I expect you have, too. Did it worry her? Does it happen very often?'

Gramps sipped at the drink, then wiped his whiskers with the back of his hand. 'Well, it doesn't happen all that often, but of course, when Emily heard it for the first time it was frightening for her, but she had James there then.' He chuckled. 'I remember the first time Ella May heard it – she clung to me all night, we spent the night under the bed, she wouldn't come out,' he laughed heartily. Alison laughed with him.

'But it really isn't funny, is it? When it starts, I must say we were really scared, well I was, anyway.'

'Yes, it is frightening, my dear, but you see I have lived with it all my life, as my father and my grandfathers have done, and so did James, but he went off the island for a few years to become a doctor, and then came back years after, bringing Emily with him. When I was at school, it used to be a ghostly joke, and we boys used to sit down on the beach all night, hoping to hear it wail. It's unnerving to anyone who doesn't understand it, and it is best to stay indoors. It passes, you know, it passes.'

'Gramps, what about the galleon? Did Emily ever see it? You said the other night that it was a bad sign, why? Is it a ghost that wails, is it a ghost ship? I am sure that I saw it out there on the horizon. I know it sounds stupid, but I am sure I wasn't seeing things, or maybe it was just a sailing ship, and I imagined it. But why did you say it was a bad sign?'

'Well, you see,' he said slowly, thinking before he spoke, 'you see, that is how I lost my dearest Ella May.' He stopped for a moment, deep in thought. 'You see, she saw the galleon. Of course no one would believe her; she saw it three times, and in all my years I have never seen or heard anyone else say that they had seen a sailing vessel out there that looked anything like a galleon. But Ella May insisted that she had seen it. It had been a stormy night, and the wailing had been loud, we were both awake, and lying in our bed, listening to the noise. Whether I dozed off or not I cannot say, but I turned to find her gone. I called and there was no answer, and then I came downstairs, the door was wide open, and when I came out, I could see her rolling in the surf. I ran quickly, down to her, and pulled her out. She said, "The ship", and died right here on the beach in my arms.

'It was such a very sad day for me,' he shook his head gently. 'I remember, I did not want to leave her lying here alone on the beach, but the shock was so great that I had no strength to lift her, and I remember running wildly along the path and banging on James's door, begging him to come quickly, even though I knew it was too late... They came running, James and Emily, in their night clothes; James had grabbed his medical bag which was always ready by the door, but it was too late. I remember running after him and crying...' he trailed off.

Alison could see the pictures in her mind. There was a quietness, and she broke into his sad reverie. 'Gramps,' she whispered, afraid to disturb him. 'Gramps, do you think that I really did see a ship out there, I mean the actual *Savannah Lady*? Do you think that it is possible?'

He was back to normal now, and he smiled, shaking his head, 'Strange things do happen my dear.' Then he nodded, 'do you believe in the supernatural?'

'Do you mean do I believe in ghosts and things? I don't really know. I have never thought about it very much, that is until now, but it does worry me. Do you think that White Lady Cottage is haunted?'

'No, no. My dear, now don't you go worrying your pretty head about such things. There are many things in this world that cannot be explained, and I can't explain this one. I think it must be the wind whistling through the trees. And you know what I think, you have a very artistic mind, and the Caribbean lends itself to such things as pirates and galleons, and your artist mind, my dear, runs wild. The sun casts shadows and the eyes see things. Just shadows. Shadows, that's all it is. Now you go on and enjoy the rest of your holiday, my dear Alison. I am sure that there is nothing to be afraid of. No one has ever been killed by a ghost.'

'Ella May?'

'Now I know Ella May said that she saw the ship, but I am sure really that after all these years, her death was really an accident.' He was nodding again as he touched her arm. 'You enjoy the rest of your holiday, my dear. And I am sure that you will come back here again. Everyone does. The Caribbean has a magic charm. 'THAT'S IT!' he said, tapping her arm with a quick and friendly gesture, 'it's M.A.G.I.C.' And he gave a jolly chuckle, screwing up his face, and his twinkling brown eyes almost disappeared under his bushy grey eyebrows. They walked to the door laughing together; the sun had come back out again.

'Thank you, Gramps, I feel a lot better for talking to you. I guess it is just my imagination, and you are right, this is a magical island, and Richard is already talking about coming back. You see, my sister and her husband, that's Robert's parents, couldn't come with us at the very last moment, and they want to come out here so much, so you see we will be back.' He was smiling and nodding in agreement.

'There, you see, the cloud has all gone. I told you it would.'

'It's magic,' she laughed, putting the half-finished glass down onto the table on the verandah. 'Well, I think I will be getting back, thanks for talking to me, you and Nick must come over for dinner again before we leave, bye.' She gave him a last wave as she went down the steps onto the sand and walked down the beach to the low rocks and climbed back the way she had come; as she looked back, she saw Gramps making his way back down towards his fishing boat.

As she came back up the steps and onto the verandah, Selena looked out of the kitchen window.

'There was a phone call for Mr Robert, Mistress. It was a Mrs Bentley. I say Mr Robert e swimmin', she say she call back.'

Alison smiled and nodded, and then sat down on the verandah on one of the sun beds. She looked out into the blue sea and could see Richard and Robert swimming. The sea was rough, with big swells, and the waves crashed onto the beach. Out further the wind was whipping up the sea into white peaks, and out on the reef the sea rolled in great white waves. There were a few people walking along the beach, and a ski boat went by, and there was a local man snorkelling amongst the shallow rocks, but what he saw she did not know. She gazed out at the wonderful Caribbean sea, with its many shades of blue and green, and silver, ever-moving, never still; sometimes calm like a pond, but the least touch of the breeze and the waves could become dangerous with an undercurrent. She watched Richard and Robert; they were both good swimmers, but the sea mastered their every stroke.

Her mind was still on the talk she had had with Nick's grandfather. He had tried to reassure her, but she felt nervous of his words; it's a bad sign, she'd seen the ship, she was sure, and she thought she would be very careful of the sea, or was Gramps right that Ella May's death was just an unfortunate accident?

A small sailboat was going by, she thought it a lovely colour and nice to paint, but she couldn't get to grips with painting at the moment, she could still hear Gramps' voice in her head. A catamaran sailed in closer to the shore, it was a daily three-hour trip with about 40 passengers on board, and some jumped into the water to swim before the lunch was served, and then they would set off again back to Bridgetown.

Her eyes were now on the horizon. She blinked, it was there again, she felt alarm rise in her stomach, she was afraid to move in case the sail disappeared. She blinked her eyes again and again, it was still there, the galleon in full sail; it was not imagination, it was there, she was in full control of her mind and her body. She stood up, it was still there. 'Richard,' she breathed and then went rushing down the steps on to the beach, not noticing the sharpness of the rock under her bare feet, and ran down to the water's edge, calling and waving frantically to Richard, who waved back; Robert waved as well. They both turned to look to where she was pointing and then looked back at her and waved; she could see that the ship was fading, and dropped her arms and her shoulders slumped limply, in a hopeless gesture; she felt drained and let out a deep sigh. She stood knee-deep as the rough surf splashed her thighs and her bikini pants, swirling all round her before rushing in and up onto the sand. Richard and

Robert were swimming towards her. She waited, hoping that they had seen it, she wondered if Gramps had seen the ship, as he was sitting just the other side of the rocks; she called to him, but he could not hear her. Richard and Robert were standing now, finding it difficult to wade in the strong current. She called to them excitedly, 'Did you see it, Richard?'

He came closer. 'What did you say?'

'Did you see it? The ship? The galleon, it was out there.'

'Is it? Where?' Robert turned round quickly, and then turned back. 'Where, Ali?'

'Oh! It's gone now,' she sighed. 'You obviously didn't see it, it was out there,' she pointed, 'out there on the horizon.' It was hopeless, she knew that they had not seen anything, and she felt disappointed; she also wondered what was going on in her head, why was she the only one who could see the galleon? Even Gramps, with all his years by the sea, had said he knew no one who had ever seen it, except poor Ella May of course.

'Well, I didn't see the galleon, Ali,' Robert sounded disappointed, 'Why didn't you call us? Cor! Its rough out there today,' he said, shaking the water out of his ears and his hair, as they started to walk up the beach, all thoughts of the galleon gone quickly from his mind.

Alison was walking beside Richard. 'Didn't you see the sail out there? It was plain enough.' There was annoyance in her tone. 'Both of you out there swimming, and you didn't see anything?'

'No,' said Richard, looking back out to sea, 'I didn't see anything. I saw you shouting but I couldn't hear what you were saying.'

'Hmmm!' she fumed. 'Damn good job I wasn't desperate then, wasn't it? I was shouting at you to look, and you didn't take the slightest notice.'

'I couldn't hear you, Ali.'

Alison clenched her lip tightly; she was annoyed. She looked out to the horizon, there was nothing now but the rough white waves curling high out on the reef and rushing towards the shore. The sea was getting rougher.

* * *

That evening the three went to a restaurant for dinner. The dining room was set high up on a rock, they had a table overlooking the beach, and below them the sea rushed fiercely in to the small rocky cove. There was just a rush roof above which protected them from the heavy rain, and the candle in the centre of the table flickered under the hurricane glass as the strong warm breeze caught it. The people on the next table moved their chairs further round the table, away from the spray of the rain, as a strong breeze suddenly blew the rain in, rustling the leaves on the trees, and the waves crashed in with a thunderous boom on the rocks below, sending sea spray 20 feet into the night air.

They looked out into the blackness of the night, to where small lights still twinkled on the fishing boats regardless of the weather, and a mass of lights twinkled on a cruise ship, rising and falling in the rough water. The passengers would be dining now, and then they would dance until the early hours and awake in the morning to find themselves docked in St Lucia for yet another wonderful day in paradise. Suddenly there was a burst of loud drumming disco music as the gusty wind blew the sound across the darkness of the water from an evening cruise ship which came in quite close; they could hear talking and happy laughter, the holiday crowd quite oblivious of the driving rain, which looked like diagonal stripes as it lashed past the lights on the deck. They would dine and dance until midnight, until the boat docked again in Bridgetown, from where they had boarded; it seemed that no matter what the weather, people still went to sea.

Alison looked up with a smile and nodded as the waiter asked her if she would like white wine; she smiled as the food that they had ordered arrived at the table.

'I had a nice chat with Nick's grandfather this morning.' She told them what he had said, and told them that she had seen the photos of Aunt Emily, and his wife Ella May. Then the conversation got around to how much they had enjoyed the company of John and Carol Turner, and Robert said that he was missing Gary and Tim. They talked about the treasure, Jack Barneby the pirate, and the galleon.

'You must have seen the galleon out there this morning, I don't know how you could have missed it. And Gramps said that his wife saw it, so it must be true. She was drowned, did you know that, Richard?'

'Err, yes, I think Nick mentioned something about it. Lovely meal this, isn't it? Do you want some more wine, darling?' He topped up her glass. He was trying to change the subject; he flashed his eyes at Robert, who was quick to catch on, with a knowing glance that Alison did not see.

'I really do miss Gary and Tim's company. Gary and I have arranged to go to football; he knows someone who can get us tickets for Chelsea and Manchester United in about three weeks' time. I think Tim is quite keen on football, he will probably come if Gary can get tickets. Do you like football, Richard? Gary might be able to get some more tickets.'

'Sure, I go occasionally, sounds good.'

'What?' Alison frowned. 'When do you go to football? You haven't been to a football match for years. In fact, I don't remember you ever going to one.'

'No, but if Gary can get the tickets.'

Between them Richard and Robert kept the conversation going, talking about anything and everything, to keep Alison's mind off wailing and galleons until they had finished their dinner. When they went out to the car, the doorman did his best to hold the umbrella mostly over Alison as she got into the front seat. Robert got into the back seat behind her, while Richard scooted quickly round the bonnet, and jumped into the driver's seat and drove off back to the cottage, which took them less than ten minutes.

When they arrived at the gate, Robert and Alison made a quick dash for the cover of the verandah; they were laughing and soaked through to the skin. Richard came quickly up behind them. 'Come on, Richard,' called Robert, anxious to get in. Alison giggled, she had had too much wine. Richard fiddled about in his pocket for the key, found it, and as he opened the door they rushed in, glad to get away from the wind, which was driving the rain onto the verandah.

Alison shook the rain out of her ponytail, and gave a little shiver as the wet cold ends touched her bare shoulders; one shoestring strap slipped off her right shoulder, and the thin and wet pink material of the dress clung to her body and her legs. Both Richard and Robert, in light trousers and short-sleeved shirts, were drenched to the skin, and they shivered even though the rain was warm and the night was humid. The rain clattered on the roof as they stood inside the door, and the wind was now strong and gusty as it whipped across the verandah.

'Wow!' Robert chuckled, wiping his wet arms. 'A tropical storm! This is the first bad day that we've had since we arrived, and it seems to be getting worse, doesn't it?'

'Yeah.' Richard closed the door. 'Let's hope that it clears by the morning, don't mind if it rains all night.' He turned the key and followed Alison, who was already in the bedroom, taking off her shoes and stripping off her wet clothes. Richard closed the bedroom door as Rob called out goodnight, and they heard his bathroom door slam. They both called out, 'Goodnight Rob.'

Alison was tired; she crawled into bed; the wine had gone to her head. Richard got into bed and gave her a kiss, then turned out the light. The room was hot and humid and the ceiling fan did little to cool the air, but despite this, they were soon asleep. Outside, black storm clouds gathered across the night sky and the rain still hammered on the roof, as the sea rolled in with thunderous waves that boomed on the shore, and the rocks sent spray high into the night air with vengeance. They slept.

Alison woke with a start as a loud clap of thunder rumbled across the sky and a bright flash of lightning streaked across the ceiling through the gap in the curtains, then seconds later, another tremendous clap of thunder and another streak of lightning flashed across the ceiling again. She ducked her head under the thin sheet that covered them.

Richard turned over, with his back to her and the window, his eyes still closed, hardly awake. 'Is that thunder?' he mumbled. 'Bad storm.'

'Yes, and the lightning is bad,' she said, poking her head up from the sheet, just as it flashed again. 'Can't you hear the rain hammering on the roof? Gosh, I think you could sleep though anything.'

'Mmm.'

She got up out of bed and peeped though the curtains. She didn't know why, she hated thunderstorms, but she just had to look out of the window. Fork lightning cracked across the sky and she jumped back quickly, holding her hand to her eyes. She peeped out again, the wind was blowing the trees and the rain was pelting down, and again the thunder crashed and the lightning flashed. She got back into bed, unable to close her eyes. Richard had gone off to sleep again, and she wished that she could sleep like him, but she tossed and turned with her head under the sheet, then she lay on her back, watching the ceiling fan as the blades were caught in the lightning flashes, and listening to the wind as it howled and blew pieces of branches off the trees, which clattered down heavily on the roof.

The night was tumultuous, the coconut palms swayed their willowy trunks and waved their feathery arms in frenzy – although they had seen many a storm such as this over the years, not one had ever snapped in half. In the mahogany tree, birds in their nests ruffled their feathers in an effort to protect their young, as the well-built nests swayed and dipped in the fearsome wind and rain. The sea was whipped up into white peaks, and out on the reef large waves gathered and rose high, rolling like a stampede of white horses racing towards the shore.

Alison lay listening to the raging storm; the thud of the tremendous waves shook the house and rattled the doors and windows. She whispered a silent prayer, and wondered if God was angry with the world. It was then that she heard it above the noise of the elements: it started low, a moaning and then the wailing, which got higher and higher, rising to an unearthly screaming, rising and falling. She sat bolt upright, anxiously shaking Richard by the shoulder.

'Richard! Richard! Wake up, it's the wailing! It's started again!'

But Richard was only semi-conscious; he could hear the rain and the thunder, but he could not bring himself to really open his eyes. 'Mmmm,' he murmured sleepily, 'it's the storm.'

Alison got out of bed and went to the window again, and just as the lightning lit up the sky she saw it – the galleon was tossing. She saw it rise and fall under a huge curling wave.

'Richard!' Her voice was a loud whisper. She slipped into

her pink towelling housecoat that was on the chair, and went swiftly to the door, opening it quietly, not knowing why; if Richard could sleep though this racket, the sound of the door opening would not make much difference. She came out into the hall and switched on the light. There was no electricity, but the lightning was as bright as day. She glanced at Robert's door, it was closed; didn't men ever wake up? She started down the stairs, tying the belt of her housecoat as she went. As she turned the bottom of the stairs, lightning flashed in the mirror above the telephone table, almost blinding her. She stood quite still and closed her eyes for a second; the wailing seemed much louder down here, she was going into the kitchen to make some tea, and then she remembered that there was no electricity.

There was an almighty clap of thunder, and she ducked and stayed bent in half with her shoulders hunched for a moment, expecting the roof to fall in on top of her. The wailing was loud – how could Richard and Robert sleep through this? Or perhaps they were both just lying there awake, they must be, surely with this racket; the whole island must be awake. The lightning flashed again, and she suddenly remembered that she had seen the galleon out there. She went to the verandah door and turned the key then turned the handle, and the force of the gale blew the door back, almost knocking her over, and the cool rain sprayed into her face.

She could see the galleon, it was still heaving and rolling out there on the reef. A sudden thought came into her head, that George Kingsley had once stood right here and watched the very same scene all those years ago... It had to be a ghost ship. A white mist swirled across the verandah, it hovered in front of her swirling and curling, and she saw clearly a women's face, it was the face of the White Lady. The red lips were parted into a smile, and the red-gold hair streamed back from the beautiful face, and the white mist swirled around her like a white cloudy chiffon evening gown, and it billowed gently, even though the wind was blowing a gale.

It seemed to Alison that it was all happening in slow motion. The Lady's smile dazzled her and she smiled back as the white hand reached out to her. Alison took it; the Lady held her fingers firmly, drawing her forward out onto the verandah and beckoning to her with the other hand, and they moved slowly and silently, even though the wind howled and the screeching of the goddess seemed to come from far away. The Lady hovered, facing her, as she went down the steps, she felt the sharp coral under her bare feet, and lightning flashed, and the thunder rumbled over head, and the white chiffon dress floated and swirled in front of her like white smoke.

They were at the bottom of the steps now, and she felt the uneven warmth and hardness of the wet sand beneath her feet, the wind blew her long dark hair back, and rain lashed into her face, and as the Lady compelled her forward, the belt of her housecoat came undone and was swept back by the wind, and the thin cotton nightdress was soaked by the lashing rain and clung tightly to her slim figure. Wind whipped up the soft sand, stinging her legs, like needles, but still the Lady drew her forward.

They were nearing the water's edge, and Alison smiled back at the beautiful face, with the blue eyes and the dazzling smiling red lips, and the Lady held her hand firmly, and beckoned as she backed into the raging surf, drawing Alison towards her. The wind whistled wildly in her ears, and she was aware of the loud wailing and screeching, the thunder clapping and the lightning bright, lighting up the sky. She saw the ship, and the cool water rushed and swirled around her thighs, and she toppled, but the Lady held her firmly, smiling as the white chiffon billowed and floated slowly, and appeared to stay dry, and the red-gold hair framed the beautiful face and fell softly on the white shoulders, and the red lips seemed to be mouthing her name, Alison, Alison, but she could hear no sound.

The Lady beckoned, drawing her deeper into the sea; she was up to her waist now and could feel rocks beneath her feet, then a huge swell lifted her off her feet and the water dragged her back toward the shore, but the Lady held firmly on to her hand; Alison's arms were stretched out to the limit, and the Lady pulled her deeper and deeper out into the raging sea. They were going out to the galleon, Alison saw it, just before a huge wave rose above her and rained white foam down on her, plunging her head deep under the deluge. She lost her grip on the hand, and she reached for it but it was not there. She struggled, fighting the water, trying to swim but the housecoat was heavy and dragging her down. Her head broke the surface and she gasped for air and the sea battered her body as she floundered round in the darkness, and another huge wave washed over her and her head went under again. There was a terrific rushing noise in her ears, she heard the Lady wailing and then it turned into a scream and high-pitched laughter. She fought to reach the surface again, but she could feel her strength leaving her as the blackness of the water engulfed her.

The wind blew the bedroom door shut with a loud bang. Richard was suddenly jolted out of his drowsiness, and turned over. 'Are you awake, darling? Was that the door slammed? God, what a night.' He opened his eyes and lightning flashed and thunder shook the foundations, rattling the windows and all the doors though the house. The lightning streaked across the ceiling, and he could see that Alison was not there, he sat on the side of the bed and yawned, then stood up and pulled at the elastic waistband on his short red-striped pyjama pants, and it went back with a slap. He stretched his arms up to the ceiling; how he had slept through this noise he didn't know, must have been too much wine. He made his way across the room to the bathroom, lightning flashed, showing him the way, he switched on the bathroom light, there was no electricity. He came out of the bathroom, feeling his way along the wall, and knocked his toe on the dressing table. He winced and swore out loud, and he made it to the door and opened it.

Robert was at the top of the stairs. 'God, what a night, I've been awake for ages. I heard someone go downstairs, I thought it was you.' He started down the stairs, and called back loudly, 'The verandah door has blown open.' He had no need to shout so loud as Richard was right behind him, although the wailing and the screaming were deafening. Robert shut the door against the elements.

'I'm not surprised,' said Richard, making his way to the kitchen. 'Alison, Alison,' he called, coming back down the hall and looking into the sitting room, and Robert opened the dining room door.

'She's not in here.'

They looked at each other, realizing that she must have gone out on to the verandah. Robert turned the handle and the wind blew the door back at him. Richard was calling, 'Alison, Alison,' as the wind whistled in their ears and the rain lashed in their faces, and then on the beach they could see a light from a torch and snippets of men's voices, which were carried away on the gale-force wind. Someone was running, Robert was halfway down the steps. Richard shouted to him as he saw someone in the water, the torchlight flashed, and the lightning lit up the beach and the huge white foaming waves as they crashed on to the shore.

Richard saw two people. No! Three, one was in the water and the other was just going in, one was holding a torch. 'Alison,' he called, but the words were lost. In a quick lightning flash he saw a sail; his first thought was these men are shipwrecked. He and Robert reached the water's edge, thinking that it was Alison with the torch, but was surprised to find that it was Gramps, dressed in fishermen's waterproofs.

'It's Alison,' Gramps shouted in despair.

Richard was already in the water up to his thighs, shouting 'Alison, Alison' hysterically in wild alarm, until his voice broke as he splashed into a dive towards her, Robert close alongside him.

Alison was fighting for breath. She could feel her lungs ready to burst as the heavy, waterlogged housecoat tangled around her legs, dragging her down. Her fingers lost their grip on the Lady's hand as a huge swell parted them, and her ears were filled with hysterical laughter that faded into the quiet and peaceful blackness of the water.

Suddenly she felt herself lifted high out of the water, and she gasped for air as the rain spattered her face and the wind took her breath away. She dipped again into the dark waters, but strong arms held her, they were dragging her though the water, and she felt herself lifted high above the raging sea. She was flying; it was God's arms that held her, she was going to heaven, and then she knew no more.

Richard and Robert watched as Nick and Joseph dragged

Alison through the raging surf. Joseph held her high up in his arms and waded through the white rushing surf and carried her up onto the beach and laid her down by the rocks where there was a little protection from the wind.

Richard, breathless and on his knees, patted her face. 'Alison, Alison,' his voice was choked with tears. Nick was also on his knees, rubbing her cold hands, but she did not move. Then water spilled from her mouth, and she coughed, turning her head to one side as the rain spattered down on her face like needles, and through her closed eyes she saw a flash of lightning, and she opened them as thunder shook the sky. A distant voice was calling her name, she was no longer in the water, where was she? And then she realized that she was on the beach but how had she got there? The distant voice was calling. It was Richard's voice. She slowly opened her eyes.

'Richard,' she whispered, and someone said, 'she's going to be all right.'

'It's all right Ali, it's all right, you're safe now.' He was leaning over her, he was all wet, and his dark hair fell over his forehead and water ran down his face and his nose and dripped into her face. She smiled a weak and gentle smile, and then moved her head. Nick was the other side of her, rubbing her hand, it was rough with sand, and then she saw Gramps, all shiny in his black waterproofs; he was holding a torch, he was wet, and his grey whiskers had gone into separate curls; he stood smiling down at her. Joseph stood, his arms folded, and breathed heavily as he looked down on her from a great height; water dripped from his black curly hair down his nose to his chin, and his strong white teeth showed a flashing smile, and his large brown eyes goggled; she saw his beige knee-length pants, clinging to strong black hairy legs, and as he stood feet apart, arms folded, she thought he looked like the genie of the lamp in Aladdin, and in the torchlight his shadow stretched to twice his length.

Looking back over her head she saw Robert; he was upside down, she thought he was smiling, but it was hard to see, as his face was in shadow. She felt light-headed; had she been drinking? Everyone was wet, well of course they were, it was raining, but why were they all out here in the rain, no one had an umbrella. And why was she lying on the beach, in the rain...?

Suddenly, she said, 'What happened?' She was bewildered, then suddenly realizing she was also soaking wet and in a thin nightdress, she sat up, helped by Richard, and quickly covered herself with the housecoat, which was wet and covered in sand; it was cold, and she shivered.

'What happened, Richard, why are we out here?' She looked round to each and every one of them.

'What happened? What did happen?' Richard echoed. 'You were very nearly drowned, that's all…' His voice rose comically but annoyed, and of course he did not feel either way, it was just his way of expressing his utter relief at knowing that she was all right. 'Come on, let's get you inside.' He helped her up, and they all made their way to the coral stone steps, shoulders hunched against the blustering gale and driving rain. Richard had his arm round Alison, and Nick held Gramps' arm, helping him up the steps as he shone the torch for them to see, until they reached the shelter of the verandah, where Selena had lit candles under hurricane shades, and was waiting with dry towels for them all. She quickly took the wet housecoat off Alison, and wrapped two large yellow towels around her and sat her down in one of the rattan chairs. Alison recovered quite quickly, but still clutched on tightly to Richard's hand.

Nick handed her a large glass of rum, which he had got from the kitchen, after searching round with a torch. She took a sip and pulled a face at him, he smiled down at her. 'Drink it, it will warm you.'

She took another sip. 'Well, thank you all,' she said looking at the bedraggled group, now all with yellow towels draped around their shoulders. 'But I don't really know what actually happened. You said I nearly drowned, surely I wasn't sleepwalking. I've never done that in my life.'

'Well, there is always a first time, Ali,' said Robert.

'No! I knowd what happen to de Mistress,' said Selena sharply. 'It shee, she had you's in her power.'

'Oh, no,' said Alison. 'Not shee…'

'Shee?' Richard frowned. 'The White Lady?'

'Could be; you nearly drowned, Ali,' Robert said anxiously.

'Yes,' said Richard, 'if it hadn't been for Nick and Joseph, you would not be here.'

'It was Joseph, not me,' said Nick.

Alison looked bewildered. 'Well, how did I get down on the beach? Oh! Wait a minute; I remember now, I came down to make some tea because I couldn't sleep, and the electric had gone. The wailing was awful down here. It's stopped, hasn't it? Listen...' They all listened; it had stopped, but no one had noticed. She went on, 'The doors were all rattling, and I remembered that I had seen the galleon from the window, so I opened the door, and it was still out there, and the next thing I knew she was there, offering me her hand.'

'Who was there?' Richard frowned.

'Sheee was!' Selena snarled. 'Sheee, de Evil One. I seed her from de window, de mist was swirling around, and I seed de Mistress following herrr, down on de beach. Sheee evil. And as de lightning flash I see de ship it break on de reef, I wake Joseph, and he runs quick, but de Mistress she already in de sea. She evil, Mr Price, I tell you sheee evil.'

Alison looked at Selena in open-mouthed surprise; in fact, they were all amazed at the venom in Selena's voice.

'You saw the ship, Selena?' Alison looked at her anxiously. 'You really did see it?'

'Yes, Mistress, I see it, out dare on de reef.' She pointed out into the wildness of the night.

Alison smiled up at Richard. 'There, see, I told you I saw it,' she squeezed Richard's hand. 'I told you,' she nodded to them all.

'And the mist, Selena?' said Richard. 'You said you saw the mist, but what made you think it was the White Lady?'

Selena held her head high, jutting out her chin. 'It shape like e woman,' she said indignantly.

'The shape of a woman?' Richard raised his eyebrows, he was flabbergasted.

'Yes!' she snapped. 'De evil one.'

'Is it the first time that you have seen her, Selena?' Alison was looking up at her as she put the rum glass onto the table. 'And is it the first time you have seen the galleon?'

'No, Mam. I seed it twice before.' Gramps had a quick intake of breath; he had seen it, too, a long time ago.

'Well, has anyone else seen it?' Richard looked round at them all. Nick shook his head slowly, and grimaced. Gramps lowered his eyes but never moved. Joseph shook his head; his large brown eyes looked afraid as an enormous flash of lightning streaked across the sky, and an equally enormous clap of thunder shook the floorboards under their feet. And they all hunched their shoulders; Alison tightened her grip on Richard's hand.

'Well, I think I saw a sail out there,' said Richard. 'As I was running down the beach, it was only in a flash of lightning, though, and in any case I was more concerned seeing you all in the sea, and dragging Ali out.'

'Was I actually in the sea? I mean deep?' Alison looked amazed. 'I don't actually remember going in.'

Nick was nodding, his eyebrows raised. 'Yes. Obviously the storm kept Gramps and me awake, and I came downstairs and made us a pot of coffee, took it up to Gramps and then came down and started to read the paper, but then the electricity went off, and the wailing was terrible. I wondered if you would all be all right, and for some reason I peeped through the curtains. I don't know why, couldn't see anything, then in a lightning flash I saw someone running down the beach. I thought it was you, Robert, so I opened the door and shouted "Robert", and Joseph shouted, "Nick ... Nick, help me", so I dashed after him, and when I got to the water's edge, he was swimming out. I thought he was in trouble, so I dived in after him. You were a long way out, Alison, but I got there just as he grabbed you, and we struggled to get you in. The waves were terrible, and we didn't know which way we were swimming, and then someone was shining a torch, and I could see it was Gramps. Thank God you had the torch, Gramps, or we might all have been lost. Then I saw Richard and Robert splashing around, but by then Joseph had a good grip on you and carried you up onto the beach.' He looked at Gramps. 'I'm glad to see you had the sense to put your waterproofs on, Gramps.' Gramps smiled through his wet whiskers, and pushed the hood back off his head.

Alison sat there with her mouth open; she took a breath. 'Well, thank you, Joseph, and you, Nick. Well, what can I say? If you hadn't come in after me...' She shook her head. 'Well, I just don't know how to thank you enough.'

'It were nothing, Mistress.' Joseph dropped his head shyly,

blinking his large brown eyes, and smiled. 'Anyway, it were Mama who saw you first. I was in my bed, but I was ewake. She see you from de window of our house and she call me.'

'Well, thank God you saw her, Selena,' said Richard. 'Otherwise...' he turned his palms upwards, and shook his head. 'In fact we can't thank you enough.' He was looking at Selena, still shaking his head.

'Hmmm.' She dipped her head shyly, her lips pressed tight together. 'I go make some tea.' She walked off, feeling proud of herself and yet embarrassed at being praised.

Robert called after her, 'There's no electric, Selena,' but by then she knew, and she felt her way along the hall to the kitchen to find some more candles.

The storm raged on and the wind suddenly changed, blowing the rain in on them, so they all went into the living room, where Selena had lit some candles. Alison took one, and was halfway up the stairs to change into some dry clothes. Nick was the last one in, and just as he was about to close the door there was the most almighty clap of thunder, and fork lightning zigzagged to the ground; and there was a loud crack. Nick poked his head out of the door again, and shouted 'FIRE!' He saw light flickering. They froze, then there was a mad rush as they went to the door.

'What is it, Nick?' Richard looked at Robert for an answer, and then saw the flames. Alison turned on the stairs, and followed Joseph as he disappeared out of the door, leaving Gramps and Selena still in the living room.

They were all on the scene together. The large mango tree had been struck by lightning and was engulfed in flames, and was half fallen over onto the bougainvillea, which was hanging over the frangipani tree, beneath it the White Lady. The whole thing was ablaze, and the wind and rain were in competition. As the wind fanned the flames, so the rain rained harder, and the rain was winning. The flames licked the hair and the right side of the White Lady. They watched stunned and helpless, and Alison thought she saw the eyes blink, and took hold of Richard's arm for comfort, but then realized it was the flickering of the flames.

Joseph was quick to get the hose, which he left every day attached to the tap; he sprayed it over the White Lady, and the flames were quelled before they took hold of the wooden-framed kitchen window. They went back into the house, leaving the smoke smouldering into the grey dawn sky, while the rain lashed down, hammering on the roof.

By eight o'clock the next morning the rain had stopped, the sky was a clear blue, and the sun was shining again. The only sign of the terrifying night was the remains of the mango tree, split down the middle, the bougainvillea burnt to the ground; and there was an acrid smell of charred wood and dead and wet leaves, and the mouldy smell of sodden earth. The frangipani tree was a sad sight, its beautiful pink blossoms scattered wet and limp on the ground. Its oval-shaped, dark shiny leaves, what was left of them, were black, charred and in tatters, and its almost bare and broken branches dripping its life's milky fluid on to the White Lady, who looked a sorry sight, burnt partly from the waist, the arm and the shoulder, and with the right side of the face charred black.

Richard, Alison and Robert were surveying the sad scene, when Jojo bounded up the steps from the beach, followed by Nick.

'Good morning, Nick,' Richard greeted him. 'It's a bit better this morning. God, what a night.' Alison was patting the dog.

Nick nodded. 'God, what a mess.' He was taking in the charred scene. 'Lucky that mango tree is some distance from the house, it might have come right through the roof. But look at the sky now. Who would think there had been such a storm? Anyway, how are you feeling this morning, Alison?'

'I'm fine thanks, Nick. How are you? How's Gramps this morning? It was a rough night for him.' She stopped patting Jojo and turned back to the frangipani tree. 'This is unbelievable, isn't it? What are we going to do with it all?'

Nick grimaced, shaking his head. 'You will have to get the tree-felling company in to remove it. I think the name is Miller or Mellors, or something like that; Gramps had to have a tree removed once, and they did a good job.' Jojo was sniffing around the charred remains of the tree, his large paws sunk into the damp earth and leaves, and his black legs were blacker as he stepped over the burnt branches.

Nick said, 'I have to go. I promised Gramps that I would take him down to the shops to buy some cigars. See you later.' He called to Jojo, and then started down the steps.

'I've got some you can have, Nick; I won't smoke them, and it will save you a trip.'

'Thanks, Richard, but it gives Gramps a bit of pleasure to go out.' He smiled. 'Even if it is only to the shops. Thanks anyway, see you later.' He went off down as far as the water's edge, Jojo following with his tail held high. Alison watched as he ran ahead of Nick and into the rushing white surf which would clean his dirty paws; he barked loudly as the waves rushed at him. She smiled, he was such a happy dog.

The three of them were still looking at the charred mess when Selena arrived.

'Mornin', Mr Price, mornin', Mrs Price, mornin', Mr Robert,' her normal airy greeting was low and cheerless.

They all chorused together in a low toneless 'Mornin', Selena', mimicking her with a smile.

She gave them a shy smile. 'Oh, dis is e mess,' she sighed, 'I get Joseph to move it.'

'No, it's too much for Joseph, Selena. I will get the company that deals with this sort of thing, and they will come out and clear it. But I expect they will be busy today, there are probably trees down everywhere after last night; we are lucky that the house wasn't damaged.'

Selena, just nodded and asked Alison if she was feeling all right, and then made her way to the kitchen.

'You know, I feel a little sorry for her.' Alison was standing with her head on one side.

'Who, Selena? Why?' Richard looked after Selena as she disappeared into the kitchen.

'No, not Selena. Her.' She half-nodded towards the Lady. 'She looks a little sad this morning, don't you think?'

'Well, so would you, if you had half your head burned off,' Robert chaffed.

'Well,' said Alison sulkily, 'I think it's a shame. Look at her with half her hair burnt and half her face blackened, poor thing. Look, there are traces of the original red paint. It's sad.'

'Hmm! Don't forget she lured you into the sea last night,'

said Robert. 'Selena said she was evil, she certainly looks it now. Best get rid of it; letting a block of wood spoil our holiday sounds daft to me, chuck her in the sea. Anyway, I'm going in to get a cup of coffee.' And he walked off, leaving Richard and Alison thinking on what he had said.

They stood for a minute or two, just looking up at her, and then Richard said a little despondently, putting his arm around her shoulder, 'Come on, let's have a walk along the beach.'

The beach was strewn with debris, branches blown down from trees were everywhere, and leaves covered the sand. The sea was still rough and came pounding in and up on the shore; it was brown and thick with the mud which had washed off the land, and there was a sour smell. Seaweed clung to the water's edge, washing in and out, and higher up on the now-dry sand, where the water had washed up in the night, black seaweed, stones and shells made a long straggling line which stretched for miles. Crabs crawled, searching the rocks for food; the rocks had now been stripped clean of the algae that they lived on, and the mighty waves still washed over them as they clung on tightly with their sharp claws. Small fish had been thrown up onto the sand and left to die. One still gasped at the unhealthy fishy-smelling air with wide frightened eyes, and Richard pushed it with his toe back into the water, maybe it would survive.

Palm leaves floated in the heavy swells; further out a fishing boat was half-submerged, and the bright pink buoy that it was anchored to bobbed up and down as if trying to save its life by tugging it back. As they walked along, the sea pounded heavily on the shore and rushed towards them with such a force, then washed back out again 50 yards in swirling white foam. Patches of yellow sand came to the surface and although they were well up on the sand sometimes their feet got wet, and the spray splashed at their white shorts and T-shirts.

As they neared the hotel, they saw that the damage had been severe: the sea wall had collapsed, and the sea was rushing into the ground-floor rooms, and thick mud from the gardens had coated the floors and halfway up the walls. People were up to their ankles, trying to salvage what belongings they could find. Furniture washed in and out of what had once been a garden; an armchair was upside down, and bedding was soaked. Beach chairs were scattered along the sand, some were tossing over and over in the surf; beach boys were trying to retrieve them, which wasn't an easy job. Trees had fallen at the back of the hotel gardens, and the swimming pool was filled with branches and palm fronds, and there were two chairs floating. Thick sand covered the patio, the chairs and the tables which were turned over, two waiters were standing them back into place and cleaning them with a cloth, and two boys were sweeping the sand from the patio back onto the beach.

They sat at the beach bar, and Richard ordered two orange juices with ice, which the barman squeezed freshly for them. The scene all around them was devastation, but there were a few people sitting around the pool and bar area, and several were back on the beach with the recovered sun beds, rubbing on suntan cream and settling themselves down for another hot and sunny day. The holiday scene was back to normal.

The tree people came in to remove the fallen mango tree. It took them several hours to saw up the branches into small pieces with an electric saw - luckily the electricity had been restored early in the morning - and took it all away on a truck.

When they had finished, Richard stood amongst a heap of wood shavings and sawdust that the men had left; he would ask Joseph to sweep it away. While he was considering this, Joseph came lumbering round the garden with a broom in his hand and began to sweep. 'Thanks, Joseph, I was going to ask you to clean this up.'

'What you do bout her, Mr Price, sir?' he nodded to the bedraggled Lady.

Richard clicked his tongue and took in a breath through his teeth. 'I don't really know, Joseph.' He rubbed his chin, 'I think we will have to chop it down.'

Joseph nodded. 'I do it, sir, I do it,' he grinned eagerly.

'Joseph! You got them eggs?' Selena's strong voice carried through the kitchen window. She had seen him come by.

'Jes' comin, Mama.' His big brown eyes goggled and his mouth opened; he had forgotten the eggs. He stood the broom up against a tree. 'Must go, back in e minute,' and he dashed off though the trees. Richard smiled to himself.

There was a large, deep hole in the ground where she had stood for 200 years. Joseph had dug her up. It was early evening, the sun was still hot, and the temperature was still high. She was lying in a forlorn state on the beach, where Joseph, Richard and Robert had carried her and dumped her. Nick was coming in with his grandfather's boat, which Tubby was driving. Richard had decided that they would take her out to the reef. So, knee-deep in the surf, which was a lot calmer now, they floated her out to the boat and lifted her into it, and the three of them climbed in. Tubby drove slowly out – there was not much room, as she was longer than the boat – and it took them a few minutes to reach the reef. Then between them they lifted her, which was difficult as the water was choppy, and the boat rocked; she was heavy, and the boat tilted dangerously sideways as they rolled her over the side with a splash. She sank deep into the heavy swell. Stephen Tubworth turned the boat around. 'That is the best place for it,' Nick said. 'That's where it should have been years ago.'

There was a loud bang on the bottom of the boat, which lifted them well out of the water. They looked at each other in alarm, catching hold of the side of the boat, and thinking that they had struck the reef. Tubby managed to steady the boat, and they looked over the side and saw that the goddess had risen again, and was face-up, looking at them through the water; a slight mist seemed to engulf the boat. Richard and Robert exchanged quick glances, and they both reached out and pushed the charred oak away from the boat just as a big swell took it, and a curling wave which had smashed down on it took it under. It floated for a second and then disappeared with a gurgling sound, and there was a big eruption in the deep water. Tubby took fright and revved up the engine, and they sped away out of the thin mist back towards the shore.

No one spoke, but their thoughts were all the same, hoping that she would not get washed up again on the beach.

It was Robert who broke the silence. 'I wonder why it has

been here so long? I wonder someone didn't get rid of it years ago.'

'Gramps said that they tried,' said Nick, as the boat slowed down to a steady pace. 'He said that he and James Kingsley once started to dig her up, but James fell backwards and cracked his head open, so they left it for a week or two, and then they tried again, and in the attempt Gramps broke his wrist. Emily said it was the evil spirit, and told them never to try moving it again. Then it was years after James had passed away, that Henry Munchester, a neighbour who lived up on the hill, thinking that he was helping, came to see Emily. There had been a storm and they had all been kept awake all night with this terrible wailing, and he asked her if she would let him dig it up and throw it into the sea. She thanked him, but explained that the statue had evil spirits and advised him not to touch it. He had laughed and said that it was nonsense, and it was about time someone did something about it, so he started to dig, and I believe he moved her a bit, and while he was digging, a neighbour, Helen Harrison, who lived next door to him, came running down the hill, to tell him that his wife had had a fall, and to come quickly. He rushed back, and minutes later she died in his arms...

'And then a week later he went out in his fishing boat, as he did every day, and was never seen again. No one knows whether he just sailed away, or whether he was drowned, but they never found a trace of him or his boat. Gramps was one who helped in the search... Emily was putting a coat of white paint on the garden gate when Helen Harrison came down to tell her about Henry. She was so upset by the news, saying that it was because he had tampered with the evil spirit, and she threw the whole pot of white paint up into the evil face of the statue, and she was shouting angrily, and Helen was almost in tears, shouting and trying to stop her, when Tom Wiley, who was just going in to see Gramps, heard the two women, and Emily shouting at the statue that she had killed the Munchesters. Poor Tom didn't know what to do to calm either of them, and said that he would get rid of it, but Emily begged him not to touch it, saying it's evil. She was so hysterical about it that he promised not to touch it. He took Emily and Helen over to Gramps' house, and Ella May made them some tea. He and Gramps went over, and Tom picked up the paintbrush and smoothed the paint which Emily had thrown all over the lady, and that is the way she has stayed all these years. And Joseph gives it a coat of paint now and again, don't you, Joe?'

Joseph nodded. 'I not heard dat story before, Mr Nick. But she evil, Maaan, she evil. Mama says she evil, we all gonna die, Maaan.' There was great fear in his eyes, and he shrieked, 'We's all goona die, Maaan! I wish we never dunned it, Maaan.' Tubby had not said a word, but his eyes were fearful too.

'Oh, stop worrying, Joseph, she's well out of reach now. Forget about her, man, she's down at the bottom of the sea.' Nick spoke with confidence.

'Yes,' Richard chuckled, 'don't worry, she's only half the woman she was, she must have lost her evil heart, that's if she ever had one. Pity the fire didn't take more of her, anyway she's back in the sea again now where she belongs, with her grisly crew.'

'Yeah, let's hope she stays there,' chuckled Robert, giving Joseph a hearty slap on the back. 'Stop worrying, Joe. It's only a block of wood after all.'

Joseph's dark eyes showed great fear and he looked around him and back out to sea, as if expecting the goddess to follow, and in the warmth of the evening, a cold shiver went down his back.

Stephen Tubworth brought the boat close to the shore. Richard jumped out, water up to his thighs, and held it steady for Robert and Nick. Joseph seemed to be frozen to the wooden seat, he moved himself slowly over the side as if in a trance, glancing out to sea with frightened eyes.

Stephen backed the boat out into deeper water and threw the small anchor over the side, then jumped into the water, half-swimming, half-wading, and followed the others up the beach, fearful like Joseph, and looking back over his shoulder for fear that he might be followed.

'Good morning, I would like to speak to the curator if possible, please.'

'Yes, I am the curator, Andrew Harrison. Can I help you?'

‘Oh, hello, my name is Richard Price, and I have a house on the west coast, and we think we have found a pirate’s treasure.’

‘A treasure?’ Andrew had a quick intake of breath. ‘Have you informed the police?’

‘Well, no. I never thought about that... But we have found a jewelled sword and a dagger, and a few other bits and pieces, and I wondered if you would be interested to come and have a look. Do you know anything about a pirate called Jack Barneby, and a ship called the *Savannah Lady*?’

‘Oh, yes, yes,’ there was short laugh in Andrew Harrison’s voice; he was beginning to get quite excited. ‘Yes, I should like to come and look at what you have found.’ They made arrangements for Andrew to come the next morning, as Richard said that they were leaving the island on Saturday evening. When Richard gave him the address, he smiled into the phone and said that he knew the house, and would be there at ten o’clock in the morning.

Andrew Harrison was a white Barbadian, a slightly built man of medium height, aged about 40. He had thinning, straight fair hair brushed back from his lean, narrow, square-jawed face, and pale blue eyes behind square rimless sun glasses. He wore beige cotton trousers and a crisp, white short-sleeved shirt open at the neck. He stopped the car, got out walked through the gate with a businesslike manner, and came up onto the verandah, where they were still finishing cups of coffee.

Richard got up. ‘Good morning,’ they shook hands. ‘This is my wife, Alison, and our nephew, Robert.’ Alison offered him some coffee as he sat down at the table with them, but he refused politely, with a smile showing a set of very white even teeth.

Richard explained how Robert and his friends had found the treasure, and told him as much as they knew about Jack Barneby. It turned out that Andrew had heard later of the White Lady, but he had never seen her, and it was his grandmother, Helen Harrison, who had come down to tell Emily about Henry Munchester who had gone missing.

'Is your grandmother still here?' asked Richard.

'Oh yes, she still lives up on the hill, she's been there all her life.'

Richard said that he would like to meet her, because she had known his great-aunt Emily.

They took Andrew Harrison into the dining room; he was amazed at the sight before him, and kept saying, 'How interesting, how interesting,' as Robert explained how he had fallen in the cellar and how they had dug these wonderful things up out of the earth. He picked up the magnificent sword – they had washed off most of the dirt and grime – and as the sun streamed through the open window, the stones shone like fire. He turned it in his hand, then put it down and picked up the dagger. He examined the locket and the miniature painting, and thought that it was painted by the young Italian artist, Giovanni Colletto, confirming what Gramps had said, he being a friend of the Fotheringays who had been commissioned to paint a portrait of their daughter Jane for her 21st birthday. She had died two days after the portrait was finished, by falling from a horse, and they were devastated. Lady Amelia had asked him to copy the portrait in miniature so that she could always wear it in her locket. She had the locket specially made to match the earrings which they had given Jane for her birthday. As you can see, she is wearing them in the portrait.'

'So it is a portrait of Jane, the daughter,' said Alison. 'I bet that's why they were in the secret drawer. I bet Lady Fotheringay put them away and never wore them.'

The box, Andrew said, was cedar, and was made by a carpenter named Thomas Atkins, who was also an artist, and was very popular at this time for his fancy carving.

Andrew Harrison agreed with Richard to take the treasure back to the museum for cleaning, and said that he would give them an estimate of the value and that he would phone Richard, who had given him the London phone number of his home and his office.

Richard said that he would like to have a valuation on the locket and the earrings, but Alison would like to keep them; but the rest of the things he could have for the museum. 'You can also have the rum barrels from the cellar if you want them. I'll have them taken out and sent down to you tomorrow, and there are also some interesting pieces here in the glass cabinet, but I haven't sorted them all out yet.'

Andrew looked into the cabinet and nodded eagerly. 'Yes, when you are ready, send them down and I'll look them over.'

Alison and Robert had come back from Gramps' house after saying goodbye to him and Nick, and now they were saying goodbye to Joseph. Selena came out to the gate to wish them a safe journey again; she had said it three or four times to Alison. They thanked her for looking after them so well, and said that they would be back next year.

'I am looking forward to that, Mistress.' Selena had tears in her eyes. 'I have enjoyed working for you.'

'Bye, Selena.' Alison was in the car with the window open, 'Thank you, it's been great, apart from the scary bits,' she laughed, leaning out and holding Selena's hand. They laughed together, and Selena wiped a tear from her eye as the taxi started to move away. Just as the taxi was turning the corner, Nick came running up to wave a last goodbye, but he was too late.

3

Alison sat at the small desk in Thomas Gordonston's art shop in Chelsea, where she had worked for three years. She enjoyed being there, she met many artists like herself, who just painted for fun and the pure pleasure of it; she also met many students who were trying to make a living from their special creations, some of whom were excellent.

They had been back from the Caribbean for six weeks now, but life was not the same in London, and she had found it hard to settle down again, plus the weather had not been good. She had been listing prices for Mr Gordonston all morning; there had only been two people in the gallery to view the paintings – they had not stayed long, and now it was lunchtime. She had remembered this morning to bring in the two watercolours which she had painted while she had been away. She had pinned them to some cardboard to keep them flat, and stood them down against the leg of the desk.

Mr Gordonston was in the back room, unpacking some new art which had come in the day before from Italy. He had looked at her work and said that they were very good, and that he would be willing to buy them from her if she wanted to sell them. But if not, he would get Edwin Spooner to frame them for her free of charge. But unfortunately, Edwin, a small and wizened little man, had called to say that he could not come in as he had a cold, so her framing would have to wait until he came back to work.

She looked up as the bell tinkled on the door, and a man in a light raincoat came in with a rush, pushing the door closed with a bang as the wind pushed it against him. He was tall and thin, with glasses. He smiled, raising his tweed deer-stalker hat at her, put it back on to his thick, straight grey hair, and pushed his wet black closed umbrella into the stand.

'All right if I just look?' he smiled politely, and began to walk along the wall, viewing the artwork.

Alison smiled back and nodded, then went back to her listing. The phone on her desk rang, she spoke quietly into it, pen poised over a note pad, and then jotted something down.

He was looking closely through round spectacles at an oil painting of a boat, when Alison asked if he needed any help.

'Yes please,' he said very precisely. 'Yes, a friend of mine left a painting of a ship here two weeks ago, might it be ready?' He spoke very slowly, pronouncing every syllable.

She smiled. 'And the name, Sir?'

'My name is Smythe, Maxwell Smythe. Oh! But of course, you want my friend's name,' he gave little chuckle, clasping his thin and white sinewy hands together in a feminine way. 'My friend's name is Rogers, Henry Rogers.'

She looked down at the order book. 'Yes, Mr Smythe, it is ready for you, if you will just take a seat for a moment.' She went into the back room and asked Mr Gordonston about the painting. He left the unpacking to find it for her.

Maxwell Smythe did not sit down as he waited for Alison's return. He wandered around the gallery, peering closely at the paintings. He was very interested in art, and knew quite a lot about it. He liked historical paintings, especially old ships; he could not afford to buy many, but found great joy in just looking. He saw the paintings that Alison had stood by the leg of her desk; he picked one up and was holding it out in front of him when she returned.

'Yes, here we are, all ready,' she smiled, holding up the painting of a ship for him to see, which was now in an ornate gilt frame.

He looked at it, saying, 'That is very nicely done, thank you.' He gave a little bow. Then he turned back to the painting he was holding.

Alison had started to wrap the painting in brown paper.

'Oh! I DO like this one, it has such a lot of movement. Oh! Yes, yes,' he nodded with approval. 'Who is the artist? Is this one for sale?'

'Oh...!' She mused shyly looking over at him, bringing up her shoulders to her ears and putting her hand to her mouth.

'I painted that, and no! It's not for sale; I just brought it in to have it framed. We have been out to the Caribbean for a holiday, and when I get the chance I like to paint.'

'Well, how strange. How very strange,' he said. 'Do you know, one of my pupils has not long came back from the Caribbean. I teach history, you know, at Longstone College. And he has brought back some wonderful photographs.' He leaned towards her, his watery blue eyes popping from behind his silver-rimmed specs. 'He says they found a treasure, can you believe that?' He put a hand to the side of his face. 'Really, can you believe that?' He looked over his specs. 'But he had some beautiful photographs,' he said, shaking head from side to side.

'Oh!' said Alison brightly, 'you must be Old ... ummm ... Mr Smythe,' she smiled gripping her hands into tight fists at her sides. 'And you must know Tim Turner,' she said, speaking quickly to cover up the mistake, and hoping that he had not noticed her embarrassment.

'Yes, of course,' he smiled, eyebrows raised. 'Timothy is one of my pupils, and he has taken some wonderful photographs. I showed them to the headmaster, he was very impressed. So is it true about the treasure, then? Well, what a coincidence.' They laughed together, then he leaned a little closer to her, wrinkling his nose, and talking from the back of his hand in a whisper, 'Don't worry, my dear, they all call me old Smythe. They think I am ancient, you see, but they will be old one day,' he smiled. His blue eyes twinkled, and she looked embarrassed again and giggled girlishly, biting her bottom lip, and then taking a deep breath and standing up to her full height of five feet four inches tall. She boldly held out her hand, 'How do you do, Mr Smythe, I am Alison Price.' They shook hands. 'And yes, we did find a valuable treasure in the cellar of our house. My nephew and Tim and his brother found it, but then I suppose Tim has told you all about it. We sent it to the museum just before we left, that was about six weeks ago, they were going to phone my husband; we have not heard anything yet.'

'Yes, young Turner told me. It was funny, I was talking to them about old galleons, I think it was last year, and the name Jack Barneby came up, so I had them all researching in the history books, and now here is young Turner coming back with all the proof. It is amazing, so we are starting the project all over again. Mind you, I don't think some of the pupils really believe that Turner found a treasure, even though he has the photographs... I do like this painting which you have done, Mrs Price,' he said, holding up Alison's ship, 'the *Savannah Lady*. I am very interested in this ship, you know. Well, in fact I quite like both of them,' he picked up the painting of the goddess. 'Could I possible purchase them from you?'

'Oh! Well,' Alison hesitated. Even though Mr Gordonston had said they were good, she was a bit surprised to think he was serious. 'Well, I hadn't really thought about selling them ... but, well ... if you really like them ... well,' she raised her shoulders, putting her head on one side, 'I suppose you can buy them ... umm. Yes.'

He was looking over his specs again, waiting for her to decide, and then his blue-grey eyes sparkled with delight as he thanked her, and she noticed the laughter lines at the side of has eyes.

'You know, I am very interested in old ships, and I have quite a collection of paintings, and a few models as well.' He viewed her painting again, holding it out and away from him. 'You know, this is very good.' He frowned, looking at her. 'Timothy said that you actually SAW this ship. It sounds incredible ... is that true?' his voice rose.

She looked a little awkward. 'Well ... yes,' she faltered. 'I know it does sound hard to believe, but yes ... I am sure that I saw a boat. Well, I must have done.' She turned the palms of her hands up to the ceiling and shrugged her shoulders, 'Or I could not have painted it like that. How would I know what a galleon looked like in detail?'

Mr Smythe held the painting out in front of him again, and then stood it on the seat of the chair, leaning it against the back, then putting the index finger of his left hand over his lips and the thumb under his chin, and stood back to get a better view, his head on one side.

'Mmm,' he nodded. 'It's excellent. Just look at the detail you have put in.'

Alison moved beside him. She could see what he meant about detail, but how had she painted it? The cannons ... the shadows of men standing near them ... had she seen men too? She had not really noticed them before. No, it must be just the stroke of the brush, but it did look like men ... the canvas basket on the top of the mast, the crow's nest, where the look-out man would have sat, the lantern alight swinging from the mast, the sails full-blown and the boat being tossed in the wind. 'Mmm, it puzzles me how I could have painted a galleon like that.'

'Aah! But, Mrs Price, this is a sloop,' he looked at her, his head down, and his surprised eyes looked up over his specs, then looking back at the painting.

'What is the difference between a galleon and a sloop, then? I wouldn't know, all the boats look the same to me.'

'Well, you see,' he pointed a long, skinny, bony finger, 'this is a one-masted vessel, fore and aft rigged with a long bowsprit. Pirates had a preference for these because they had a shallow draft, and they were easily manoeuvrable in channels, and they could carry up to fourteen cannon. Look, you have painted half of them in, and a crew of about seventy-five. Well I must be going, I only get an hour for lunch.' He picked up the painting he had come to collect for a friend, and she followed him to the door. 'Let me know when you decide about selling the paintings. I'll pop in again next week.'

Alison was cooking chicken for the evening meal, and Richard was making a pot of coffee.

'He really did like my painting.'

'Hmm, he can't know much about art if he wants to buy them, although you do paint very well, darling,' he added quickly, but he really couldn't believe it. He put another spoonful of coffee in the percolator.

'Aaah, don't be like that, Richard, they are not that bad. I put a lot of time into my painting, and even Mr Gordonston said he would be willing to buy them, and he has offered to frame them for me free of charge, but Edwin wasn't in today, he's not well, he has a cold.'

'Well, I didn't say they were bad, darling, it's just that I thought you sold Rembrandts and Gainsborough, and things, you know all the old oils. What do they call them...?'

‘Old Masters,’ she corrected. ‘But there is all the other stuff that comes in too, we have a lot of students’ paintings, and there are abstracts too and portraits; you never know, they may be the Rembrandt of the future. We get all sorts; we had a lot of Italian stuff in yesterday. Mr Gordonston has been unpacking nearly all the morning, Michael was helping because Edwin was away. Michael could frame my painting, but I would sooner wait until Edwin comes back, and then Old Smythe came in and wanted to buy them. And,’ she grimaced, ‘I made the mistake of calling him old Smythe. I felt such a fool,’ she smiled.

Richard smiled to himself. ‘So you might be a great artist yet, you never know,’ he looked round at her, raising his eyebrows. ‘Alison the Great, painter of phantom galleons...’ he trailed off, and his face changed; she could tell there was something wrong.

‘What’s the matter?’ she looked at him and closed the oven door and came round the kitchen table. ‘Richard? What is it?’

‘Oh well, I have something to tell you. I’ve been wanting to tell you ever since I came in. I don’t really know how to put it nicely ... you see, Nick phoned me just as I was leaving the office.’

‘What, Richard? What’s happened?’

‘Selena ... died.’ He winced, biting his lip.

She held her breath, then whispered, ‘Selena ... oh no. Oh my God,’ she put her hands to her cheeks. ‘How ... was she ill? What happened?’ She took a tissue from the box on the side table, and wiped her eyes.

Richard looked down at his hands. ‘Well ... Nick said ... That they don’t really know. Joseph found her in the garden, right where the Lady had stood.’

Alison caught her breath. ‘Oh, I can’t bear it, Richard... Do you think, the Lady...’ She held her breath waiting in anticipation, looking deep into his eyes.

‘Nick said that the doctor couldn’t understand it. She apparently hit her head, possibly on the ground, but they said the ground was soft – it had been raining – and the doctor said that it could not have been a blow to the head that killed her, and it was not a heart attack. There seems to be no explanation, they are having an inquest.’

'When did it happen?'

'Some time yesterday morning, I suppose. Old Tom Wiley came down to play cards with Gramps, and Joseph rushed over to ask for their help. Selena was supposed to have been cooking the lunch for them. Gramps told Nick that Joseph is devastated.'

'Have you phoned Joseph?'

'I tried, but there was no reply from the house.' He turned his hands up hopelessly.

Alison stood quite still, staring into space, and then suddenly she burst into tears, covering her face with her hands. 'Oh, Richard,' she was mumbling though her hands, 'oh, Richard.'

He came and put his arms around her, holding her close, kissing her hair. 'Alison, Alison, don't cry.' He cuddled her head and tears welled in his eyes as they clung together.

'I liked her so much,' she mumbled into his chest. 'And I thought that she would be with us for years,' she sniffed again and pulled away from him. 'She was the only one who understood what I felt about the Lady, and she was the only one who said she had seen the ship.' Suddenly she stopped and looked at him; her vision was blurred, she reached for tissues and wiped her eyes quickly. 'RICHARD! She saw the ship!' She held her throat. 'Do you remember that night, she told us she saw the ship.' Her arms came up in goose bumps, remembering the night she was nearly drowned, and she rubbed her arms and shivered. 'Oh, Richard, what are we going to do? Just say she takes someone else, the Lady I mean. I bet it was the Lady who killed her. Oh, poor Selena,' and she burst into tears again. 'She always said "shee" was evil.'

'But she isn't there now, Ali. Here, cheer up,' he handed her a glass of water. 'It couldn't have been the Lady. Selena tripped in the garden, she must have done, there can't be any evil now.' He was also trying to convince himself, and he really didn't feel too sure.

'It's her evil spirit, she is evil, and we must do something!' She wiped her tears.

The phone started ringing. 'Yes, Ali told me about Smythe. He wants to buy them and have them framed. Coincidence her meeting him, wasn't it? Yes, he liked Tim's photos. Oh, so he has started the lessons again, on Barneby I bet; Tim will be taking the class next. Old Smythe will be out of a job.' He laughed. 'Ali liked him. Gentle soul she called him. Yes, right John, we would love to come, bye.'

'John and Carol have asked us for dinner on Saturday at eight. Robert's going, so they have asked Sue and Peter. Should be nice, eh? Feeling better now?'

She nodded. 'Did you tell John?'

'Yes, he was surprised, and said that he was sorry.'

'We must send some flowers, Richard.' He nodded.

It was nice to see Sue and Peter; they had not seen them for nearly a month. They talked and talked about the holiday. Tim showed them all the photos and kept them in fits, telling them all about Old Smythe, how he had gone on about the photos and the treasure. 'He was holding up Alison's paintings, showing the class. We had a good laugh.'

'Oh, did they think that they were funny, then?' said Alison in surprise.

'Oh, no! I didn't mean that, it's just the way he talks, he's so, so, weedy. Well, you know, you have met him, Ali.'

'Well, yes, but I thought he was a kind and gentle sort of man, but he is a bit ... umm.'

'Weedy,' said Tim, wrinkling his nose with a smile.

'Eccentric,' smiled Alison. 'I'd say harmlessly ... err ... odd but nice.'

Sue and Peter were intrigued when they saw the photographs.

'Gosh, just look at the size of those rubies.' Sue's eyes were nearly popping out of her head. 'They can't be real, can they?'

'And this is the barrel of rum which we found in the cellar,' said Tim enthusiastically. 'You can see the name painted on the side.'

'Yes, and if Rob hadn't got trapped down in the cellar for five hours, we would not have found anything, would we?'

'Gosh! Was it as long as that?' Sue looked at her son in surprise. 'You didn't tell me you were down there nearly all day.'

Robert had a twisted smile. 'Well ... didn't wanna worry you.' He wrinkled his nose.

'How did you get on with the museum, Richard?' John asked, looking down the table.

'Oh, Andrew Harrison, the curator, rang me. He said the sword and the dagger are priceless, and he has had everything cleaned and says it looks fabulous. It's all displayed in a glass case and it is being advertised on the radio and in the papers as a special pirate's horde, and people are flocking to see it. No doubt the museum is doing well, I don't know what the entrance fee is, though, but Andrew Harrison sounded delighted on the phone.'

The conversation got around to the White Lady and the wailing. Sue and Peter were fascinated.

'Sounds a bit weird and eerie.' Sue wrinkled her nose.

'Yeah, it is a bit eerie, Sue.' Alison wrinkled her nose in the same way. 'And the first time that we heard the wailing and the screaming was terrible. It was three o'clock in the morning, and then there was this banging on the door. Well, I was really scared.' She had a little chuckle.

'You were scared?' said Robert. 'What about the night of the storm when you were nearly drowned?'

'Well, what about you getting trapped in the cellar, then?' said Richard. 'We were worried, and I walked the beach so many times looking for you, and Alison was going frantic, she thought that you had got drowned or something.'

'Yes, and you rang up, Sue, in the middle of it all. We had only just found him,' said Alison. 'And to be honest, I was frightened to tell you over the phone.'

'Sounds like some holiday,' said Peter. 'Nothing but disasters.'

'Yeah, but we'd do it all again, wouldn't we?' said Robert with a cheeky grin.

'Hmm, sounds like a dangerous place to me,' Sue grimaced.

Alison smiled. 'Yes, it does sound a bit strange, but we really enjoyed it, didn't we, Richard? I think we would go again; it has not really put us off, has it, darling, and I just loved the cottage.'

'Well, we have booked into the hotel again for Christmas,' said Carol, getting up to pour more coffee for Peter.

'That's a good idea, Richard. We could go out for Christmas, couldn't we?' Alison looked a little sad. 'But it won't be the same without Selena, will it?'

‘Well, we could go, I suppose. The weather will be better there than it will be here. If you want to go I’ll phone Joseph tomorrow and make some arrangements.’

‘Can you come, Rob?’ Gary nodded.

‘We can all come,’ said Peter. ‘That’s if it is all right with you, Richard. I know Sue would just love to go to the Caribbean, she has been asking me ever since you went out there the last time.’

‘It’s super,’ said Robert, ‘the best holiday ever.’ His face was beaming at the suggestion that he would be able to go again.

‘Yes, but of course you don’t find a treasure every day, do you?’ Richard smiled then looked across the table at Peter. ‘Yes, of course you can come, we would be pleased if you did, wouldn’t we, Ali?’

‘Yes, of course,’ Alison smiled at her sister; Sue’s face was beaming like a child with a new toy.

‘Well, that’s all settled then. You arrange your air tickets, Peter, and I’ll make the arrangements at the cottage. I’ll phone Joseph tomorrow.’

4

Gramps guided his fishing boat skilfully into the shore. The water was calm today, and he felt happy with his catch, a small tuna, four large snapper and some flying fish. He had been out since the very early hours of the morning, and he was still quite fit for his age, but he had now engaged Tubby, Stephen Tubworth, to help him haul in the nets. He was tall, about six feet, strong, slim and athletic. He jumped easily over the side, holding the boat steady, while Gramps climbed out slowly; he stood thigh-deep in the water, holding the boat steady, while Tubby lifted the heavy white plastic bin, half-full of water with the snapper and the flying fish still flapping around in it, and put it onto the beach. He then lifted the tuna and laid it beside the bin on the sand; it flipped its tail as he left it. Then he went back to the boat, drove it out into deeper water and anchored it to a small buoy. Then he swam back to the beach, lifting the bin onto his shoulder, walking with ease to Gramps' house, where he had a small van waiting to take the fish to a man that would buy them for his small stall which was at the side of the road. This made Gramps a very small living, and a few dollars for Tubby to buy a beer.

When Gramps got to his house Joseph's girlfriend was there already, cooking his breakfast; she had seen him coming off the boat. He liked her and he was getting used to her, but he had to admit that he missed Selena. He remembered when Selena had first come, she had only been seventeen. She had been bright and happy, and she would sing to herself while she worked. She had made such a difference to his and Emily's life. But this girl was also bright and a good cook; he could smell the bacon before he got to the door.

She turned from the stove as he came though the door,

with a cheery, 'Good mornin', Mr Cotton. Have you had a good catch dis mornin'?'

'Tuna and snapper,' he smiled, lifting his nose into the air. 'That smells real good, girl.' He smiled again as he went through to the bathroom to wash his hands and change into clean shorts and T-shirt, throwing the fishy ones into the laundry basket.

He sat at the table and she placed eggs and bacon in front of him and sourdough bread, and a big mug of coffee. She flashed him a smile; her teeth were very white and even, she had a beautiful face and light brown skin, large sparkling dark brown eyes, and long, glossy black, thick curly hair, which she had tied up tight onto the top of her head with a red scarf. From her ears small gold earrings dangled as she moved about. She was slim and small and delicate, and her name was Albertina Guttenpetal – Gramps was so shocked when she had first told him her name – her father was of Dutch decent, and she had come from Aruba, an island in the Dutch Antilles. Gramps said that he had been to the small island north of Venezuela years ago, when he was a lad. His father had gone there looking for work in 1929; they had the largest oil refinery in the world there then, but when it had closed down they had come back here to Barbados.

Albertina said that her father still worked at the refinery, as it had opened up again. But she wanted to visit other islands, and had been to St Lucia and St Vincent, but she liked Barbados the best, and now she had been here a whole year and she had met Joseph and she was staying.

Gramps found her bright and refreshing to talk to, and he called her Petal; he said he couldn't get his whiskers around a name like Albertina Guttenpetal, and now even Joseph called her Petal.

She took Gramps' plate away, and began to clear the table. The phone rang in the living room. She wiped her hands on a tea towel and went to answer it. 'Mr Cotton, it your grandson, Mr Nick.'

Gramps was always pleased to talk to Nick, and was pleased when Nick said that he was coming for Christmas, and also that Petal had got a job at White Lady Cottage if she wanted it; there would be five people to look after at Christmastime.

He told Petal and she was so delighted to have a full-time job as housekeeper, that she came and kissed his whiskers. It made him laugh, this beautiful little brown-skinned girl really was a breath of fresh air.

'You know, Richard, I've been thinking about us all going away at Christmas. Do you think we ought to go?'

'Well, of course we should go. Why not? I've booked the tickets now, and so has Peter, besides you can't put Sue and Peter off. Anyway, why the sudden change?'

'Well, Sue thought it was a big joke. She spoke to me on the phone earlier today. But say we get there and something else happens ... I mean like ... Selena for instance?'

'Oh it won't. I'm sure that was an accident, but I must say that the thought had crossed my mind too. I spoke to Nick on the phone about it the other day, he mentioned an exorcist.'

'An exorcist!' She sat up straight. 'That's a bit drastic, isn't it?'

'Well, I remember Nick's grandfather saying that she only wailed when a ship was in trouble, or about every two or three years, whichever. But don't forget, we were only there for a couple of weeks, and it happened twice, didn't it? I think it is a problem, but I think we ought to go out; we can't disappoint the others, can we? It probably won't happen again. Don't worry. We'll sort it out.'

5

'Ooooooh! It looks beautiful.' Sue marvelled at the island as they got the first glimpse from the air. She sounded like a child on a, Sunday school outing, as if she had never been anywhere before. She turned her head, looking over the high back of the seat, to Alison. 'Looks lovely, doesn't it?' she said excitedly. 'Look at the beach! Look, Robert.' He was sitting in front of her and she was tapping him on the head.

When the Boeing 747 finally touched down on the runway and taxied to a standstill, and they stepped out into the afternoon sun, Sue and Peter couldn't believe the heat, even though there was a strong breeze blowing across the tarmac. In the terminal, after the passport check, a smiling porter took their baggage out to a waiting minibus. Peter was glad that Richard had arranged it and knew where he was going; he felt strange, never having been in the Caribbean before.

Sue couldn't believe the cottage. 'Ooooooh,' she said, 'isn't it lovely, Peter?' But Peter was already at the back of the minibus with Robert and Richard, helping the driver to get the luggage out, then Joseph came to help and Richard introduced him to Peter, and he was all smiles and glad to see them all again.

Alison walked through the gate and up onto the verandah, Sue close behind her, still 'ooooohing' at this and that and gazing out onto the sea view, and when Alison stopped she almost bumped into the back of her.

A beautiful brown-skinned girl came out from the kitchen with a dazzling smile to greet them.

'Good afternoon,' Alison smiled, shaking the girl by the hand.

'Good afternoon, Mistress,' she gave a little dip, hardly a curtsey.

'You must be the new cook and maid. I am Mrs Price, and this is my sister, Mrs Bentley.' The girl smiled and shook hands, dipping again.

'And what is your name?' Alison asked.

'Albertina Guttenpetal, Mistress,' she dipped again.

Alison was not often stuck for words, but for a second she was stunned. The girl was still smiling. 'Yes, Mistress, I know, it shocks most people ... my father is Dutch. Now everyone calls me Petal.'

'Thank God,' Sue muttered through her teeth.

'Yes, thank goodness,' said Alison, 'you look far too pretty to have a name like Albertina Gutt ... sorry, what?'

'Guttenpetal,' she laughed. 'A lot of people call me Albert or Berti, but I prefer Petal. Can I get you a drink? Most people are thirsty when they first arrive.'

'Yes please,' Robert was puffing as he came down the stairs after humping a heavy bag up to the bedroom.

'Yes please. Cola; five please.' Richard came through the door. 'By the way, I'm Richard Price, pleased to meet you.' They shook hands. 'Albertina, isn't it?'

She nodded with a smile. 'Yes, Sir. But dey calls me Petal.'

Sue glanced at Richard. 'They call her Petal,' she sniffed and stuck her tongue in her cheek. 'I'm not surprised,' sniffing and turning up her nose. Albertina smiled and went off to the kitchen.

Richard had phoned John and Carol, who had walked along the beach from the hotel, and Robert, Gary and Tim came up out of the sea, and then Jojo bounded up the stairs, followed by Nick, carrying a huge bunch of flowers for Alison. Gramps was following slowly behind him; he could hear loud and excited voices, and there were lots of kisses and hugs and handshakes, all pleased to be together once again.

Alison had arranged a sandwich lunch, and Petal came though the door carrying a tray, followed by Joseph who set a tray of wine glasses on the table, and went back for the ice bucket and Coke for the boys.

Nick had them all intrigued. 'I have organized the Ghostbusters,' he announced, taking a sandwich.

'The what?' squealed Tim with a hearty laugh, throwing his head back into the chair, and then coming forward again, and plonking his large bare feet down heavily on the wooden deck. 'Spooks Men! Ha, haaaa, are you serious?'

'Yes, it's true,' said Nick. 'They are the M and D Psychic and Paranormal Research Group Ltd. And their names are Clive Marshall and Ian Douglas, and they investigate hauntings.'

'Are they American?' asked Richard.

'No, British, but I met them at a party in California about two years ago. They are back in the UK now, and when I phoned, their secretary said that they had been sitting around for two weeks in a Scottish castle. Now if that is not spooky, I don't know what is,' he chuckled.

'What do they actually do?' asked Alison.

'Well,' said Nick, 'I am not really sure, but when I was talking to this Clive Marshall at the party, he said they have this computer that can pick up sounds, and sometimes voices, from the other side.'

'Good heavens, the dead?' said Gramps, raising his bushy grey eyebrows. 'Do you mean that I will be able to talk to Ella May after all these years?'

'Voices from the other side,' Sue wrinkled her nose. 'It can't be true.'

'Oh, yes,' Nick nodded. 'They have been listening to voices for a few years now. Sounds weird, but it is a legitimate business.'

'When are they coming?' Robert was most intrigued.

'They are waiting for me to call them. They were very interested when I explained, and they can be here this week if you want them, providing that they can get a flight of course, and start work on Friday, if that's OK with you?'

Richard said that it was OK.

'Work!' Sue frowned. 'Is that what they call it? God, it does sound weird.'

'Can we come and watch?' said Tim eagerly; his eyes were wide and sparkling. 'Maybe we will see a ghost, wouldn't that be fun?'

'Tim,' said his mother, looking at him with disgust, 'why is it that you always want to do such weird things? Sounds very creepy to me, ghostly voices.' She shrugged as a shiver ran down her spine. Peter looked across at her and smiled. She grimaced.

Gary and Robert were both interested, and Robert said he would find out if they could watch, and he would let them know.

'I don't know if I want to watch or not,' said Sue, moving her eyes round to look at them all. 'What do you think, Ali?'

'Well, I think it sounds very eerie and a bit daunting, but I think I would have to watch. And I would really have to see something to believe it.'

Alison was showing Sue around the garden. 'And this,' said Alison, as they came back to the house, 'is the frangipani tree.'

'This is where the figurehead stood?' said Sue, peering at it closely.

'Yes, and that is the mango tree which was struck by the lightning. You can see it is beginning to grow back, and also the bougainvillea is beginning to flower again.'

Sue was staring into the space, as if trying to visualize the goddess. She could smell the delicate perfume from the pink blossoms. 'These would be lovely for flower arranging. You would only need one cluster in a glass bowl, they are beautiful. So this is where she stood? Weird isn't it? However did you cope with all the strange things that happened the last time you were here, Ali? I think I would have packed up and gone home.'

Alison shrugged her shoulders. 'Well, I was scared,' she nodded, raising her eyebrows, 'and Richard and Robert were not too happy about it either, but then what could we do? We coped.'

They stood just looking at the space under the tree. The garden was quiet; they could hear the sound of the sea shushing on to the beach and the birds twittering, it seemed so peaceful, and Alison's mind went back to the time when she had stood right here with Selena. Poor Selena, she looked down at the ground, she must have died right here, and a little shiver ran down her spine as Selena's voice echoed in her ears, 'Sheee evil'. Poor Selena, she felt a tear touch the corner of her eye as she imagined Selena's round, black, shiny, smiling face.

'Oh!' exclaimed Sue, jumping almost a foot off the ground, and holding her hand to her fast-beating heart as Jojo came up behind them, pushing his nose between them. Sue looked down, 'Oh! It's the hound of the Baskervilles. You're not kidding, and it's SPOOKY! You really got me going there, Ali.' The dog was looking up at her, a smile on his face, showing a set of white teeth, and a long pink tongue hanging out the side of his mouth, with his tail wagging fast and so hard against her leg that it hurt.

Alison bent to pat him with a laugh, 'Good boy, Jojo. Without him we might never have found Robert.' She looked round for Nick, who was down by the water's edge talking to a man; he had not noticed that the dog was gone, so she sent him away, pointing. The dog ran off as he heard Nick whistle, and he waved. Alison and Sue waved back.

It was Friday. Clive Marshall and his team had arrived on Thursday and were staying in a small hotel on the west coast, not too far from White Lady Cottage. He had spoken to Richard on the phone, and they had arranged to come about nine o'clock in the evening. Clive said it would take them some time to set up their equipment, and they would be ready to start the ghost hunt about ten o'clock. He had also said that they could all watch.

The Turners arrived at White Lady Cottage at half-past seven for dinner, and they were all sitting round the table on the verandah chatting and finishing off glasses of wine. Petal had cleared up the kitchen, and Richard said that they could stay and watch with everyone else if they wanted to.

It was a sultry, moonlit night and very humid; the sea shushed in gently on the shore, and the tiny whistling frogs kept up their nightly ritual that would go on until the dawn.

Tim, who had been standing down by the gate for about 20 minutes, came running up onto the verandah and announced with excitement that the Spooks Men had arrived. In the light that shone out from the verandah, the car stopped at the gate and four tall, handsome men, aged somewhere between 30 and 40, got out and came through the gate.

'Well?' Alison mused, 'no long grey beards?'

'Wow.' Sue grinned.

They were all wearing jeans and T-shirts; three carried soft leather bags, and one was carrying a large oblong black leather box with a handle, which seemed very heavy as he put it gently down on the wooden deck of the verandah and came forward with a smile to take Richard's outstretched hand.

'Good evening, I am Richard Price.'

'Clive Marshall, pleased to meet you, and this is my partner, Ian Douglas.' He smiled and said good evening with a Scottish accent. Toni Borsini was obviously Italian, and Steve Palmer a Londoner. They all shook hands, and Richard introduced his wife and the family.

Richard showed them round the garden to the frangipani tree, and explained that the figurehead once stood there. He told them about the storm and the mango tree catching fire, and he gave them a rough outline of the *Savannah Lady*, Jack Barneby, and the terrible wailing, and pointed to the spot where it seemed to come from.

Clive Marshall said that the spirit was most probably still in the soil. And Richard also explained about Selena and his wife almost being drowned.

'Mmm,' Clive Marshall nodded, 'sounds serious.' They made their way back up on to the verandah. Clive then explained that the computer system could pick up any sound, even sounds not heard by the human ear, and that he was going to put microphones and audio tape and video cameras around the garden at different angles, and any sounds would be recorded. Ian had the most sophisticated camera equipment, and in the past had taken some most unusual films. 'But we will also use a laptop computer, which is linked to a base unit, and the monitor has a needle that moves at the slightest sound and can detect movement and a drop in temperature, which is usually associated with any presence of ghostly activity. The computer records where it happens and the time it occurs, and how long it lasts.'

'You were in a castle last week,' said Nick. 'What happens when you are not there, like now? Do you leave some equipment set up until you go back?'

'Oh no,' Clive smiled. 'Since I met you a couple of years ago, we have expanded the business. We have forty people working in different places, plus us, and I now have a central office in Scotland, with a secretary and a young girl assistant, and they are kept pretty busy with calls, you would be surprised.'

Clive and his team began setting up the equipment around the garden, watched closely by Tim, who was following them around and helping by plugging into the electric sockets through the kitchen window. Toni was spacing out small lights and hanging them in the trees.

'Do you need light?' asked Tim in surprise.

'Yes,' said Clive. 'Light doesn't seem to affect ghosts – if there are any, of course. We get reports of ghosts being seen at all times of the day and night, but it is quieter at night and easier for the computer to pick up any sounds.'

Toni Borsini, who was somewhere amongst the trees, called, 'I'm all set. OK, Steve?' and Steve called back, saying he was ready.

Ian sat on the grass, his back against a large manchaneal tree and his camera trained on the frangipani tree. Clive switched on the monitor in the heavy black leather case.

They all stood waiting; they did not have to be told to be quiet, but there was complete silence, except for the sounds of the tropical night, creatures, and the shushing of the sea.

Alison was holding her breath; she thought she would never breathe again. They waited. It was one o'clock in the morning. Sue yawned, they were still standing in silence, leaning against trees and part of the balustrade, and Gramps had found a tree stump to sit on. Robert looked across at Gary, who was leaning against a tree a few feet away. Their eyes met, but there was no reaction. Sue yawned again, putting her hand to her mouth; just the movement of her arm against her breast seemed to shatter the long silence. As another hour went by Richard looked at his watch and then down at Ian Douglas, poised and ready to flash his camera; he had a slight movement, but then there was nothing again.

It was two forty-five that Clive took a breath, stretching his body. 'I think we had better call it a day.' His voice shattered the silence and Sue jumped. She was very sleepy, as they all were; there was a shuffling of feet, and a clearing of throats as they all moved stiff and aching limbs, and Rob made a quick dash to the loo. Peter lit a cigarette. 'We'll try again tomorrow night,' Clive nodded at Richard, 'if that is all right with you. There has been nothing out there tonight, or it would have broken the infra-red beam, but the needle on the monitor hasn't even twitched, so we will try again tomorrow.'

Richard said it was OK. Ian packed his camera away, and Clive asked if it would be all right to leave the lights, which they had dotted around the trees, so it would be ready for another session.

The next night the Turners had dinner in the hotel and arrived by taxi. The Spooks Men were already setting up the equipment for another session. Again Tim watched closely, and decided when he left college that he was going to be a Ghostbuster. To which John said, 'Why am I spending all this money on education, when all you want to do is chase ghosts?' to which Tim replied, 'It would be a lot more fun than being an accountant,' and John certainly had to agree, although he did not let Tim see him smile.

Tonight they were prepared for a long session. Alison had directed Joseph and Robert to put chairs out in the garden, and large cushions for Gary and Tim and himself, and they lifted an armchair between them and put it out for Gramps. Peter and Richard had found and moved an old garden bench which had stood beneath the trees for years. They covered it with towels and settled themselves down. Joseph had asked if he and Petal could watch again, and they sat at the back of everyone on the tree stump which Gramps had used the night before. The chairs had been put in a sort of semicircle, like a theatre audience waiting for the curtain to go up. There was much chattering and giggling while the Spooks Men set the scene, until Toni called, 'All set, Steve?' and Steve called back, 'All set.'

The chatter stopped as Gary called, 'Overture and beginners, please.' There was some tittering and then total silence as they waited, listening and yet not hearing the sounds of the night.

Alison was sitting closest to Clive; she noticed that he never took his eyes off the monitor, and Ian sat just a few feet away in the same place as before, with his camera set on a low tripod, ready to flash at anything that moved.

They waited.

The sounds of the tropical night were oblivious to them all as they concentrated their minds on ghostly activities that might suddenly happen; no one wanted to miss anything. They waited in anticipation.

There was just the wafting of a breeze, and Alison saw Clive raise his eyes quickly and gave Ian a nod. He stiffened, his finger poised on the camera button. She glanced at the monitor in front of Clive without moving her head and hardly daring to blink her eyes, but she could not see if it moved. Her eyes fell to her wristwatch, and in the dim light she could just make out the time – it was almost three o'clock. She was aware of the silence and the tension, and she wondered if everyone else felt the same. They waited until three-thirty, then Clive moved, breaking the intense silence, saying that they had better call it a day. He told them that the needle on the monitor had moved fractionally, but nothing to speak of, and asked Richard if it would be convenient to try again tomorrow. He thought it would be a good idea to do it again, if Richard was in agreement.

'We usually give it a week,' said Clive, 'but we could keep on for months. Sometimes you get lucky and sometimes you don't, but it is worth another try. There was something there, but very, very faint.'

Alison had asked Petal to get a meal for five at seven-thirty. And while she was preparing it, Joseph and Robert put out the chairs and cushions again. The Spooks Men were setting up their equipment, and just about fifteen minutes later the Turners arrived, and then Nick and Gramps. As Nick came through the gate he glanced at the spot where the White Lady had once stood; for some reason he imagined her there.

Alison plumped up the cushions behind Gramps as he sat down, and asked if he was comfortable. They all took a seat; the silence was tense again, as they waited anxiously.

Sue closed her eyes, she felt drowsy. Carol, sitting next to her, took a long, quiet breath in, and tried to ease her back without a movement. Peter turned his wrist over very slowly and glanced at his watch, and then looked up quickly as he saw Clive nodding gently to Ian, Toni and Steve, watching him through the trees for a signal. They quietly adjusted their recording equipment and gave each other the thumbs-up signal.

Alison was sitting close to Clive again; she couldn't quite see the monitor, but she could see him listening in to the headset, and his eyes were alive with excitement.

'We got something,' he whispered to Ian. Ian raised his eyes and moved his thumb on the camera button.

The wailing was low and slow to start, rising and falling like a siren, then a loud wailing, and then to a screaming crescendo. They all cringed. Sue's eyes flew open wide with alarm. She grabbed at Peter's hand and the other gripped the chair until her knuckles went white. Carol pressed her back hard against the chair and held her breath.

Alison strained her neck and could just see the needle on the monitor quivering. The hot and humid temperature changed suddenly to a chilling cold breeze, and she rubbed the tops of her arms with her hands as a chill went down her spine, her eyes darting in all directions around the garden.

Tim sat bolt upright, his eyes wide, his arms bent up across his chest and his fists closed tight under his chin. Gary and Robert scanned the garden for any movement. And Richard and Nick, sitting together on the garden bench, felt themselves pushed roughly aside, as something unseen came between them; they looked at each other in alarm.

The wailing got louder, and the screaming was like an animal tortured and in the greatest pain, and then there was a sparkling like a firework just before it goes out – and there, right where the White Lady had stood, he manifested: Jack Barneby, Pirate, in all his splendour: a tall and handsome man. He looked so real they were all wide-eyed, alarmed, astonished and speechless.

He wore a three-cornered hat; his long raven hair hung straight to his shoulders and was tied back with a leather thong; a dark green frock coat, with large pockets and gold buttons; a beige waistcoat; black pantaloons, tucked into long black shiny boots, which turned over with large flaps at the knee. He stood before them waving the jewelled sword in his right hand, furiously, as if in a fighting stance. They all sat absolutely motionless, not even daring to breathe, not even daring to blink in case they should miss anything, their eyes glued to the image before them.

The wailing and the screaming were deafening. Alison gripped the arms of her chair and took her eyes away for a split second, not daring to move her head; she saw the needle on the monitor, it was going wild; she saw Ian flashing the camera continuously, and from the corner of her eye it seemed that Clive was suspended in mid-air.

What happened next, no one was quite sure. Jack Barneby seemed to groan and just fizzle out slowly, as if consumed by a flame, but there was no fire; and in a brief moment before he was actually gone, a man's deep voice bellowed in pain and then stopped abruptly, and all at once there was a total silence...

Gramps felt his old heart leap, and beat frantically. He put his hand over it, glad to feel that it had not stopped. Everyone else was stunned and still, as if made of stone. Only the sounds of the tropical night creatures disturbed the peace, and not a leaf moved as the mist swirled under the frangipani tree and then wafted away into the still and humid night...

Toni, switched off the tape recorder with a loud click, and Steve took off the headset.

Clive Marshall took off his headset and suddenly threw his arms in the air, and shouted excitedly, 'Woweeee, we got it, we got it!' He switched off the monitor and Ian looked up at him with a surprised broad grin. He'd seen Clive excited before, but not like this.

'Yeah, yeah,' chuckled Ian, getting up from the cushion where he had been kneeling for hours. 'Yeah, that was great, the best we've had in the last three months. Hope we have some pictures.' He smiled. 'I've taken a whole roll of thirty-six?'

Petal had been clinging on to Joseph; she was petrified. 'Voodoo, voodoo,' she whispered hoarsely. Joseph was holding her tight, the whites of his eyes also showing fear; he knew that the white people did not believe in such magic.

'It not voodoo, Petal, it not!' He was trying to calm her, but she pulled away from him and flew down the coral stone steps and ran down to the water's edge. He ran after her and caught her, holding her tight in his arms; they were both breathing heavily, and he tried to calm her, telling her over and over again that she had nothing to fear, and that it was a white man's magic tricks, and that Clive Marshall had all the magic hidden the black leather box.

'Voodoo,' she whispered. Her eyes were wide and afraid, and she began to fight him to get away, but he held her close, and in a few minutes he managed to calm her down by kissing her and stroking her hair. She was shaking as they walked back along the beach; he had his arm around her shoulders, and he felt her shiver as they passed the coral stone steps and went into the gap a little way beyond them, up past the gate of White Lady Cottage on their way up the hill to their own little coral stone cottage, which had once been the home of Joseph's grandfather, and Selena's home.

They went inside and shut the door on the evil night, shutting out the sounds of the night creatures and the birds, which began the dawn chorus. It was only then that Petal felt really safe in Joseph's strong arms.

On the verandah the excitement continued. Richard and Peter were pouring champagne – no one was going to bed at this early morning hour; even Gramps sat comfortably in the armchair which Robert and Gary had lifted up on to the verandah for him.

'Wow,' Tim said to Ian, 'you got some good shots, wasn't it terrific? Can I have some pictures when you get them developed? My teacher will go mad when I show him, pictures of Jack Barneby. Did you see the sword; we found that in the cellar. It was like watching a film, wasn't it? I should like to see it all over again, wouldn't you? Do you think that we will?'

Ian smiled and nodded. 'Oh well, I don't know if you would

ever see that again. You might, though. These things just happen and you have to wait patiently; sometimes it takes weeks or months – sometimes we take on a job and get nothing – but when it does happen, you feel lucky and glad that you have been patient and waited.'

'How many times have you seen anything like that?' asked Tim eagerly.

'Not many,' said Clive, who had been listening to them. 'As Ian says, sometimes it takes months, and considering I have been working with the supernatural for twenty years, I could count on one hand the times I have seen anything as good as that. I would say that was one of the best, wouldn't you, Ian?' Ian nodded with a smile.

'Well,' Richard sipped at the champagne, 'I would never have believed it if I hadn't seen it with my own eyes ... I find it hard to believe even now.'

'Or me,' said Peter. 'It was so real, absolutely unbelievable.'

'Well, I feel a bit scared, knowing that he's out there running around the garden,' said Sue. 'I never thought that I should see such a thing.'

'Me neither,' said Carol, 'it doesn't seem possible.'

'Well, I really can't believe what I have just seen,' said Alison, partly to the girls and to Clive, who was standing drinking a glass of champagne. 'Was that actually the pirate Jack Barneby? It was so real, and he has been dead for two hundred years or more. But why Jack Barneby? Why wasn't it the White Lady? She is the one that wails, well, we think so, anyway.'

'Yes, can you explain that?' said Robert as he and Gary joined the circle.

'Well,' Clive nodded, 'it's not the first time that we have seen such a good example of an apparition like this, but I can't explain why it wasn't the White Lady.'

'Can you explain the apparition, then?' said Gary.

'Well, yes,' said Clive, 'in a way, but of course, it is only theory. It's called the Stone Tape Theory, where images can be stored in the fabric of a building, sort of like a video tape recording, so that in the right conditions a scene can happen just as it occurred two hundred years ago, so maybe what we have just seen is the right condition at this moment, but it may never happen again. But as I say, it could happen, it just depends on conditions.'

No one spoke, they just let what he had said sink in for a moment. Then Tim said, 'It possibly wasn't the White Lady, because it is an object, and not a person.'

'Oh no,' said Ian, 'objects can manifest themselves, too. The *Flying Dutchman* has been seen many times. One captain even followed it into a harbour, and it disappeared before the crew's eyes; and also there was a double-decker bus that raced round the corner of St Marks Road and Cambridge Gardens in Kensington; it caused motorists to mount the curb and run into a wall, but when they removed the sharp bend in the road, it was never seen again. And we have all heard tales of phantom coaches, which feature heavily in folklore.'

'And animals,' said Toni, 'are quite often seen. I had a dog that died five years ago, and I can still hear him bark in the garden, and I have often looked out to see if there is a dog there, but there is nothing, and none of my neighbours have a dog. But cats feature a lot; they roam around houses and pubs and all kinds of places. Animals never seem to leave the homes of their owners.

'Well, if objects manifest,' said Tim, 'why wasn't it the White Lady that we saw? She is made of wood, so why was it Jack Barneby?'

'I know,' said Gramps. They all turned to look at him. 'Possibly he manifested, is that the right word?' He looked at Clive, who nodded. 'Possibly he manifested because it was his blood that was spilled over the figurehead. The legend says that he fell forward onto the dagger and slumped over the figurehead, cursing all women, and to him she was a woman.'

'Yes,' said Nick, 'that could explain it.'

Clive bit his lip, nodding in agreement. 'Mmm, it's possible. Do you want to try again tomorrow?' he said to Richard. 'Mind you, we might have done it, we might not get anything; you see, it's all to do with an electronic energy force, and if it has burnt itself out, as I think it may have done, then we have finished the job. The apparition won't appear again, but maybe it will, perhaps in many years to come, so if you want to try again to make quite sure it has gone, well, it's up to you.'

Richard looked around him. 'Well, what do you think?'

'Yes, we'd love to see it again,' said Tim enthusiastically, 'wouldn't we?' Gary and Robert nodded eagerly.

'Tim!' said Carol. 'The idea is to get rid of it, it's not a show.'

'I know, but I bet you would like to see it again, wouldn't you, Mum?'

'Well,' was all Carol could say, raising her eyebrows.

There was a short discussion, and there was a unanimous 'Yes'. And they decided for what was left of the night that they should all go to bed, but no one felt tired.

It was mid-morning. They had all slept late, but Nick had asked them over for a sandwich lunch, and they were now sitting on the beach in the shade of Gramps' fishing boat. Gramps was still sleeping in his own bed.

'What I can't understand,' said Alison, 'is why it was Barneby that materialized.'

'Because his blood was on the figurehead,' said Richard.

'But it's not there any more,' said Alison.

'No, I can't understand that, either,' said Sue.

'Well, you don't understand anything,' said Peter.

'Oh, Peter! Don't be nasty. I am beginning to wonder if this guy Clive is genuine. He could have rigged the whole thing; he knew we wanted to see a pirate, so he fixed it, like one of those holocaust things.'

'Hologram, Sue,' Peter clicked his tongue, shaking his head in despair.

'Well,' said Nick, 'it does seem funny, as Ian said last night; objects do materialize. I think that Barneby and the White Lady are one and the same. I think that when he died his spirit must have gone into the figurehead, if he fell over on top of it.'

'But it's not there,' said Alison.

It was the only topic of conversation, and they argued about it this way and that, but in the end there was really no explanation.

* * *

It was three days later when Clive rang Richard from England. 'Sorry to tell you, but we did not get anything on the photographs. Ian was disappointed, but this sort of thing has happened many times before. There is something there, but lost in a cloud of ectoplasm.'

Richard frowned. 'What's that?'

'Well ... it's a kind of translucent sticky material.' Richard grimaced in the receiver, he was none the wiser.

'Well, we all witnessed the materialization, didn't we? That was something.'

'Yes, but we have nothing on film to prove it,' said Clive. 'But there was something on the recordings apart from the roaring, when we played it back. It revealed the sounds of footsteps, of more than one person, and there is heavy breathing, and something that sounds like a sigh, but I can't be positive. There is also a metallic sound, could be a sword being drawn, I can't be sure, but I will send you the disc anyway. When are you due back?' Richard said January, and Clive said he would send the recording to the Chelsea flat.

6

Robert had talked a lot about White Lady Cottage, and Belinda was looking forward to being there. He had mentioned about the wailing, but had not made much of it, and he had not mentioned anything about the apparition. He didn't want to scare her and put her off before she even got there, although he thought perhaps she would have found it quite fascinating, and he had made mental plans to take good care of her, thinking back on what almost had happened to Alison and Gramps' words, but then that had all happened almost ten years ago, and Richard and Alison had been out to the cottage many times since then, with no problems. He had been to Barbados twice before when his parents had joined Richard and Alison, but now for the last two years they had been saving hard to get married. He had a good job that paid well in a publishing business; Belinda was a physiotherapist, and on their return to England she was to have her own private practice in a medical centre.

They had met at a party in London three years ago, and now with the help of both their fathers, they had a small flat in London to go back to, and between them up until last week they had been decorating and furnishing it; now they were both in need of a holiday, especially in the warmth of the Caribbean sunshine. He knew that Belinda was going to love being there.

The flight had been good, and they were coming in to land; she gripped his hand with excitement as she pointed out the bright blue sea below them and a stretch of golden sand.

The drive to Belinda's home took about an hour, and Alison blinked behind dark glasses, she had a hangover like she had never had before, but she had promised Belinda's mother, Pat, that she would go over and help take out the flowers in the marquee.

She arrived, just as her sister, Sue, and Pat were going into the marquee.

'Morning, sorry I'm late,' she said as she got out of the car, and then, leaning back into it slowly to retrieve her handbag, which was on the floor, the bending made the blood rush to her head and she felt dizzy. She took off her sunglasses.

Her sister pulled a face, wrinkling her nose, as she came closer. 'God! You look awful,' she blurted out.

'Thanks, Sue, that's all I need,' Alison said gently, nodding her head. Her eyes hurt and she winced, even the slightest movement was sickening, and Sue never did have any tact. Instead of 'how do you feel?' it was 'you look awful!' So much for making anyone feel good. Alison blinked in the bright sunlight; she gave them a slight smile, but even that hurt.

'Oh, it doesn't show that much, does it?' she put the sunglasses back on again.

Pat shook her head with a chuckle, 'No, of course not.'

'It does. You look *awful*, doesn't she?' smirked Sue?

'Let's have a cup of coffee before we start to tackle the flowers, shall we?' said Pat kindly, walking towards the house. 'Come on into the kitchen.' Alison held her head as she sat down. The kitchen smelled of freshly ground coffee, and Alison took a deep breath, winced at three mugs chinking together as Pat took them from the cupboard, and poured the coffee from the percolator jug. She put a mug in front of each of them. Alison sat with her hand against her cheek, thankful just to sit down and grateful for the coffee. She had already had two cups before she left home and felt that she really could have done with a day in bed. She didn't know how she had driven the car, but she had promised to help with the flowers, and couldn't let Pat and Sue down.

After the coffee, they went down into the huge marquee, which had looked so beautiful yesterday, but this morning looked quite forlorn and bedraggled. The pink and white carnations were still bright in their containers in the centre of each table, but the tables were now brown and bare wood, after the caterers had stripped them of their snow-white tablecloths, sparkling glasses and silver cutlery. Beside the carnations on each table there were silver helium balloons with white ribbons, wavering gently on long strings, like graceful swans, stretching their long necks to reach the pink and white striped canvas above them. The caterers had collected all the empty glasses and coffee cups and saucers, and stacked them in large containers near the front entrance to be collected later. The strong smell of alcohol, stale cigar and cigarette smoke, and the perfume from the flowers which adorned the marquee poles, hung heavily on the air and did not do much for Alison's condition. The gilt chairs with red plush seats were strewn higgledy piggledy away from the tables, some knocked over, as if a whole mass of people had suddenly jumped up and were in a hurry to get away. Confetti and streamers were scattered across the dance floor, and one lone blue feather, which had come from someone's hat, lay in the middle.

Alison took a deep breath as she helped Pat and Sue to remove all the flowers, which included climbing up on chairs and ladders to remove the pink and white flower arrangements, which were twisted around the poles. Alison found this a dizzying experience, but thought better not to say anything, or Sue would have chided her again. They loaded all the flowers into their cars, and later they were to distribute them to the local hospital and the hospice, and to some near neighbours and friends who had not been wedding guests.

They were back now in Pat's kitchen. She was cutting small pieces of wedding cake that would go with the flowers to friends and neighbours, and Sue and Alison were wrapping the pieces in white paper napkins printed with silver bows and bells. Pat wrapped the top tier of the three-tier square wedding cake in silver foil, and put it back into the box in which it had arrived, saying that she would keep it for the christening. They laughed, and Alison winced at the sudden noise.

'It does keep a long time,' Sue's loud voice rang through Alison's head. 'I kept mine for Robert's three years, didn't I, Ali?'

Alison nodded her head very gently, hardly moving her eyes; she could not answer. The strong smell of alcohol from the marquee, and the sweet perfume from the flowers, were still in her nostrils, and now the pungent smell of rich fruit cake and the strong coffee in the kitchen, made her feel she could take no more.

'I am so sorry, Pat,' she put her hand to her head, 'I think I will have to go and sit down for a while, I feel terrible.'

'You look terrible,' snorted Sue, she looked disgruntled. 'But you can't possibly be *that* bad, Ali. Gosh, it was a super day, and we all had plenty to drink, and we are all right.' She looked at Pat, shrugging her shoulders and raising her eyebrows.

Alison gave Sue a furious look. Her sister had never been very compassionate. 'You just wait until you have that extra drink, Suzi dear! And then you will know how it feels.'

'I know how it feels, Ali, and you learn over the years, and you should...'

Pat cut her short. 'Come on, Alison,' she put an arm round her shoulders, 'come and sit in the lounge, it's cooler in there, and I'll bring you a black coffee.' She showed Alison into the lounge, and she sank down into a deep armchair, and laid her head back, feeling her whole body relax. Pat pulled the curtains and left the room. It was very quiet.

Pat took a mug of black coffee in to Alison and returned to the kitchen where Sue was just wrapping the last of the wedding cake. 'She will be all right when she has had a rest.' She started to make a fresh pot of coffee.

'Mmm,' Sue grimaced, 'I don't know why she should be so bad, and she seemed all right when she left yesterday, although I suppose we did have a long day, didn't we? I wonder how they are getting on? I suppose they are flying right now.'

'I hope that they will be happy,' Pat said, pouring two mugs of coffee and handing one to Sue.' 'It's a big step in life when you get married, isn't it?' They were sitting at the table, it was half clear now that the cake wrapping was finished. 'Would you like a piece of cake, Sue?'

'No thanks Pat,' she smiled. 'I think I have seen enough cake for one morning. Oh, I am sure they will be OK,' Sue said in her normal casual way. 'My Robert is a sensible boy, and your Belinda is a lovely girl, he will look after her and she, with her nursing training, will look after him and bathe his knees if he falls down the cellar again.' Sue smirked and went rambling on in her happy-go-lucky manner.

'The cellar, why did he fall down the cellar then?'

'Yes ... Well, you see my Robert went on holiday with Ali and Richard. We couldn't go, you see, Peter's business and all that. Didn't Belinda tell you? About the wailing and all that?' Pat shook her head. 'Well, I'm always telling him to look where he's going. He fell in the cellar, trying to get his shorts on or something... I'm surprised Belinda didn't tell you about the wailing, but then perhaps he didn't tell her, about the ghost, I mean. I hope she can cope with it, it's ever so eerie.'

Pat frowned. 'Sue, what are you talking about? Ghosts and wailing in the cellar.'

'Ooooh! Yes, the wailing is awful... You see, what happened was... Well, my Robert went with Ali and Richard as I said, and my Robert found the treasure, you see, we saw it in the museum. Ooooh, it's lovely, you should see it, you wouldn't believe it. I expect he will show it to Belinda, she won't believe it either. It's all because he lost his shorts in the cellar.' She was rambling on, telling Pat all about the ghost of Jack Barneby, the sword, and the wailing. 'Oooh, it was awful,' she kept on saying. 'And then suddenly he appeared right there in front of them.' 'Who? Robert?' Pat was fascinated, puzzled and confused. 'Belinda has never told us anything about all this.'

'No, not Robert. This pirate, Jack. He was right there.'

'Well, that was all ten years ago anyway, and we have been out to the cottage with Ali and Richard a few times now, and it seems all right now the Lady has gone, and Ali and Richard have been out a lot more, and they haven't had any problems. Well, not since the Lady has gone anyway.'

'What lady? Did she live with them?' Pat was trying to understand Sue's rambling.

'Oh, no, she was in the garden, she's been there for years.'

'Oh, she lives there in a cottage in the garden, does she?'

'No! No no,' Sue shook her head with a frown. 'She stands in the garden, but I haven't seen her, because she is gone now. Richard got rid of her.'

Pat sipped the hot coffee, she was thoroughly confused, she frowned. 'Where has she gone then?'

'Richard chucked her in the sea.'

'What! An old lady?' Pat had to grin; Sue was spinning her a yarn.

'No!' Sue, chuckled. 'The Lady was the figurehead of a ship.'

'Oh! Ha ha ha,' Pat burst out laughing. 'I thought you were talking about some old woman, Ha ha ha.'

Alison sipped the coffee that Pat had brought her. Her head was throbbing, and she could hear Sue's voice chattering away in the kitchen, even though the door was closed and the words were muffled, but once Sue got talking there was no stopping her, she was still going on and on...

'Well, I am surprised that my Robert has not told you all this. I bet he hasn't told Belinda either or she would have told you, wouldn't she?' She wrinkled her nose, 'I expect he didn't want to worry her, but we will see when they come back, won't we? But I am sure she will enjoy the cottage, it is lovely – right on the beach, and the sea so blue. I'll organize a dinner party when they come back. I'll ask Ali and Richard, and John and Carol, Gary the best man's parents, you'll like them,' Pat nodded with a smile. Gary had been best man to Robert yesterday, but she had only met him a few times and didn't know him well.

'It's not long ago since he got married, is it, Sue?'

'No, it was February. My Robert was his best man. It was an awful day,' Sue clicked her tongue, 'sleet and windy, we were all frozen, shame really. I wore a fur coat it was so cold, although you are not supposed to wear them now, animal rights and all that, but June, the bride, and the bridesmaids, all wore little fake fur capes over blue velvet dresses, it was very pretty, and they needed them. She's a lovely girl, June, didn't you think so? Pretty, got lovely hair.'

Alison could stand no more, Sue's voice had been droning on and on. She stopped as Alison came into the kitchen with the empty coffee mug, which she put onto the draining board, and Pat asked her if she felt better.

'Yes, thank you, Pat. What can I do to help?'

'Well, we have to deliver the flowers and the cake. Do you think you can drive?'

'Yes, of course, I feel a lot better.'

Sue clicked her tongue, and lifted her chin looking annoyed. 'Of course she can drive.'

* * *

Petal was there to meet them at the cottage door, a big welcoming smile on her pretty face.

'Hello Petal,' Robert shook her hand warmly. 'Gosh, it's good to be back here again.' She smiled up into his face, he was more handsome than she remembered; it had been about four years since she last saw him and he looked even taller.

'This is my wife, Belinda,' he smiled proudly as he introduced them. 'Mrs Bentley, this is Petal, and she's a super cook so you will have to watch your figure,' he chuckled.

Petal was stunned by Belinda's beauty as they smiled at each other and shook hands; she stared at the pale flawless face, the silver blonde hair, and the deep violet eyes smiled back at her as she held the delicately slim hand. She felt numbed by this tall and elegant woman. She had a fixed smile on her face and everything around her seemed to stand still, until this beautiful creature gently pulled her hand free, saying, 'Hello Petal, I have heard a lot about you.' Petal was suddenly aware of what she was doing; she had seen pictures in books, and Mrs Bentley was a fairy queen. She curtsied low, the smile still fixed on her face, as her soft dark brown eyes looked up into the deep violet eyes which shone with happiness. She was holding her breath, although she did not realize it, when Joseph came bustling through the door, a suitcase in each hand which he had taken from the taxi driver, a big smile on his face. He dumped them at the bottom of the stairs, and shook Robert by the hand enthusiastically, he was so pleased to see him again, and Robert proudly introduced his wife.

Joseph looked down from his great height with a huge grin on his face, his big brown eyes goggled as he said 'Married', looking at Robert, and then taking Belinda's small hand gently in his. His thick curly hair brushed the ceiling as he bent forward in a bow, grinning from ear to ear, his strong teeth white against the blackness of his handsome face. The smile was surprised and shy as the deep violet eyes looked up at him and the pink lips smiled and said, 'I'm pleased to meet you, Joseph.'

'Yes, Maaam,' the shy smile still on his face, he turned away and with a suitcase in each hand, he looked back over his shoulder. 'Good to see ya, Maaan,' he drawled, with a big grin. 'Me and Petal wait for to see ya, bin a long time, Maaan.' Robert nodded back with a pleased smile. 'Good to be here, man,' and Joseph went up the stairs to their room.

As the days went by, Belinda could still not believe the beauty of the Caribbean. Every day was warm and sunny, and with the help of plenty of suntan cream, her pale complexion now had a golden glow. They had been swimming in clear blue water, and had walked hand in hand along the golden beach; they were in love and had eyes only for each other. Today, they walked along the beach, hand in hand to the Sunset Hotel, and sat at a beach-side table. The hotel was not very busy, June was really out of season, but more people were starting to come out at this time of the year. Some guests were lying out on sun beds now under green umbrellas on the soft golden sand; some swam in the sea, which today was rushing in, and children squealed and played in the white fluffy foam.

After lunch, they walked back to the cottage, hand in hand again along the water's edge, the cool waves caressing their feet, the hot sun on their backs, Belinda wearing a large straw sun hat to protect her delicate skin. Then they turned away from the sea, walking up on to the soft sand and then up the coral stone steps, which Belinda found sharp and hot under her bare feet. She was glad to reach the verandah. Discarding the straw hat, she lay down with her feet up on a sun bed under the shade of the mahogany tree.

She waved her arms in the air dreamily, and stretched lazily. 'Why is it called White Lady Cottage? It's more than a cottage, it's a house, isn't it?' She was looking up at Rob, her beautiful face all screwed up, with one eye closed against the brightness.

He scratched his ear thoughtfully, frowning. 'I think I told you some time ago about the White Lady, didn't I?'

'Well, I don't remember.'

'Well...' He told her about the time he was in the cellar. 'And if it hadn't been for Jojo, I might still be there now,' he chuckled.

'And you might never have met me, and you would have been too late for the wedding,' she mused. 'Who's Jojo? Is that Joseph?'

'No,' he chuckled, 'Jojo is a dog. He belonged to Nick Cotton's grandfather, and when he was a puppy he was a devil. He was always running away, and Nick spent most of the time chasing him, and he used to come bounding up the these steps...' He stopped.

'And that is when you found the treasure? Must have been exciting. You will take me to see it, you promise? Now, why is it called the White Lady?'

'Yes, I promise I will take you to see it...'

'Rob, is there something the matter?' She could see in his face and hear in his voice that he was keeping something back. 'Is there something you don't want to tell me?' she frowned, shaking her head. 'Why is it called the White Lady; was she someone special?'

'Well,' Robert wiped his chin with his hand and screwed up his face thoughtfully. He knew he would have to tell her some time about the goings-on. 'Well, it was the figurehead of an old pir...' he was going to say pirate ship, but changed his mind. 'An old sailing ship, and it used to stand in the garden.'

'But where is it now?'

He smiled. 'Out there,' nodding towards the sea. 'Joseph dug it up, and Richard, Nick and Joseph and I took it out there one evening, and dumped it. Apparently it used to be red, but someone had painted it white. It was damaged in the fire.' He was getting in deeper trying to avoid saying anything about the wailing, which was all so long ago now.

'Oh, you had a fire? Was it bad? Was there much damage? Did it get burnt, is that why you had to dig it up?'

'Yes, sort of. We didn't like it,' he said quickly.

'But why? Suddenly you didn't like it? After it had stood there for years?' There was surprise in her voice.

Robert took a breath. He was about to tell her when Petal called, to ask if they would like cold lobster for dinner, and would they like a cup of tea now, to which they both replied, yes please.

Robert gave a sigh of relief. Thank heavens for Petal, she saved him a lot of explaining.

The thought of cold lobster salad took Belinda's mind off the subject of the White Lady, and they chatted together over tea.

Belinda moved away from the table to sit on the sun bed again, and Robert was about to join her but the phone was ringing on the hall table, and he went in to answer it.

He came back a few minutes later. 'That was Gary, he just wondered how we were getting on. He said the weather's not very good, it's been raining ever since we left. He said they are going to Majorca for a couple of weeks, he said it was a belated honeymoon,' Robert chuckled.

Belinda smiled, 'Oh that will be nice for them, they will be glad to get some sun, it feels so much better when the sun shines, doesn't it? Shame they had such bad weather on their wedding day, I think it must have been the worst day of the year. When are they going?'

'Saturday.'

'Oh…' She thought for a minute. 'Rob … why don't we ask them to join us out here? We have had a good week on our own, and it would be nice for them and company for us. What do you think?'

A slow smiled crossed Robert's face. 'You know … I was very tempted to say that to Gary. I think it's a great idea, but I didn't know if you would agree. Shall I ring him back?'

She wrinkled her nose, and nodded with a smile, 'Yes.'

7

There had been a lot of rain in the night, and the morning was dull and overcast, with heavy black clouds low over the sea.

'I don't think we are going to get much sunbathing today,' Belinda put down her coffee cup and looked up at the sky.

'It might be a good idea to go to the museum,' said Rob. 'I'm sure you girls would love to see the treasure.'

Their eyes lit up and they both nodded. 'Can we go now?' asked Belinda.

'Well, I don't think the museum is open this early,' said Rob, 'but I could give Andrew Harrison a ring; he might give us a private viewing. I'll try, though it is a bit short notice.' He went off into the hall, and was just about to pick up the receiver when the phone started to ring, and he snatched it up quickly. 'Good morning, White Lady Cottage.'

The voice on the other end shouted, 'HELLO ROBERT, Nick here. Sorry I didn't phone sooner, I've been a bit tied up, but I left a message with Petal, did she tell you?'

'Hello Nick, nice to hear from you. Where are you, still in New York?'

'No. LA.'

'What are you doing in LA, Nick?'

'Working, travelling round. I was in Boston last week, I am down here now sorting out some antique insurance problems. I've been here ten days, but I am going back to New York tomorrow. I knew you were there at the cottage; I phoned Tubby and he said he was delivering fish to you, got a girl-friend down there, so I hear?' He gave a sexy chuckle.

'No...' Rob smiled into the phone again. 'My wife. We are on honeymoon,' Nick could hear the delight on Rob's voice.

'HONEYMOON?' he shouted. 'You old devil. MARRIED?

How long? How long? When was the great day? What's she like? I bet she is a stunner.'

'Nearly two weeks ago now.'

'Any luck?' Gary was calling from outside.

Rob called back, 'Just a minute, Gary.'

'Gary!' Nick shouted into the phone. 'Did you say GARY! JEEESUS CHRIST!! You didn't marry him ... did you...?'

'Yeah! He's on his honeymoon, too.' It went quiet. 'Nick! Nick! Are you there?'

'Yeah ... Rob!' Nick was stumped for words. 'Fancy ... you and Gary, married!'

'Yeah,' Rob explained. 'Well, they got married in February. The weather was bad. But they didn't have a honeymoon then, so we invited them out here; we have already had a week on our own.'

'Oh! He's got a wife! Then?'

'Well...! Yeah...!' Rob's mouth was open, 'Oh, Nick ... you didn't really think? ... Oh bloody hell, Nick, he's a good friend, but...' There were hoots of laughter from both ends of the phone.

Then Nick was saying that he planned to come out for Christmas, and that he was looking forward to meeting both their wives, which caused more hoots of laughter, and then he rang off. Rob came back on to the verandah, still laughing, and when he told them that Nick had thought that he and Gary had married each other, they fell about.

'Oh, I wish you had called me while he was still on phone,' said Gary, 'we could have kidded him along.'

'Well, any luck with the museum?' Belinda mused.

'Oh, gosh. I haven't got hold of Andrew yet.' He turned to go back into the hall, and called back, 'Oh! Nick sends congratulations.'

They arrived at the museum before ten-thirty, and Andrew Harrison was there to meet them. He was surprised to find that they were all on honeymoon together, and when they explained he congratulated them and greeted both their wives warmly.

Belinda and June could not believe how the sword and dagger gleamed and sparkled as Andrew opened the cabinet.

'It's fantastic,' Belinda's violet eyes shone as she put her finger delicately across the hilt of the sword and took a breath. 'I've never seen such stones, and just fancy it being down there in the cellar all that time.'

'I should like to go and have a look down in the cellar,' said June, 'we might find something else. Just to find some simple little thing would be exciting.'

'You girls wouldn't want to go into the cellar.' Gary raised his eyebrows, a surprised look on his face.

'If you do,' said Rob, 'don't expect us to fish you out. It's full of termites and spiders.' He ran his fingers like a spider up Belinda's arm.

'That's enough,' she shuddered. 'We've changed our minds.' She and June looked at each other with girlish grins.

'You were rescued by a St Bernard, weren't you?' June had a smirky grin.

'No,' said Rob, with a hearty chuckle, 'I think Jojo is a Heinz 57. But when he barked at me, I thought he was a Cruft's Champion. I could have been down there all night, you know, if it hadn't been for him.'

'Oh...! Rob, I didn't know that,' Belinda looked at him in surprise.

'You haven't had any more trouble with the Lady or Jack Barneby, have you?' Andrew asked casually.

Rob and Gary froze.

Belinda looked away from the glass cabinet. 'Who is Jack Barneby? Is he a neighbour?' and before either Rob or Gary could get their breath, 'He is the guy who had all this stuff on him,' Andrew nodded at the glass cabinet. 'When George Kingsley fished him out of the sea, it was his blood that was on this dagger as he slumped over the figurehead of the ship.' He casually flung his hand out towards the cabinet. 'That is what all these ghostly happenings are about. You haven't seen him again, have you?' he looked searchingly at Gary and Rob.

There was a tense silence for a moment, as Gary took a deep breath and Rob bit his lower lip.

'No...' Rob looked vague.

June looked at Belinda, and frowned. 'I saw someone hiding in the trees the other night, perhaps it was him. I only really got a glimpse, but it certainly was someone, and they had a hat on, that is for sure. I told you that, Gary, didn't I?'

Gary was about to say something, but Belinda said, 'Who's George Kingsley? Perhaps it was him, perhaps he wanted to see you about something, Rob. But wait a minute, it was three in the morning, we had just come back from the night club; why would anyone want to call on us at three in the morning, and then hide in the garden and not come out? Seems funny.'

'A drunk, possibly, or some local on drugs? Andrew bit the inside of his mouth hard, and squeezed his toes up inside his shoes, knowing full well that he had put his foot in it by saying the wrong thing.

'It's OK, Andrew,' Rob sniffed, 'it's a long story. Come on, I think we should be going, I will tell you about it when we get home.' They started to walk towards the door, thanking Andrew for his time and Rob suggested that he come up to the cottage for dinner one evening. Gary walked to the car with the girls.

Andrew followed close behind Rob; they were just at the top of the steps.

'I am sorry, Robert,' he winced, feeling awkward. 'I can see I shouldn't have said that.'

'Oh, it's all right; they would have to be told some time, it was just that we had not told them in case it worried them. But Richard and Alison haven't had any trouble for years now, and the White Lady is not there. I don't think there is any problem now, but the other night June was convinced that she saw someone under the frangipani tree, and she mentioned a three-cornered hat, so she must have seen something. But Gary passed it off – he told her she had had too much to drink ... and she had, really,' he smiled, scratching his head.

Andrew grimaced. 'Well, I am sorry anyway, it just came into my mind. I was up visiting my grandmother just last week, and she was talking about the old days. You know how old people like to reminisce; about Bill Cotton and Ella May and Emily Kingsley. She said she had not seen her recently, and told me to go down and tell her to come up for a cup of tea. My grandmother is getting on for ninety now, and she rambles a bit, but most of the time she is very with it. If I had known you were here on the island, I would have come in to see you.' He grimaced again. 'I really am sorry for dropping you in it. I shouldn't have mentioned Barneby.'

'Oh, don't worry.' Rob gave him a friendly punch on the shoulder. 'I'll sort it out.' He chuckled, 'I got married for better or worse; better to get the worse over now.'

'Rob, what's all this about George ... umm? And this Jack ... what's his name, and did he say ... ghosts?' They were in the car, on their way home. 'Who has been giving you trouble? You never told me, I didn't know.' Belinda gave June a puzzled look, then turned back to Rob, who was in front of her, driving. 'Do you owe them money? This George and Jack Barns?'

'Barneby.' Rob stopped at the traffic lights.

'Do they live here in Barbados, then?' Rob gave Gary a smirky grin; the lights changed and he drove on, glancing in the mirror. He saw the puzzled look on his wife's face and he could see she was getting ready to ask more questions.

Gary looked over his shoulder at the girls. 'No! Neither of them is asking for money.'

'Do you know them as well, then?' June leaned forward and pulled at the back of his collar.

'No, not to speak to.' Gary grinned sideways at Rob again, sniffed and rubbed his finger under his nose. June knew that gesture, he was lying.

They were passing the harbour and June mentioned that there were two cruise ships in the port. Gary looked and pointed out a container ship, out on the horizon, saying things like, it was bringing in produce to the island, as they did not grow very much here and there was hardly any industry on the island to speak of... He was just trying to change the subject. Belinda had been quiet for those few minutes as Rob drove on.

'Well, if it's not money they want, what is it? I think you are being a bit cagey, Rob. Why?'

There was a stretch of golden beach before them, and Rob pulled the car over and stopped under the shade of some tall trees which lined the edge of the beach. Belinda raised her eyebrows, 'Why are stopping here, Rob? Where are we?'

'This,' he leaned back, switched off the engine and took his hands off the steering wheel, and took a breath. 'This, my darling, is Brighton Beach.'

'But why have we stopped? Phew! It's a bit hot without the air conditioning.'

He took another breath and let it out again irritably. 'Well, open the door, then. Let's get out and sit on the beach in the shade.'

'But why? Why stop here?'

'Because, my darling wife ... I am going to answer all your questions, and I can't do it while I am trying to concentrate on the road.'

Gary sniffed and grinned. 'Now, now, boys and girls, wait a minute, this is not your first married tiff, is it?' He lifted his eyebrows in a comic fashion and looked from one to the other. They all smiled.

They sat on the sand a few yards from the car, under the shade of the tall mahogany trees and coconut palms, facing the ultramarine, deep blue and silver sea; each ripple sparkled like a diamond as it was caught in the sunlight. Several people were bathing, and the happy squeals of children fell on their ears, as two little girls ran splashing into the water.

'Now! My darling wife,' Rob bowed his head comically at Belinda, 'just what is it that you want to know? Eh?'

She smiled at his comic gesture and then frowned. There was agitation in her tone. 'About this guy, George, and his friend Jack, what's it ... Barn. And about the cellar and the treasure of course, and about this lady in a white dress, that you said used to wander around the garden. You were hedging about that last week, and I never did get to the bottom of it, you only told me snippets.' Rob was about to start, then she went on, 'And what did Andrew say? Something about this being a ghostly business, isn't that what he said?' She looked at June for confirmation and June nodded.

Robert looked at Gary, making a hopeless gesture with his hands and his head, and sighed.

Gary blew smoke into the air, sniffing and twisting his mouth sideways, then grinned. 'Well, go on then, tell them.'

Rob thought for a minute; where should he start? 'Well, first of all, the White Lady isn't a lady.'

'You can say that again!' said Gary, still grinning and drawing on the cigarette.

'Shoooosh!' June shook her head at him.

Rob went on. 'She is, I mean, it is a block of wood, and Barneby isn't a man.'

'Oh, yes, that's very easy to understand,' Belinda said sarcastically. 'And what about this George, what is he, then, a monkey? Andrew said he saved someone from drowning.'

'Fished him out of the sea, that's what he said,' June put in, raising her eyes.

'Hmm,' Belinda lifted her chin. 'Perhaps he was a dolphin, then,' she chuckled. 'Come on, Rob, get on with it, who is Jack?'

'I'm trying, I'm trying. Jack is ... Jack Barneby,' Rob was wishing he had never got into this. 'Wait a minute, let me start at the beginning. It all, umm ... started when we read the scroll.'

'Scroll,' said Belinda, 'what scroll?'

'No, I think it all started when we dug under that rock,' said Gary.

'What rock?' Belinda frowned.

'Do you remember that terrible smell, Rob?' They both began to laugh. 'I think we let the genie out of the bottle.' They were laughing, and the girls sat there, just looking at them.

'Been there since 1700 and something,' Rob spoke through his laughter. 'I remember Tim falling flat on his back. I can see him now.'

'Look, you two! Can we join in? Now come on, Rob! Tell us about it, and stop messing about.' Belinda was getting quite annoyed. 'Now come on.'

'I'm trying to tell you. Well, it all started when Richard met Gary's father at the hotel and I met Gary and Tim.' He tried to explain everything clearly, Gary helping out with the odd bits and pieces. He told them how they found the treasure and about the wailing. June and Belinda listened intently, but when he got to the bit about Jack Barneby materializing...

'Rubbish!' June butted in, 'I don't believe that for one minute.'

Belinda was looking at Rob's face, and she knew that he

was telling the truth. 'Really, Rob?' She was astonished. 'It sounds absolutely unbelievable.'

June had second thoughts. 'There you are,' she poked Gary on the arm playfully, 'I told you there was someone standing under that tree.' She stopped and put her hand to her mouth, 'Oh God, do you think that I actually saw ... a ... ghost? I actually did have the most creepiest feeling this morning; I went down to look at the tree, and I felt that someone was watching me, and then there was that strange buzzing noise. I told you about it, didn't I?'

Gary said nothing.

Rob went on, saying how they had dumped the White Lady into the sea.

Gary nodded. 'Yes, but that was after Alison was nearly drown...' he stopped, not finishing the word, as Rob looked daggers at him.

'Sorry...' He raised his eyebrows, clenching his teeth, and ducking his head, sucking in air with a hissing sound. He looked at Rob. 'Sorry, but you did say that you were going to tell them everything.'

Rob went on to tell them about Alison's experience and finished up with, 'Well, after Clive Marshall had been, it all seems to be OK now...'

Belinda and June sat in silence, and Belinda could not think of another question to ask.

It was lunchtime when they got back to the cottage. As they came through the gate June saw Joseph sweeping the path near the frangipani tree. She stopped, and they smiled at each other. 'Hello Joseph.' She looked at the tree, 'Have you noticed any footprints around or near this tree?'

Joseph had a surprised look. 'No, Maaam.'

When she explained why, she noticed his eyes widen; he looked fearful, almost on the edge of panic. 'Joseph?' She was about to ask him what was wrong, but all she managed to say was 'Oh,' as she heard Petal saying that the lunch was being served. She walked off, leaving Joseph to his sweeping. She did not see his wide-eyed gaze as it followed her up the garden, and she did not see the way he peered gingerly through the shrubs at the trunk of the frangipani.

After lunch they sat at the table chatting, the girls still asking a few questions about the White Lady and the ship.

'Has this verandah always been here?' asked Belinda, looking around her.

'I suppose so,' Rob looked around him. 'I should think it must have been renewed over the years. But I would think that there had always been a verandah here. Why?'

'Well, I was just thinking that George Kingsley must have stood right here when he saw the ship go down in the storm... Alison saw it from here, didn't she?' She looked out to sea, squinting behind sunglasses. 'What's that out there on the horizon?' They all looked up quickly.

'A sail boat,' said Gary.

'Well, she must have seen it from here, mustn't she?'

'Yes, I suppose so,' Rob looked at her quizzically, and then he gazed out to sea thoughtfully.

8

The early morning was quiet with a cool breeze; the birds were singing and the frogs were still at their nightly whistling. The sky was a light grey-blue dotted with white fluffy clouds and a few dark rainclouds; the sea was rough and pounding on the shore, rolling back to leave the beach strewn with thousands of small coral stones.

Belinda brought June a cup of tea and sat opposite her at the verandah table.

'Thanks, Belinda. I wonder what's going on out there?'

Belinda squinted her eyes against the brightness, shading them with her hand, looking out to sea where the seagulls were swooping and circling, their screeching cries drifting faintly across the water on the light breeze. 'I expect the fishermen have thrown some fish over the side.'

'Yes, but there are several boats out there; that's not normal, is it?'

Belinda was still squinting. 'I don't know. Wait, I'll get the binoculars.' She went quickly into the dining room and opened the drawer in the sideboard below the glass cabinet. With a casual glance she saw the scroll and the piece of wood with the name *Savannah Lady* painted on it, and in front of this, the ring. She picked it up and just put it on the tip of her finger; it was miles too big. She had seen it before, but had not paid much attention to it – they seldom came into this room, they spent most of the time outside. The ruby eye of the falcon sparkled as she moved it; she shrugged her shoulders, she suddenly felt quite chilly. Just then June called her to bring the binoculars quick. She almost threw the ring back in the cabinet, picked up the binoculars, and went quickly to the door. It was hard to open, it seemed strange, but she came out and the dining room door slammed hard behind her; she looked round with a frown.

‘Quick, give me the binoculars,’ June had her hand outstretched. ‘Quick, it looks like a boat out there is cut in half. Yes, yes, it is,’ June’s voice rose with amazement, ‘and there are two other boats out there now, looks like they are all climbing into one, look.’

Belinda took the glasses from her. ‘Oh yes, looks as though they are going to tow the two halves away, they are throwing ropes across.’

‘Look!’ June was pointing. ‘There’s a ski boat going out there now.’

‘What are you two up to?’ Gary came to the top of the coral stone steps and took a towel off the back of the chair, Rob following him. ‘Gosh, it’s far too rough for swimming this morning; we got wet but didn’t swim. What are you looking at?’

Belinda told them there was a boat cut in half, and Gary took the glasses from her. ‘Good God, yes. What the hell’s happened?’ He could see that the boats were towing the two halves in, and they were also dragging something else behind them. He put the glasses down, and he and Rob went upstairs to shower and shave, and the boating incident was soon forgotten, and the girls continued to watch out at sea.

After lunch, the afternoon was too hot to sit out. The sun had come round on the verandah, so they went up to their rooms. With the fans going it was cooler, they had a nap and would all be ready by 7.30 for a quick drink before going to a restaurant for dinner.

Rob was the first to get up. It was five o’clock; he came downstairs still yawning. The sun was still blazing hot; it hurt his eyes. He went into the lounge, turned on the fan and sat down lazily, even though he had had two hours’ sleep, then he got up again and went to the kitchen. He took a glass from the cupboard and filled it to the top with ice, and then took a Coke and poured half into the glass and went back into the lounge, glass in one hand, bottle in the other. He sat down again and picked up the television monitor and flipped through the channels, not really interested in anything special.

He flicked past ‘Barbados, a fishing boat’ and flicked back

quickly, it was the world news. 'Struck by a piece of driftwood, it was later identified as a large oak carving, the figurehead of an old ship, possibly a galleon which had been wrecked. It is believed that the rough seas have dislodged it from a dangerous reef which is marked on nautical maps and now surrounded by beacon bells, as a warning to shipping.' There was an interview with two fishermen: one was saying that they thought it was a shark, it had lifted them high into the air out of the water and the boat had come down heavily on top of it with such a mighty force that the fishing boat was so badly damaged that it had been cut clean in half, and they felt lucky to be alive. The other fisherman was saying that the sea had been quite rough out near the reef in the early hours of the morning.

Rob had heard enough, so he switched off the TV and walked out on to the verandah, crunching his hands nervously deep in the pockets of his shorts. He looked out to sea; it had to be her, 'she' was back, and he was in no doubt now that what June had seen near the frangipani tree had been Jack Barneby. In his mind's eye, he remembered the day they had dumped her over the side and she had risen again. He remembered the eyes looking up through the water as she finally sank into the deep. But now she was back, and Barneby's ghost was here again after all these years.

He shivered, his hands still in his pockets were tight into fists. It was eerie; he thought back to when the mist had engulfed the boat and Tubby had sped out of it, and now it was threatening to come back. He hunched his shoulders as a creepy, cold feeling ran down his spine; he remembered how Joseph had reacted. His thoughts turned now to Belinda and June, and then went back to the night that Alison had almost drowned. He shivered again and went upstairs to get changed ready for dinner. Belinda was in the shower, but he had made his mind up not to say anything, he would talk to Gary alone.

Rob turned the key in the lock, and the click seemed to shatter the stillness. Belinda had already taken off her shoes and was halfway up the stairs, June following her.

'Do you fancy a nightcap, Gary?'

He looked at him in surprise, it was not like Rob to want to drink whisky. They never had a nightcap, especially after being out all evening and drinking wine.

Rob raised his eyebrows knowingly, and Gary knew there was something up; he wanted to talk.

'Yes,' Gary smiled brightly, as if he really needed a drink. 'Good idea, just fancy a whisky,' as if it was a thing that they did all the time.

The girls both turned at once on the stairs. 'Whisky!' Belinda looked most surprised. 'You're surely not going to sit up half the night drinking, are you? Besides, you don't drink spirits.'

'Oh, only a quick one. You go on up to bed, darling, be there in a minute. Just a quick one, eh, Gary?'

June gave Gary a look of disgust. 'How can you want to drink whisky at this time in the morning, after you've been drinking wine all night?'

'Easy,' Gary said airily, shoving his hands into his pockets, and almost dancing from foot to foot as if he couldn't wait for a drink. 'Be up in a minute, darling, good night,' he almost sang the words.

June sniffed and Belinda clicked her tongue with annoyance as they looked at each other helplessly, and went off up to their rooms. Both doors banged.

Rob had already gone into the kitchen and was opening a bottle of white wine, he knew Gary would not really want whisky; neither of them did. He came back into the lounge with a bottle in one hand and two glasses in the other.

'Wine?' Gary raised his eyebrows questioningly.

'I thought you would prefer it. Let's go out onto the verandah, it is too warm in here.' They sat in the rattan chairs, the coffee table between them.

'Yes, wine,' Rob grinned, as he poured it. 'I think we have got enough spirits. She is back.'

'What!' Gary gasped. 'How do you know?'

Rob smiled. 'Cheers,' he lifted his glass. 'It was on the telly. I have been wanting to talk to you all evening, and I didn't want to say anything yet in front of the girls. But I watched the news before we went out, and what we saw out there this morning, you know with the boats, it was the Lady, she floated up to the top and split a fishing boat in half. The news said it was the figurehead of a ship; it has just got to be her. They will have diving equipment out there tomorrow, you bet.' He looked at his watch, it was gone one o'clock. He nodded, 'I mean today.'

'I wonder what else they will find? Maybe the *Savannah Lady* is still down there. Maybe still hanging on the reef.' Gary drew hard on a cigarette. 'She must have come up with a great powerful force, to split a boat in half.' He sat thoughtfully for a moment. 'Do you think we ought to say something, I mean to the police or the coastguard, or whatever? We probably know more about the *Savannah Lady* than anyone. The scroll is still in the cabinet, isn't it?'

Rob grimaced, tipping ash into the ashtray. 'Well, I have been thinking about that all night. I couldn't concentrate over dinner, and I don't really know what to do. I mean, who would believe that Alison got lured into the sea, and...' he was shaking his head, 'and a pirate materialized right there in front of our eyes, here in this garden, a ghost... Who would listen, I mean, who really believes in ghost stories? It sounds so fantastic. Who would believe a statue wails in the night? They would think we were mad or making it up.' He shook his head. 'I don't really think we ought to say anything just yet, let's see what they find.'

Gary nodded. 'They surely would believe the wailing; people around here have heard it for years, and there must be old wives' tales about the guy you told me about, Munchings or something.'

'Munchester, I think Nick said.'

Gary lit another cigarette, offering one to Rob, but he shook his head. 'What about Andrew Harrison's grandmother? She could verify that story.'

'Yes, but she is old,' said Rob. 'She probably wouldn't remember anyway, and when we last heard the wailing it was about ten years ago, and now I would expect if there was wailing people around here would not take much notice. They'd say it was a police siren or someone had the television on too loud; they'd say it was a hoax. People are more sceptical these days; they wouldn't be sitting in their houses afraid of a ghost, they just wouldn't believe it.'

'Mmmm, you say, that Grandmother Harrison is old, but then Gramps was in his eighties, and he was very with it, wasn't he?' Rob nodded.

They sat discussing the White Lady and the possibility of whether it was a ghost that split the fishing boat in half, or whether it had just been an accident in the rough sea; and then, coming to no conclusions, they eventually went to bed, leaving the bottles and the glasses, and the ashtray brimming over with cigarette ends.

The telephone was ringing loudly on the hall table. Belinda left the coffee she was making in the kitchen, and rushed to pick up the receiver. It was six o'clock in the morning, and she hoped that the bell had not woken the others.

'Hello,' she whispered.

'Hello Belinda,' the voice on the other end bellowed, as if he was shouting from England; it was Richard. 'How are you enjoying the sun over there? It's pouring with rain over here.' She was sure that they could hear him upstairs in the bedrooms.

'Oh, it's wonderful, thanks,' she whispered, smiling into the phone, 'but the time is going so quickly, and...'

'Yes, we saw it on the telly,' he said. 'I hope she won't start her nonsense again, but don't worry, Robert can handle it. I'm sure he will know what to do.'

'Handle what? Do what?'

'Well, the Lady. We saw it on the telly. You know, the whaler, it was her, wasn't it?' He stopped, realizing she didn't know what he was talking about. 'Oh! Em, umm, is Robert there?'

'No, he isn't up yet. He and Gary sat up late last night talking.'

'Yeah, I expect they were discussing what to do about her. Anyway, ask him to give me a ring, will you? I'll be in the office. Thanks, bye.' The line went dead.

Belinda shrugged her shoulders and looked up to the ceiling, not knowing what that was all about. She went back to the kitchen, and the kettle had already gone off the boil.

* * *

June came tripping down the stairs, almost singing a happy 'Good morning' to Belinda, who was just passing the bottom of the stairs with a steaming cup of coffee.

'Morning, June. I have just made a pot of coffee. It's a lovely morning.'

June smiled. 'Every morning is a lovely morning out here.' She tripped off to the kitchen and came back with a cup of coffee and joined Belinda on the verandah, sitting opposite her at the table.

The early morning sun in a pale blue sky filtered through the leaves of the mahogany tree and a slight breeze wafted across the quiet beach, bringing the smell of the warm salty air off the ever-rolling sea.

The phone was ringing again, and Belinda went into the hall to answer it. 'Helloooo,' she sang out; she smiled to herself, she must have caught the happy, early morning feeling from June.

'Hello, Nick Cotton here, can I speak to Robert please?'

'No, sorry, not at the moment,'

'Is that Belinda?'

'Yes.'

'Oh, hello, are you enjoying Barbados, with the sun and the sea. I bet it's great, can't wait to get there, and I am looking forward to meeting you. I will be down there at Christmas. Anyway, would you tell Robert that I called. Tell him I saw it on the news last night. I tried to bell you then, but there was no answer. Sorry, have to go. Tell Robert I'll call him back later. Bye.'

'Bye,' she said, but he had already gone. She looked at her reflection in the hall mirror above the table, made a puzzled face at herself, looked at the receiver and then put it down and went back out to June.

'There's something funny going on.' She looked at June with a frown.

'Well, are you going to let me in on it, then?' said June, and Belinda told her about the phone calls.

Robert and Gary finally surfaced, about ten o'clock, and came down to coffee and toast, which Petal brought out to them.

Joseph had been in twice to see if Mr Robert was about, he

must speak to him urgently. Then as Robert came out onto the verandah, Joseph was watching for him and beckoned him to come.

'Mr Robert, Sir, could I speak to you, please?' His eyes were goggling, and Robert could see the anxious look on his face and they went off round the side of the house.

'I told you there was something funny going on,' Belinda was talking to June, but she was watching as he disappeared round the corner with Joseph.

'What is going on, then?' Gary was buttering a piece of toast.

'I don't know yet,' said Belinda, 'but something is, something to do with the news.'

Gary didn't look up.

'Oh, Mr Robert, Sir,' Joseph's eyes were almost popping out of his head, 'have e seed de news? Oh, Maaan, she back. Maaan, she back. I knowed she come back, Maaan. I tell Mr Richard and Mr Nick years ago. I phone you... But you's all out last evening. It on de news agin dis mornin, Maaan.'

'I know, I know, Joseph, but try not to worry so much.' He wrinkled his nose. 'It will be OK, besides, we don't even know yet if it is her; let's wait and see. Anyway, that thing won't be here in the garden again, will it?' He touched Joseph reassuringly on the shoulder.

'But she evil, Maaan, she evil,' he was almost hysterical. Tears welled in his eyes.

'Joseph get a hold of yourself, calm down.' He gripped him tightly by the shoulder. 'It's just a block of wood, that's all, and it floated to the surface. The sea is rough, it's just got dislodged from the reef, that is all, and it unfortunately happened to strike a fishing boat ... it was an accident.'

'De Mrs Turner, she asks me if I seed de footprints under de frangipani tree. I seed nothing, but de eerie feeling it still dare, de wailing will start again, I know it, Maaan,' his voice rose, and the whites of his large brown eyes were fearful.

'No, it can't wail, it's not here, it's somewhere down in Bridgetown now, you bet, being analyzed, and they are going out there to investigate what is on the reef. Now stop worrying, I'm going to have my breakfast. And while you are here in this part of the garden, trim that bougainvillea back, it's getting very untidy.'

Joseph watched Robert walk away round the corner of the house, his eyes still wide with fright. He looked nervously at the bougainvillea which climbed up the wall near the kitchen. He would have to stand very close to the frangipani to trim it back. He took a deep breath and edged closer to the frangipani, looking for footprints, the garden broom ready in his large hands. The hair prickled on the back of this neck as he took a slow step nearer and then jumped back with a shriek as a bird flew from a branch, and he swiped at it with the broom, his breath came in short bursts, his heart beat faster, and the sweat poured down his cheeks. How Mr Robert could not worry about the evil one, but could worry about the bougainvillea. He shook his head in hopeless despair.

'What is going on, Rob?' Belinda looked bewildered as he came back and sat at the table. She poured him a mug of coffee. 'Richard phoned early this morning,' she wrinkled her nose and frowned. 'He sounded quite mysterious. He said something about a whaler, and he was sure that you could handle it, and then Nick Cotton, he is the guy who owns next door, isn't he? He has a nice voice. Said he was coming down here for Christmas, and was looking forward to meeting me and June.' She smiled at June, who perked her chin up with a smile. 'He was saying something about he had seen the news, and come to think of it, Richard said that too. Anyway, Nick Cotton said he would ring you back, he sounded as if he was in a hurry. What's the matter with Joseph?'

'Nick is always in a hurry,' Robert sipped at the hot coffee, and lifted his eyes over the rim of the mug at Gary, who had a slightest flicker of the eye.

'Well,' Rob began slowly, 'it's to do with the boat that we saw out there yesterday. It was hit by a large piece of driftwood, and it chopped a fishing boat in half, and we are all worried that it is possible that the White Lady has surfaced again… I did tell you about Alison almost getting drowned, didn't I? Well, it was because of the White Lady, and it also happened to Gramps' wife, Ella May. She was also drowned all those years ago. Well, that's what everyone thinks, anyway. And Joseph's mother was found in almost the same place as the Lady stood.'

There was a long silence; Belinda and June sat with open mouths.

A large ship, which looked a rusty red with a blue hull, sailed slowly towards the reef; it had a large crane in the middle of the deck. They watched, taking turns to look through the binoculars, as the activity out on the reef increased during the morning. The crane was swinging out, dipping into the sea and then swinging back across the deck; they could see divers in the water, and around the ship several small craft had gathered, bouncing up and down on the heavy swell. Even the salvage ship dipped and rolled, standing well away from the dangerous reef, or it could be dashed to pieces on the coral as the long arm of the crane stretched out.

'Let's get a ski boat and go out and watch, shall we?' said Gary. 'After all, it was our Lady, and we pushed her over the side.'

'You didn't.' Rob looked at him with wide eyes.

'No, but I feel I was really involved.' He gave Rob a cheeky grin.

The ski boats came by often, and a loud whistle got their attention.

The man drove at speed, the boat lifting high in the front, bumping down hard into the waves, it was a rough ride. They counted 14 boats hovering round watching as they were, as the crane swung tirelessly in and out, creaking and cranking and squeaking, as the rusty metals rubbed together. It dipped and grabbed pieces of rock and old wood. There were three divers in the water, and at least 12 men on the deck of the salvage ship, *Four Winds*, which was painted in large black letters on the side. A diver's head appeared. He guided a rope basket onto the hook of the grab; it was no easy task in the heaving swelling water. The basket was lifted high, water cascading back into the sea from it as the crane swung it up and over onto the deck, where it was steadied by the men and lowered as gently as possible onto the heaving deck. They could not see very much, but it revealed pieces of rusty metal and something that looked like a lamp. But nothing was really discernible from their point of observation.

The diver went down again. They looked on as the water swelled, lifting the ski boat, and it swayed and dipped from side to side. On the deck near the crane was a tall man in a light blue T-shirt and navy shorts; he was built like a house, and had red hair and a red beard. He was wearing a headset and keeping in touch with the divers, deep below the surface. He was shouting into a small hand-held microphone, but his voice was distorted in the cranking of the crane; no doubt below, in the silence, he was coming though loud and clear.

They had watched for an hour, and not really seen anything; the ski boat bounced and dipped dangerously from side to side. The sea was getting rougher, and they asked the driver to take them back to the shore. Rob paid the boatman, and they both jumped out over the side into the cool rushing surf; it felt so good after sitting out at sea basking in the sun. They dived and wallowed in the sea for about five minutes cooling their bodies, then came out; it was really too rough for swimming.

They came up to the girls who were on the lawn, flat out on white wooden sun beds. June lay in the full sun, her tan getting darker. Belinda had pulled her bed under the trees, and had to keep moving as the sun came round; she envied June her dark complexion. They sat up as Rob and Gary approached, anxious to know what was going on, but Gary said it wasn't very interesting and they went off to get dry swimming trunks. June and Belinda went back to their sunbathing. The sun had moved round again, and Belinda pulled her bed under the frangipani tree; this was the third time she had moved to the shade. She lay looking up through dark sunglasses at the beautiful pink clusters of its blossoms, smelling their delicate perfume. She closed her eyes behind the dark glasses, and pulled the large straw sun hat down over her face and relaxed. It was so restful, so peaceful, so tranquil, she half-dozed, aware only of the shushing of the sea, it seemed so distant. She heard a buzzing bee and a bird twittered, but the garden was still, not a leaf moved.

'This is the life,' June mumbled. 'Do you want some more suntan cream?' She was waving the plastic bottle in Belinda's direction, still with her eyes closed.

'No thanks.' She was in a drowsy, semi-conscious state, and she thought June's voice sounded far away.

There was a crack somewhere above her head, and Rob and

Gary heard the scream as they were just coming down the garden path; they started to run. June was quickly on her feet, looking at the huge branch of pink clustered flowers and dark green leaves, under which Belinda was buried and was fighting to get out. Rob and Gary quickly lifted the heavy branch, which luckily had fallen mostly to the side of the sun bed, and June gripped her hand and pulled her out. The sun hat was flattened but still half on her head, and she grabbed at her sunglasses as they began to fall. Standing now, she gave them all a vague smile and said, 'Thanks.' Robert put his arm around her and asked if she was all right. She nodded, rubbing her arm and her leg; a few long scratches were beginning to bleed. Rob held her tightly, she was quite shaken. Over her head Gary gave Rob a knowing look – it was no accident.

'Are you all right, darling?' he caressed her hair and cupped her face in his hands and gave her a friendly kiss on the mouth. He looked at her anxiously. 'Are you OK?'

She smiled, pulling away from him. 'Yes, I'm fine, thanks,' she was breathless. 'Just a bit of a shock, that's all,' she chuckled, looking down at the scratch on her arm. 'Lucky I had the hat over my face.' She brushed a wisp of hair from her eyes. 'I wonder what caused that to suddenly fall?' They all stood looking at the frangipani tree. High up the broken branch dripped a white, milky substance through the dark green leaves onto the towel on which she had been laying.

Petal was on her way down the garden with a tray of ice-cold lemonade. Her eyes opened wide with surprise when she saw the long scratches on Belinda's arms and legs. June was dabbing her leg with a towel, it was beginning to bleed more.

'I bring you sometink to put on dat, Mistress,' she said, and after they had taken their drinks, she ran away back to the house for some antiseptic cream.

June and Belinda sat down on the bed June had been lying on, and Robert and Gary stood looking up at the broken branch. It was still dripping the white, milky substance, the tree's life blood. They listened, their eyes and ears alert. They looked at each other – the buzzing or humming was not a bee.

* * *

Petal answered the phone. She was pleased to hear Mr Nick's voice. She smiled into the receiver when he asked her to clean Sandridge House for him and fill up the fridge; he would be arriving tomorrow late afternoon. She called out to Mr Robert, saying that Mr Nick wanted to speak to him. Rob left the verandah and went to the phone. They talked for a while, and Rob wished him a good flight, saying he looked forward to seeing him. He put down the receiver with his hand still on it; it rang again, making him jump, and he snatched it up quickly. It was Richard.

'Look, Rob, I know it's your honeymoon and all that, but would you mind if we came over for a week? I was just lucky to get two Club Class seats on the Saturday flight; they are all fully booked. I have booked into The Sunset, but we'd like to come up to the cottage a couple of times, if you and Belinda don't mind.' He went on to say that they had watched the news, and they just had to be there to see what was going on.

Robert told him to cancel the hotel and come and stay at the cottage, and that they wouldn't mind a bit ... they had already had a good week on their own, and they were enjoying the company of June and Gary. And that it had not yet been officially identified as the *Savannah Lady*, but both he and Gary was sure that it was, as Jack Barneby was back. June had seen him, although she had not realized that she had seen a ghost. It was just a few days before the accident that Belinda had had under the frangipani. It was too much of a coincidence.

Richard asked if he had told Belinda the situation yet, and Rob said that he had now explained everything so that Belinda and June would be prepared if the wailing started again, but he had not told her that the cause of the broken branch was not just a natural thing. Both he and Gary were convinced that it was Barneby. He also told Richard that Nick was arriving tomorrow, and Richard was pleased; he had not seen Nick since last year. They went on to talk about general things ... how was Alison? The weather? Richard said he would be pleased to see some sun, and then they rang off, Rob saying he was looking forward to seeing them on Saturday.

* * *

Nick had arrived the previous day, and been so tired that he had slept through the night and most of the day. It was now early evening, and he came up the coral stone steps from the beach, Jojo bounding up before him and going straight to Alison, wagging his tail excitedly, his mouth open in a wide smile showing a pink tongue and a set of very white teeth; he was a happy dog as she made a big fuss of him. Nick was surprised and pleased to see Richard and Alison, who had arrived just about an hour ago.

There was a lot of happy chatting and laughter as they all got together again, and Robert opened a bottle of champagne to celebrate the gathering of the clan. And then the conversation got around to the White Lady, and the possibility of Jack Barneby's ghost coming back. The men sat at the table, and Belinda, June and Alison sat on the sun beds; it was still very hot in the evening sun, but the mahogany tree shaded the verandah and there was a slight cool breeze. Petal came out with another bottle of champagne and told Robert that there was a Mr Harrison on the phone.

After Robert had spoken to Andrew he came back to the table, a sombre look on his face.

'Well, it definitely is our White Lady. Andrew has it down there. They have cleaned it up and he says there is no doubt. He says he has got several pieces to be cleaned yet; there's a compass and a lantern and several pieces of carved oak. He has a whole team working on it now, and the pieces keep coming in. He is very excited, and he has met the Captain of the salvage ship, Captain Hanson, I think he said his name was, and he says there is part of a ship hanging over the reef, but he has not identified it yet as the *Savannah Lady*, as there are several wrecks down there. His thoughts on the Lady are if, of course, it is the *Savannah Lady*, that she has been caught in a crevasse for years, and has been dislodged after all this time, with the recent rough seas. He says the divers are having great difficulty, as the undercurrent is so strong. And the reef is hundreds of fathoms deep, and the water is dark and murky. He described the reef as a mountain under the sea, and in rough weather as the waves dip, the top is almost to the surface, but the rocks are hidden; he says that even with his ship and his equipment, he cannot get too close.'

'Well, can we go down to the museum and see what they have brought up?'

'I asked him that, Richard, and he said that it would be better to wait until he had more to show us. The cleaning is a delicate job and takes time. He will ring us some time in the week.'

Nick was lying on his back in bed, his hands behind his head and his elbows spread wide across the pillow. He was watching the ceiling fan spinning round; it flickered as it caught a moonbeam which streamed through a gap in the bedroom curtains. He could hear the waves thundering on the beach. It was a hot tropical night, and it felt good to be back here again, especially now that Richard and Alison had arrived; that had been a great surprise. He had liked Belinda and June, both stunners in different ways; he thought the guys had chosen well, a smile touched his lips.

He had met many nice girls over the years, but had never met anyone that he wanted to spend the rest of his life with. Sometimes he felt quite lonely ... but he had plenty of friends. And now there was Paula ... he liked Paula... Yes, he liked being with her, he liked her style, and she was good company. Mmm ... he bit the inside of his mouth, but not the marrying kind, but... Mmm. He nodded gently. She was nice, a good friend, no ... lover ... mmm, yes, lover ... in a sort of way, not serious though. She might like to come out here for Christmas. She might ... he considered for a moment, yes he would ask her... No! He had a quick change of mind. No! He would not ask her, it was not a good idea, might make things a bit too serious, keep it as it is now, he had toyed with these thoughts before.

Gramps, he thought, the house was quiet without him here, and he missed him still, even though it was a few years since he had passed away. He missed Gramps, he had come here to this house for years on vacation, and had lots of fishing stories to tell his friends back in New York. How he had been in his grandfather's fishing boat, and they had caught a big tuna fish; he showed them photographs and they thought he was lucky to come to Barbados. Yes, he missed Gramps.

He could hear the clock ticking loudly on the bedside table, close to his ear. He thought he could hear a church bell then the pitter-patter of raindrops, as a gust of wind blew them onto the window pane. The church bell chimed again; funny, he had never heard a church bell before. He opened his eyes and looked at the luminous hands on the clock, it was faint, he could only just see it, as the fan flicked flashes of bright moonlight. He reached out and switched on the lamp, saw that it was almost three in the morning, and switched it off again quickly, the light too bright for his eyes. He closed them; sleep would not come.

There was that bell again; he sat up on one elbow. It wasn't a church bell, it was a ship's bell. Eight bells. The watch... What did that mean? He had been here by the sea for years, but knew nothing about shipping. He heard it again, and then the low moaning. The White Lady flashed into his mind, but she wasn't there any more, then he felt a cool breath close to his ear, and a loud whisper, 'She evil'. His eyes flew open, and he jumped up quickly, turning on the bedside lamp, knocking the clock on to the floor. It was Selena's voice.

His heart was pounding, but he was quite alone in the room, there was no doubt that it was Selena. Had he dozed off? No, it was not a dream. The noise of the clock falling on to the floor had started Jojo barking down in the kitchen. The moaning got louder. He swung his legs over the side of the bed and went to the window, pulling the curtain back sharply. He saw white sails out on the horizon; he shook his head. They were billowing. He opened the window, it must be the silvery moonlight playing tricks with his eyes; the wailing started; he could hear voices shouting; it must be Richard.

He quickly grabbed the shorts and T-shirt that he had been wearing during the day, pushed feet into his trainers, the laces were still tied, and then rushed down the stairs and opened the door. The wailing was getting louder, rising and falling like a siren. He ran along the narrow sandy path, towards White Lady Cottage, Jojo bounding after him and then passing him, and he was already standing at the gate, wagging his tail anxiously, when he got there. Nick opened the gate and the dog dashed through. Nick glanced at the frangipani as he went through the gate; the wailing was coming from there, and the tree was shaking; the rain was coming down heavily now, and thunder rumbled across the sky. Richard, Rob and Gary were coming towards him, and Richard was shouting above the wailing. The hard rushing sound of the rain hammered on the roof and rustled the leaves of the trees, as the gusty wind got stronger. Jojo was barking and running round in circles.

'Nick! What is it, Nick? She's not there any more.'

'It's coming from the frangipani,' he cupped his hands round his mouth. 'It's got to be Barneby, are the girls all right?' The wind slammed the gate shut behind him as he let go of it, and thunder rumbled across the low clouds; the bright moon of ten minutes ago was gone. A quick flash of lightning made them all wince, and Jojo dashed for cover in the cottage and sat panting behind a chair. They were all under cover of the verandah now, and as lightning lit up the sky Alison glimpsed a white sail just disappearing. She hunched her shoulders, taking a deep breath and clenching her teeth, her hands were clenched into tight fists. 'Richard, look,' she shouted, as another flash of lightning lit up the sky, but her words were lost.

The wailing and screaming got worse; there was nothing that they could do. June and Belinda stood close together by the door, ready to run in if necessary, but they were too scared to go into the house on their own, and really too afraid to be out there on the verandah, but at least they were all together. They both had their hands clapped hard over their ears. The rain was lashing down in torrents, and the wind, now at gale force, whipped up the sea into raging white peaks, and it thundered on to the shore, in competition with the thunder and lightning which streaked across the sky with vengeance.

Suddenly the rain stopped abruptly and the wind died down, and the wailing, to their relief, slowed down to a low moaning and gradually died away, as if a battery had run down. For a few minutes there was utter silence; the night was still, and they watched as a fine mist swirled and wafted across the garden towards the frangipani tree.

They all sighed with relief, and the silence in the darkness hung heavy on their ears, then a cloud moved and the bright moon shone across the water, which heaved and fell like the chest of a gigantic, sleeping giant. It was peaceful, and they began to relax in the stillness, with just the slow sound of raindrops dripping from the gutters and from the leaves; even the frogs had stopped their nightly whistling. They strained their ears for the slightest sound; there was none.

Belinda said she was going to make some coffee, and Alison looked at her watch. It was three-fifteen.

'I wonder if that was the time that he died?'

'Who?' Richard frowned and they all looked at her.

'Barneby, of course.'

'Why, Ali?' Robert sounded surprised and puzzled.

'Well, each time that we have heard the wailing, it has been about three in the morning.' Gary glanced at his watch. 'Do you remember when you and Gramps came banging on our door? It was three o'clock in the morning, then, do you remember?'

Nick nodded and Richard and June checked their watches. It was now twenty past three.

'No, it can't be the time that he died.' Nick shook his head. 'Because George Kingsley and my great-great-grandfather apparently dragged him out of the sea in the morning. He must have died somewhere around six or seven, or maybe even later.'

'What time did the ship go down?' asked Gary. 'I remember reading something about that in the scroll; have you still got it here?' He looked at Richard and Robert.

'Yes, as far as I know.' Richard nodded towards the dining room. 'I didn't send everything down to the museum, I felt I ought to keep a few bits here.'

Gary went into the dining room just as Belinda came out with a tray of coffee. He switched on the light and went to the cabinet, opening the glass door, and took out the scroll still tied with its faded blue ribbon. In his haste, he caught the ring and knocked it onto the floor; he picked it up, putting it just on the tip of his finger, and looked at it. Suddenly the dining room door slammed and it shuddered the window. He looked quickly round the room, which had an icy chill all of a sudden, and felt that he wasn't alone. He shrugged his shoulder in a chilly shiver, put the ring back into the cabinet, and closed the glass door quickly. He rushed swiftly across the room; the dining room door was stuck fast. He pulled with all his strength, and called loudly to Robert, tugging frantically at the door handle.

Robert opened the door. 'What's the matter? Couldn't you find it?'

Gary rushed out, almost knocking him over. 'Did you have trouble opening that door?' he flicked his finger back over his shoulder.

'No, why?'

'Well, it slammed shut, and I couldn't budge it and it suddenly went strangely cold in there,' he shuddered.

Rob grimaced with a smile. 'Don't tell me that Barneby is sitting in the dining room. You have left the light on.' Gary put his arm round the door and switched it off quickly. Robert noticed he looked a bit pale. 'You all right?'

Gary nodded; he had beads of perspiration on his forehead, and Rob thought it was just the heat of the night as they joined the others on the verandah.

Gary unrolled the scroll with shaking hands. 'It says something about George Kingsley here.' He scanned the scratchy handwriting. 'Here, Rob, you read it.' Rob took the scroll and frowned; something had really shocked him. He began to read, and Gary sat down and took a mug of coffee off the tray.

'There you are.' Alison looked up and looked into all their faces, 'George Kingsley saw the ship go down in the early hours of the morning, and I bet it was three o'clock. I thought I saw a sail out there when the lightning flashed,' she shook her head, 'but I can't understand how we can hear the wailing, not now, anyway, now that the figurehead is gone.'

'Wind in the wood,' Richard said absentmindedly.

'Richard?' She stared at him. 'Come on. There isn't any wood, she's not there any more.' Her voice rose with annoyance.

'Well, then,' he sighed, 'I can't answer that. I suppose ghostly happenings just happen, they can happen anywhere, at any time... Clive what's-his-name said that.'

'Marshall,' said Nick, thoughtfully. 'You know, that frangipani was shaking when I came in through the gate, and it wasn't so windy then.' He walked to the end of the verandah and turned the corner, disappearing round the house. Richard,

Robert and Gary followed him, the four stood between the frangipani and the mango tree, and they saw a few gold sparks. Robert described them later to the girls as looking like the dying ends of a firework.

'Do you think he was standing there all the time, and we were round here on the verandah, and we missed it?' Gary looked at each and every one of them and there was a communal intake of breath.

'Shall I contact Clive Marshall again?' Nick gave Richard an inquiring look. 'Since he was here the last time, things have been better, haven't they?'

Richard nodded, rubbing his chin thoughtfully. 'It has been better, I agree, and I think it might be a good idea to call him in again,' he raised his eyebrows, looking round at them all for confirmation. 'We can't go on like this, can we?' They were all in agreement, shaking their heads in despair.

'Well, I suppose in my grandfather's day,' Nick grimaced, 'I mean when Emily was here, they just put up with it, thinking it was ghostly happenings, and most probably shivered in their shoes; it is quite nerve-racking. But with today's high-tech equipment, there must be something that we can do. I will give him a ring in the morning, if you like. When would you like him to come, providing he is free of course, and not chasing some headless horseman in Timbuktu?'

Alison collected the coffee mugs, put them on a tray and took them into the kitchen. Belinda went with her, to make some more, when Joseph and Petal arrived.

'Oh, Maaan,' they heard Joseph's deep voice saying, 'she back agin, Maaan, I knowed she'd be back. Petal is real scared, Maaan.' He was sort of talking to Robert, but his large brown eyes goggled at everyone.

Petal trotted off to the kitchen. June followed her, leaving the men to sort out what they could do.

Alison looked round as Petal came through the kitchen door; she looked really scared, her pretty brown face was pale.

'Oh, mistress,' she sobbed, talking to Belinda, 'I not want to come here, but Joseph he want to come, and I not want to stay by my own.' She was wringing her hands tightly together, 'It start all over agin, Mistress, I is scared, scared, it awful eerie, and...'

'Now! Stop it, Petal!' Alison was sharp. 'I know it is very frightening. I don't like it ... neither does Mrs Bentley nor Mrs Turner. But no one has been hurt, have they? I know that it's eerie in the middle of the night, but we haven't had any trouble for years, have we?'

'No, Maam, but I's scared,' she sobbed.

Belinda sympathized. 'It's the first time Mrs Turner and I have heard the terrible noise, and we are all a little scared, Petal, but a ghost can't do any of us any harm, can it? It's just not real, is it?' She spoke kindly, trying to convince Petal and herself.

'No, Mistress.' She lowered her long black lashes, not really convinced, and then looked up with large brown sad eyes. 'Even de fire in de tree ain't stopped it... He back, Mistress, an he strong.'

'Yes, but it doesn't worry me as much as it used to.' Alison was sharp as she poured coffee into the mugs. 'And as Mrs Bentley has said, a ghost is not real and it can't hurt you.' She suddenly had pictures in her mind of the night she was lured to the sea by the lady in the swirling white misty dress; was it really a ghost? It had seemed so real then, but she would never know. 'Now come on, Petal, pull yourself together,' she encouraged. 'Take this tray of coffee out on to the verandah.' Petal picked up the tray, her hands trembling, and Alison followed her out. Belinda looked at June with the slightest of smiles, and June raised her eyebrows with tightened lips.

It was early evening. Andrew was sitting in the museum at a workbench, still examining parts of the excavations. He turned the rusty iron lantern around in his hands; it was badly damaged. He tried to remove some of the barnacles, which had clung to it for years. On the bench in front of him was a heavy black iron ring; attached to it was a piece of red rusty iron lattice-work grill, obviously part of the hold. Next to it lay a spoke from the ship's wheel, and the backstaff, used for calculating latitude. Apart from the cleaning, it was intact. He had been discussing these pieces with the Captain, Stefan Hanson, who said that his divers could find nothing else, and they would be packing up and leaving in the morning; one of his crewmen would be in a little later with a few more objects, but it was the last, and it wasn't much.

He walked to the corner of the workshop, eyeing the figurehead as it stood propped up against the wall. 'This is the biggest thing found from the *Savannah Lady*,' he touched it lightly, nodding his approval. 'Der carving ist very good. Der face is quite beautiful, even though it is a little disfigured; it is good for you at the museum that it floated to the surface.' He shook his head. 'But I cannot understand how it could have split a fishing boat into two halves. The boat must have been old or faulty, not unless there was some almighty eruption under the water, which I suppose could have sent it up with such a force that it came up out of the water like a rocket.' He shook his head again. 'But never in all my years at sea and in the salvage business, have I ever encountered such an eruption that could do this sort of damage. The two fishermen were very lucky.'

He turned back to Andrew. 'My divers say that there is nothing left down there now, and the reef is dangerous, endlessly deep and dark; they had trouble seeing even with their strong lamps. They say that the ship was caught in a chasm and partly broken up on the reef. They describe it as a mountain under the sea, and the water is endlessly deep and dark. They could see the mast, but it was wedged into the rock so tight that even the crane could not move it, our cables were not long enough, and they say that there are other ships down there, but too deep to explore... Also, two of my men reported hearing an eerie screeching. They could not make out what is was or where it was coming from, and one man refused to go down any more, he said it was like nothing he had ever heard on this earth.'

After the Captain left, Andrew went back to the bench where Pete had been cleaning some metal. It looked like part of a bracket, it had a hole in it where it had been attached to something or bolted down; it wasn't very special to look at, but all things that were hundreds of years old were very special to the museum and had to be preserved. He ran his eyes over the rest of the stuff that Pete had cleaned and had yet to clean.

He heard the phone ringing; Duncan answered it in the

outer office. It was for Pete, who was sitting outside on a bench, smoking a cigarette. Duncan called to him, and he came in. The workshop was quiet, and Andrew looked up from the bench as one of the officers from the *Four Winds* came struggling through the door with a heavy cardboard box, which he dumped on the end of the bench, and stood back.

'Phew,' he was out of breath. 'It's not so heavy, it's just awkward, that's all.'

Andrew smiled and wished him, 'Good evening; all finished now, I hear?'

The man smiled. 'Afraid so, we can't find another thing. How is it all going?' He looked down at the iron ring on the bench. 'I should think that used to be the lock for the hold, possibly to keep the slaves in. God, imagine being locked down in the hold and knowing the ship is going down and you have no chance of survival.' He shuddered, shrugged his shoulders and left.

Andrew gave a nod and began to unload the contents of the cardboard box; there was a small keg, which would once have contained gunpowder, with the V and the H and Y, which would have once read *Savannah Lady*, painted on the side. There was an oblong wooden box, badly damaged, one side completely missing. 'Tom Styles' had been carved roughly into the lid, it was still visible, and obviously a sailor's ditty box. It also had a broken iron lock. There were a few pieces of black unidentifiable objects, and a piece of oak carved into some sort of a pattern, a large padlock with a key still in it, encrusted with white chalky coral, barnacles and soft, green-black seaweed.

Andrew winced as he lifted it up; it had a soft and slimy texture, and the whole cardboard box had a vile seaweed, dead, fishy smell. He pulled a face. He took the last metal box out and put it on the bench; then taking the cardboard box, which someone had lined with supermarket bags to stop the bottom from falling out, to the bin out in the back yard. The smell was atrocious and clung to his nostrils for ages afterwards.

He went back to the bench and examined the box; it was metal, he could tell that, it was black and green with age, and battered on the corners, with fossilized limpet shells stuck to it and strands of seagrass curled around it. He turned it round in his hands; it was about six inches long, three inches wide, and about two inches deep. There was a rose engraved on the lid, well-worn but still visible as a rose. He held it under the brightness of the table lamp on the bench to get a better look, and adjusted his glasses. As he turned it over it rattled; there was something inside. He tried to open the lid, but it was shut tight, possibly damaged.

Just then Duncan came through from the outer office. He nodded to the stuff on the bench, 'Anything interesting?' Then saw the box in Andrew's hand.

'What have ye there?' His strong Scottish accent was curious, and his keen blue eyes were eager to see the box. He came closer to the bench, leaning across to get a better look.

Andrew looked up, a smile touching the corners of his lips, as he raised the box in hand. 'Silver, I think.'

'Yeah ... how do you know?'

Andrew showed him the rose on the lid. He had rubbed at it with a silver cloth which was always at hand on the bench, the years of grime had not come off easily, but the silver shone through. 'I suppose it was the rose emblem, made me think it might be silver. It's a bit battered now, you wouldn't put that sort of thing on an ordinary metal box.' He handed it to Duncan. 'Here, I can't open it ... have a go, there is something inside,' he shook it gently.

Duncan took it from him and sat down on a chair at the other side of the bench. He took a small screwdriver and carefully began to prise the lid open. He was used to handling precious antiques and tried to lift the lid with as little damage as possible; it was moving just a fraction, just a little more pressure and it opened; he had made just a few scratches. Then he sighed, as if making a noise would shatter it; set it down very gently onto the bench and pushed it gently across to Andrew to do the honours.

Andrew put his thumb to the front of the lid, and lifted it carefully. They gasped: the inside of the box and the lid were bright, shiny silver, as if new. 'Not a bit of water has seeped in, in all those years.' Andrew looked at Duncan's face; he was equally amazed.

'It's in pretty good condition, considering silver is a soft metal.' Andrew took out a piece of yellowed paper neatly folded and put it onto the bench. They looked at each other, both feeling the excitement rising within their stomachs, and then back at the contents of the box – five gold coins, a broken piece of quill and a small china pot containing a black dry powder. Andrew knew that when they analyzed it, it would be ink. There was a large white pearl, held in a claw, on the end of a golden stickpin, and a small button. Andrew thought it might be ivory, probably from a shirt, and a flat silver disc, which he picked up and turned over and found that it was a small picture frame, a little bigger than a locket. There was a miniature painting of a woman, head and shoulders: her hair was dark and pulled back severely, she was wearing a black dress off the shoulder showing a deep cleavage, and round her neck was a diamond necklace.

Duncan frowned. 'I wonder who she is?'

They both heard the back door open and close again; it was Pete, coming back in after his ten-minute phone call.

'Anything interesting in the box?' He meant the large cardboard box that he had seen the officer deliver; then, looking at their faces, he came closer to the bench. 'Wow, that's something, a change from pieces of wood. What is it?'

Andrew spread his hand over the few pieces for him to see, and Duncan lifted his head, the sandy brown mop of curls flopping over his forehead, and looked up at him, saying, 'The box is silver.'

While Pete Lester was examining the silver box and the contents spread on the bench, Duncan picked up the piece of aged yellow paper and opened it. The creases were worn and torn, and it was very fragile; he looked at it and began to read the thin and scratchy words. He frowned and read it again.

'Look at this, Andrew. What do you make of this? It's in rhyme, I think.'

Andrew, hearing the uncertain tone in Duncan's voice, left Pete examining the silver box and its contents, and came round the bench. Duncan handed him the paper.

Andrew read the rhyme and then read it again, then read it out loud.

Upon Scotland's golden sandy shore.
We paced from rock, some twenty score.
And there where beam meets green, upon high ground
A shadowed cross will be found.
And be ye there when sun goes down where beam upon three ______

'Mmm, not finished, looks as though someone was caught in the act,' said Pete, rubbing his chin. 'More treasure, do you think?' He inclined his head, and nodded gently.

Duncan raised his eyebrows and pressed his lips together. 'Maybe,' he came round the bench so that he could see the scratchy writing again. 'I wonder why it wasn't finished?'

'Maybe he was writing it when the ship went down.' Andrew laid the delicate piece of paper down on the bench in front of him, so that they all could see it.

'Nay, come on,' Duncan frowned, throwing back his curly head. 'Who starts to write poetry in the middle of a storm, when the water is rushing around yer kilt, for goodness sake?'

Andrew smiled. 'Well, something disturbed him. Even if the ship was going down, he had time to put it in the box and shut the lid down tight, didn't he? And the lid was tight, wasn't it?' He raised his eyes, looking at Duncan. He leaned back, lifting the front legs of the chair off the floor, looking thoughtfully back at the paper. 'You know, I would think that the ship stopped in Scotland. I bet they hid something. Treasure. It's got to be treasure.'

'Could be they stopped for food or water.' Pete glanced first at Duncan, but was talking to Andrew.

'No,' Andrew shook his head. 'Whoever wrote this was making a note, so that he would know where to go back at some later date. It's possible that the ship anchored there in Scotland, and then ran into the storm.'

'But why in rhyme?' asked Pete.

'Dunno ... perhaps he was a poet ... or ... perhaps, it could be a way of remembering; didn't you used to do that when you were at school, put things into rhyming slang, like...' he bumped the legs of the chair down onto the floor, and looked at the paper '...like, for instance, shore rhymes with score, and beam with green... If you kept repeating it over and over, you wouldn't forget. Would you?'

'But why keep the paper? But then I suppose he was going to finish it.'

'Scotland?' Duncan frowned, twisting his mouth up one side. 'But the ship went down here in the Caribbean, didn't it? It could never have sailed from Scotland in a day. It takes Concorde three and a half hours...'

'Not Bonnie Scotland, you twit,' Pete laughed.

Andrew smiled. 'No, not Bonnie Scotland. Scotland is a district on the east coast of the island on the Atlantic side, where the sea comes in rough with continually white rolling surf. It is very dangerous, not good for swimming; in fact, just thinking about that, I don't think you could anchor a ship too close and get into the shore. But it is beautiful, with rolling green hills, very similar to your Bonnie Homeland.' He mimicked the Scottish accent.

Duncan McBride lowered his long fair eyelashes and looked a little embarrassed. 'I didna know there was a Scotland anywhere else. Do ye think that this Jack Barneby really stopped there to picnic or something?' He winked his eye to cover his embarrassment.

It was gone seven o'clock and now dark outside, and they all knew that they would be working well into the night. Andrew looked at the rhyme again. 'I think I had better have a word with Richard Price about this?'

Richard was driving the car, Nick beside him. 'Wonder what Andrew has turned up? He sounded quite eager on the phone.'

'Well, it must be something special,' said Robert from behind him, 'or he wouldn't ask us to come down.'

'I thought he said he wasn't ready to show us anything yet,' Gary sounded surprised. 'Must be something special.'

Richard parked the car in a shady spot under the trees, and they made their way across the tarmac drive, which was in need of repair, then up the steps and into the museum through the enormous iron doors which were studded with black iron bolts; the museum was originally a prison. They walked up the slope and through the cobblestone arch, then across the lawn, which supposedly had once been an exercise yard, and then into the coral stone building

They reached a door which took them through to a lawn and gardens; two large cannons stood either side of the entrance. Around the perimeter of the lawn was a concrete walkway surrounded by heavy wooden doors; these once upon a time had been the prison cells. They stood in front of one, which had a notice, NO ADMITTANCE, and went in.

Andrew, Peter, Duncan and Mike all looked up as they entered, and Andrew came round the workbench to shake each one of them by hand. A big grin on his face, they knew he had found something good. His blue eyes shone behind his square rimless specs.

'Oh, come in, come in,' he beamed. 'Just come and look at this, I can't wait to show you.' They followed him across the large open room, the old wooden floorboards squeaking under their tread, to the bench. Duncan was polishing the silver box

'I can see that you have cleaned her up.' Richard walked past the bench to the corner of the room and stood in front of the White Lady. Andrew came to stand beside him.

'Yes, we cleaned the old girl up, but there are still traces of the white paint in the crevices; as you can see, we can't get into them. But God knows what kind of paint they used originally, it's unbelievable that the red is still so bright.'

Richard looked into the forlorn face with its now half-burnt hair, which was still red-gold; the cheeks were still pink and shiny and the lips still red; the blue eyes looked paler. He felt a chill run down his spine, as they looked back at him, and he hoped that no one noticed as he cringed and stepped back.

Nick was standing at his side now. 'There is something strange about her, isn't there?' He spoke almost under his breath.

Robert wandered over. 'Mmmm, block of wood,' he murmured.

'This is what I wanted to show you,' said Andrew, taking their minds off the Lady, and they followed him back to the workbench, where Duncan was showing the bright silver box to Gary. 'It was a little battered, and pitted black. Duncan said he would still have to work on it, but didn't think it would come up much better; he said it was good, as silver is a soft metal and normally wouldn't stand up to much battering. It's probably been shielded by the rocks.'

Robert's eyes were wide as they gathered round the bench again. 'To think that has been under the sea all those years and it still looks good.'

'Was there anything in it?' asked Gary.

Andrew nodded, his blue eyes seemed to dance with joy. 'Look at this.' He unfolded a soft cloth to reveal the five gold coins. 'Doubloons,' he said, 'and a tie pin and a miniature painting.' Then with a big smile, he handed the plastic pocket, in which he had put the yellowed paper with the rhyme on it to protect it, to Richard. 'And this, what do you think of this?' His face lit up as he waited.

Richard looked at the clear plastic and then looked back at Andrew. 'It's in rhyme,' and he began to read out loud. When he had finished, there was silence as they stood thoughtfully round the bench, taking in what they had heard.

'What do you think?' Richard looked at Andrew in surprise. 'Is it more treasure?'

'Surely not,' Gary breathed, and his mouth fell open in disbelief.

Andrew had a wry smile; he pushed the square rimless specs further up onto the bridge of his nose, raised his eyebrows comically and nodded. 'Well ... I think it could be the clue to another treasure,' he twisted his mouth, biting the inside of his lip, his blue eyes twinkling. They all moved as one with a gasp, their mouths open in surprised disbelief. Andrew looked over his specs, smiling at the surprise on their faces. 'But there again,' he tipped his head slightly sideways, pursed his lips and nodded, 'I could be wrong, it might be nothing at all.' There was a short silence. 'But I think it would be a good idea to take a drive over to the east coast and have a look along the beach.'

Nick was flabbergasted. 'What the hell ... where would we look? What would we be looking for? We can't dig up the whole beach.'

'Like looking for a needle in a haystack,' Rob grimaced, and Gary looked at him with a smile; he'd said that before.

'Yes, where on earth would we start, Andrew?' Richard straightened his back and stuck his hands in his pockets.

'Well, I have given this quite a bit of thought before you arrived, and if it is more treasure, as I think it must be on the east coast, which is the Scotland District ... not Bonnie Scotland,' he looked at Duncan, who smiled and cringed, moved uneasily in his chair and looked down at the floor. 'The rhyme says something about the sun going down.'

Andrew picked up the plastic cover and looked at the rhyme again, and rubbed his chin. 'It says, paces twenty score, that's, um...?' He looked up. 'Who's good at figures?'

'Four hundred paces,' Richard volunteered.

'Yes, but from where?' said Nick.

'I don't know yet.' Andrew scratched at his eyebrow. 'But no one is going to count out four hundred paces for nothing, there must be something there.'

'Yes, but where would you pace from? Where would you start? There is a long coastline over there.'

Andrew twisted his lips, biting the inside of his mouth again. 'Mmmm, well, I think it might be over there at Cattlewash, there is a lot of open ground there.'

'Yes, but over two hundred years, someone might have built a house over the treasure.'

'No,' Andrew shook his head, 'they would have to dig the foundations, and it would have been found, and I have heard of no such thing. This Scotland,' he tapped at the plastic with his finger, 'I bet it is at Cattlewash.' He looked at his watch. 'Sundown is about six thirty.' He looked at Richard. 'What are you doing now? Could you spare an hour or two, we could go over and take a look. I don't know what we will be looking for or where we will start, but we could wait for the sun to set ... what do you think? Let's see if there is a shadow.'

Richard nodded. Nick said, 'OK by me.' Rob and Gary grinned at each other, agreeing that it sounded interesting.

Pete said he had an appointment and would stay to lock up the museum.

Duncan got the minibus and brought it round to the front door of the museum. They all piled in, Duncan driving, Andrew next to him; Richard sat with Mike; Rob and Gary sat at the back. They were excited and joking about finding more treasure.

'Do you remember when Tim was dancing about with the sword?'

Robert laughed, 'I can still see Alison's face now when she saw us all come up filthy dirty, she nearly had a fit.'

Richard looked over his shoulder. 'So did I.'

The minibus trundled on slowly, rolling and bumping over the rough uneven surface of the road. Andrew gave Duncan instructions on which way to go. Duncan had not long joined Andrew's team at the museum, and therefore had not been over to the east coast of the island before.

Eventually they rolled into Cattlewash, driving along the coast road, which was long and stretched out straight in front of them. To their left, the long golden beach stretched for miles and the rough white Atlantic rollers continually followed each other closely, until they crashed heavily on to the rocky shoreline. To their right there were rolling green hills, with craggy patches of grey coral stone rock which rose high above them, and skinny black-bellied sheep grazed quietly on the hillside.

Duncan, parked under the shade of a clump of bushes and trees, which grew in the sand at the edge of the road, and they got out, looking around them.

'What are we looking for, Andrew?' Richard adjusted his sunglasses and then stuffed his hands deep into the pockets of his white shorts, and they all gathered around Andrew, hoping that he had a lead.

Andrew stood with his hand shading his eyes, then he took off his rimless glasses and put on his sunglasses. He first looked out to sea, at the white rough rolling surf, then he gazed along the long stretch of flat golden beach, which stretched for miles. Close on the water's edge were flat black and slippery rocks, which were hardly visible as the white fluffy surf rolled over them, and up on the beach a few large boulders were dotted here and there. But there was one very large one, right on the water's edge, which must have been about 15 to 20 feet high, rounded and smoothed over the years by the sea and the elements, like a huge cannonball. He then turned to his right, looking up at the green grassy hills and craggy coral stone rock. High above the hills, seagulls swooped and swirled; their high pitched screams could be heard above the pounding of the Atlantic ocean, but there was a serenity and tranquillity, over all, as the sheep grazed quietly on the hillside in the hot early evening sun, and thin, bony brown cows walked slowly across the road close to where they stood in front of the car, and began munching noiselessly on the sweet, green grass which grew out of the sand in patches under the shade of the trees.

Andrew turned round and looked at the sea, and then he turned round again and looked up at the hills. They all followed his gaze, but no one spoke.

'Well,' he said at last, 'I don't really know where we should start, but I am sure that we are on the right stretch of beach. The rhyme says...' he looked at the notebook in his hand where he had copied it down, then up at the hills again, 'the shadow of the sun, when it sets, should be about over there,' he pointed with a pencil high up on the green hills, and shaded his eyes with the notebook. 'The sun should be setting soon,' he muttered to himself, biting the end of the pencil, 'and then, I think the shadow ... mmmm, yes, should fall ... yes, about there.' He pointed again: they all looked up to the hills, where the rocks and boulders had laid for hundreds of years, touched only by the elements, the scorching sun, the rainy season, and the wind which blew continually off the ocean.

Andrew rubbed his chin, 'It says paces from rock to sea,' and turned completely round.

'It must mean sea to rock,' Duncan was the first to speak. 'They must have landed on the beach and walked up.'

'Yes, it would have to be something that was outstanding, and something that would be standing for a long time, a special rock.' He scanned the beach, his eyes resting on the huge rounded rock.

Mike nodded. 'Yes, they must have come from the sea, and if we are in the right place, I'd bet it was from that large round rock down there at the water's edge; it must have been there for ever.'

'Yes, I think you are right, Mike, but I don't think Barneby intended to leave a treasure here for too long. He would want to come back and collect it.'

'Perhaps he had already collected it,' said Gary.

Nick nodded. 'That's possible.'

'No, I think it means rock to sea.' Andrew was not really listening to them. 'He would have buried the treasure in a safe place, and then counted the paces back to the sea, where he obviously had a rowing boat waiting to take him back to the ship.'

'That sounds sensible enough,' Robert nodded to Gary. 'And then, when he comes back to collect it, they pace from the sea to where ... umm,' he turned from the sea, looking up at the hills. 'It could be anywhere.'

Gary nodded again. 'Do you think Barneby wrote this rhyme, Andrew?'

'No, I would imagine one of his crew wrote it down and was planning to steal it.' He looked down at the rhyme again. 'It says twenty score, that's, aah...'

'Four hundred paces,' said Richard. 'But Robert is right – from where?'

'I would suggest that we start to pace from that big round rock on the water's edge and...'

Richard butted in, 'Well, let's get started, then.' He moved a few steps away from the car onto the beach.

'We had better wait until we get a shadow somewhere,' said Andrew. 'We need some sense of direction, but I think it will be somewhere up there, on the hill, where the palm trees are.' He looked at his watch. 'I should think they would cast a shadow in about thirty minutes. The sun is beginning to go down, we will just have to wait.'

Mike and Duncan settled themselves down on the sand under the shade of the thick sea-grape bushes, which grew in clumps at the edge of the road; the car also offered a little shade. There were a couple of bench-type seats with table attached under the trees, and a noticeboard that said 'Picnic Area'. Whether people came here to picnic was a wonder; the whole area had a quiet uninhabited feeling.

Richard and Andrew walked the short distance back to the car and stood with their backs leaning against the very hot bonnet, while Nick, Gary and Rob stayed where they were on the beach, a few feet from the car.

The beach was deserted, except for a couple in the distance walking a dog, and a native man who was standing on a rock a few feet out, knee-deep in the rushing white foam with a fishing rod. The waves passed him and thundered down onto the flat hardened sand into a mass of white foaming soap bubbles.

The three stood together in silence, looking at the vast space of sea, sand and countryside around them. A strong warm breeze came from the sea and ruffled Gary's thick curly hair, and tugged at Rob and Nick's white shorts.

Nick looked up as the excited cries of seagulls caught his attention. He watched them swooping, swirling and gliding. Even though the sea rushed and thundered on the beach, there was a quiet and peacefulness, and he felt as though he was suspended in space.

'Eerie, isn't it?' Robert broke into his silent thoughts. He wasn't looking at either of them; he was still looking out at the vast space of the ocean. But Gary nodded just the same. Nick turned to look at the sea and Rob looked up at the seagulls and then turned his gaze back to the sea.

'Amazing isn't it, that Jack Barneby could have been standing right here, looking for somewhere to stash his loot, just like we are now?'

'Except we have no loot to stash,' Gary mused.

'Well, you know what I mean.' Rob tossed his head, 'I can just imagine him giving orders to dig right here,' he pointed down towards his feet.

Nick chuckled.

'Dig? Orders to DIG?' Gary's eyes narrowed behind his sunglasses.

Rob looked surprised. 'Well, you don't suppose that he dug a hole himself, do you? He was the Captain, for God's sake. He wouldn't be doing the digging, he probably came ashore with a dozen members of the crew, all armed with shovels.'

'Mmmm, I suppose so, I never thought of that. But if I was burying my gold, I would want to do it myself. I wouldn't want anyone else to know, would you?'

'Gold?' Rob frowned. 'Who said anything about gold?'

'Well, you wouldn't write a rhyme about burying a load of old junk, would you?'

Nick grinned. 'Oh you two,' he sighed, shaking his head as he walked away, leaving them arguing about hidden gold and pirates. He was still grinning to himself when he reached the car, where Richard and Andrew stood talking.

Rob and Gary watched him go. Then Gary sauntered slowly after him, saying that he was going into the shade, leaving Rob standing with his hands in his pockets, staring out to sea. His eyes darted from left to right, unseen behind his dark sunglasses, and he became deep in thought as he watched the waves, which seemed to crash noiselessly and in slow motion on to the beach as he daydreamed. His imaginings went back in time, to 1721.

There was a deep swell on the water as the *Savannah Lady* dipped and rolled, and the sea lashed at her bow and sprayed away into streaks of white foam. She slipped easily and silently on course, with Sam Jackson at the helm, chewing at the clay pipe which seemed to be perpetually stuck in the corner of his ugly wide mouth, his unshaven chin jutted out, and his heavily wrinkled face was screwed up against the wind as he scanned the waters before him. Above him the sails billowed full in the sun and the light breeze, and the black Jolly Roger fluttered high on the mast. She was still running with the wind from the Dutch East India man o' war, which had fired half of her 60 cannons across her bow over three hours ago, but had done little damage. She was lost now, far beyond the horizon though still surely in pursuit, but the *Savannah Lady* ploughed on, seemingly well out of danger. The crew that were not on watch sat quietly around the deck, mostly in the shade away from the rays of the fierce Caribbean sun, which beat down on the scrubbed white deck. One man sat carving a piece of wood that was taking the shape of a galleon; a group of six sat in a corner playing cards; others played dice, some dozed, and some sat enjoying their clay pipes. A few polished their muskets and flintlock pistols, paying special attention to the trigger action and making sure that they would not fail to fire the next time they would be needed.

Captain Jack Barneby sat in his cabin, writing the events of the day so far into the ship's log. He omitted to write any details of the very early morning encounter with the brigantine *Edwina Rose* off the coast of Havana, Cuba, when six of the *Savannah Lady*'s cannons had blasted away her main mast and topsails, and then rammed her in the darkness of the early morning. Then the ruthless, cutthroat crew had boarded and surprised the sleeping and unarmed crew, attacking and killing most of them, including the Captain.

Jack Barneby had enjoyed his personal encounter with Captain Michael Tompkinson, who had been no match for him with a sword. Sir Hugo Fotheringay had stood on the deck of the *Savannah Lady* and watched as Jack had easily run him through, and then pushed the good Captain over the side, his huge bulk splashing into the water, where the waiting mouths of the hungry sharks had devoured a good breakfast in minutes, including the sharp sword which he still clutched in his hand. Then Jack sent the first officer over the side with a wound to his right arm; his blood-curdling screams were high above the clashing of steel on the deck, as sharp teeth bit into his body and took him below the waves.

Captain Barneby had intended to keep the *Edwina Rose* and put Ben Pellers in charge of her as Captain, but in the bloody skirmish Ben Pellers had been killed, and the ship was sinking slowly, with a gaping hole in her hull where they had rammed her. After forcing half of the *Edwina Rose*'s crew to jump overboard into the circling gaping jaws, dripping in blood from their fellow crew members, he forced another group to help with the transferring of her cargo of tobacco, spices and sugar onto the *Savannah Lady*. He then discovered sacks of silver and a chest full of gold coins hidden away in the Captain's cabin. Twenty men had been captured and were now locked away in the airless stinking hold, without food or water, while the sun blazed down on them through the iron grid. Some would probably die of their wounds or of thirst, and those that survived would be forced to join the crew of the *Savannah Lady*, taking the places of dead men. If they refused, as one man did, the sharks would feast again.

Captain Barneby closed the logbook with a loud slap and stood up from the desk, his head bent slightly under the low oak beams. He was a well-built man for his 36 years, with broad shoulders and a narrow waist. He was handsome, with keen brown eyes and long straight raven-black hair; his lean, rugged features were clean-shaven and sun-bronzed from years of seafaring. But he was meticulous about his appearance and insisted upon clean white shirts twice a day of the finest cotton with frilled fronts and wide sleeves, which narrowed to neat cuffs at the wrist, over which he wore a golden yellow silken waistcoat and a wide brown leather belt with a large silver buckle, which he had taken from a dead nobleman in a fair fight. He stuck the jewelled dagger and a musket into the belt, and had the sword at his side; his black pantaloons were tucked into the tops of long black leather boots which flapped over at the knee. His dark green frock coat was thrown over a chair.

Old Peg, as he was called, polished the boots every day to a brilliant shine, until he could see his grizzled beard and ugly, toothless grinning face in the leather. Old Peg had lost his left leg in a sea battle years ago, shot off by cannon fire from a pirate ship – he had been a merchant seaman when they were attacked – and he now had a wooden stump to replace the leg, but he managed to walk around the rolling decks without complaint. Some said that he was a relative of Jack Barneby; he had spent many years on several ships as Jack's aid, and Jack looked after him well.

Jack stood in his cabin by the desk, his hand on the jewelled sword which never left his side; any man who had ever dared to take it from him was now dead, for no man had ever matched his swordsmanship.

He knelt down in front of the oak-and-iron-bound sea chest, which he had that morning confiscated from the *Edwina Rose*, and slowly lifted the lid. His dark brown eyes twinkled and an amused smile touched the corners of his lips as he looked down at the bright and shiny golden doubloons which filled the chest to the brim. He ran his large right palm greedily over the warm golden coins, he stroked them lovingly with long, sun-bronzed fingers, gently and delicately, as he would caress the soft body of a beautiful woman. He took a long slow breath, and a soft and sensuous feeling ran through his whole body. Hunching his shoulders, he scooped up the shiny gold in both hands, and his brown eyes sparkled under black lashes and a wide smile came to his lips as the precious gold fell through his fingers with a jingling clatter back into the chest.

He got up off his knees, then bent again and dragged the heavy chest nearer to the desk, then sat down in a chair behind the desk and leaned down, taking up a handful of coins, and began to count them, putting them into stacks in front of him on the desk. He thought that the crew had done a good job when they attacked the *Edwina Rose,* and being a fair man, they were entitled to a share of the bounty - he grinned to himself - but not a share of this precious gold. He would have to find a safe place to hide it, and he would give them a share of the silver.

He had hidden treasure many times before, which one day he planned to collect, but never had he ever had such a fortune in gold aboard his ship, and now that they were in the Caribbean he would have to find a quiet and safe island to hide this precious hoard. He knew he would have to find somewhere quickly, the crew could get mutinous; they knew that the gold was on board, and it was only a matter of time.

There was a knock on the door. It startled him and he quickly covered the counted coins with a large map, which was at hand on the desk. Then he stood up, slamming the lid of the chest shut before coming round the desk and calling 'Come in!' Then, realizing that the door was bolted, he slid the bolt and opened the door cautiously, then sighed with relief.

'Oh, Hugo, come in.'

'Can I talk to you, Jack?'

Jack nodded. 'Yes, come in and close the door quickly.'

Sir Hugo Fotheringay entered the cabin, and Jack slid the bolt on the door once again.

Hugo had admiration and respect for this handsome rogue, as his eyes ran down the clean appearance of Jack's crisp white frilly shirt and rested on the hilt of the jewelled sword in the scabbard at his left hip. He knew that the blade was of the finest steel, and so sharp that it could cut a single hair in two; Jack kept it razor-sharp.

He remembered the night that Jack had taken it from him. He had almost been killed, and he often wondered why the ruthless rogue had let him live, when all others around were being slaughtered. It was the first time that they had met, and he had been wearing the sword when Barneby and his cut-throat crew had stormed the palace. It had been a ceremonial dinner given by the King, but at the very last minute the King was unable to attend. A party of one hundred of the most important people in the land were seated with their wives at the long table in the candlelit dining room, dressed in their finest attire. They had dined and sipped fine wines in crystal glasses from the royal cellars.

The ladies were just about to retire to another room while the gentlemen took port wine and brandy and smoked the King's cigars, when there was a sudden outburst as the pirates came noisily down the long hallway that led to the dining room; there were screams of pain as the King's guards were taken by surprise and struck down. As the dining room doors were flung open, every man in the room stood up from the table, a drawn sword in his hand. There was sudden uproar as steel clashed and flashed in the candlelight, and women screamed and swooned as jewellery was snatched from their persons by rough and filthy hands. Steel glinted as men fought face to face, swords swishing, with curses and abuse amongst the anguished cries of pain and the smell of blood which filled the room as the surprised men were hacked to the floor.

Hugo pulled the jewelled sword from the belly of a hairy, filthy pirate, and turned quickly as he heard Amelia's anguished cry, 'HUGO!' There in front of him was the handsome Captain Barneby, with a roguish grin on his face, sword in his right hand, as he stood back from kissing his wife. Amelia was shocked and surprised, and looked helplessly at her husband, and as Hugo lunged forward with the jewelled sword in hand, Barneby pushed her roughly aside, raising his sword to protect himself. Hugo and Barneby were locked in battle, circling each other slowly at first and then clashing the blades with venom…

Hugo could still hear the ringing of steel in his ears, as he stood in the dim light of the cabin now, facing Jack, his mind reliving the past. He thought what a good thing it had been that the King was called away so suddenly, for had he attended the function he surely would have been kidnapped and held to ransom, or slain right there in the dining room.

Hugo looked at Jack, now facing him in the cabin with a stream of pale sunlight coming through the window behind him, his handsome face now in shadow, but his mind went back to the night he had faced him in the King's dining room, swords wavering in each of their hands. He remembered seeing the stones, how they had glittered and sent dancing shafts of light around the room, reflecting off the low candlelit chandeliers. The clashing of steel and the cries of men and screams of mercy were lost, and it seemed that he and Jack were alone, and everything seemed in slow motion as they circled each other, not taking their eyes off each other's face. He remembered looking into those brown, twinkling, devilish eyes. Jack was playing with him, and suddenly and without warning, he had pinned Hugo in a corner against the wall, the point of steel under his chin as he slowly and carefully took the jewelled sword from his grasp, grinning roguishly. Then he had stepped away with the dagger, which he had taken from the sheath in his belt, throwing his head back with a low and menacing chuckling.

'We will meet again, my friend. I will let you live.' He leered. 'You will have your chance to challenge me for your sword.' He smiled, a charming smile, leaving Hugo standing alone in the corner stupefied, then suddenly becoming aware of the noise and the smell of sweat and bloodshed, and the thought that the pirates were leaving with joyous shouts of victory. The once-beautiful dining room was in chaos, with men left dead and dying; the armed guards had not stood a chance and were left in the hallways, some dead and dying, some rolling in pain from their bleeding wounds. The women, their clothing ripped to ribbons, sobbing and afraid, knelt over their dead and dying loved ones, trying to comfort those in great pain.

He looked around the room for Amelia and saw her at the end of the table with Lady Mosebury, who was attending to a vicious cut on her husband's hand with a small lace handkerchief. He made his way to them amongst broken glass, crockery, wine bottles and sheets of white tablecloths which were strewn across the floor and the table. Amelia was dazed, her dress torn, hair hanging in bedraggled ringlets; she was splattered with blood, but he found luckily it was not her own. She came towards him unsteadily, her arms outstretched, and he towards her, stepping over the bodies of people who had once been his friends. He took her in his arms and held her tightly, both thankful just to be alive; he could feel the warmth of her small, trembling body even now, and the smell of the perfume which she used to put in her hair. The room had gone strangely quiet ... they clung together... 'Oh my darling, my darling...'

'Have a seat, Hugo, my friend.' Jack's voice broke into his reverie, sounding a long way off. He blinked his eyes, as if waking from a long sleep. Jack was nodding to the armchair; he moved towards it, feeling numb, and his long, gaunt face looked even paler. Being at sea for three years had not changed his complexion or his ways; he still looked down his long, sharp nose, and his thin lips rarely smiled. He would never make a pirate – his manners were far too impeccable, and he gave the impression of being weak and delicate. His voice was quiet and cultured, and his dress, as was Jack Barneby's, was immaculate. They made a perfect pair, but in appearance only. Sir Hugo would always be the perfect gentleman, whereas Jack just played the part. But, Hugo had to admit, he did play the gentleman very well.

Sir Hugo enjoyed the excitement of the sea, the plundering of ships and then hiding the treasure in remote places, but he did not agree or want to be part of the killing of innocent men, although he was an accomplished swordsman, and he could hold his own in a fair fight, he would not kill for the sake of it. But he had been no match for Jack Barneby when they had fought at the palace, and he had lost the ceremonial sword, but he would win it back one day, and he knew that he would have to kill Jack.

The sword had been in his family for hundreds of years and had been handed down from father to son as each in their turn had come of age. It had been carried through the years only on ceremonial occasions, and never used as a weapon, until the first night that he and Jack had met. But since then, in Jack's hand, it had killed many good men, and one day he would get the chance to win it back; and that day would have to come soon, as his eldest son Edward would soon be of age, and he would have to hand the sword over to him.

He looked now as the stones sparkled at Jack's side, and his thoughts drifted to his son, and then again to his lovely wife, Amelia. He had been thinking about her a lot just lately. He might even give up the sea and pirating and go back home to England.

His thoughts were interrupted as Jack's voice came from the distance. 'Look at this, Hugo.' He had the lid open on the chest, showing the gold.

Hugo blinked.

Jack knew, of course, that it was safe to show Hugo the gold, as he was already one of the richest men in England, as Jack was himself, from the plundering of ships and houses over the years. But Sir Hugo had inherited his great fortune, and he really had no more need of money; but the sight of so much gold must surely be a temptation for any man.

Jack was talking about hiding the booty. 'As you can see, Hugo, the lock on the chest is broken and I cannot get any man here on board to mend it. It would be too dangerous.'

'It is also too dangerous to keep it here, on board.'

'I know,' Jack nodded gravely. 'This is the biggest fortune we have ever taken, and the men know that it is here, although they have no idea of the value; to them it is gold, and I do not trust any of them. Even Maxwell could incite the men to mutiny. We have to hide it or bury it, as we did the silver and jewels in Cuba. Also, if that Dutch Brigantine should catch up with us, I do not want to be caught with this much gold on board.

'Maxwell tells me that in this morning's skirmish we lost four men besides Ben Pellers - he was a good man - and there are seven wounded, two of them not able to carry out their duties, and also that a ball from the Dutchman's cannon has given us a very slight seepage in the hull.'

Hugo looked anxiously at Jack.

'Oh, it's nothing much to worry us as yet, but we will have to find a safe careenage to repair the hull. The caulker is down there now, filling it with oakum and sealing it with hot pitch, it will hold. But at the moment I think that this gold is of much more importance. Do you not think it so, my friend?'

Hugo looked at the chest and watched as a streak of sunlight came through the window as the ship rolled. It lit up the gold for a moment, and then disappeared again as quickly as it had come. He raised his fair eyebrows, and his watery blue eyes opened wide with concern, 'But where, Jack? Where could we hide this much gold without anyone knowing?'

Hugo thought for a moment. 'You know, Jack,' his eyes lit up, 'with this much gold you could afford to have a sword fashioned much as mine,' he nodded to the jewelled hilt, still referring to it as his. 'You could have one fashioned to your very own taste, even better,' he nodded to the hilt again. His tone softened. 'You know, Jack, I would really like to have it back in my possession again. My son will be of age quite soon, and as you well know, it is my duty to hand it over to him.'

Jack put his head on one side, a pathetic lopsided grin on his face, his right eye squeezed up. He spoke slowly. 'You know, my dear Hugo, you can have it back at any time, but you should never have lost it in the first place.' There was amusement in his tone. 'I have told you, my friend, you will have to challenge me.' His eyes twinkled with delight. 'Just name the time and the place; I will be ready to accommodate you.'

'Oh! But Jack...' Hugo seemed to go quite limp, 'you know that I am no match for you, and now that you have the gold... Jack! I would willingly give you my share...' His eyes seemed close to tears, he was pleading. 'Jack? Please.' The word came out so softly it was hardly heard. 'Jack! Please... I'm no match...'

'Precisely, my dear Hugo, precisely.' Jack raised his eyebrows with a charming smile, and his voice was light and apologetic. 'But to purchase a magnificent prize would not give me so much pleasure, and I am awaiting your challenge... Are you afraid to challenge me, Hugo?' He spoke slowly, his eyebrows raised again, and he lifted his chin high, waiting for the answer which did not come, and his voice rose then fell again quietly. 'Good. I need you, my friend, I need you...' he nodded slowly; there was a tense moment.

'But Jack!' Hugo's watery blue eyes looked pleadingly into keen and dancing brown eyes, and he saw the amused smile curl at the corners of the handsome, roguish face, and he felt a tight and tense smile as his own lips pressed hard together, and he nodded his head very slightly, knowing that Jack was right. He took a deep breath, and then turned his attention back to the chest. 'How much is there?'

Jack winked his eye and relaxed. 'Tell you when I have counted it.' He smiled. 'We have these six sacks of silver,' he nodded to the bulkhead, where a row of sacks stood. 'I suggest we distribute some amongst the crew; it will keep them quiet for a while until we have decided what we will do with the gold. They deserve their share, do you agree, my friend?'

He nodded. 'I agree,' and then, without another word, he turned and unbolted the heavy oak door and left the cabin, leaving Jack staring at the closed door. He sighed and bolted the door again, then went back to his counting.

He spent hours counting the coins, and then, as he reached the bottom of the chest, he found that it was layered with gold ingots. He breathed in slowly: the small shock of seeing it gave him an even more pleasurable feeling in the pit of his stomach, and for a moment he sat quite still with his hands clenched into tight fists, as a feeling of sheer joy ran through his whole body. He began to scoop the coins back into the chest, smoothing the last of them across the top just to feel the warm gold, smooth under his palms, and then he closed the lid quietly, took a deep breath, filling his lungs with the smell of gold, and leaned back in the chair contentedly, his hands closed together as if in prayer.

A knock on the door roused him and he went to unbolt the door, his hand ready on the pistol at his belt. It was Old Peg; he had brought a jug of ale and a pitcher of cold water for washing, then left to go back to his chores.

He sat drinking the ale then knelt in front of the chest; he had to secure the broken lock. He did the best that he could with a piece of metal, making quite sure that it would not fly open, and then pulled the rug from the bed and threw it casually over the chest, so that it could not easily be seen by prying eyes. He lay down on the bunk, and his mind was alert; he hung one hand over the side of the bunk, resting on the chest with a feeling of contentment and eventually fell into a deep sleep.

The next morning Jack rose early, swinging his long legs over the side of the bunk, touching the precious chest to assure himself that it was still there. He went to a small basin on a stand and poured cold water, splashing his face, and drying it on a piece of material which he kept solely for that purpose, then he unbolted the door, bellowing to Old Peg to bring him a clean white shirt. He noticed that the ship seemed unusually quiet; there was not much movement under his feet, her timbers hardly creaked, and there was no noise from the deck above.

Old Peg hobbled through the door, pushing it back with a loud bang against the bulkhead, and the stump of his wooden leg clonked heavily over the oak boards as he held out a crisp white shirt, into which the Captain slid his arms.

'Top o' the mornin' to ye, Capt'n, Sir, it be a still day atop, Sir.' His Irish brogue sounded the 'Rs' as his smile widened, showing black and missing teeth. The Captain stepped back and tightened his nostrils as Peg came close, and he caught the smell of his breath, a mixture of stale rum and tobacco and the strong and sour odour of his sweating body.

Jack buttoned the shirt across his broad chest. 'You say there is no wind, Paddy?' Jack was the only one who had ever called him Paddy.

'Aye, Capt'n, Sir. That be right.'

Jack buttoned his silk waistcoat, and pulled the leather though the silver buckle belt. Old Peg held out the green frock coat for him to put his arms in, lifting it up and over his shoulders. Jack stuck the glittering dagger and the pistol into his belt, and adjusting the scabbard, put his hand on the shimmering hilt of the sword and marched swiftly past the faithful Paddy up the stairway aloft to the deck, where Sam Jackson was leaning lazily on the wheel, smoking his clay pipe.

'Morning, Mr Jackson.' He looked up at the clear blue and cloudless sky.

Sam Jackson jumped immediately to attention, taking the clay pipe from his mouth.

'Gud mornin', Capt'n, Sir.' He shook his head, 'It ain't a gud one, Sir, we be becalmed, Capt'n, Sir. Bin like this since after midnight, Sir. Not a breath o' wind, Capt'n, Sir.'

Jack looked up again at the sky. The sun was coming up, it was going to be another scorching Caribbean day. He looked down at the scrubbed white deck below him and then up at the sagging canvas, waiting in readiness for the slightest breeze to touch it. The black flag clung limply to the mast, the hollow eye of the skull and crossed bones intermixed in the lifeless folds. The *Savannah Lady* eased with the gentlest movement as the still water lapped at her hull, and her timbers barely creaked. Jack looked around him. They sat quite alone in the vast blue ocean, as the early morning sun crept higher into the silent, clear blue sky.

The figurehead looked down into the depths of the still waters; her sightless blue eyes did not see the large fish which swam in the cool shadow of her voluptuous bosom. Above her on the deck the mariners moved, finding little shade as the sun got higher in the sky and beat down on bronzed, sweat-soaked, smelling bodies and unwashed clothing.

Captain Barneby knew that if this weather kept up for days, which it could quite well do, they would soon be short of drinking water. He called Jim Maxwell to him and instructed him to put the men on half rations until they could replenish their supplies; the barrels of salt beef and pork would also run low. Now that they had taken the prisoners from the *Edwina Rose*, there would be more mouths to feed.

He came down the stairway to the hold where the prisoners were kept. Looking down through the grating, he could see that they stood or sat, sagging and lifeless, under the heat of the sun. The smell of sweat and urine was nauseous and rose high on the still air. He tightened his nostrils in disgust, but he felt for them, crammed together in little space, with little food, where rats brushed their legs in the darkness and men got bitten and cried out in pain. Weak fingers poked through the iron grating, begging for his attention, and dry, throaty whispers begged for water, which he was now unable to give them. He walked away. It worried him; he must set them free. He would need more hands when the wind came again, and he had no use for weaklings. He called Maxwell to him again. 'Give the prisoners a little water and a bite to eat.'

Maxwell looked surprised. 'But, Sir, you told me to put the men on half rations.'

'Don't question me, Mr Maxwell. DO IT.'

'Aye aye, Sir.'

The Captain walked down the stairway to his cabin, unlocking the door and closing it and bolting it from the inside before going to the chest, unwinding the metal strip, lifting the lid, and looking down on the precious gold. He picked up a handful and then let the coins fall back into the chest; he took a deep breath and ran his fingers over them thoughtfully, then he called to Old Peg.

Jack Barneby was in his cabin, lying on the bunk. He had been there for hours, both hands tucked behind his head, his elbows spread wide across the pillow.

The lantern above the heavy oak ornate desk to his right moved slightly. He watched it; it moved again and began to swing gently to and fro. The *Savannah Lady* was stirring herself to a gentle roll, she was speaking to him. Her timbers creaked and it was music to his ears; she heaved and rolled gently as a swell lifted her hull. He sprang up off the bunk and grabbed at his leather boots, pulling them on. He reached for his belt, pushing the sword down into the scabbard and tucking the dagger and the pistol into the belt. He walked swiftly out of the cabin, up the stairway and out on to the quarterdeck, taking the ship's log, a quill pen and an ink pot.

Sam Jackson got quickly to his feet and grabbed at the wheel as he saw the Captain approach, straightening his shabby grey sweat-stained shirt with one hand, and moving his lips so that the clay pipe moved from the left side of his mouth to the right. His thick grey-whiskered chin stuck out, and his eyes screwed up as he announced, 'All's well, Capt'n, Sir.'

'Thank you, Mr Jackson ... thank you.' Barneby looked up at the sky, twisting his mouth and biting the inside of his lip. There were a few clouds sailing by, and a gentle breeze wafted across his face, turning the beads of perspiration on his forehead quickly cold.

'Wind's a-comin' up, Capt'n, Sir.' Sam stood at the wheel as if making ready to go. 'I see ... Mr Jackson ... I see.' His deep voice bellowed, shattering the silence, echoing back off the water.

'MR MAXWELL ... call the men to attention.'

Even Jim Maxwell was startled by the sudden command, jumping quickly to his feet, he began yelling and roaring orders to the crew, to get their asses off the deck and form lines. In a flash the deck was alive with wild cries and the thunder of running feet, as they were ordered to form lines in the waist of the ship, in front of the quarterdeck, and pay attention to their Captain.

They stood now in lines in utter silence.

Captain Barneby stood tall, his feet firmly placed, a stern look on his face as he surveyed the assembly before him. They were a good crew, living and working together for some time. They worked hard – he admired the scrubbed white decks and the general cleanliness of his ship – but he could not say the same for the crew, as he looked upon the scruffy, ragged, sweat-stained clothing and hairy unkempt appearances, but each tanned and weatherbeaten face was turned towards him now and quietly awaiting his command. He rocked gently back and forth on the toes and heels of his knee boots, his tanned hands clasped behind him, but said nothing.

Sir Hugo heard the roaring and the commotion on the deck above, and, thinking that the Dutch East India Man-o-War had caught up with them, they were about to have another bloody skirmish, came running up onto the quarterdeck, sword in hand.

Jack turned, raising his eyes inquiringly, and sniggered as Hugo stopped dead in his tracks, put the sword slowly back into the scabbard, and stepped closer to Jack and faced the awaiting crew.

Jack turned a little towards him, speaking out of the side of his mouth quietly, 'I have decided to divide the silver.'

Hugo gave a tight smile and nodded in agreement, and then the Captain turned back to address the crew.

'Men...' His voice boomed across the deck and echoed back from the sea, 'you have done well... Our encounter with the *Edwina Rose* was a success, and we have acquired much silver.'

Each man turned to look at the next, and a mumble went through the ranks. Maxwell yelled for silence, as the Captain continued.

'You will be rewarded. You are entitled to a share of the spoils. Every man will receive the same. The two cabin boys will each receive a quarter-share.'

There were loud hoots and whistles of joy and excitement. The Captain held up his hands for silence, and the noise ceased at once.

'MEN! You may come up here to receive part of your share,

and the rest you will be paid when next we reach an English port, which should be in next March, given that we have a fair wind to take us on our way.' There was loud murmuring again, and the Captain held up his hands.

'You can come up here in twos, giving your name to Sir Hugo Fotheringay. He will write it into the ship's log.' He held up the heavy brown book for them to see. 'Please sign your name or make your mark.' He handed the log to Hugo.

The Captain put up his hands for silence once again. 'While we are here still without the aid of the wind to see us on our way, you have my permission to drink a rum or two. Mr Maxwell will see to it.' There was much merriment, shouts and hoots and whistles, and some danced arm in arm.

'But!' the Captain held up his hands again.

'But... I warn you all now, and take heed of my warning, any man ... and I say again, any man ... who is drunk when called to his post, which could be at any time should the wind come up suddenly, and it will, it will ... will be whipped, keel-hauled and thrown to the sharks.' He smiled inwardly; he knew he would do nothing. When the storm came he would need each and every man, but the smiles of excitement and merriment drained from their ugly faces, and there was a slumping of shoulders as a silence fell across the deck, then sour looks and murmuring undertones.

'Mr Maxwell?'

'Sir.' Maxwell stepped sharply forward.

'Pick two of the strongest men.'

Maxwell pushed amongst the men and found Nathan Burns and Jonas Perkins, who he edged forward with the rolled-up whip which he carried in his right hand. They came to the front, looking up at the Captain, who ordered them to go below to his quarters and bring up four sacks of silver.

With a nod and a grin and a 'Yes, Sir', they scurried away. There was shuffling and murmuring, then Burns and Perkins came back to the quarterdeck, and the mumbling and muttering stopped, as the whole crew turned towards the Captain, wide-eyed with anticipation.

'Lift them high,' Barneby ordered quietly, and Burns and Perkins raised their strong, muscled hairy arms, holding a sack in each hand, marked 'Silver', high above their heads for all to see. There was a sudden uproar of whoops and joyous shouts and whistles and hoorays, and the noise was deafening.

Jack and Hugo smiled at each other. Jack held up his hands, but the noise did not cease; his voice boomed out.

'Men ... you did well, this is your share of the spoils.' His voice was lost in the excitement; there was laughter and jumping for joy, and caps were thrown into the air, until the roaring of Jim Maxwell brought them all to order.

The Captain ordered Burns and Perkins to put the sacks down on the deck. When he slit them with the jewelled dagger, the silver coins spilled across the deck and the noise rose again, and as two of the coins rolled down onto the deck below, where the crew were standing, there was a mad scramble as two of the hands left the ranks and dashed forward, sprawling across the deck. Both were immediately grabbed by the scruff of the neck by Jim Maxwell, who pushed them roughly back into line and handed the coins back to Sir Hugo, who was leaning down over the rail of the quarterdeck.

They were then organized to go up and receive their share, and each man came away, happily jingling coins in his pocket. The excitement began again as one man played a hornpipe on a wooden whistle which he had made himself, and another joined in drumming out the rhythm on the deck with the wooden handle of a knife. Some clapped, one played a fiddle, there was singing and shouting as the rum took effect; the hornpipe music got two of them dancing, one pretending to be a woman, curtseying and tripping daintily on his booted toes.

Jack and Hugo smiled down on the exuberance of the crew. Jack hoped his threat had not been heard; he could not keel-haul them all.

'That should keep them quiet for a while. Hugo, my friend, come, let us go below.' Hugo's tight-lipped smile widened as he followed Jack to his quarters.

Jack settled himself in the chair behind the desk, crossing his legs and lifting his feet up onto the corner of the desk, while Sir Hugo slumped down into the only comfortable arm-chair, opposite him. They sat in silence for a short while, each with their own thoughts, enjoying a large cigar, and listening with pleasure to the party spirit above them.

Jack lazily took his boots off the desk and reached for a flagon of Jamaica rum. They had stolen 50 barrels of rum and coffee, and spices a few weeks ago from a ship named the *Rebecca* off the coast of Haiti. She was bound for the Americas and two days out of Hispaniola. He filled two silver tankards and pushed one across the desk to Hugo, then he sat back, putting his feet back up onto the desk; they sat quietly, discussing the gold, trying to decide on a safe hiding place, coming to no real decision.

They fell into silence once again, and the gentle motion of the ship, and the rum, made Hugo drowsy. His head began to nod, his chin sank deep into his chest, and the rhythmic sound of his heavy breathing filled the cabin.

Jack looked at him; his deep brown eyes were wide and alert, his mind still on the gold. His eyes darted around the cabin, from the oak chest to the heavy black oak beams above him, then to the oak door and the great iron bolt that secured it, down at the oak boards on the deck, then back to the oak chest. His thoughtful gaze went again to the beams above him, and he tapped his fingers nervously on his knee, his mind was on the gold. He would have to get the chest ashore, find a safe place, for it ... somewhere, where he ... and Hugo, could come back...

In Spain they had buried a chest, but not half the value of this, in a cemetery. He had four of the hands dig a new grave in the middle of the night. They had put a cross on it and marked it 'Dearest Mother, Mary Smith, aged 96'. They had added a bouquet of flowers and cried mock tears over the grave, and then they went off with roars of laughter, trampling over well-kept graves and kicking at headstones, disturbing the peace of the warm Spanish night. The noise startled the old gravedigger, who spent every night dozing in a small hut at the entrance to the graveyard, watching out for grave robbers. He challenged them with a musket, but after much friendly bantering, they assured him that they had not robbed a grave; one sobbed and wailed with mock tears, saying how he was missing his old and beloved mother, and the old man had sympathized, without knowledge of the language. Jack had offered him rum from a silver flask, which he carried in his pocket. The man drank gratefully and died happily...

His eyes fell upon the chest again, and he began to think of the places where he had hidden treasure: a few hidden trinkets in South America, and a box of uncut diamonds in North Africa, which he had hidden in the wall of an antiquated church high on a hill; afterwards running the priest through with the jewelled sword and leaving him hanging upside down by his ankles, swinging from the church bell. He looked at the now-sleeping Hugo; he had been so shocked, telling Jack that he would go to hell for such an outrageous deed. He smiled. One day he would go back and retrieve those treasures, and many more which he had stashed away... And when he got tired of sailing, he would one day take a wife, and live in a big house, a big house like the sleeping Hugo, and have servants to wait on him, and he would become a gentleman of leisure ... he would be rich... Rich, even richer than the sleeping Hugo...

Hugo started and jumped with a loud snort, and his eyes flew open as Jack slid his boots off the desk and clumped them down onto the floor. Then he heard a heavy tread on the stairway, and Maxwell's voice as he banged on the door, telling the Captain that a strong breeze had suddenly sprung up.

Barneby unbolted the door, and was past Maxwell and almost to the top of the stairway, when the man perched 60 feet above deck in the canvas called, 'LAND ... HO!' Jack consulted the chart, looking up and then straight ahead to where the lookout man was pointing; he took up the telescope and raised it to his right eye. He could see in the distance a strip of white surf and a strip of gold - it must be sand. Beyond that he could see a haze of green which could be trees or hills, he was not sure,

Hugo struggled to his feet drowsily, blinking the sleep from his eyes, and came up onto the deck as quickly as he could, shading his eyes with his hand.

'What is it, Jack? Is it land? Where are we?'

The Captain did not answer him, he moved the telescope along the distant shore line, looking at the Atlantic rollers as they smashed against hidden rocks and swirled into white surf before running up onto the sand. The rugged shoreline seemed deserted as the *Savannah Lady* ploughed steadily and slowly on, rolling and dipping in the swells.

'Steady as she goes, Mr Jackson.'

'Steady, Capt'n, Sir.'

'A point to starboard, Mr Jackson.'

'A point to starboard, it is, Capt'n, Sir.'

'Steady as she goes.'

'Aye, Capt'n.'

Jack Barneby took the telescope from his eye. 'Yes, it is land, my friend, look!' He answered Hugo's question, handing him the glass.

'Do you know where we are, Jack?' Hugo looked at the scene though the telescope.

'Barbados!' Hugo took the glass from his eye and looked at him with surprised eyes, and then looked through the telescope again.

Jack shaded his eyes. 'It is an island east of the main chain of the Leeward and Windward Islands ... we are moving towards the east side of the island.'

Hugo looked at him and chuckled with pleasure at the sight of the land ahead of them; they had been at sea for months. He looked through the telescope again. He could make out the beach more clearly now, but it would take a long time yet before they reached it.

Jack turned, bending his head close to Hugo, and whispered, 'We should find a suitable place for our hoard.' He did not mention the word gold, in case Sam Jackson should overhear.

Hugo smiled one of his rare smiles and looked at Jack knowingly, then raised his eyebrows again. 'Barbados, eh?' He nodded with a tight-lipped smile. 'I have heard of it. There were Amerindians here for a thousand years.'

Jack's keen brown eyes darted sideways, and a look of concern crossed his face. 'You know this land, Hugo? Hostile savages, you say?' He turned to the helmsman. 'Change course, Mr Jackson.'

'No! No! Jack,' Hugo clutched at Jack's arm, shouting quickly. 'No! No need for that – they are here no longer, they are long gone.'

'But how can you know that?' A deep frown creased Jack's forehead.

'Because the first civilized people to land here were the

Portuguese. It was they who named this island Os – Barbados – after the bearded fig trees which grow along the beaches. I would expect that is the greenery which we can see from here, and if, as you say, this is the east side of the island, this would be the Scotland District, because I am sure those are green hills; they look too high for trees. It was our countrymen who named this side of the island. The English settled here in 1605; they landed on the west coast, they called it Holetown – that is over a hundred years ago now, Jack.' He put his hand to his mouth thoughtfully. 'They may not all have been Englishmen, some must have been Scottish, that must be why it is so called, do you not think so, Jack, eh?' He lowered his voice to a whisper, putting the back of his hand to his mouth, 'A good hiding place I think, Jack,' he nodded, and winked his eye.

Jack looked at Hugo with wide-eyed amazement, then inclined his head with a frown.

'You seem very well informed about this remote island, my ... dear ... Sir ... Hugo,' he spoke slowly, his voice rising, and blinked his eyes with astonishment. 'Is there more I should know before I decide to drop anchor?' There was a light air of disbelief in his tone.

Hugo grimaced and scratched his fair and thinning hair.

'Mmmm, well, I only know what I can remember my tutor telling me when I was a boy. Now let me think,' he scratched his head again thoughtfully, then put his hand to his mouth, 'yes, I think it was in a geography lesson, or was it history? I really cannot recall.'

Jack took a deep breath, heaving his chest, and grimaced with annoyance, pulling himself up two inches taller; his patience was running out.

'Never mind what lesson it was, Hugo. Get on with it, Sir! What else can you tell me, and what else should I need to know?'

Hugo turned his gaunt face towards Jack with an irritated frown, then looked back to the island. 'Well, as far as I can remember,' he rubbed his chin, 'the island has fresh spring water, so we should be able to replenish our barrels. There will be fruit, of course, coconuts; look, you can see the palms from here. Also, I am sure there will be bananas and mango, and of course we will be able to get a supply of fresh meat.'

'Fresh meat!' Jack was startled. He turned quickly to Hugo and beamed with delight. 'Meat, meat?'

'Yes, well, of course we will have to find it first, and then shoot it... It was the Portuguese that brought wild pigs to the island, and when they left, well, they just left them here to multiply. They were a good source of food for shipwrecked mariners; a lot of ships get wrecked on the reefs, did you know?' Jack shook his head while still looking through the telescope.

'As I said, the English arrived to find the island uninhabited, except for the pigs of course.' He raised his shoulders in a matter-of-fact manner, and his polished voice went on, 'And, I would suppose the English ... being mostly small farmers ... well ... I would suppose ... that they caught some, and started breeding them...'

'And about these ... hostile Amerindians, what about them?' Jack had a worried look on his face, taking the telescope from his eye.

'Oh...' Hugo flicked his hands up in a genteel manner, 'they just left ... no one ever knew why...' his eyebrows were raised, and his voice airy. 'But then, when the English settled, King George gave the Earl of Carlisle permission to colonize the island. He was a friend of the family, you know, my grandfather knew him well.' He turned to Jack raising his eyebrows again with a tight smile, and looking down his nose. 'It was the Earl who appointed Henry Hawley as Governor, my family knew him too.' He nodded. 'They say he was a good man...'

'But Hugo, there seems little life here,' Jack interrupted, putting the telescope to his eye again and scanning the beach and the green hills beyond. They were a lot nearer now, and he could see clearly the coconut palms and other trees, but whether they were bearded fig trees or not, he did not know. 'I can see no signs of life, Hugo ... look!'

Hugo took the telescope. 'I can't see anything either, Jack. I think the English must have settled on the other side of the island. There is much sugar grown here, you know, and they bring in hundreds of slaves from West Africa to work on the plantations. I suppose when the white man first came here they found it much too hot to work on the land. I remember

Mr Weatherstone telling me that they brought African slaves here all the time, perhaps they still do.'

Jack, nodded thoughtfully. 'Mmmm, maybe there still is a slave trade here, I must look into that,' he rubbed his chin. "There might be a lot of money to be made. Hugo, my friend,' he smiled, 'although on second thoughts, I do not relish a stinking ship.'

'No, Jack...' Hugo had a look of disgust, flexing his nostrils. 'The odour from the hold, where we are keeping the prisoners, is enough.' He put a finger under his nose. 'We are getting a lot closer now, Jack. Look, you can see much more of the beach and the vegetation, even without the telescope.'

Jack decided to take a chance. 'Hove to, Mr Jackson.' He took up the loudhailer, and bellowed, 'Mr Maxwell. Prepare to weigh anchor.'

Maxwell's voice could be heard yelling orders to the men, who scurried to their posts, quickly climbing and pulling in the canvas.

The Captain then turned the loudhailer up to the man in the crow's nest shouting instructions, and asking if the man could see life on the island. He signalled that all was well.

Sam Jackson moved the pipe from one side of his mouth to the other. 'Aye, Capt'n, Sir, the men can now man the windlass.' Barneby nodded.

Men hung in the rigging; the Captain watched, and when the last of the canvas was furled on her yards, Jack yelled orders to the boatswain to get the scurvy crew to drop anchor, securing the *Lady*. She swung round and her timbers creaked in protest, and she strained as the anchor cable tightened. The men in the rigging came down, and the lookout man in the crow's nest slid down with agility to join his mates on the deck.

'Mr Maxwell, get Burns and Perkins.'

'Sir...' The boatswain roared out the names down the deck, and Nathan Burns and Jonas Perkins came running.

Jack turned to Hugo. 'Go below, my friend, and show them where the chest is,' he grinned, winking his eye. Hugo nodded and the two men followed him.

While they were gone the Captain ordered Maxwell to pick out four men to row the long boat; he told him to arm them with a shovel and a pick, also to lower empty water barrels onto the long boat. 'We have work to do, Mr Maxwell! Get to it, man!' His command rose clearly and sharply.

As they waited on the deck the afternoon sun blazed down. Jack mopped the sweat from his brow with the back of his hand, as they waited silently for the chest. Cries from the hold could be heard as the prisoners called for water from below; it was even hotter in the hold when the ship came to a standstill, as the unrelenting sunbeams shot down through the iron grating, as fingers burned on the metal, clawing to get out.

Maxwell began bellowing orders again, and the long boat was lowered and ready to go. Hugo joined Jack by the entry gate, and Burns and Perkins struggled along behind him at last with the heavy sea chest. The Captain ordered them, with the help of other crew members, to lower it into the long boat. This took some doing while they waited in the heat.

'And be careful with it,' growled the Captain, 'or I will have you all flogged and thrown to the sharks.'

Hugo waited with bated breath, and twisted the jade and ruby ring nervously round and round on his finger, hoping that they would not drop the precious load into the sea. He noticed Jack watching him, and his thin lips tightened as he flicked a speck from the cuff of his silk shirt and wiped his neck with a silk handkerchief.

'I hope this will be a safe place, Jack...' His tone was low and almost a whisper, sceptical and condescending. He raised his nose in a superior manner and sniffed. His blue eyes were now cold, narrow and squinting as he gave Jack an odious look, his mind quickly darting back in time to the many other places around the world where they had stashed their precious hoards of jewels and silver, which he had personally arranged to steal and then helped to collect. Collect ... yes, collect, that was a nice word. Collect, so much nicer than steal. He wondered if Jack ever intended to share it with him. He thought not ... but he would come back one day with a ship and collect the ill-gotten gains; he would return for the gold. He returned to the present and watched as Jack supervised the lowering of the precious chest. He did not truly trust him – he nervously touched the sword at his side – he would one day have to kill him... Jack broke into his thoughts.

'Yes, Hugo, old friend, I think this will be an ideal place, and you can trust me, my friend, your share will be safe.'

Safe! How had he known? thought Hugo. How had he known what he was thinking? He frowned. Jack must have read it in his face.

'No one,' Jack whispered, 'no one, my friend, will ever know where this chest is hidden ... or what secret it contains. No one, my friend, but you and I.' He grinned slowly. 'Come now, Hugo,' his command was sharp, as he went towards the rope ladder, 'I have spied a sail, far out on the horizon. I think it might be the Dutchman, and we must make haste to get ashore.'

Hugo glanced quickly to the horizon but saw nothing, and then followed Jack down the rope ladder into the long boat. The crew manned the oars and pulled swiftly away from the ship, while Maxwell and the rest of the crew watched enviously from the deck.

There was a good swell on the water, and Jack looked up at the blue sky, where a few dark clouds were beginning to gather and a light wind whipped the sea into small white peaks. Although the sun was still blazing down, Jack knew the signs well enough; there was a storm brewing. Only last year he had lost a ship, the *Sea Hawk*, in similar circumstances, off the coast of the Carolinas. They had seized her in the early hours of the morning, while her crew slept, and taken over the ship. It had been hot and still, as it was now, and in just a few hours the storm raged, and she broke her back and sank with a cargo of linseed, hams and flour - and a treasure chest of silver, a dowry being taken by the Honourable Lady Clarissa Pitman to her betrothed, Sir Harold Montague-Hope. Jack sighed. The Lady Clarissa, she had been such a beauty, and so willing with her affections - he smiled at the thought - but alas, she had perished, along with 40 of his crew, who now slept in the deep. He and Hugo had escaped death in a crowded long boat; Boatswain Maxwell had pushed three men over the side to make way for them. Will Logan had been taken by a shark, and Jack shook his head as a picture of the man's face appeared in his mind. He could still hear the man's screams ringing in his ears as his body sank under the swells of circling blood, minus a leg.

He closed his eyes for a second, shutting out the sight of the sea, and came back to reality as the long boat neared the shore, rising high on the fast-rushing tide and dropping heavily, shipping a little water, and then rose again, as the oarsmen deftly steered her between the hidden slimy rocks close to the shore, where grew thick wavering sea-grass as the foaming white surf rushed up on to the golden sand.

Burns and Perkins went over the side and held her steady, while the Captain and Sir Hugo jumped over thigh-deep, the white foam swirling around and filling their long boots. The Captain shouted instructions over the noise of the roaring sea for Burns and Perkins to bring the chest up onto the beach; they struggled to get it up and over the side of the boat. Jack signalled to three of the oarsmen to help them and then to follow, leaving one man to manage the boat. Stumbling and splashing through the surf, the five men dropped the chest heavily down onto the wet and hard flat sand, away from the water's edge, beside an enormous round rock, which stood at least 20 feet high, half in the water and half out.

'You two stay here and guard the chest well,' the Captain commanded Burns and Perkins.

The Captain gave orders to the other three men to go and find food and water and bring it back to the long boat. He told them that there were wild pigs to be found on the island; they were not to shoot at them, causing alarm to anyone who was in earshot, but to take a few piglets alive if possible, or use their swords. 'Take the water barrels, you will find fresh water here, and we need it badly in this heat.'

'Come, Hugo!' Barneby walked off up the beach, leaving the seamen unloading the two barrels from the long boat. Hugo followed obediently, his long polished boots soaked and squelching inside with each step. It felt very uncomfortable, but he did not complain, he knew that Jack must be feeling just the same, but that he only had thoughts for hiding the gold as quickly as possible. He turned and looked out to the horizon, but could still not see any sign of a sail; he hurried, wincing after Jack with each step. He knew that Jack would not stop or speak until he had found a suitable hiding place.

They came to the top of the beach, where green fresh grass grew through the sand, and clumps of the beaded fig trees grew in abundance, and beyond them green grassy hills swept up to great heights. In places there were patches of craggy grey coral stone rocks, and gorse bushes grew green and tinged with rust brown, scorched by the ever-blazing sun. Coconut palms waved their feathery fronds in the warm salty breeze, and above them seagulls swooped and cried, the only living creatures ever to have disturbed this peaceful paradise.

Jack had a satisfied grin, knowing that he must be the first white man ever to have set foot here. Followed by Hugo in his squeaking, squelching boots, he began to walk and part-climb on the steep grassy slope, clambering over craggy rocks in search of a place he knew he must find as quickly as possible, to hide the chest. He stopped high on the hillside and looked down at Burns and Perkins as they sat patiently beside the chest. They knew that if they moved, the Captain could easily pick them off with his pistol. From this distance, the two huge men looked like dwarfs on the long golden beach, with the vast rolling ocean behind them. The long boat still rose high on the waves, falling heavily again into the white surf, and way out to sea the *Savannah Lady* strained at her anchorage, and he knew that Maxwell would also be straining his eyes through the telescope, watching their every move.

Jack was looking around him. His sharp eyes did not miss anything; he had to find a safe place.

Hugo was also looking around and spied a large mahogany tree growing at an odd angle out of the side of the hill, its long trunk leaning towards the sea. 'Jack! Jack! Look at this … this could be a good hiding place, what do you think?' he started to walk towards the tree.

'No…' Jack's voice rang out, echoing in the emptiness. 'The rock is too hard, we would never be able to dig into it; besides, the tree might die.' He walked closer to Hugo. 'What I am looking for is a crevasse in the rock,' and just as he said it, 'Haaa … look here.' Hugo turned, looking at Jack and then to where Jack was nodding, to the rock just above him, where a wide gap split the rock in two. He climbed up, his long legs covering the short distance in three strides.

'Come up, Hugo,' he called but Hugo was already by his side.

Jack moved a few small boulders and the gap in the rocks

got bigger; the rocks had obviously fallen at some time, and one was wedged across the top, making a roof. They peered into a small dark cavern.

'This, my dear Hugo, would make an excellent hiding place, don't you think? In time the grass will grow over it, and no one would ever find our precious chest.' He smiled as he emphasized the words and began to laugh, and Hugo joined in; their voices echoed off the coral stone and around the cavern, and were lost in the cries of the swirling seagulls.

Jack cupped his hands and yelled loudly, gesturing to Burns and Perkins, who were looking up, shading their eyes with their hands. They could not see him clearly, as he was half-hidden behind a large tree and a dip in the hillside, plus they were looking into the sun; they could hear the hollowness of this voice but could not make out the words, but they could see him waving his arms, instructing them to bring up the chest.

Jack and Hugo watched for some time as the two burly men struggled, climbed and stumbled, sometimes lifting the heavy chest then dragging it behind them in the scorching heat of the early evening sunshine. Jack smiled as he watched them sweating and straining their bare backs, one also carrying a pick and the other a shovel.

He nodded gently as they finally dumped the chest almost at his feet. Sweat glistened on their bare, sun-bronzed bodies and heaving hairy chests. It dripped from their foreheads and soaked their eyebrows and beards. Both men were spent, but he gave them little time to recover, ordering them to start moving the rest of the rocks and boulders away from the crevasse to make it wide enough for them to stow the chest inside. When he thought that they had done enough, he ordered them to stop. The men looked at each other; exhaustion showed in their faces, and for no more than a moment, they were allowed to rest.

Burns sat down wearily on a low rock; he was breathing heavily and his limbs ached.

'Come on, Burns, no time to sit about, you are not finished yet,' the Captain commanded. 'Take hold of that handle, and help Perkins put the chest into the cavern.' Burns looked up at his Captain defiantly, his face screwed up, sweat running into his eyes and dripping off his chin, there was a hideous look of hatred on his face.

'Burns,' the Captain bellowed. Nathan Burns stood up slowly, his broad chest heaving, loathing the Captain; his huge muscled arms hung limply at his sides and he cursed under his breath, then clenched his large hands into fists as he had done many times in his life, ready to fight, but his strength failed him, drained by the heat of the sun. He slowly took hold of one handle of the chest, and he and Jonas Perkins lifted the chest inside the cavern, and put it down with a hollow clatter.

Barneby looked in and told them to put it further back; they had to go down on their knees and drag it to the back of the cavern with great difficulty, where the roof was very low for two men of their bulk, broad and over six feet in height. He told them to position the chest so that the lock was facing the entrance; it was difficult to manoeuvre in such a cramped space, airless and dusty, as they struggled with the heavy chest. Then they crawled out wearily one after the other and flopped down onto the grass, their great chests heaving with exhaustion, coughing and spluttering from the dusty dry coral stone atmosphere.

Barneby gave them no time to rest, kicking at Jonas Perkins to get up onto his feet. 'Come on, you lazy livered swine, get on your feet; your job's not finished yet.' He ordered them to replace the rocks that they had removed, so filling up the gap and enclosing the chest.

Now the two men stood aside, once again exhausted from their efforts, wiping the sweat from their brows and breathing heavily.

'We should mark it in some way, Jack,' said Hugo. 'If this grass grows up over it as you hope it will, we will never ever find it again.'

Jack considered for a moment, rubbing his chin. Hugo was right. He looked around and saw a few round white boulders. He ordered Burns and Perkins, now recovered just a little, to roll them over in front of the rocky entrance, and put three of them in a line. The men did as they were told; it was fatal not to obey the Captain.

'There you are, my dear Hugo, now you will be able to find

it again. All you have to do is look for three round rocks of the same size.' A smirk caught the corners of his mouth, as all four stood looking at the blocked-up entrance.

No one spoke; the warm wind whistled in their ears, and only the mournful cries of the swirling seagulls disturbed the loneliness of the hillside.

Jack was the first to move away. Hugo followed him, then Jack stopped to let Burns and Perkins lead the way. He thought it would be safer to walk behind the pair – Jack rarely turned his back on any one of the crew. Just at that moment a family of wild pigs rushed out of the gorse bushes, startling them all. Barneby was for a moment taken off his guard as Perkins, regaining his energy, suddenly lifted the pick axe and lunged at his Captain with great force. Jack's reaction was as quick as lightning, and in a split second he had drawn the sword from the scabbard, and the pistol from his belt with his left hand in almost the same instant, stepping back, firing at Jonas Perkins' heart. It was more by luck than judgment, as Perkins had his arms way above his head, and the weight of the axe pulled him down to the ground; he fell at Jack's feet, flat on his face, and stayed there very still.

Hugo stepped back in alarm, sword in hand, as Nathan Burns came at him with the shovel raised in a violent attack, but Jack's quick action and skilled swordsmanship caught him across the neck, and he fell screaming and writhing on the ground, holding his neck as the blood spurted out through his fingers like a fountain, and then he lay still on his back, looking up at them with wide and unseeing eyes, as Hugo and Jack watched his very last breath leave his body.

Jack's eyes twinkled as they both stood like statues, and a slow smile twisted his lips as he said quietly, 'Now no one will ever know where our precious chest is hidden; that is, no one, Hugo ... except you ... and me...' He smiled slowly; his tone was soft, but there was a threatening air in his manner. They faced each other. Hugo raised his sword ready to defend himself, and Jack waved the jewelled sword in front of him, almost under Hugo's nose.

'Oh, no, my friend,' he spoke softly, his smile menacing, 'not you too, my DEAR Hugo ... surely you want to live long enough to collect your share of the gold ... and just think for a moment that you have to hand this,' he wavered the sword, 'over to your son.' The smile lingered on his lips as he moved the sword just a fraction, and Hugo flinched. The sun caught the stones, and shafts of light sparked like fire. Jack waited for Hugo to realize his fate.

From way down on the beach the four waiting seamen caught the glint of steel and the sparkle of the stones, but of course did not realize what was happening. Ben Commings looked back to the *Savannah Lady*, waiting for a signal to move out, which never came.

High on the hillside Hugo's eyes never left Jack's face, and he realized that he was holding his breath; he let it out slowly, easing the tension between them.

'Sorry, Jack,' his voice wavered shakily, 'I thought ... I thought ... that you were ... going to...' He bit his bottom lip nervously, and his gaunt white face twitched. Jack surely would have killed him, he knew that.

Jack, still smiling, ran his tongue across his top teeth and sniffed. 'Kill you ... Hugo? Is that what you thought?' Then he began to laugh softly then loudly, throwing his head back. 'Hugo, you amaze me,' he said between laughing, 'you really amaze me. Come, come, my friend, put away your weapon.'

Hugo slowly lowered his sword, slipping it back into the scabbard; Jack smiled, putting a friendly arm round Hugo's shoulders. 'You and I have a lot more plundering to do yet, and what would I do without you? Eh? When we next reach a port, only you know how to organize such elegant and lavish parties; the rich flock to you like bees to a honey pot, and we will have many more days such as this, hiding, what did you call it, our ill-gotten gains.' His manner got enthusiastic. 'Do you not find hiding such treasure exciting, my friend, eh? Just think of retrieving it, when the time comes, eh? And sailing it back to England, and presenting it to your wife! How is your wife? My dear Hugo ... such a beauty, if I remember. You are a very lucky man, eh? Do you know that I am thinking of taking a wife for myself some day...? Now! What do you think of that, eh? Me! Ha ha, me! With a wife and settling down,' he chuckled. Hugo said nothing, but his cold blue eyes watched Jack carefully, ready to defend himself should Jack change his attitude, and suddenly catch him unaware.

Jack still had the forced smile on his face as they made their way slowly down the steep hill, his arm still companionably around Hugo's shoulders, the other carrying the jewelled sword. They came to rugged rocks in their path and clambered over and around them, and walked on the grassy slope again until they reached the beach, then they both turned and looked at the place where they had been. The sun was going down, and two palm trees that were crossed now shadowed the rock where they had hidden the chest; leaning towards the sea, their feathery branches waved slowly in the light breeze.

The two men faced each other with a contented smile, the tension now gone between them. Barneby grinned, 'Marked with a cross, Hugo.' Jack put away the jewelled sword and they walked in silence towards the rushing surf, where the other crewmen awaited them. They had caught five piglets, which squealed in a rope net, and two large pigs which they had killed; and the water barrels were full.

They waited while the men held the boat out in the surf, and just as Hugo was about to walk into the water, Jack said. 'Four hundred.' He raised his eyebrows, 'And you, my friend?'

Hugo turned slowly, a surprised look on his face, and smiled a rare smile. How had Jack known that he had been counting the paces back to the big rock? 'Three hundred and ninety-nine,' he said quietly, almost mouthing the words, although with the rushing of the surf, the men in the long boat could not hear their conversation.

Jack's handsome face creased and he threw his head back and laughed. 'Well, we won't argue over the size of your boots, will we, my friend?'

Hugo shook his head, a tight smile on his lips. Jack was a remarkable man – and how had he known that he had been counting the paces? How had Jack counted so accurately when he had been talking all the way down? He truly was a very remarkable man.

Jack saw the puzzled look on Hugo's face. 'Are you wondering how I counted, my dear Hugo?' A slow smile caught the corners of his lips. 'I counted on the way up to the jutting rock, see there,' he nodded with a wink. 'We walked another thirty paces on.'

They waded out into the surf and climbed clumsily into the

rocking long boat, where the four men sat with their hands ready on the oars. The Captain growled orders to pull for the ship.

'But where are Burns and Perkins, Sir?' One of them dared to ask.

The Captain looked at the man with sadness in his eyes. 'Alas ... they are no longer with us ... God rest their souls ... they are both dead. Hostile savages attacked us. Me and his Lordship here had to run for our lives, did we not, Sir Hugo?' Hugo gave a slight nod, thinking to himself, what a good actor Jack was. Jack went on, a sadness in his voice; he shook his head in sorrow, 'Two good men, two of the best, so sad, so sad,' he shook his head. 'But they fought bravely, put up a good fight they did, to enable us to flee to safety, did they not, Sir Hugo? But they were hacked down by savages, who will no doubt have borne away their bodies by now for their boiling pots, and will leave the bones for the buzzards to pick clean.' He bowed his head in sorrow again. Then he lifted his head and looked searchingly at the four crewmen, who sat with their mouths open and their eyes wide in disbelief. They had seen no one and had heard nothing, but not one of them would dare to question the Captain. Ben Commings was the only one who had glimpsed the flash of steel; he said nothing.

As the oarsmen pulled silently for the ship, Hugo looked back at the place on the hill; the sun was lower in the sky now, and the shadow of the two coconut palms now made a very definite cross, roughly near the entrance of the cavern. He took the silver watch from his pocket and looked at the time; it was fifteen minutes past six o'clock.

Jack had also noticed the cross and noted the time by the sun going down. 'What time do you read on your timepiece, my friend?' And before Hugo could answer him, he had snatched the watch from his hands, pulling the chain, which made a small tear in the pocket of his silken waistcoat. Hugo gasped and grabbed at the chain, which got caught around his finger and almost took the jade and ruby ring from him. Hugo winced and rubbed at his finger, taking in a quick sharp breath at the pain, while Jack noted the time and quickly stuck the watch into his pocket.

'Jack! My watch if you please!' Hugo frowned with annoyance as he held out his hand, pleadingly.

'Do not distress yourself, my dear Hugo, if it is the time you want, you only have to ask.' He patted his pocket with a chuckle and then looked towards the ship, they were almost there.

Hugo gave Jack an odious look and just sat there, looking at the back of his head. He was rubbing his finger; the ring and the chain had torn the skin. He knew it was useless asking Jack for the watch, he would get the same answer as he did when asking for the sword and the dagger.

His very body was shaking with rage, and he was trying to control it. He raised his hands, about to hit Jack across the back of the neck and push him into the water, and then he thought better of it. But he would get back at this thieving rogue, he would kill him, kill him, kill, kill, the word seemed to spin around inside his head. He could feel his face getting redder, and felt that the rage in his body would burst out of the top of his head; he would wait his chance and finish him for good, and then go back to collect the gold. But he knew he would have to wait, catching him off-guard, when he was least expecting it, but he would surely kill him, kill him, kill this thieving...

'Are you not coming aboard, my friend?' Jack's voice shattered his mind; he was looking down at him from the deck of the *Savannah Lady*. Hugo was sitting alone in the long boat, but for one crew member, who was waiting for him to alight.

'Are you daydreaming, my dear Hugo?' There was a sarcastic tone in Jack's voice, as he smiled charmingly down at him. Hugo glared up at him, stood up carefully in the boat, grabbed at the rope ladder and began to climb.

As he reached the deck, Jack was telling Maxwell about them being attacked by savages. He could not discern the look on Maxwell's face, but he was sure that the man would not believe a word of the Captain's story, although Jack could spin a good yarn. All of a sudden his attitude changed, and he bellowed, 'Get this ship under way, Mr Maxwell, quickly, before those savages reach us.'

Maxwell and Hugo looked towards the beach, and coming towards them were two canoes with dozens of black men paddling fast.

Hugo looked at Jack; he could not believe his eyes, and Jack had a look of surprised alarm as he hurried towards the quarterdeck, yelling orders as he went. The sailors scrambled up the ratlines to unfurl the yards, and were all at their posts, two at the windlass pulling up the anchor; so used were they at getting the ship under way at short notice that the sails were full blown and caught by the strong breeze, and Sam Jackson steered her away out to sea – the canoes were soon left far behind.

The sea was now whipping up into white peaks as a few grey storm clouds gathered in the sky, but the ship pitched and rolled peacefully now in the heavier swells.

Hugo stood on the quarterdeck, his face ashen with the thought of the two men callously struck down by Jack and how near he had come to death himself. One move and Jack would have run him though without blinking an eye, and he would be telling Maxwell how the savages had struck him down with Burns and Perkins. He looked at the sky; if the storm broke they would be needing the two extra hands. He twisted the ruby ring nervously, it was a bad habit. He was still raging inside at the thought of losing his watch, and he knew that he would have to challenge Jack Barneby soon, but the thought made him very on edge. Jack was an excellent swordsman, but the time would come when he must be challenged, and he would surely have to kill him quickly to get his sword back, and now the rogue had stolen his silver watch, as easily as stealing a rattle from a baby. Catch him off-guard, that's what he must do, catch him when his back was turned, although that was a coward's way to think – but it was the only way, maybe creep up on him when he was sleeping. He had to kill Jack Barneby, he had to. His eyes were hard and venomous as he left the deck and went down to his cabin. He could still hear Barneby and Maxwell yelling orders, but their voices faded as he closed the cabin door.

Hugo slumped down sulkily on his bunk, chewing at his bottom lip, still raging inside but annoyed at himself for being so weak. He was not a fighter, but he had seen Jack Barneby kill men in cold blood many times. He had killed one man himself, but only in a duel, and it had worried him for months afterwards – and although Burns and Perkins had attacked their Captain first, neither man had been armed with a sword or a pistol, and to slaughter two good young men, to stop them from talking sickened him. But had they not attacked, Barneby would surely have killed them anyway, and probably he would have killed him too, had he not had a sword to defend himself. But he would get his own back one of these days.

His thoughts turned now to the gold; he did not know just how much there was. Jack had not told him, as he said he would... The gold ... he was a rich man, did he need more? No! But he would get a ship and come back and steal it, leaving Jack with nothing, and then he would sail away to where Jack Barneby would never find him. He would take Amelia and the children to the Orient. He wondered why he had ever craved the life of a pirate; he was a rich man. A gentleman. He was not of this scum. A rich man, and his wealth had been acquired honestly, by his grandfather's hard work, his father's, and his own. He was a rich man, a very rich man, he had no need of this ill-gotten gold, which innocent men had had to pay for with their lives. He was not a pirate, never really had been; he could not kill just for the sake of it, and for gain... No, he shook his head. He had had enough of this rough seafaring life, and decided now that he would go back home to England, he would go back to Amelia ... but how, he did not know yet.

He got up from the bunk, not knowing how long he had been lying there. The lantern above him was swinging hard; he knew there must be a good swell on the water, and the ship rolled. As it surged forward, he groped his way to the desk and fell into the chair. He took a paper from the drawer, opening the oblong silver box, which had been his father's. He took out a small quill pen, and opened the silver lid of the small porcelain pot, which fitted snugly into a slot with a silver clip to stop it from rolling about. He dipped the pen into it, and sat thoughtfully with the quill poised over the paper before he began to write.

He had to remember the exact location of the chest, which he intended to steal; he smiled. No ... collect, that sounded better. And one day he would kill Jack and retrieve his sword. His mouth twisted into a smile, and a shiver ran down his spine at the ugly thought of running Jack through. The quill touched the paper and he began to write in rhyme, easier, he thought, to remember; he would recite it to himself over and over again, and learn it off by heart. He thought then of Jack – should anything unforeseen happen to him, he would hide the paper in his belongings. He knew that Amelia would eventually receive his chattels, and then his sons would surely seek out the treasure. Edward would be 17 now and James 15; he imagined them two strong young men, well educated; why did he ever leave them? He shook his head in despair... What a fool he had been. Amelia had been through a lot; the death of their daughter, Jane, in the riding accident, had shocked her so... He thought of his daughter, she had been so beautiful, like her mother. Oh why had he been so stupid, why had he left them, was not his family and his wealth enough for him, why had he wanted more? And why had he wanted this? This ... he looked around the small and dingy cabin, shaking his head, and thought of his lovely house in London. He shook his head in despair. Why? What a fool he had been. He loved to be on the deck with the wind blowing the salt air in his face, but here below deck, it was dark and dingy, with a mixture of smells: wood, paint, and sweat, not only his own. It was hot, fetid, airless and reeking of sour ale and wine, stale cigar smoke, and urine. The stink from the galley of grease, meat, dead fish, and rotting vegetables; the foul smelling of the hold with its cheeses; rum and tobacco mixed with the sweetness of molasses and salt beef in brine and the bilge water which seeped through the planking and collected in the bottom of the ship. The foul stinking water was pumped daily to the deck and ran out through the scuppers; the smells seeped through her timbers, blending with the nauseating noxious smells of livestock – chickens and a goat, which was kept for fresh milk for the Captain and which roamed about fouling the deck with its droppings, and now piglets. Out of the corner of his eye he saw a large roach, he put out a booted foot but it was too quick for him and it disappeared between the boards. Even though Barneby kept a reasonably clean ship, it was impossible to control the vermin.

The lantern swung from the low beam, leaving him in the darkness and then again in the light, making his writing difficult. The ship pitched and rolled, and the silver box with the ink pot slid to the right side of the desk and down onto the floor, the contents spilling out. He picked up his cravat pins and the five gold coins which he had taken from the chest, closed the lid on the inkpot, and put the silver box back on to the desk. The ship rolled again and the box began to slide, and he steadied it with his hand. He went back to writing his poem; he read it through and was just about to add the next line, when suddenly the cabin door flew open and Jack Barneby burst in.

'Come, Hugo, do not delay,' he was breathless. 'I need another hand at the helm, the swells are great and Jackson needs help holding her steady. The wind is strong and we are running into a storm.' Jack turned away as quickly as he had come, and rushed back up onto the deck.

Hugo folded the paper in half quickly and put it into the silver box, out of Jack's sight; but Jack had been far too concerned with the matters of the ship and the storm to notice. He put the quill pen quickly into the box, and as he shut the lid tightly the feather of the quill broke in half. He got up unsteadily as the ship rolled and the box slid to one side again; he caught it, pushing hard on the lid so that the contents would be secured, and then put it into the drawer. Then with great difficulty, as the ship rolled flinging him from side to side, he managed to grab at the door – the motion of the ship almost flung him backwards – then holding the door frame and anything which he could get a purchase on, pulled himself forward, gripping the stair rail. Hand over hand he pulled himself up the stairway using all his strength, and finally made it to the helm, where Sam Jackson was fighting with the wheel.

Although in the cabin he had been thrown about, Hugo had not realized the weather atop was this bad: the rain lashed at his face, stinging his pale cheeks, and the wind roared in his ears. As she pitched and rolled he grabbed frantically at the wheel for support, and the heavy waves splashed up and over the bow, the gale-force wind blew her; she was listing to port, and the torn sails flapped with loud clapping noises as the crew battled against the elements. The storm was growing worse.

Sam Jackson clenched the clay pipe firmly in the corner of his mouth, as he and Hugo between them fought to keep the ship upright. They had been in bad storms many times, but the wind and the rain were torrential, and Sam wondered just how much the *Savannah Lady* could take. The sailors battled with the rigging, and tackle that was strewn across the deck slid from one side to the other.

Hugo could see the Captain flinging his arms about, his mouth moving; but the orders he gave were unheard by the men as they slipped and slithered, unable to get a good foothold on the slippery deck as the mountainous waves washed over them, and the thunder rumbled and forked lightning cracked across the sky. The rain lashed down, stinging bare backs, and the wind tossed the ship like a cork; she creaked and groaned under the impact of the waves, as a bolt of lightning streaked across the sky and crackled as it hit the water, followed by a rumbling, and then the most tremendous clap of thunder, which shook her very timbers. So close overhead was it that Hugo ducked, almost losing his grip on the wheel, and as the lightning flashed again, he saw the most enormous wave curl over the deck. The *Lady* groaned in pain, men were flung over the side, and there were screams of pain as a cannon broke loose, sliding down the deck, crushing four men against the bulkhead then sliding over the side into the raging sea, leaving a gaping hole in her balustrade as another huge wave caught her broadside.

In a flash of lightning he saw the reef, the black shining jagged rock which loomed up one minute and down under the waves again. He shouted to Sam Jackson, his words lost, it was too late, and there was a creaking and grinding as her hull struck the coral stone, and above the tumultuous uproar Hugo saw and heard the terrified screams of men as the main mast fell, crushing them and entangling them in the rigging. Some slid down the slanting deck to certain death into the raging Caribbean Sea, as the next huge wave came, washing her on to the reef again. The wheel spun fast, and Sam Jackson was flung over the side.

Hugo hung on to the wheel as the deck slid from beneath his feet, and a rope caught around his wrist, binding his left hand tightly to the spoke of the wheel. He heard his own voice screaming out in pain as he dangled, held only by the rope around his wrist, the weight of his body tightening the rope. He felt the snapping of his wrist bone as the waves tipped the *Lady* hard over to port, completely on her side, and his body now swung and slithered from side to side, as he desperately tried to get a foothold; but with each pounding of the thunderous waves he hung free, dangling by his broken wrist. Another tremendous crash of thunder, and lightning lit up the sky; he saw Jack clinging to a rope. He screamed out his name and his voice wafted away into the wind and rain, and his wrist snapped, leaving his hand clutching the spoke, and his body slipped down the vertical deck into the raging torrent. He heard his own scream ringing in his ears, and water filled his lungs as he went deeper and deeper and the Caribbean Sea enclosed him forever.

Robert came out of his daydream as he heard Andrew calling his name, and all thoughts of Jack Barneby were gone.

Andrew was pointing up onto the hillside to where the shadow of the tall palms seemed to make a cross. Robert started to follow the others as they walked across the deserted road, Andrew's two men bringing up the rear, each carrying a shovel.

The hill was steep and grassy; they had to clamber over a few boulders and sharp coral stone rock – luckily they were wearing trainers. The climb was not too difficult, but the heat was exhausting as they made their way slowly and roughly to the centre of the cross; they had counted about two hundred paces and stood together in a group.

'Well, now what?' said Andrew, looking around him. 'This should be the place. What does it say, Gary, you have the poem written down – 400 hundred paces was it, to where the palms cross?'

Gary checked the paper, 'Yes, but I have only counted a hundred and ninety something.'

'I made it one ninety-eight,' said Richard.

'Two hundred,' said Nick.

They all agreed that they had made it roughly 198 to 200.

'Yes, that is what I made it,' Andrew nodded. 'But I had

already counted roughly two hundred paces from that big round rock down there back to the car. I guess they had to start from somewhere, and if we are in the right place, it must be somewhere near here.'

Gary looked down at the paper again, and read through the rhyme. 'Yes, it does say twenty score, that's four hundred paces, and it says from rock to rock, but which is the rock up here?'

They all looked around them; it seemed all grass, one or two coral stone rocks, but nothing that stood out as a landmark. Above them black-bellied sheep grazed on the hillside; they looked like goats, with flat black and tan coats and lopped ears. One looked down at them with its sad eyes, but it did not seem to mind that they were there and it went back to chewing the grass, the others quite unaware that they were being watched. Higher still on the hilltop, seagulls swooped and swirled their high-pitched cries eerie in the quietness. The hillside had a desolate and lonely feeling, a strong warm and salty wind swept through the long grass with a rustling sound; no one spoke. Looking down far below, they saw two thin and bony brown cows walking lazily at the side of the road near the minibus; they looked small from this height. Richard was the first to speak.

'Well, where do we start?'

'Well,' Andrew clicked his tongue uncertainly, and drew in a breath. 'Well, we are here under the shadow of those palms,' he rubbed his chin, turning to look about him, 'and I reckon this is roughly four hundred paces. So let's all poke about here and see what we can find; it has got be a rock that stands out.'

They all agreed and began walking round, kicking their feet in the grass, no one really knew what they were looking for. Duncan and Mike dug shovels into the grass, but all they struck was coral stone rock.

It was hot on the hillside, and Mike sat down on a rounded rock and took off his baseball cap and ran his arm across his balding head; his plump red face streamed with perspiration. 'Well, I don't think there's anything here, Andrew. We seem to have covered almost every rock, and there is nothing.'

'I think you are right,' Nick nodded wearily, putting his

hand to his aching back. It wasn't easy standing on a steep slope; he pulled himself up to his full six foot height, and then plonked himself down heavily on a rock beside Mike. 'I think we had better call it a day, Andrew, I need a drink,' he swallowed hard.

'That's a good idea,' they all agreed. Richard looked at his watch. 'Yes, I think we should give it up, Andrew. Let's come back again tomorrow, the girls will be waiting for us – we promised to take them out for dinner, and the light is fading.'

They agreed to come back the next day, and started to make their way slowly back down the hill to the minibus. Duncan got behind the wheel and drove them back to the museum where Richard had left his car, then the four drove back to White Lady Cottage.

High on the hill Andrew stopped. They were roughly where they had been the previous day. Mike leaned hard on the shovel, dumped the bag off his shoulder, and took out a bottle of Cola. 'Good job we brought a drink with us today,' he said. He took the cap off his head, wiped the sweat from his bald head, then replaced the cap. 'Thank goodness there is a bit of a breeze too.' He was quite fit for his 57 years, but he was a big man and the climb had taken its toll.

Richard was also swigging from a bottle. 'We need a breeze.' He pulled a face, the drink was warm. 'Where do you think we should start, Andrew?'

Nick shaded his eyes from the blazing sun and pushed his sunglasses up on to the bridge of his nose, as he looked up to the top of the hill. 'I suppose we are looking for an outstanding looking rock, aren't we, Andrew?'

'Yes!' Andrew nodded. 'I think so. I counted from that large round rock yesterday, and I think this must be roughly the spot, don't you? It did say from rock to rock, didn't it?'

Everyone agreed that they were looking for a rock. There were a lot of rocks scattered around them, but they knew that it had to be something a bit unusual.

'There are hundreds of rocks over here,' called Duncan. He was poking about in the grass, further away from the group, and his voice echoed off the quiet hillside.

'It must be a special rock,' Andrew called back, raising his voice. 'And it must be marked in some way.'

'How many paces did you make it up here, Richard, I mean from the beach?'

'Well, today I made it two hundred,' said Richard.

'I made it two hundred and two,' said Robert.

'Me too,' Nick nodded.

'And me,' Gary put in.

Andrew nodded biting his lip. 'I made two hundred, but we had to go around those gorse bushes, didn't we? How many paces do you think we took going around them? And we must still be in a straight line, we can't be much out. We are roughly in the same place as we were yesterday, but you know I think we must be too low. Let's go up a few paces.'

'I think you are right,' said Gary. 'It must have been at least six or eight paces round the gorse bush, maybe even ten. I think you are right, we haven't come far enough.'

Mike called to Duncan and signalled that they were going up a bit. Duncan waved back and came quickly towards them.

'Find anything?'

'No,' said Andrew, 'but I think we are too low.'

'Well, we are in the same spot as we were yesterday,' said Duncan, 'because those are the same three round rocks where Mike and Nick sat down.'

'Three round rocks?' Andrew frowned. 'What? Three rocks, together? All the same size, where?'

'Just over there, you can't really see them clearly, they are sort of in the grass, and there is a wall of rocks above them. I should think there has been a rock fall at some time or other.'

They followed Duncan; the whole group stood together, looking at the pile of smallish rocks which seemed to take a cone shape. At the foot of this three larger round rocks stood a little apart; over the years the grass had grown over them.

'I don't think that they look natural, do you?' asked Andrew. 'This lot look as if they have been piled up, and if they had fallen, surely these three would not have landed right here together; and they are all exactly the same size. No,' he shook his head, 'they are not natural, they have been placed here. What do you think?' He looked at one and then the other; they all considered.

'And all very round, and the same size. No,' Rob shook his head, 'it doesn't look like a rock fall, does it?'

Richard bent forward. 'Let's see if we can move a couple of these smaller ones'

Andrew turned to Mike and Duncan, 'See if you two can get a spade under them.'

Mike and Duncan dug spades into the solid rocks.

'No,' said Mike, 'it's solid, it's been there forever.'

'Wait a minute,' said Duncan. 'There is a bit of movement here; what we need is more leverage. If we all got something and tried to get underneath it, we might do it. That is, of course, if you think we are on to something, Andrew. What do you think?'

'Well, I am not totally convinced, but it does seem strange, a cone-shaped pile of rocks and three identical ones at the bottom. Seeing as we are looking for a marker, I think it would be worth a try.'

'Yeah, let's give it a try,' said Gary, 'there are lots of pieces of wood around. Let's see if we can find some really solid bits and all have a go together.'

They began poking around in the grass for pieces of wood or rock which they could hold, or anything they could get to wedge under the rock which Duncan had eased. It was hard work in the heat of the morning, and it took them a long time, but eventually the rock began to move a fraction, and they stopped for a breather. Then they started again, and eventually they managed to lever the rock and prise it free.

They were all exhausted, but Robert laid down on his stomach and tried to peer into the gaping hole. He could not see anything, so he sat back like the others to get his breath and cool off a little from his efforts. There was a sound and they all looked towards the hole as the rocks began to slip a little.

'Well, let's just have one more go, now that we have got our breath back, shall we?' said Nick. 'Let's have a go at the top,' he pointed the stick which he was holding up to the top of the pile of rocks. 'They look a bit smaller up there, maybe they will be easier to move. Don't forget, the whole weight is probably bearing down on these,' he pointed the stick again at the bottom of the pile where they had removed one.

Andrew looked at them. 'Are you game, guys?' they nodded.

Robert looked at Nick. 'That's a fine, solid stick you've got there, Nick, where did you find that? It looks like a leg bone.' He laughed; suddenly it went quiet and they all looked at the stick in Nick's hand.

'I believe you are right,' Nick gasped as he held it in two hands, looking down at it. He grimaced. 'It is, you know, it's probably the leg from one of those sheep.'

'Let me look.' Andrew took it from him and examined it with a professional eye. It was black from years embedded in the earth, green from age and grass-stained. He turned it over and over in his hands, and suddenly said, 'It's a human bone, a shin bone.' His eyes lit up; he looked at Nick eagerly. 'Where did you find it?' His mind jumped automatically to a body – maybe he would have another exhibit for the museum.

Nick looked around him a little bewildered. 'Well, I don't really know. Umm, down there I think.' He pointed a little way below where they were standing.

Andrew started a few paces down the hill, the bone still in his hand, looking around and kicking his feet about in the grass. Nick followed him and said, 'It was somewhere about here, I think.' The others gradually wandered down, looking about them in the grass.

Andrew was on his knees, scraping at the earth.

'Find anything?' Nick called. 'Want some help?'

Andrew looked up. 'I don't know; come and look at this.'

Nick went down on his knees beside Andrew, and looked at the white dome-shaped piece of rock that he had scraped around. Rob came near, then Gary, followed by Duncan, Richard and Mike; they were now all looking down at Andrew as he scraped away at the dry, hard and parched earth, revealing a white smooth rock.

'What is it?'

'I don't know, but it's not coral stone. It's too smooth. I think it might be a skull.'

'What?' exclaimed Nick, sitting back on his heels; he took his hands away quickly, not wanting to touch it, as Robert bent down beside them.

'A skull,' he said. 'Do you really think it might be a skull? Do you think someone has died up here, of the heat?'

'Do you think someone has been murdered up here?' Duncan

was looking over Andrew's shoulder, trying to see what he was doing.

'Well, if someone was murdered,' said Andrew, 'it was a damn long time ago.' He had nearly scraped away most of the dusty earth. He now got his fingers under the object and eased it gently out of the ground. They all took an intake of breath as Andrew held the top half of a human skull in his hands.

'Could it be a monkey?' asked Richard.

'No,' Andrew shook his head gently. 'No, no. It is human,' and he held it in his hands as if it was so precious and delicate. He laid it gently down in the grass and began to scrape into the dry dust again. Just below the surface he began to uncover more white bone. They all began to scrap away in the dust. Andrew suddenly said, 'Stop!' as Mike was about to dig into it with a spade.

'I think we might disturb something special here. I think we should get Tom Blakeney and his crew up here, don't you?' He looked at Mike. 'I think this skull is very old, and as we are here looking for treasure, this could quite possibly be one of the pirates.'

Mike nodded. 'I think you are right, Andy. Let Tom Blakeney sort it out, his crew are experts at this sort of thing.'

'Who is Tom Blakeney?' Richard asked, giving Robert an enquiring glance, and then turned back to Andrew, who was still sitting on the grass beside his precious skull.

'He is the guy who looks into civilizations through their material remains,' he smiled. 'In other words, he is an archaeologist, and I would suspect that this skull is hundreds of years old. He and his team will come up here and excavate everything properly; we might damage something, but he will uncover a whole skeleton or even more if they are pirates and they killed each other, which is more than likely.'

Andrew marked the spot by putting a handkerchief over the place where the half skull had come out and placing four heavy stones at each corner, so that the wind would not blow it away. Then he turned the Cola bottles out of his bag and placed the half skull and the leg bone into the bag. They then counted six strides up the hill back to the three round rocks, and began the task of trying to remove them again, as Andrew seemed more sure than ever that this must be the place of the treasure. They worked hard, managing to move a few of the rocks, but they made slow progress, and the heat of the mid-morning sun exhausted them; but after almost an hour, they had made a fair-sized hole. Robert climbed up and looked down into it.

'Looks like a cave,' he said, 'can't see anything. It's too dark.' He was standing on the smaller rocks about four feet off the ground; suddenly they started to roll under his weight, and he jumped clear as they fell. There was a shout from Duncan, and they all scattered sideways as they watched the rocks roll down the hillside with a thunderous rumble. Mike had a fit of coughing, and when the dust cleared they stood looking into the gaping entrance of the cave.

Richard wafted the dust away from his face as he neared the entrance to the cave. They were all shaken by the sudden rock fall, then Rob and Gary moved closer. Andrew followed, and then Nick, Mike and Duncan. They stood in silence, peering into the darkness.

'Can't see anything, can you?' said Robert. No one answered. Then he moved forward, ducking his head, and took a couple of steps inside. Gary followed him, and they went in a little deeper.

'We can stand up in here.' Rob's voice was hollow in the darkness. Richard walked in, but they couldn't see anything. 'I wonder how far it goes back?' Duncan took a step forward, putting up his hand as he almost hit his head. 'The roof gets lower here.'

Gary snapped on his lighter, and they could see that it was just a very small cavern; there was not much depth.

Duncan, who was the tallest, was down on his knees, unable to stand. 'Put the light down here, I think I can see something.' Gary bent down and went forward, holding the lighter, crawling on his hands and knees.

'Its a sea chest!' They all heard the excitement in Duncan's voice, and 'Ouch!' as he hit his head on the low roof.

'Yes,' Gary called out, 'it's here. It's a chest, but God knows how they ever got it in here.' The lighter went out, he flicked it and flicked it. 'Anybody got a light?'

Mike produced a box of matches and struck one. It didn't last long, and they were in darkness again.

'Give us some more light,' called Gary, 'and hurry up, it's stifling in here.'

Mike struck another match, and Nick went outside and came back with a dry palm branch.

'Here, try lighting this.' It took a long time to catch, and then went out again.

'Let's tie this handkerchief round it,' said Richard, already binding the handkerchief round the end of the stick and knotting it tight like a bandage. 'Anybody got another one?' Andrew gave him one, and he bandaged it over the top.

'Hurry with the light!' shouted Gary.

'Hang on,' Richard shouted back as Mike put a match to the handkerchief. Nick held the stick low and forward giving them enough light to see. 'This is a good idea.'

Richard grinned. 'I used to be a Boy Scout.'

'I wish I had thought to bring a torch,' said Andrew, 'but I thought we would be digging treasure out of the ground.'

'We can't move this thing,' Gary called, 'it's solid, and there is hardly any headroom. God knows how they got it in here, we can't budge it.'

'Throw that rope in,' Duncan's voice came back hollow and strained out of the darkness, 'I left it outside there somewhere.'

Mike went out and came back with the rope and threw it in to where Gary and Duncan sat on their knees, with their heads bowed, in the flickering light. Duncan reached for the rope, they tied one end to one of the handles on the chest, and they crawled back out.

'Hell, it's hot in there.' Gary wiped the sweat from his head and took a deep breath.

Duncan followed him, holding the end of the rope. 'It's far too heavy to move, and I suggest that if we all pull on the rope, we may be able to move it. It's an old wooden sea chest, I think; it's hard to tell. You know the type with iron bands around it, I think, but och ... is it heavy and the roof is too low.

They all took hold of the rope and pulled. They could feel the chest moving. They pulled again and hung on like a tug-o-war. It took about five minutes and finally they pulled the chest out into the first sunlight it had seen for over 200 years.

They sat one behind the other, still holding the rope, puffing and laughing, and sweating and getting their breath back. Then they excitedly got up and knelt down around the dark brown oak chest, with its two black and rusty iron bands across the domed lid which was covered in coral dust and cobwebs.

Andrew tried to open it, but the lock was bound with rusty metal, and was impossible to move with his hands.

Mike carried a strong Swiss Army knife with all the gadgets on it. He gave it to Andrew, who managed to free the lock. Andrew looked round at them all with a satisfied smile, then slowly lifted the lid, the hinges creaking with dry rust.

They waited in silent anticipation and then gasped, looking down into the wooden chest, revealing its secret and seeing the light of day for over two centuries. Andrew picked up the yellow faded paper which lay on the top, and unfolded it. He read: 'Sorry Hugo, you have sailed far, but my need for gold is more than yours. Jack'. They sat in fits of laughter looking at the old rusty anchor.

Down in the museum workshop, Andrew, Mike and Duncan were busy analyzing the letter written by Jack Barneby. They looked into the handwriting, ink and paper with magnifying glasses, and decided between them that it was definitely dated around 1700.

Andrew also had a team of contractors with a bobcat up on the hillside to bring the heavy chest down, and had sent Mike Jennings and Duncan with them to supervise the operation. He had given the company strict instructions to be extremely careful, and the chest was now in the workshop; it would be cleaned and the wood preserved, and then put on display.

Andrew had contacted the archaeologist Tom Blakeney; he had been up there with him and shown him the place where they had found the bones, and come away leaving Tom and his team scratching around in the grass with small brushes. Tom had since then phoned Andrew, to say that they had unearthed the rest of the skeleton, and they had also found another skeleton; part of the rib bones were sticking up out of the ground, and he was surprised that one of them had not found it. The skull had broken away from this body, and rolled further down the hill. They had uncovered leather belts with buckles, and a gold chain, which had obviously been around the neck, plus a ring, maybe an earring. They had also found a pick axe and a spade nearby. He said that it was getting interesting and that they were still searching.

Andrew had laid the letter flat into a plastic folder to protect it. The half skull and the leg bone which Nick had used as a lever had been put carefully down in the corner next to the damaged figurehead, where it was waiting to be cleaned and treated with preservatives before going on display in the showroom. He thought he would display it in a large glass case, as he now had several pieces from the *Savannah Lady*, and also a ghost story, which he would have properly written up and displayed alongside.

Andrew pushed the buttons on the phone, and Richard answered. 'Hello, Richard, I wanted to ask you about the guys that do the ghostbusting. When are they coming? I should like to come over and bring a camera, if that is OK with you? I might bring Duncan.'

'Yes, sure, I will let you know. I'll get Nick to contact them, but I don't know if you will get any pictures. The guys that do the ghostbusting have the most sophisticated camera equipment, but they got nothing. I told you he sent me a disk, didn't I? I will let you hear it when you come over, it's not very good but it is something.' Andrew said he would pop over, and they rang off.

Clive Marshall was pleased to hear from Nick Cotton again, and he relished another week in the sunny Caribbean. He told Nick that they had just had four weeks in Ireland, trying to contact a lady in a green dress who roamed round a tower in a large country house, leaving windows wide open. 'Of course, it had to be a green dress for Ireland. But we were lucky enough to get a sighting, and the people who live in the house have not had any more ghostly experiences so far.' He said that it had been bitterly cold and raining all the time while they were there, and that a spell in the Caribbean was just what they needed, and that they could try and get a flight tomorrow.

Nick explained that Tim and his parents were arriving and that they did not want to miss anything, so if he could arrange a flight and be ready to start working on Monday evening, it would be great. Clive rang off, then Nick dialled the number and spoke to Richard, telling him the arrangements.

On Monday evening they were all assembled on the verandah of White Lady Cottage. Robert and Richard were pouring drinks while they waited for the Spooks team to arrive. Sue and Peter had arrived in the afternoon. Sue, as usual, was chatting away saying how nice it was to be back here in the warm, as it had been such terrible weather in England, cold and wet. She held out her glass for more wine as Richard came close with the bottle.

Belinda and June, standing together, both admitted that they were a little apprehensive at the thought that they might see a ghost, but also both said that they were a bit excited about it anyway.

'Did you actually see a man, Rob, or was it just a shadow?' June was asking as he came over to fill up their glasses.

'Yes,' he smiled, 'definitely a man. I told you, Belinda, it was a pirate, and there was no doubt about it. If Clive can get him back again you will see. And stop worrying, you both look as if you had seen a ghost.' He laughed. 'Sorry, I didn't mean that, just a figure of speech.'

'Oh, you will find it quite fascinating.' Sue had been standing close by and overheard. She was bubbling over with excitement.

Tim shouted, 'They're here!'

Sue jumped, spilling her drink, and her hand went to her throat in alarm. 'Gosh! I thought he meant the ghost!'

June laughed. 'Well, I shall have to see it to believe it.'

Richard and Nick went forward to greet Clive and the team, and gathered round watching as Clive unpacked some of the latest recording equipment.

Tim was interested in Ian's new camera, and showed him the one that he had just bought, and asked which Ian thought was the best position for him to sit, in case anything happened, as he wanted to get the best shots.

Ian pointed to a spot, and said that he couldn't be sure if

Tim would get anything, as the last time he got a couple of smudgy pictures, which had not come to anything. But he showed him a snap of a carriage and horses which he had taken when they were investigating down in Devon the previous year. It was not a good photo, but you could make out a wheel and part of a horse. Ian said he was hoping for more this time, as the apparition of Barneby had been so clear when they had seen it the last time, and he should get better quality with his new camera.

Clive looked at his watch, it was almost midnight. He twisted the knob on the monitor and listened into the headset that he was wearing. He nodded to Ian, who nodded back to say that he was ready, and then called to Toni, who answered, 'I'm ready.' Steve's voice came from somewhere in the bushes.

The mumbling stopped almost immediately, and all eyes were fixed on the frangipani tree; their ears were strained for the slightest sound, and you could have cut the tension with a knife. Only the loud whistling of the night tree frogs, and the shushing of the sea as it rolled up on the beach filled the humid air.

Belinda looked up at the black velvet sky, studded with a million stars. The moon was just peeping through a cloud, and in the stillness a bat flew high and swooped low over the garden. June ducked, but it was not really so near, and then it swiftly disappeared into a tall mahogany tree.

Belinda turned to her right and smiled. June grimaced nervously and Gary, sitting next to her, saw the look and reached out for her hand.

Clive was about to give up. They had sat in silence for ages, when suddenly the needle on the monitor quivered and there was a rustling sound and whispering. They all looked at each other. Realizing that it was not any of them, they became alarmed and again sat with their ears strained and eyes wide.

The tension was unbearable. Petal was gripping Joseph's hand so tight that he winced.

Belinda felt a silent scream in her throat, her eyes fixed on the frangipani tree, and she felt for Rob's arm. He did not look at her, but squeezed her hand firmly.

The whispering continued and then something chinked – it sounded like metal, then a scraping sound like a sword being drawn, and then a swish.

Clive, now glued to the monitor, lifted his eyes only to glance at Ian. He then looked back at the monitor, the needle was quivering fast and then moved sharply to the right as a man's deep voice shouted, and everyone jumped. Sue lifted right off the chair; her heart was beating so loud she put her hand there and held it tightly. The tension was so great, she sat stiff, holding her breath, and the sound of her heart drumming in her ears was frightening.

Clive bent his head low over the monitor and put one hand to his ear, holding the headset closer, trying to get a clear reception, his eyes wide as he listened. The needle quivered, moving from left to right in one swift move, and stayed hard over to the right, and a roaring noise sounded around the garden and clear words, 'A CURSE ON WOMENFOLK!'

It went quiet, and they watched as a thin mist swirled across the garden and gathered like a white cloud, taking a human form, and the face of the figurehead appeared in a thick white swirling mist, then faded, the face disappearing into the white cloud. Then, before their unbelieving eyes, a pirate materialized, and there was a loud hushed intake of breath as Jack Barneby stood before them, dressed in a dark green frock coat, a three-cornered hat, golden yellow waistcoat, white frilly shirt and black pantaloons tucked into long black boots. His face appeared sun-bronzed, young and handsome in the dim lights which Clive had put round the garden. He stood six feet tall and broad-shouldered. He was not transparent, but appeared solid as any other man, and at his side the stones on the hilt of the magnificent sword glittered, and the jewelled dagger sparkled from his leather belt; beside it he carried a heavy flintlock pistol.

Tim sat mesmerized, holding his breath, his eyes so wide it was hurting. He was taking in every detail, and he suddenly remembered that he was holding his camera. He was afraid to move in case he missed something, but then he lifted the camera and began flashing away, hardly waiting to focus, and then Jack Barneby suddenly lunged forward towards Alison and

Belinda, who cringed back in their chairs. To Tim it was so fantastic, looking at a man who had lived 270 years ago, looking tall and handsome and healthy, not a bit pale and gaunt or ghostly, not even frightening ... just a man, dressed as a pirate. A pirate, as he had seen so many times in swashbuckling films.

Gary sat with his arm round June, he could feel the stiff tension in her body. He was afraid to take his eyes off the figure before him, but he did manage a quick glance over June's head at Tim, and he smiled to himself. He knew that Tim would never get over this. When he looked back Barneby was pulling the sword from the scabbard – there was no metallic sound, but he noticed how the stones glittered. He had a quick flash thought of the time when they had first found it and Tim was swishing it about down in the cellar.

Now Jack Barneby was swishing the sword in front of him. He pointed it at them and bellowed in a deep voice, 'ATTACK!' He spat out the word loud and clear, and lunged forward, brandishing the sword and swishing it over Alison and Belinda, who jumped back. Robert grabbed at Belinda, and Richard and Nick grabbed at Alison as her chair almost toppled over; the sword seemed to go right through the three of them. Richard felt a shiver run through his body.

'Richard.' Alison's voice was a tiny squeak as she hunched up her shoulders in fright, grabbing at his arm.

'Death to all women,' Barneby's deep voice bellowed clear into the night, as the mist seemed to engulf him, and he wafted away into the trees. There was total silence, but the sound of his voice seemed to ring through the garden long after he had gone.

No one moved, no one dared to breathe, and then there came the sound of boots, walking and metal, which could have been knives chinking together, or coins clinking. They listened, and then it faded away and their ears felt heavy with tension ... the whistling of the frogs was the only sound in the tropical night.

Clive was the first to move. He took off his headset with a satisfied grin.

Toni came hurrying out of the bushes, flinging his arms into the air with excitement, yelling, 'Yahooo, we got it, we got it!'

Clive turned to Richard, who still seemed in a stunned trance. 'Wow! That was great, wasn't it?' He had a huge smile on his face. 'Didn't you think that was just great, eh?' He looked at each and every one of them, but still no one had moved, they sat in stunned amazement.

'Well, I have shot a whole roll of film,' said Ian. 'Let's hope that we have got something.'

They all slowly began to move, stretching their backs and their arms, as if waking from a long sleep, and suddenly everyone was talking at once.

'I hope I got some pictures,' Tim said excitedly to Ian. 'Wasn't it fabulous? I don't even know if I had the camera focused, I was so enthralled with it all.'

'Well, I can't believe what I have just seen,' said Nick. 'It seemed to go on for ever. How long did it last, Clive?'

Clive checked the monitor. 'Ninety seconds; a minute and a half.'

'I can't believe it,' Alison was shaking her head. 'A minute and a half, it seemed like a film.'

Steve Palmer came up the garden path. 'Christ, what a sight. Blimey ... I never saw a sight like that before, it must have been the best we've ever done, don't you think so, Clive? How long did it last?'

'Ninety seconds. Yeah, I think it was the best.' Clive smiled, and looked round the garden. The moon had come out, everything was still, and the only sounds were the whistling of the frogs and the shushing of the sea, and a sobbing, as Petal clung to Joseph.

'It not right, it not right. He come back, Joseph, it voodoo, an I is scared. It ain't right,' she sobbed and sobbed into Joseph's chest. He tried to comfort her, talking to her gently and kissing her hair. 'Petal, Petal. It OK, it OK...' he whispered.

Alison came and tried to help. 'Look, Petal, it can't hurt you. It's not real, and we are doing this to try and get rid of Barneby. It's too eerie, none of us like it. Take her into the kitchen, Joseph, and make her a cup of tea; in fact, make us all one.'

Alison moved across the verandah to where Clive, Toni and Peter stood together. 'Did you say, Clive, that we might have seen the last of our ghostly friend? I hope so, as it is not comfortable living here with him hanging around. I must say that it doesn't worry me as much as it did, but it is still a very eerie feeling. Personally, I don't think Jack Barneby will ever leave this place; it seems he had been here for years, and it is the first time anyone has tried to do anything about it. The people around here are afraid of the White Lady and the wailing, such as Petal and Joseph for instance. Joseph's mother, Selena, even died because of the Lady, and still no one has tried to find out why, or do anything about it until you arrived, Clive. But then I suppose they couldn't afford to do anything, could they?'

Richard put the empty drinks tray on the table. 'Yes, I can't understand it. People have just listened to the wailing and the screaming in the night over many years and just cringed in their beds, afraid even to try and find out what has caused it.' Clive nodded, and Richard went on. 'They say that she only wails when a ship is in trouble out there on the reef, but we have never seen a ship in trouble out there, in fact, I don't think anyone had ever seen a ship out there, do you, Alison?'

'No...' she took a deep breath, 'it seems that I am the only one who has seen the sail, but Nick did say that he thought he saw a sail out there the night of the storm. It could really have been any ship, but there was not one in trouble on the reef or we would have heard of it on the news or in the papers, wouldn't we?'

Richard bit his bottom lip. 'What do you think about getting it exorcised, Clive?'

'I don't really know, but seeing as we had such a full and clear apparition here tonight, I think it most probably will go away. Of course, I am not completely sure of that, but there was a lot of energy there.'

'Well,' Alison smiled, 'after seeing him there tonight, I think it would be a shame to see him go, but we can't possibly live like this, can we? When we come away on holiday, we want to relax.'

'Well, I think you can tonight,' Clive smiled.

'Yes, what's left of the night.' Richard looked at his watch, 'It's four o'clock in the morning.'

* * *

The next morning Clive arrived on his own, about nine. Nick, John and Peter had come across the beach and now all the men were standing together, looking at the frangipani tree. It looked so peaceful in the morning sunlight: the garden was quiet, and the birds were singing, and there was nothing to show the events of the night before, except for the empty chairs and cushions where they had sat and experienced a most fascinating and alarming sight.

'Is there anything to show where he appeared?' said Tim, looking further into the tree and the bushes around it. 'I remember the last time there were a lot of gold sparkles, but I don't remember seeing any last night, do you? You would think that the ground would be burnt, wouldn't you?'

'No,' Clive answered him. 'I was just looking for that, but there are no scorch marks, no fallen branches, or even any sign of the grass being flattened, there's nothing.'

'And yet it all seemed so real,' Richard had a surprised look, shaking his head.

The day went on in the usual lazy way. They walked on the beach and swam in the sea, the men went to play nine holes of golf. Petal cooked a light lunch, and in the evening Nick booked a restaurant for them all and they went out to dinner. They were back by eleven o'clock, and when they arrived Clive and the Spooks Men had already set up their equipment.

Clive introduced a Mrs Dahl to Richard. 'I hope that you won't mind,' he said, 'but Cheetra is a medium, recommended to me by the priest. I went to see him about the exorcism, he said to try Cheetra first. He was sure she could help, as she had helped with this kind of thing in the past. She may be able to talk to this spirit for you, and send him away.'

Cheetra Dahl looked up at Richard with a smile. 'I hope that I will be able to help you, Mr Price.' She was a small and very petite Indian lady, dressed in a brown, red and orange sari. She had dark brown eyes which shone with enthusiasm, and her thick black hair was tied up into a shiny bun at the nape of her neck. She wore large golden earrings which dangled nearly to her shoulders, and rings on most of her slender fingers.

'I think I may be able to contact this spirit and talk to it. Mr Marshall has explained to me about the wailing and about the White Lady, which you no longer have here, but we do have to feel sorry for these unwanted spirits sometimes – poor souls, they are unable to rest. Sometimes talking to them can help both sides and we can find out what makes them so troublesome.'

Richard had his doubts and saw the smirk on Rob's face as he looked over the head of the tiny Cheetra Dahl. But then he turned his attention back to her and said, 'Well, anything is worth a try. We can't carry on like this, even though we are getting used to it. This terrible wailing must have been going on for years, and no one has ever tried to find out why it happens or what it is, and I must say that it is certainly very nerve-racking.'

Petal offered Clive and his team soft drinks while they were waiting for everyone to return from the restaurant. She also met Mrs Dahl, who asked if she might have an armchair to sit in when she tried to contact the dead.

'The dead!' Petal looked scared. Clive jumped in quickly and said 'Spirit'. He smiled, and Petal went away to ask Joseph to take the large carver chair out from the dining room. Andrew arrived with Mike, Duncan and Pete.

They were about ready to start; it was midnight and everyone took their places. Cheetra Dahl sat a little apart from them all in the large armchair with its high back, which made her look very small.

They waited and waited in total silence, much the same as they had done the night before. Cheetra sat with her eyes closed and her fingertips on her temples, and concentrated as hard as she could.

Suddenly they heard a low moan and what sounded like the shuffling of boots. It seemed to come from the direction of the frangipani tree, and then from the bottom of the garden. The moaning got louder, then there was the terrible wailing again.

Petal, who was terribly afraid, clung to Joseph, her large brown eyes wide as she watched, praying hard that none of them would come to any harm and thinking on what the Mistress had said about it not being real. But the wailing got to such a pitch that she pulled away from him and put her fingers into her ears.

Everyone's nerves were tense; they waited and waited for the mist as they had seen it last night and for Jack Barneby to appear. They heard words, but they were slurred and difficult to understand, like a badly tuned radio.

Clive turned the knobs tuning in the monitor, as the sound got worse, he tried to adjust it. Then through the wailing came another voice. Everyone tensed and strained their ears, trying to make out the new voice, and the screaming and wailing gradually calmed down to a low moaning, and then dead silence.

A voice said loudly, 'Jack'. They all looked around. The voice came from Cheetra Dahl, then there was a long silence. Cheetra sat very still, she said, 'Hugo', but her voice had changed to a deep growl. 'Hugo!' The voice was deep, loud and clear. There was a draught which blew across the garden; it rustled the leaves in the trees, it swirled around the frangipani and a slight mist seemed to rise from the ground. As it got thicker, Jack Barneby appeared, just as if a television had been turned on. He was having a conversation with someone, but the words were incoherent, muffled and muddled. Then a sharp word. 'JACK!' All heads turned as one, to look at Cheetra. She was breathing heavily, but she had not moved; and then they turned back to Barneby. A mist was gathering near him, and another figure came through, very faintly at first.

Tim gasped in a loud whisper, 'It's Hugo Fotheringay! Look!' No one answered him, but his eyes were popping out of his head with excitement. He gripped the chair to stop himself from jumping up and rushing forward.

'JACK!' The voice came loud and clear from Cheetra; it was short and sharp, and the two figures then began to fade into the mist and were gone. Cheetra was breathing heavily, every muscle in her thin and fragile body seemed strained. In her own voice now, she was saying, 'Go. Go. Why can you not rest in peace?' It seemed then that she was listening to something. 'But I command you to go ... rest ... rest...' Then she gave a short sharp gasp, and jumped as if she had been struck a forceful blow, slumping back into the armchair exhausted, her hands clutching at her heart.

There was a shocked and tense stillness, then Belinda, who was the nearest to her, got up slowly and went to her. Just as she touched her hand, Cheetra sat up slowly, holding her head, then her eyes opened as if she was waking from a long sleep. Her eyes focused, seeing Belinda, and she said, 'Did anything happen?'

Andrew was still receiving things from the *Savannah Lady*, and his people in the workshop had been slowly and carefully cleaning and restoring each piece.

Duncan had polished the oblong silver box with much loving care to a brilliant shine, and it was amazing, after being under the sea for such a long time, how good it looked. The engraved rose and the letter 'H' on the lid were a little battered and so were the corners, but generally it was in good condition.

They had it now on display in a glass cabinet, with the sword and the dagger; the box was left open, showing the two gold cravat pins and gold doubloons. Andrew told Duncan that rich people often possessed doubloons from Spain, which were worth much more than any other gold coins; but these two were special, minted in America, and American doubloons were very rare – these two were bright and shiny and newly minted. They also had displayed beside the box the paper with the rhyme, laid flat for all to see and carefully protected with a plastic cover. The half-broken quill lay beside it, with a small card explaining that it had been written by Sir Hugo Fotheringay, a distinguished gentleman of great wealth and owner of an Oriental shipping fleet, who had turned to piracy, joining the notorious Jack Barneby on the ship the *Savannah Lady*.

Duncan had also polished the oak chest inside and out, and cleaned the iron baton of red rust. Pete had cleaned and polished the anchor, and they had put it back into the chest as they had found it. This had also been put in the display case with the lid open, and Jack Barneby's letter to Sir Hugo was laid flat in front of it, also in clear plastic.

There had been many visitors to the museum since it had all been on the television and great write-ups in the papers, with photographs of Captain Hanson and the salvage ship the *Four Winds.*

Andrew spoke to Robert on the phone, saying how amazed he was to have seen the apparition last night. He had been so enthralled by it all and it had happened so quickly, that he had just sat there mesmerized, but he was so pleased when Robert had said that Clive had phoned to say that Ian had got something, but he had not seen the photos as yet. Robert told him that if they wanted to come again, Clive would be there at eleven thirty. Andrew said they would come.

They were sitting waiting for Clive to say he was ready; Cheetra Dahl was comfortable in the armchair. Andrew had met Mrs Dahl some years ago, and had found her conversation very interesting. He asked her what she thought about the wailing, and why it always seemed to be about three o'clock in the morning.

'Well, I can't really say for sure, but I may be able to ask the spirit, if he is here again, but I must say in all my years of experience as a medium, that I have usually found that it is only one specific person who triggers off the spirit, and usually it is a child. Children seem to have psychic powers and can call up spirits, and they do not even know why they are doing it. Also, people with lively imaginations can quite often be very psychic.'

Alison listened to Cheetra with interest. 'Who could possible be calling up the spirit of this pirate? As far as we know, this wailing had been on going for years.'

Cheetra's deep red lipstick parted in a slow smile, showing a set of very white teeth.

'Well, I can't tell you that, but who do you think would have a lively imagination, and could trigger off such a phenomenon? If it has been happening for years, it is possibly someone who has stayed in this house. If it has happened in the night, it is possible for someone to dream and drum up a spirit. Maybe there are times when it doesn't happen. Do you know if this wailing goes on when you are away in England?

Or does it just start up when you arrive? Think about it ... I really cannot answer your question as to why anyone would want to contact a pirate.'

Alison said nothing, but she thought: Robert was young, maybe he was fascinated with pirates and dreamed about them; and then there was Gary, and then Tim, but he had only just arrived. But could any of them be psychic?

'How would you know if anyone was psychic?'

'Well,' Cheetra smiled, 'you wouldn't know. People just don't go about with "psychic" written on their foreheads. It might be someone who had seen something quite unexplained, and it is playing on their mind. That's the sort of thing that could trigger this sort of thing off.'

Alison's eyes widened. She said nothing, but she knew that she was the only one who had seen the ship. She began to have a worrying sensation in her stomach. It couldn't possibly be she who was awaking Jack Barneby, could it? Could it? She bit her lip and clenched her hands. She was about to mention it to Cheetra, but then Clive called to say he was ready to start.

They waited in anticipation, wondering what would happen this time.

Suddenly there was a terrific flash, and the crash that followed made them all jump with alarm; that is, all except Cheetra, who still sat with her fingers pressed to her temples, her elbows on the arms of the chair.

Someone swore. They held their breath, and then Steve came bursting out from the trees, holding his hand.

'What's happened?' Clive looked up in alarm as Steve pushed his way towards him, holding his hand, his face pained.

'I don't know,' he sounded breathless. 'Something pushed me from behind with such force, that I stumbled forward on the sound equipment and got an electric shock. I have burnt my hand. It's not much, but it gave me such a jolt.' He was shaking.

'Here,' said Richard, offering him his glass of wine, 'drink this. It might make you feel a bit better.'

Steve took the glass and sipped gratefully at the wine. His hands were shaking still, but as he sat down for a minute or two he said he felt better. 'I really don't know what pushed me, but it was a great force, and I never saw anything. I am sorry, Clive, but I am sure I have blown the sound recording gear at my end. You can carry on with Toni, but, of course, if anything shows you won't get the full force.'

'No, it's blown mine as well.' Toni got up off his knees and came out from the trees, throwing his hands up in a hopeless gesture.

They were alarmed at the sound of a roaring voice. It was coming from Cheetra Dahl. She sat shaking in the armchair, her fingers still pressed tightly against her temples and her eyes closed – then she began rocking back and forth violently.

'Death to all womenfolk,' she bellowed. Belinda grabbed at Rob's arm. Alison wrung her hands together. June and Sue grabbed at each other and Carol stood with her eyes wide and her hand clamped over her mouth. The men all just stood staring at Cheetra, and as they stared, fear in their faces, the shadow of Jack Barneby stood over her and seemed to engulf her whole body.

Ian lifted the camera and flashed it continuously.

'Death...' she moaned loudly in a deep voice that trailed away into a chilling whisper. She sat bolt upright; she seemed to be in his power. She stared straight ahead and sat very still, and then suddenly collapsed back into the chair, her mouth open and her eyes wide, staring up into the star-studded sky.

Nick moved cautiously towards her and put his hands under her head to support it, then Richard moved forward, standing in front of her, looking helpless as Alison and Carol knelt before her, each taking a hand and rubbing it, trying to bring her round; even with the humidity, she was cold.

'What's happened to her?' Richard was bewildered.

Nick looked up at Richard as the others gathered round. 'I think he has possessed her.' His voice was a hushed, bewildered whisper.

Suddenly Cheetra took a deep breath, moved her head, which Nick was still holding, and sat up slowly, blinking her eyes; she looked at them all in a dazed state.

They were relieved to see her move, but alarmed again when she narrowed her eyes and said 'Death to all womenfolk'. They all took a step back, alarmed at the deep growl in her voice. 'Death...' she breathed, and her voice trailed away weakly.

'She is possessed,' Clive said anxiously, his eyes wide with alarm. 'He's possessed her. Quick! Do something.'

'What can we do?' said Richard.

'We must bring her round,' said Alison anxiously, looking at Carol. They both began to rub her hands hard and roughly, trying to get some reaction. Richard patted her cheeks; her dark Indian complexion was pale and opaque.

'Slap her hard, Richard,' said Nick anxiously. Richard gave him a quick glance and decided that he could be right. He gave Cheetra a hard slap across the face.

'Ouch!' She sat straight up, holding her hand to her face, looking at Richard in surprise.

There was a gasp from them all as a thin mist seemed to surround her, and then wafted away into the dark, airless, humid atmosphere of the tropical night.

'What happened?' asked Cheetra in surprise, still holding her face. The colour was coming back into her cheeks, and she seemed perfectly normal again.

'I think he possessed you,' Clive said quietly. 'Do you remember? How do you feel?'

Cheetra beamed. 'No? Really? Did he? Barneby? That's wonderful,' she smiled round at them all, looking pleased with herself. 'You mean he really possessed me?'

'Wonderful?' Alison questioned with a frown. 'You think that it is wonderful to be possessed by a demon?'

'I don't know. What happened? What did I say? Did I change? Did you actually see him?' She seemed delighted. 'He was very violent, wasn't he? I know. I know from the way I feel.'

'Does this sort of thing happen very often?' Alison was still holding her hand and could feel her trembling.

Cheetra took a deep breath and pulled her hand away. 'It has only ever happened to me once before. I must say it is quite frightening, I think more so for you than for me. I seemed to know at the time what was happening. I could not describe the feeling, and it seems that I cannot really remember what I have said once I have come out of the trance. Did I say anything?' She suddenly realized that her face was stinging. 'Gosh, who hit me?' She put her hand to her cheek, then smiled.

'I did, I'm sorry.' Richard looked a bit sheepish. He glanced at Nick, then smiled. 'I was told to. For a moment, we thought you were dead.'

'Were you a boxer?' she smiled, holding her cheek.

'Yeah! Once only.' Richard grinned. 'But I got a good hiding, so I soon gave it up. Did the trick though, didn't it?'

They all relaxed, relieved to see that Cheetra had come to no harm, and began to make their way up to the cottage.

'Do you want a plaster for your hand?' Alison could see that Steve was looking at the burn across his palm.

'No, thank you. I think it will be OK, thanks. I think it was the shock more than anything; it did give me quite a jolt. But do you know, I can still feel that push in the back, as if someone gave me a good punch in the kidneys, but there was absolutely nothing there.'

'Maybe this is the last of him, then,' Cheetra was saying to Richard, 'maybe he has now used up all his source of energy. But I'll try again, perhaps tomorrow, if Mr Marshall is coming again.'

'Oh, no, no, certainly not.' Richard shook his head. 'I wouldn't put you through all that again. I think you have done enough, and you have no idea what a fright you gave us.'

'I am so sorry to have worried you, but I really must try again, now that it has come this far, I have to talk to this spirit,' she smiled.

Tim was feeling very excited. He could not stop talking about the events of the night. They had not gone to bed until five o'clock, long after the Spooks Men and Cheetra Dahl had left. They had all sat on the verandah in the moonlight.

Clive, Toni, Ian and Steve had also sat up for the rest of the night; they had endless cups of coffee in Clive's room. He had been very worried about Cheetra Dahl being possessed, and said that he thought it would be dangerous for her to try it again; but she had insisted, and they would try again if there was not too much damage to the recording equipment. Ian said that he hoped that he had got some pictures, as he had taken several of Cheetra during the possession. It was now eight o'clock, and they said that they were too tired for breakfast, so they each went to their rooms and slept until six in the evening. Then Toni and Steve got together and checked over the recording gear. They found that it was not as bad as they had thought and although there had been a huge flash, it had really only blown a fuse. They met for dinner, afterwards making their way to White Lady Cottage for another session.

Cheetra had already arrived and wanted to try again, although Richard had begged her not to do it. Clive had also said it was dangerous, but she was stubborn and said she must try for her own peace of mind, and they should not worry about her.

They went through the same routine again. The night was hot and humid and the tension hung heavy on their ears. They were now used to the waiting and nothing disturbed the stillness of the starry night, only the whistling of the tiny tree frogs.

Clive shifted his position, braced his shoulders and took a deep breath. The movement jolted the silence, and he said, 'I don't think we are going to get anything tonight,' and Cheetra, who had been concentrating hard, had to agree. And they decided that Barneby had hopefully gone to his rest at last and their services would no longer be required.

Over the next few days, they had mixed feelings about Jack Barneby. Richard was pleased to think that with the efforts of Clive and Cheetra Dahl together, it had not been a waste of time.

Tim said he hoped that he had got something on film to prove that it had all happened. He was longing to see Marie and tell her all about it; he had spoken to her every day on the phone, and wished she had been here to see it all. He also wished that he could see it over again.

Alison felt relieved; she also felt a bit sad, as if she had actually taken Barneby's life. She had said so to Richard and Rob. They both said that she was stupid to feel that way, and Robert reminded her that he had almost taken her life when he had enticed her into the sea; she agreed that he was right, but still felt uneasy about sending him away after all this time.

* * *

Clive and the team stayed on in the hotel for a few more days, enjoying the warmth of the Caribbean sunshine, and then took a flight to New York. Clive had received a message from his secretary in London, telling him that there was a job in a recording studio, where they were getting interference from ghostly voices on the discs, and there was no explanation for it, and it was ruining their business.

The days at White Lady Cottage went on as usual. Belinda and Robert cancelled their flights back to England, saying that they had to stay and see if anything else developed with Barneby; after all, Clive could not be really sure that he was gone. They decided to stay another week. Gary thought that was a good idea, and why shouldn't they stay for another week in the sun? If Barneby did come back, they wanted to be there.

Alison was sitting at the bottom of the coral stone steps with her easel set up. She had been there for about three hours and had just finished painting a fishing boat which was pulled up on the beach in front of her. She had also captured the two fishermen as they had lifted the cage off the boat; they had been out in the very early hours of the morning and dropped it into the sea, and there were dozens of lively fish jumping about, which, she suspected, by now they had sold on a market stall in the street. She added a little more blue paint to the stripe along the side of the boat, and sat back with a sigh, looking critically at her work.

Tim had been sitting on the step behind her, watching for about half an hour. 'That's very good, Ali, I wish I could paint like that.'

She turned and smiled. 'Thanks, Tim; you could paint, if you tried.'

'No, I wouldn't have the patience. It's too slow for me. You are a good artist.' He nodded gently. 'Quiet here this morning, isn't it? Where is everyone?'

'They're all over at Nick's, I think.' Alison wiped her brushes. 'And I think Belinda and June went to the shops.'

Tim sat with his elbows on his knees and his chin resting on his hands. 'I am glad that Rob and Gary cancelled their flight this week, or I would have been here on my own, just with Mum and Dad.' He sighed again. 'I wish Marie had come. I've missed her.'

Alison shut the paintbox lid. 'Well, I expect she has missed you too, but perhaps she'll come out next week. Why don't you give her a call?'

'Yes, I might do that,' he sighed, 'but I know she can't come.' He sat up, straightening his back. 'Oh, look!' He pointed out to the horizon. 'There's a sail boat out there, looks like a two-masted job.' He wrinkled his nose, holding his hand above his sunglasses. 'Looks a bit unusual, doesn't it? Look!'

Alison also shaded her eyes. 'Oh! My God, Tim!' She put her hand to her throat in alarm. 'It's the Galleon!' She jumped up and just managed to catch hold of her painting as the easel fell flat back onto the sand. 'Look, Tim! Look! Can you really see it?'

'Well, of course I can see it.' Tim had surprise in his tone. 'Yes, it looks like a galleon. I can see the sail and it certainly does look strange; must be a very old ship.'

'Yes, Tim, yes,' said Alison with nervous excitement. 'Yes, it is, it is. It's the same ship I have seen many times, and I am glad that you can see it too.'

Tim squinted. 'Maybe it's a ship that comes out of Bridgetown at certain times, and that's when you have seen it. It's probably the Jolly Roger – the galleon which goes up and down on day trips; it does a night cruise too, I think, and you have dinner on board.'

'No! No! I am sure it's not; it is not a normal ship... Look! Oh, it's gone.' She turned round and looked at him in despair.

Tim was still shading his eyes. 'Yes, it certainly seems to have disappeared, and I would say, from the height of the sail, it could not have gone over the horizon that quick.' He looked at her, surprised. 'It does seem strange ... it just disappeared, didn't it?'

'Oh, Tim,' she beamed, 'I am so glad that you have seen it.

I am sure that Richard thinks I am quite mad, I must tell him. Here, hold this.' She handed him the sketchpad, and started to rush along the beach towards Nick's cottage, calling over her shoulder, 'Tim, take my paints and things up, will you please?'

'How much?' asked Ian, holding a handful of American dollars to the girl over the counter.

The girl looked at the packet. 'There is nothing to pay, sir, nothing has come out. I think the film must have been faulty.'

The short round man standing behind the counter beside her looked over the top of his specs. 'Yes, I am sorry, sir, we do get faulty film sometimes ... hope it's not the end of your vacation,' he smiled. 'Hope you have time to take a few more. Would you like to buy a new film?'

Ian took the packet of photos from the girl and thanked her. He took them out of the packet and grinned, then looked at the couple behind the counter and beamed with delight.

'They're great, thanks. Fabulous!' He walked to the door, and as he opened it he smiled back at them, almost jumping for joy.

The girl looked at the man beside her and shrugged. Leaning over the counter, she called, 'Have a nice day.'

The man looked at her and grimaced. 'Well, I ain't never seen anyone so excited about a set of blurred and misty photos afore. Usually they complain like hell; looked like a lot of smoke to me. Ah well,' he shook his head and grimaced again. 'He's English...' he sniffed. 'Funny accent, though.'

She smiled. 'Perhaps he was photographing a fire.'

Fifth Avenue was busy with honking traffic; the cab stopped and started several times as busy shoppers crossed in front when the lights changed. At last the driver stopped outside the hotel. Ian sorted out the dollars for the cab fare, paid the driver and leaped excitedly out of the cab, slamming the door behind him. Darting and dodging, he passed people on the sidewalk. Almost running through the lobby, he pressed the button on the elevator, dancing impatiently from one leg to the other. The doors finally opened and he got out on the tenth floor, then banging on the door of 1014, he almost fell in as Clive opened the door.

'We've got him, we've got him!' He went excitedly down on his knees, quickly spreading the photos out on the floor.

Clive went down on his knee beside him. 'They are great,' he exclaimed, picking one up and then scanning the rest. 'Look at this one,' he held one up, 'it's almost a perfect face with eyes and nose. I have never seen anything like it.'

'Look at this one, then,' Ian handed it to him. 'It's got a frock coat and buttons, see, it even looks a bit green – and that is definitely part of a three-cornered hat. I know they are misty and smudgy, but they are good, don't you think? And, do you know, I got them for free! The girl even apologized because nothing has come out,' he laughed.

Clive went to the phone and called first Toni and then Steve, telling them to come down. He then called the reception and asked the young man there to book four seats the next day on a flight to Barbados. 'We are going back,' he smiled.

Alison was surprised to see them when they arrived at the cottage. They spread all the photographs out on the verandah table, and were looking at them when Nick and the rest of the party joined them.

'God, these are fabulous,' John was saying. 'Just look at this one: you can almost make out the whole figure.'

'But what is all this mist?' asked Alison. 'It didn't seem so misty when we watched, it appeared quite clear.'

'That is ectoplasm,' said Ian.

'What's ectoplasm?'

Clive answered. 'It's a misty cloud, as you can see; luminous, shiny and sometimes very dense and sticky. It's hard to explain, but it happens with apparitions; it always seems more dense in photos, when you get them back, of course. This is about as good as you will get. Ian has taken many films, but I don't think we have ever seen anything this good.'

They were all looking at him intently with puzzled looks, but he did not go on to explain any more about ectoplasm.

Nick was holding one up. 'Look at this one, with the hat and a face.' Tim looked over his shoulder. He was more fascinated than any of them, and hoped when he got his film back tomorrow that he would have something to boast about. He knew that his friends would never believe him. In fact, it was really a waste of time telling anyone about these experiences. He could remember when he had gone back to school and told them all about finding the sword, the only one who took him seriously was Old Smythe; the boys had just jeered, saying that he was kidding them. But if his pictures came out he would pop along to the college and see Old Smythe – he must still be there – and he would get a great kick out of seeing his face. If his photos did not come out, he would ask Ian for a set of these ... he would ask Ian for a set anyway.

Richard held up a photo; he turned it upside down and the right way up again. It was just a white cloud. In fact, that is what he thought it was, a white cloud. He passed it to Peter; Sue was looking over her husband's shoulder.

'Ooooh, look at that one,' she said. 'I wonder who she is? Looks like a woman in a white chiffon evening dress, doesn't it, Peter?'

'Where?' Alison looked over, taking the photo from Peter.

'Well, look there,' Sue pointed. 'See, amongst all that white mist, that looks like a woman's face, doesn't it?'

Alison gasped. 'Richard, look at this, this is what I saw that night.'

Robert looked over her shoulder. 'You mean the night you nearly got drowned? I'll never get over that night either, it gave me such a fright. I have never been so worried in my life.'

Richard took the photo from her, looking at the thick white cloud. He turned it this way and that and said, 'It must be the White Lady.'

'It can't be,' said Nick, 'she is not here.'

'How can it be?' said Gary.

'Let me look.' Ian took the photo from Richard. 'Oh, yes, this is the one I took when Cheetra was possessed.'

'Oh, no! That can't be Cheetra.' Robert took the photo from Ian. 'No, look, that is not a woman's hand.'

Clive took the photo and looked at it closely. 'There is something there, could be a ring on the finger.'

'It's the White Lady!' Alison gasped. 'Look how the mist swirls, it looks like white chiffon, as Sue said, and it's just as I saw her.'

'Yes, I know,' said Ian. 'But that definitely is the shot I took of Cheetra, when Barneby overshadowed her.'

'But Cheetra is not in the picture...' Alison was bewildered.

Steve Palmer adjusted the bandage around his hand so that it would not get in the way when he was recording. The burn on his palm was still sore and worse than he had first thought, the skin had now split and the wound was open. He had got some cream and bandages from the pharmacy while they were in New York.

They had set the same scene so many times before, and the audience were waiting to start, with Tim playing the fool, pretending to take tickets and tear each one in half as they took their seats. In the bright moonlight the garden had taken on a silvery hue, and the night was hot and humid.

'Where is Cheetra?' Clive asked. 'Hasn't she arrived yet?'

'I don't think so.' Belinda looked around at Alison, 'I haven't seen her, have you?'

'No.' Alison looked surprised. They had all been so enthralled with talking about another session and talking about the photos that they had not noticed that she was not there.

'Well, can't we start without her?' said Andrew, who had been most interested in the photos and had asked Ian to get him a set printed for display at the museum.

'I think we should wait for her,' Clive said. 'I really do think that she can contact this spirit and put it to rest.'

They waited until midnight, but there was no word from Cheetra Dahl. Richard had phoned a couple of times during the evening, and there had been no reply from her house. He came back to his seat; Clive looked up and Richard turned up his palms, silently saying that there was still no answer.

There was a rustling in the frangipani tree. Clive checked the monitor.

'He's early tonight,' Sue whispered loudly. Peter nudged her arm, telling her to be quiet.

Clive watched the monitor and although there was still a rustling, the needle never moved.

Alison looked at her watch: almost two o'clock, the time was dragging... Behind her, Sue yawned, making a loud hushing sound. Alison turned round and shushed her quietly.

The time dragged on and Alison looked at her watch again. Clive saw her and then said that there was nothing, and that they ought to call it a day. There was shuffling and stretching and yawning, as they all moved stiff and tired limbs.

Clive spoke to Robert and Gary: 'I really think he has gone, there was not a fraction of movement on the needle tonight.'

'What was that rustling then?' said June.

'Probably a rabbit,' said Gary.

'They don't have rabbits on the island, do they?' said Rob.

'Well probably a tree rat, then.'

'A rat?' said Sue. 'Where? Eeerrrr.'

Clive packed up his monitor; he told Richard that he would ring him tomorrow, to see if he wanted to make any more arrangements. They all made their way wearily to bed, saying that they would sleep late in the morning.

Sue gave Robert a kiss goodnight, and told him not to stay up all night. She gave instructions to Belinda. 'You make sure he goes up to bed, Belinda, dear, it's not good for him to stay up all night and it is not fair on you.' Belinda smiled with a nod. She knew if Rob was going to stay up all night, there was nothing she could do to prevent it.

'Now, Robert, you are listening to me, aren't you?' His mother was nodding at him as if he were a child.

'Yes, OK, Mum.' He gave her a kiss and a tired smile, but knew she was only doing it in his best interests. As she went out through the gate, he and Gary sat at the table with June and Belinda, and smoked a cigarette. They had one drink and then they all went to bed.

Alison turned over and looked at the bedside clock, it was just gone five. She blinked her eyes, closed them again, then looked at the clock again. She had only been asleep for an hour and a half. She closed her eyes again and lay on her back, listening to the tree frogs as the faint light of the early morning came through the gap in the curtains. She watched the ceiling fan as it rotated and felt the coolness as the blades cut through the air.

She heard a low moaning and turned her head towards the window, straining her ears, then relaxed, it was the wind in the trees. She closed her eyes again and listened to the twittering of the birds and the shushing of the sea on the shore, and the moaning. The dawn was coming up, and the faint grey light seeped into the room; she could make out the dressing table and the chair by the door with her housecoat draped across the arm. The low moaning, no, it was not a moaning now, it was humming, and although not loud she could hear it above the frogs and the sea.

She got out of bed quietly and peeped through the curtain, looking out across the silvery grey water, and then to the coconut palms in the garden. Everything was still, there was no wind; she listened, and the humming was still there. She slipped into her housecoat, quietly opened the door and crept down the stairs, wincing as they creaked under her feet in the quietness of the house. Funny, she had not noticed them creak before. The house felt hot, and she opened the verandah door and stepped outside, the warm salty sea air filling her nostrils.

She stood at the balustrade, looking out at the silvery sea rolling in and gently splashing onto the shore in a mass of soft white foam, a contrast to the early morning sky which was bright pink, as the rising sun tinged the clouds with pink and apricot and lavender blue, putting a pink and golden haze on the sand and the trees in the garden and the walls of the house. She saw fishing boats far out to sea, and there was a cruise ship on her way to the harbour in Bridgetown. The bright lights sparkled yellow and gold out across the water, while her passengers slept peacefully in their cabins.

The night frogs still whistled; they would not stop until the morning light was bright. She cocked her head – she could still hear the humming. She looked at her watch; it was gone five-thirty. She walked to the end of the verandah, turning the corner. Something was compelling her to go to the frangipani tree. She stopped in front of it and turned her head quickly, as Selena's voice was close to her ear: 'She evil'. A cold shiver ran over her and she rubbed her arms, turning to look around her. In her mind she could see Selena as they had both stood right here in front of the White Lady. Poor, poor Selena. 'Why ... why?' she whispered to the space where the Lady had once stood. She looked around her again; she had the feeling she was not alone, but she saw nothing.

A voice startled her. 'Good day to you, Madam.' She turned quickly, her first reaction was annoyance.

'Oh, why don't you just go away?' There was a sharpness in her tone, as Jack Barneby bowed low, a charming smile on his handsome face.

She looked surprised but not afraid.

'I would be happy to oblige you, my dear lady, but I cannot. You have control of me and will not let me go.'

The surprise was still there. 'What do you mean ... I will not let you go?' She frowned. 'I don't know what you mean,' she was shaking her head. 'To be honest, I would be very glad to see the back of you.'

Jack Barneby's forehead creased into a deep frown. 'Methinks that I do not understand your meaning, madam. What is it that you say... You would like, to see my...' he hesitated. 'My back...' He looked astonished. 'But why...? He started to turn around, a most puzzled look on his face, and then he stopped as she spoke.

'I mean ... I would like it if you would go away from this place and leave us alone.' A small smile curled the corner of her lips as she thought of what she had said to him about his back – he had not understood modern-day speech.

Jack Barneby raised his eyebrows and spoke in a light and airy voice. 'But, my dear lady, I cannot leave you, I am in your mind.' There was a confused look on his handsome face. 'I cannot leave you, madam. Only you, my lady, can make me take my leave...' A slow smile crossed his lips as he leaned towards her, and she noticed his long black eyelashes, as his brown eyes twinkled at her sexily.

Alison did not think it was strange, having a conversation with Jack Barneby, a man from the past, 270 years old, standing here in the garden, tall and handsome. A ghost? A man who hated women ... was he flirting with her? It all seemed perfectly normal and she did not feel afraid.

'You must leave! Why do you keep coming back? Why?'

'Of course I do, dear madam, you paint pictures of my ship

and you paint pictures of my figurehead, and you will paint pictures of me.' He bent his head down to her level and smiled again right into her face. 'You will not let me rest, madam, I cannot go away.'

He came closer and she stepped back, blinking her eyes several times; he was still there. 'I never painted a picture of you.'

'Haa! But I am sure that you will, madam,' he smiled roguishly. 'I am sure that you will.'

She blinked her eyes again and again.

'Ha, haa,' he laughed loudly. 'You see I am still here. I cannot leave.'

She looked at this handsome pirate with an artist's eye; so close to her now, with his charming manner. She could see why people took him for a gentleman. He stood tall, much taller than Richard. His appearance was immaculate: clean-shaven, and his raven black hair was tied back beneath the black three-cornered hat; he was broad-shouldered and the dark green frock coat fitted him well over a golden silk brocade waistcoat. He had chosen his colours well, he had good taste and he had a neatness about him. The jewelled sword hung at his side, and the dagger and a pistol were stuck into his belt.

He saw her looking at the sword, and she stepped back as he drew it from the scabbard. 'Magnificent, is it not, madam?' He moved it deftly with a sweeping gesture and Alison stepped back, keeping her eyes on the sword in case he should suddenly lunge at her and try to kill her. Then he held it up in front of him, looking at it lovingly. 'Beautifully majestic ... is it not, dear lady?' He breathed the words with desire; a slow smile touched his lips and his dark eyes glinted through long black lashes. 'See how the stones sparkle,' he was drooling over the sword. Then, suddenly, as if coming out of a trance, he said lightly, 'I won it in a duel from Sir Hugo,' he smiled like a naughty schoolboy who had just played a prank, and then he winked. 'He will have to challenge me to win it back. But alas, alas, I will kill him, there is no doubt, his skill with a sword will never match that of mine. Sir Hugo...' he leered slowly, 'is weak ... I have his watch too, look!' He smiled impishly, taking the silver watch from his silk brocade waistcoat pocket, and dangling it by the chain for her to see. She noticed his hands were sun-bronzed, and the fingers long and slim; and as the watch twisted on the chain she noticed the time, three o'clock. He chuckled and put the watch back into his waistcoat pocket, then he put the sword back into the scabbard. He stood with his hands on his hips, and his eyes twinkled as he looked down on her with a roguish smile.

'Well, madam, what are you going to do about me?' he grinned; the grin broke into a charming smile, and she noticed his white even teeth. His dark brown eyes twinkled sexily at her, and she thought him very handsome. He certainly had a way with the ladies – she could imagine them fluttering their eyes over their fans and melting to his charming manner.

'Well, madam, have you decided?' His voice was deep, and the smile touched his lips again.

'Decided? Decided what, exactly?'

'Decided what you are going to do about me? Are you going to let me go?'

'What I would like you to do is to go away and leave us alone. Your horrible moaning and wailing keeps us awake in the night.' She sounded like a little girl with a sulky voice, telling a friend that she did not want to play. 'And you have frightened everyone around here for years. In any case, why ask me to release you, why me?'

'Because I am in your dreams, madam,' he smiled, taking off the hat and bowing low; the large black ostrich feather sweeping the ground made tiny lines in the dry dust. 'I am your servant, madam,' his eyes twinkled, 'as I was Emily's. Emily kept me here, a charming lady, but Selena, she did not approve of my manner, she told me so. I talked to them both quite often.'

'You talked to Emily and Selena?' Alison said in surprise.

'Yes.' He had sadness in his eyes. 'But neither of them would tell me to go, they would not let me rest ... and now, dear lady, I am here because of you. I cursed all women and now I am their slave and unable to be the man that I once was, a proud man! A fearless man! A man that was feared by men!' His voice was deep and discerning, and then his mouth softened into a slow smile and his eyes twinkled as he looked at her passionately.

Alison could see why women could not resist him, he was a charming rogue. And she was sure that he did not really hate women. 'Why are you always under the frangipani tree?'

'Because my blood is here, dear lady, spilled over the *Savannah Lady*, which they brought to this very spot after the great storm when my ship was destroyed. It is the only part of my ship that survived, and so I stay close to it, but I am longing to go back to the sea.'

'But it is in the museum now.'

'Yes, I know,' his deep tone was irritated. 'I have been there, but I cannot see the sea, and I dislike being shut up in a stuffy room. I need the fresh sea air in my face, madam!' And then his eyes softened and his tone became pleading. 'I should like to come back and spend my days in the garden, dear lady, where I can look out to sea and feel the breeze and the salt air as I watch my ship sailing on the horizon; she is awaiting my return.'

'Why don't you go back then, and stop wailing and moaning and threatening women? Why do you hate women so much?'

A stern look crossed his face and his tone was bitter. 'Because, madam, the cause of my death was a woman, interfering in men's business, running and screaming, and for the first time I was taken off guard. And to be killed by a boy ... a child ... I curse all womenfolk! Curse on them, I say!' His eyes flashed violently and his deep voice rang through the garden.

'If you hate women so much,' Alison was indignant, 'why are you here talking to me?'

'Because, madam, it is you who will not let me go!' He roared, and she cringed.

'I?' She questioned quietly in surprise. 'I ... won't let you go?' Suddenly her voice was raised in anger and she snapped back, 'GO! GO!' She flung her arms about, 'For God's sake, go! Get out of this garden, go on, get the hell out of here and leave us alone. Go ... and for God's sake, leave us in peace. Go back to your damned ship, and stay out there on the reef, go! Go on ... go! NOW!' Her body was shaking with rage.

'Thank you, dear lady,' he breathed with a charming smile, his tone softened. 'I will willing go. I long to get back to my ship. I long to get back to the sea. I will go, and I thank you, my most gracious lady.' He bowed low, his feathered hat again sweeping the dusty ground. He stood tall and with a charming manner, bowing his head. 'Farewell, my lady,' he took her hand and brushed it with his lips. 'It has been a pleasure to converse, with you this day, but I do not even know your name...' He began to fade slowly, and his voice trailed off.

'Alison,' she whispered with her hand still outstretched towards him. She watched as he faded, becoming transparent, and his voice faded into the distance, her name ringing in her ears long after he had vanished. 'Alisooooon...' She stood quite still, staring at the place where he had stood; she felt numb, and she was completely alone, surrounded by touchable silence.

'Alison? Alison?' She could hear her name as Richard came walking down the garden towards her. 'Morning, darling, you must have been up early. Who were you talking to?'

'Oh!' She turned a glassy stare on him.

'Who were you talking to?' Richard looked around the garden for Joseph, although he knew it was too early for him to be there. 'How long have you been out here, Ali?'

She looked at her watch: it was just gone five-thirty. 'Oh, about three or four minutes that's all, did I wake you up?' She sounded sleepy; her words seemed a little slurred.

Richard ignored the question. 'Who were you talking to?' He looked around the garden again, it was quiet except for the rushing of the sea and the birds twittering in the trees. The early morning was warm and tranquil, but in another hour the sun would be scorching down again.

'Jack,' she said casually, 'Jack was here.'

'Jack? Jack who?'

'Jack Barneby, of course, silly, who else?'

'Jack Barneby?' He gave her a stupid look, with his mouth open and his eyes wide. 'Are you all right, Ali? Didn't have too much to drink last night, did you?'

'No! Of course I'm all right,' she looked up at him with a slight smile. He saw a twinkle in her eyes. But she looked far away.

'Oh, all right then,' he chaffed. 'Go on then, I'll go along with it. What did he say?'

'Well … he said that he would go away if I asked him to … so I did. I said please go away and stop pestering us with your wailing and moaning in the middle of the night. Then he said he had been waiting for me to tell him to go … so I did. And now he has gone … I think he was very grateful to me for letting him go, and he bowed to me and said "Farewell, my lady", and then he was gone and I don't think he will come back.'

'Gone where?' Richard asked lightly with a smile, looking at her with his head on one side.

'I don't know…' she grimaced, 'back to the sea, I suppose. He said he had been longing to go back to the sea and his ship, and he didn't like the stuffy atmosphere at the museum, and that is why he came back here. He wants to feel the fresh sea air on his face, and would we mind if he stayed here in the garden, but if I told him to go he would go back to his ship, because that is really where he wants to be, and the ship was out there again, waiting for him, we both saw it.'

'We … who's we?'

'Well, Jack and I, of course, we both saw the ship.'

'Jack and I?' His mouth stood open.

'Yes. He showed me the sword too, it really is magnificent, and he was waving it about, you know, like fencing. And he laughed as he showed me Sir Hugo's watch, and he said that he would have to challenge him to get them back. He was a bit smug, he said Hugo hadn't got a chance against him, or something like that; I can't remember his exact words. But he said he would kill Hugo, and he kept calling me madam and dear lady, and my lady,' she smiled. 'He really was quite a charmer, a real ladies' man, and very handsome too.'

'You didn't happen to notice the time on the watch by any chance, did you?'

'Yes,' she smiled, looking up at him, 'three o'clock.'

'Oh Alison.' He clicked his tongue with annoyance. 'Come on, let's go in and have a cup of coffee.' He put his arm round her shoulders and coaxed her along, suddenly realizing that she was wearing her housecoat. He looked at her in surprise, 'You are not even dressed.'

'No, well, I came out when I heard him moaning again, and then we got to chatting, but I think he has gone now. He said that Emily had kept him here and would not let him go, and he used to talk to her every day, and also he talked to Selena, but he did not like Selena, because she despised him. But I am sure he has gone now ... shame, though,' she giggled, 'he really was a charmer. Said he was killed by a boy, because a woman distracted him.'

'Yeah.' Richard nodded nonchalantly as they came into the kitchen.

'Oh! Morning; you two are out early,' said Belinda brightly. 'Been walking on the beach?' She went straight to the kettle, filled it with water and switched it on. 'Robert is just coming down,' she said over her shoulder, 'we are going for an early morning swim, it looks lovely out there, doesn't it? Who was that guy you were talking to in the garden, Alison?'

'What guy?' Richard said quickly.

Belinda turned round. 'The guy in the green coat. I saw you from the window; he walked off down the beach to the water's edge.' She saw the surprise in Richard's face. 'Well, you must have seen him, Richard. Gosh, he walked right past you. I was wondering why on earth he had a big coat and boots on in this heat.'

Richard's eyes widened as he looked from one to the other.

At the museum, Andrew had got three strong men who were working in the garden to lift the chest with the anchor in it and move it to a different position. They had now got quite a large display of artifacts from the *Savannah Lady*. The local people were most interested and flocked in through the front door daily; they also had visitors from other islands who came over on day trips, and a lot of very interested people who were on the island for a holiday; one couple had come from Miami just for a few days to see the exhibition. They said that they had watched the activity out on the reef through binoculars, and so many pieces had been shown on the TV, and today they had come to see for themselves.

Andrew phoned Richard to tell him how well it was all going.

Richard said it was great news. 'You must be rolling in the money with all those visitors,' and they had a laugh. Andrew said that there would be no more as the *Four Winds* had packed up and left. But he had found it very exciting to keep receiving bits and pieces.

Richard told him about Alison, he was quite worried. Andrew could hear it in his tone. 'She is quite convinced that she was talking to Jack Barneby, and she is sure that he has gone away. I do hope she is right. I can't really believe it, but she doesn't seem to be kidding, and also Belinda is convinced that she saw someone talking to Alison and she said he was wearing a dark green jacket or coat, I think she said ... and big boots.'

Andrew was thoughtful for a moment. 'You mean she thinks she actually talked to him? He didn't harm her, then?' He frowned. 'You don't think the two of them are having a game, do you? I mean Alison and Belinda, of course.'

'No, they are both quite serious, and Alison came to no harm. Mind you, I never thought of that. He doesn't like women, does he? But she said he was charming, a real ladies' man, but he hates women because it was a woman that caused his death.' Richard grimaced and shrugged his shoulders. 'Don't know who that could be.'

Andrew shook his head. 'No... Shame about Cheetra, though, isn't it?'

'Cheetra? What about her? I haven't seen her.' Richard was concerned. 'She was supposed to be here last night, but she did not turn up. I kept ringing, but there was no answer; we waited ages, why? What's happened, then? I phoned again this morning.'

Andrew raised his eyes in surprise. 'Well, I thought you would have heard; they found her floating in the sea.'

'What? Is she dead?' Richard spoke softly, his strength seemed to leave him and there was a strange empty feeling in the pit of his stomach.

'No! Luckily two fishermen picked her up. She is in the hospital, and they say she keeps saying something about a lady in white dragging her into the sea. The doctor says she has been in the water a long time, so it probably happened last night.'

'But she is all right, isn't she?'

Andrew nodded into the phone. 'Well, when the police phoned me she was still unconscious and they were trying to bring her round.'

Richard had a quick flashback to the time when Alison was lured into the sea. He told Andrew about it, and then he went on to tell him about Ella May, and Andrew said he had heard the story about Ella May. It had happened many years ago, his grandmother had been a friend of the Cottons and he remembered that she had mentioned it. 'We really must do something about Barneby, Richard, it's getting worse. We must get together on this. I don't know what we can do, but something must be done. I will pop in and see you.'

When Richard told Alison, she was very concerned about Cheetra Dahl, and said they must go to the hospital. 'But I am sure that he has gone now, he told me so.'

'Oh you can't say that, Alison.' June looked at her sceptically. 'Look what he has done.'

'Yes, you must have been daydreaming, darling.' Richard wrinkled his nose and looked at her kindly.

'No, no, I wasn't. I wasn't, honestly.' Alison was shaking her head. 'I know that none of you believe me, but he was as clear to me as you all are. Belinda saw him too, didn't you, Belinda?'

'Well...' Belinda was a bit reluctant to say. 'Well, yes. I did see you talking to someone, but I didn't really take much notice, it was just a quick glance.'

'Well, you saw a man, didn't you? In a green frock coat.'

'Well, yes, but I thought it was a man in a green jacket, not a frock coat. Well, you must have seen him, Richard, he walked right past you.'

'Are you kidding?' Richard shook his head. 'But then, just thinking about that, who would be walking down to the beach in any kind of coat in this heat? You would have to be a nutcase.'

'Or a ghost,' Tim mused.

'Well, I am not a nutcase,' said Belinda, 'he definitely was wearing a coat or a jacket. And it was green.'

'It was a dark green frock coat,' said Alison. 'Did you see a three-cornered hat, Belinda?'

'No, it was only a quick glance, but he might have been carrying something. Yes, I think it may have been a hat, I am not sure. To be quite honest, Alison, you were facing this way and I just glanced out of the window, and I didn't want you to think I was spying on you.'

'So you actually did see me talking to him?'

'Yes, just for a sec, then he walked away down towards the beach, well he almost bumped into you, Richard, you got there just as he turned away. I didn't see his face.'

There was utter silence; they were deep in thought.

'I wonder if there is anything to show where he stood?' said Tim. 'I'm going down to look.' He started to walk away and they all followed. Standing near the frangipani tree, they looked at the ground, trying not to disturb any dust. 'Where were you standing, Ali?'

'Right here, and I remember that he took off his hat and bowed low, and the feather in his hat scraped through the dust on the ground, making fine lines.'

Tim looked closely. 'It does look as if something as been scraped along just here.'

'No,' said Gary, 'that is where Joseph has been sweeping.'

'I don't think so.' Tim shook his head.

'Well, he stood right here,' Alison smiled girlishly at June and Belinda. 'He really was quite handsome.' All three giggled.

'What else did he say to you?' Belinda was curious.

'Well,' she smiled, lowering her eyes shyly, 'he was a bit of a ladies' man. Old-fashioned.'

'Was he sexy?' June rolled her eyes. 'Did you fancy him? What did he say?'

Alison chuckled, she knew the girls were on her side. 'Well, he certainly was a charmer, he called me madam, you know ... like ... when men really had respect for ladies,' she smiled, shrugging her shoulders and fluttering her eyes sexily at the men. 'You know,' she turned back to June and Belinda, blinking her eyes and waving her hand like a fan in front of her face, 'when men were chivalrous. Oh, and yes, he kept calling me dear lady.' She put on a very cultured voice, 'and madam. He really was quite, quite charming.' She clipped the words, flicking her fingers daintily in the air.

The girls tittered and giggled, the men stared at her, and Richard snapped. 'Really, Ali, you ought to go and have a check-up with the doctor.'

'Oh! Don't be so stupid, Richard,' said Alison sharply.

'Yes,' said Belinda, 'she is only telling you what the man said.'

'Man!' Richard shouted. 'It's a ghost. You're telling me that I'm stupid when my wife is having a conversation and flirting with a guy over two hundred years old. A ghost ... oh, come on.' He shrugged his shoulders and turned his head away.

'I know, I know,' Alison frowned with annoyance. 'I know how it sounds, Richard, that Jack Barneby is getting to me. But he was here. Right here.' She pointed her finger to the ground. And as she did so, a black feather floated down and stopped at her feet.

Richard took a breath and raised his eyes. 'Getting to you? I think he is getting to all of us...' Alison bent to pick up the feather. 'Look, Richard...' He looked, and then looked around nervously.

Cheetra Dahl lay quietly in a private room in the hospital with her eyes closed; her dark skin looked grey, Richard and Alison stood at the bedside and then glanced at each other.

'I am not asleep.' She opened her eyes slowly, they smiled down at her. 'I am feeling a lot better.'

'Well, that is a good sign,' said the nurse who was just going out; she smiled at Richard and Alison, 'Please don't stay too long.' She closed the door quietly behind her as she went out.

Cheetra told Richard and Alison that she had vague recollections of what had happened, and she remembered the fishermen lifting her out of the sea. It had been the day before yesterday, and she had been unconscious most of that time. But now she was feeling much better. She told them that she lived in a small cottage very near the beach, and she had been sitting quietly thinking about the pirate Jack Barneby; she had not meant to go into a trance, but suddenly there was banging on the door, and in her dream-like state she had opened the door. There was the face of a smiling woman, she was surrounded by a swirling white mist and she was beckoning her to follow. She had taken her hand and she was leading her across the sand towards the sea.

She remembered entering the water and as she got deeper and deeper, the image of the lady in white had become that of the pirate, and he was standing on top of the waves. He held her hand and was dragging her out to a ship, she could see the white sails billowing in the distance, then her head had dipped into the water. She tried to hold on to the hand but it was no longer there, and she had heard deep laughter which changed into a hysterical screaming, and then the blackness came over her. The next thing she remembered was the faces of two black fishermen and she knew that she was in a boat. They were patting her face, and shaking her, saying, 'Lady, lady, wake up lady.' She had closed her eyes and could not open them again, but she could hear the panic in their voices; they had sounded far away and then she had slipped into unconsciousness. 'But I feel better now,' she smiled weakly at them. But Alison thought her dark features were looking very pale.

After they had left, she lay with her eyes closed and rested. She must have dozed off, and she woke with a start to find the young doctor leaning over her. He smiled kindly, taking her pulse. 'How are you feeling now?'

'Oh, a lot better now, thank you, doctor.'

He smiled, looking at the chart, which was fixed to the end of her bed. 'Well, it seems that your temperature is back to normal, and I think you can go home after lunch. Can someone come and pick you up?'

She nodded. 'I have a niece who lives in the town.'

He smiled again. 'I would really like to know what happened to you; were you swimming?' She nodded. 'What at night? Alone? Do you usually swim at night? You were in the water a very long time, you were lucky that the fishermen happened to see you.'

She looked at him thoughtfully. 'Yes,' she hesitated, 'and I must have got out of my depth. I am very grateful to the fishermen, do you know who they were?'

'Yes, the nurse has got their names and a telephone number.' He smiled, knowing that she would be all right. 'You rest here until after lunch. And don't go swimming on your own again at night,' he scolded, then smiled at her again and left the room.

Clive was convinced that they would have no more trouble

with Jack Barneby. When Cheetra phoned him and said that she would like to try and contact him again, he said that they were finished with the case, and that he believed that Barneby had truly used every bit of the electrical force. He also asked what she thought about Alison's experience of meeting him in the garden. She said that she didn't know anything about that, but it sounded most intriguing, and said that they must try again. She felt she must try once more and that she would go and see Alison and talk it over with her; she had to know what he had said and how he had appeared.

Clive had a word with Richard, saying that Cheetra had phoned him, wanting to try to contact Barneby again. But Richard was not keen to let her go into a trance again. Clive said she had insisted and he had tried to talk her out of it, but she had said that she must try again, so they had agreed to one last session only, as everyone was due to go back to England anyway in a few days.

Richard came off the phone feeling very worried about Cheetra. Afterwards he phoned her.

'I have to try again,' she told Richard, 'for my own peace of mind, to make sure that this poor spirit is at rest. Clive is sure that you will have no more trouble, but I beg you to let me sit in on your last session.'

Richard agreed, but said that he thought it dangerous; and here they all were, assembled and ready to start again.

Cheetra had arrived an hour earlier, and she and Alison sat quietly in the dining room with the door closed, talking about the experiences that they had both had with the White Lady.

'She was swirling around in front of the door when I opened it,' Cheetra said.

'That is exactly what happened to me,' Alison nodded earnestly. 'But, of course, it all happened about ten years ago, that was when Nick Cotton's grandfather was alive. He said it had happened to his wife years before, but unfortunately she was drowned.' Then she went on telling her what Barneby had said to her in the garden.

'Amazing.' Cheetra shook her head. 'I have no explanation for these happenings, and I have had many years as a medium, but this one is most intriguing.'

'Do you think that he might have appeared to Selena?' asked Alison.

'Most probably,' Cheetra nodded. 'Perhaps it was just the very shock of seeing him which killed the poor woman.'

'I never thought of that,' said Alison, 'although I did not feel shocked or surprised. He was just suddenly there. He was not frightening, in fact he was most polite. I don't even remember having any unusual feelings about him, he was just as a normal man, although his English was very precise; he kept calling me madam and dear lady,' and then she made Cheetra laugh about seeing the back of him. 'He hadn't understood that.'

'Most intriguing...' Cheetra shook her head gently. 'In fact, for me it is exciting, and I can't wait to try to contact this pirate again...' Her eyes wandered around the room. 'This is a nice room, it is very cool in here. Have you noticed how cool it is in this room? Have you got air-conditioning in here?'

Alison grimaced. 'No...' she said thoughtfully, 'but it does always appear cool in this room, in fact, sometimes quite cold. I had a very funny feeling once, I thought something touched me. I was looking over there in the cabinet ... oh look, I have to show you this, we still have a few things left here which belonged to Aunt Emily. Richard had not got the heart to give everything away to Andrew Harrison.' She took Cheetra to the glass cabinet and opened the door. 'Oh!' she gasped, 'The ring is here.' She frowned. 'I am sure Richard sent that to the museum. It was in the museum. I remember telling Sue not to touch it. That's strange, I wonder who brought it back...' she thought for a moment, putting her hand to her lips. 'We believe that this ring belonged to Sir Hugo Fotheringay.' She gave it to Cheetra and then stopped and looked around the room, as the curtains blew in from the window and a strong draught made them both shiver.

'Are you sure that you have not got air-conditioning in this room?'

'No,' Alison said with concern, 'but it does seem colder in here, doesn't it? And look at the curtains blowing, the window is not even open.'

'Freezing,' said Cheetra. Her eyes widened, watching the curtains blowing in away from the window. The breeze swirled around them, ruffling Alison's hair, and a cold creepy feeling went down her back.

She jumped as Cheetra boomed out in a deep commanding voice, 'Who is there? Who is there?'

She seemed to be listening, her eyes darting round the room. 'Speak! Speak to me!' A smile came to her lips; she turned to Alison, 'He says I have his ring. Who are you?' And then suddenly Cheetra's hand jumped upwards as if it had been hit from beneath; the ring flew into the air and disappeared. The two turned in alarm as the glass cabinet suddenly fell from the wall down onto the polished sideboard, knocking the silver tray with the tea set on it and the silver candlesticks to the floor, and the glass shattered across the whole of the room. They moved quickly to a corner.

Alison was frozen with fear, she stood open-mouthed, gripping hard on the back of a chair, her knuckles white, her heart beating fast. There was a chuckling voice around the room; the breeze stopped, and there was a strange silence. Alison, her eyes wide with fright, looked into every corner of the room and whispered, 'Has ... has ... it gone?' The beating of her heart was drumming in her breast and in her ears.

Cheetra was now composed. 'I thought I could feel a presence in here. I said it was cold. Be gone spirit, go from this place. Rest, go to your rest,' she boomed, with a deep voice for such a small woman, making the sign of the cross with her fingers. She turned round in a circle, and then stood silent for a few minutes; she listened, her head on one side.

Suddenly the door burst open; the women turned quickly and Joseph put his head round the door. 'I hear a crash, Maam.' His eyes goggled as he saw the smashed glass and the cabinet half-hanging over the sideboard.

Alison's voice was hoarse. 'Get a brush, Joseph, and clean it up please.'

'Yes Maam.' He was about to go out.

'Joseph.'

'Maam?'

'Take the cabinet and everything that was in it, down to the end of the garden, and burn it.'

'Burn it?' His voice rose in surprise and his forehead wrinkled in a frown.

Alison took a breath. 'Burn it, Joseph, burn it right now.'

'Yes, maam.'

He dashed out and came back with broom and dustpan and a black plastic garbage bag.

Cheetra and Alison went out onto the verandah.

Alison swallowed hard. 'Do you think that Jack Barneby is here in the house?'

'No,' said Cheetra. 'You have more than one restless spirit here. I was holding his ring. He was angry, saying "disturbed me", and I got the name Herga.'

'Hugo,' Alison corrected. 'It must be Hugo Fotheringay.' She looked around her, her eyes filled with fear. 'Two spirits?'

'Hugo. Yes you are right, that is what he said. It wasn't very clear.'

'But I heard nothing.' Alison looked around. 'Has he gone? Oh Cheetra, this place is becoming more and more eerie. If we cannot rid ourselves of these terrible things, I am going to ask Richard's father to sell the house. We love Barbados, but it is getting impossible for us to stay here. It is getting worse.' She shook her head in despair. 'Even though we have all found this fascinating, every one of us is on edge.' She held her hand to her forehead. 'Oh Cheetra, what have we done?'

'Exactly. What have you done? Sit down.' They sat at the table. Alison still looked wearily around her.

'It is all right,' Cheetra touched her hand kindly, 'there is no one here, and we are quite alone. Now tell me, when did it all start?'

Alison took a breath. 'Well, about ten years ago, really, since then we have not had any trouble, and it just seems to have started all over again.'

'But can you remember the very first time?' Cheetra gave her time to consider.

'Well ... yes, we had only been here a few days and it was in the dining room. I suddenly felt cold and a draught blew the door shut tight and I could not open it, and then it did open and I rushed out. I was still holding the scroll... It was the first night that the Turners came up here for a drink... They had gone home and Richard and Robert took them back in the car.'

'But what happened? Think ... think.'

Alison pulled a face. 'Nothing, just a drink ... the boys were in there looking at the scroll. I know! Tim knew all about the *Savannah Lady*. He told us about it, and they went down on to the beach and said that they had found a cross marked on a rock and they had dug a hole. Then it was after that they found the sword in the cellar ... and...'

'Have you got the scroll?' asked Cheetra.

'Yes,' Alison hesitated, 'it's in there on the sideboard.' She had noticed it there when the cabinet fell. 'Shall I get it for you?' She was a bit reluctant to go back into the dining room.

Cheetra saw the apprehension in her face. 'It's all right, Alison. I assure you there is no one there now.' Alison went to get the scroll; she snatched it quickly and rushed out of the room.

Cheetra was reading. 'That's it!' She snapped her fingers. 'I bet those boys dug up a grave, and the spirit is angry. He told me just now, when he said, "disturbed me".

'Alison, how strongly do you feel about this Jack Barneby and this Hugo, and Emily?'

'I don't quite know what you mean. I think about them a lot, quite a lot, I suppose ... mostly I suppose when I am sitting quietly painting. And when I look out to sea I imagine this pirate, and I see a sail of a ship.' She stopped. 'But I don't conjure them up on purpose, if that is what you think ... and Tim also saw the sail, just the other day so...' She looked at Cheetra in alarm. 'It isn't me ... is it? I mean, me that's making him stay here ... it can't be me ... it's been going on for years. No. No...' She shook her head in despair.

They had been sitting in silence for over an hour, ears strained to every sound.

Alison flinched, moving her head to one side, as she felt a breath close to her ear. 'Shee evil,' it was Selena's voice. Then a deeper voice. 'Madam...' She looked around, had any of them heard the voices? No one had moved, was she going mad? Her heart thumped and alarm bells rang in her head; she reached for Richard's hand.

Cheetra frowned and murmured. Her voice was clear and

dainty as she said sharply, 'Selena?' It was a clear and demanding voice.

'Shee evil, Miss Emily,' Selena's voice was harsh and guttural.

Joseph suddenly jumped to his feet and shouted 'Mamma?' No one dared to turn round. He stood with his hands on each side of his cheeks, his mouth open and the whites of his large brown eyes showing. Petal held tightly to his arm, her face pale in the moonlight. Her eyes, like Joseph's, were wide with fright, and she breathed, 'Voodoo.'

'Tell Joseph,' Selena's voice again. Joseph was speechless, with great fear in his eyes.

Alison felt a cold prickling all over her body, and she gripped Richard's hand so tightly he winced and frowned at her. She knew no one would ever believe that she had heard Selena's voice before Cheetra had said, 'Selena'. Emily's voice again, it was clear and sharp. Nick moved his eyes back and forth, he caught Robert and Gary; he raised his eyebrows questioningly, and Gary shook his head; it was hardly a movement.

They waited for Cheetra to go on. But there was nothing else. She moved slowly, coming out of the trance. She shook her head, taking a deep breath, and straightened her back, looking straight at Richard. 'He is gone, I cannot reach him at last. I am sure he is at rest...' She smoothed back her hair with both hands. 'I am sorry that I could not give a performance here tonight.' Her words were slurred, as if waking from a deep sleep; she took another deep breath and blinked her eyes. She smiled round at them all, and then realized that they were all staring at her.

'What's the matter?' she smiled, hoping that something had happened. 'Did anything happen? I know I could not contact the pirate. Was it someone else?'

'You mean you don't know?' Clive frowned with amazement.

'No! I know it wasn't the pirate, and I know it wasn't violent. What happened?'

'You contacted Aunt Emily and Selena,' said Alison quietly.

Cheetra gasped, then her face beamed with delight. 'Who are they? What did they say?'

'Well, they didn't say much,' said Richard, 'but there was a noted difference in your tone. Emily we only know from seeing her photograph, but Selena, well, Selena's voice was perfect, it was as if she were here.'

'Oh, we must try again.' Cheetra was beaming with satisfaction and Alison had no doubts that she could contact the other side, for she had no recollection of what she had said, but Alison knew that Selena was here right close to them now.

'When can we try again?' Cheetra was really keyed up.

'Oh no!' said Richard. 'We are not drumming up any more spirits, after what we have been through with Barneby. I hope we are rid of him, and enough is enough, never again.'

'But it was my mudder's voice,' Joseph was still stunned. 'You have to do it all agin, Mistress Dahl, please,' he pleaded, holding his arms out to her.

Cheetra was alarmed. 'I contacted your mother?' and she breathed. 'Really, I am amazed.'

Richard explained that Selena was Joseph's mother, and she had died in mysterious circumstances right by the frangipani tree.

'Mistress Dahl,' Joseph had tears in his eyes.

'No, Joseph, no! No! You must not, it's not safe. No!' Petal was almost in tears and quite aggressive. No one had ever seen her like this.

'Oh no, no!' Richard was adamant. 'Petal is right, it is not safe to mess with these things, and if you want to contact more ghosts, you are not doing it here!'

'Well, the monitor never registered a thing,' said Clive, 'so I think we might have seen the last of Jack Barneby. Let's hope so, anyway.'

'Hooray!' exclaimed Alison, although she did have mixed feelings – in a way it was sad, and he had been quite a charmer.

The nightly sessions had been interesting, a little fearful and exciting. It got the adrenaline going, it had fascinated them all; a thing that not one of them had ever imagined could happen. Their days had been full of discussions as to how Barneby appeared, now that the White Lady was no longer in the garden. Everyone had his or her own opinions as to how to get rid of him. Alison, in a way, felt sorry, but he did have to go. They were all convinced of that.

* * *

As the taxi drew up at the gate, Joseph lifted the cases with ease, putting them into the boot. They were saying goodbye to Petal and Joseph, and Richard was just getting into the front seat next to the driver; the phone rang and Petal ran off to answer it.

'Oh! They are just leaving.' She put her head out of the door and called, 'Mr Price, Mr Price, the telephone.' Richard asked who it was; she called back, 'It's Mr Harrison.'

Richard said he would not be a minute, and left Peter sitting in the back of the taxi between Alison and Sue.

'Don't be too long, Richard, it is too hot sitting in here,' Alison called as he turned away.

'Hello, Andrew,' he was breathless, 'you just caught us, we are leaving.'

'Oh, I am sorry. I just got on to wish you bon voyage, have a safe trip, that's all. Keep in touch, and I'll see you at Christmas.'

'Thanks, we are all looking forward to coming back. Let me know when you have completed the full display of the *Savannah Lady*.'

'Okay,' said Andrew. 'I am still here at the workshop, working on some pieces.'

Richard smiled. 'You're late, don't overdo it. Well, Andrew, thanks for ringing. I must go, the taxi is waiting.'

Andrew put the phone down and went back to what he was doing. He thought he would miss them all now; still, Christmas would come round quickly enough. He thought how lucky they were to be going back to London. He had not been to London for three years and now he had not got the time, and he had not got a lot of money to spare anyway – he might manage a long weekend in the islands, maybe the Grenadines, or St Thomas. Just a few days away. He put the magnifying glass over a wooden handle of a rusty knife; the name, almost worn off and hardly readable, looked like Max something.

Hours went by, he looked at his watch. Richard and Alison would be well on their way by now. The workshop was quiet, now that everyone had gone. He often stayed late, but not this late. The showroom was in semi-darkness except for the small security lights, which were kept on all night, and Bob Commings, the night watchman, sat in his office across the courtyard, watching the security cameras as they flashed continually in every part of the museum.

Andrew picked up the knife again, twisting it in his hands. The loud ticking of the clock on the wall was the only sound. He looked up at the time, a minute past three in the morning, the time had just seemed to slip by. He put the knife he was studying down onto the bench and sat back in the chair. He was tired; he yawned, stretching his arms above his head, then brought them down limply with his elbows on the bench. He took off his specs and rubbed his tired eyes; sitting under the bright electric lamp did not help. He must go home.

He was pleased with the display in the showroom, which they had put together. It was almost finished; the White Lady would be the last piece to go on exhibit; she had been cleaned and preserved. Mike and Duncan had done a good job. They would put the Lady out early in the morning; she had taken a long time to clean, and although she was now back to her original colour there were still traces of the white paint, which had been impossible to remove from the folds in the red dress and the curls in the hair.

He reached out, about to turn out the table lamp, and heard a sudden movement behind him. He swung round quickly in the chair, startled for a moment, and sat looking at the White Lady, who was standing in the corner. He felt a chill, and a creepy feeling came over his skin. He was quite alone, but afraid to move. Tension hung heavy on his ears; he listened, he stared at the Lady. Did he imagine the slight mist ... or was it a trick of the light? Did the mouth have a slight smile, which he had not noticed before, and did those unseeing eyes blink?